BETWEEN FRIENDS
& LOVERS

Also by Shirlene Obuobi

On Rotation

BETWEEN FRIENDS & LOVERS

A Novel

SHIRLENE OBUOBI

AVON

An Imprint of HarperCollins*Publishers*

BETWEEN FRIENDS & LOVERS. Copyright © 2024 by Shirlene Obuobi. All rights reserved. Printed in the United States of America. No part of this book may be used or reproduced in any manner whatsoever without written permission except in the case of brief quotations embodied in critical articles and reviews. For information, address HarperCollins Publishers, 195 Broadway, New York, NY 10007.

HarperCollins books may be purchased for educational, business, or sales promotional use. For information, please email the Special Markets Department at SPsales@harpercollins.com.

FIRST EDITION

Interior text designed by Diahann Sturge-Campbell

Library of Congress Cataloging-in-Publication Data has been applied for.

ISBN 978-0-06-330731-5 (paperback)
ISBN 978-0-06-330730-8 (hardcover library edition)

24 25 26 27 28 LBC 5 4 3 2 1

For the "strong" girls. For the girls who seem to have it all together even when they're falling apart. For the Megan Thee Stallions of the world, who everyone knows how to consume but no one knows how to protect. You deserve to be cherished too.

BETWEEN FRIENDS
& LOVERS

CHAPTER ONE

Jo

Surviving as a Black girl in high society is pretty easy, as long as you know the rules.

One: arrive with your pedigree at the ready—your degree from a prestigious university, the smattering of letters behind your name, your association with friends powerful enough to confer you relevance. Announce these clearly enough and often enough that no one asks why you're here, but with enough humility that you're not seen as a threat. (Anecdotes that begin with *when I was in medical school* or *my dormitory in Cambridge* often do the trick.)

Two: be intentional with your hair. Keep it straight on the days you want to blend in—dealer's choice on whether you rock a lace front, U-part, or a silk press, because let's be real, hardly anyone in attendance will know the difference—and only bust out the Afro when you want to stand out. Be aware that standing out might not always be in your best interest, and relish the irony that existing in your unaltered self is considered a statement.

Three: adopt a standard Midwestern accent. Strip your voice of AAVE and go for more Channel 7 News, though you can throw out the occasional *biiiitttchhhh* for laughs in select social situations.

And, most importantly, number four: never, ever make a white woman cry. Because white women's tears are salt sowed into fertile land, the fertile land being your friendships, your peace, your livelihood, and whatever else you may hold dear. The cuter and younger the white woman, the more potent the tears. The more witnesses, especially of the straight male variety, the more devastating the impact.

All this to say: I was screwed.

Ashley Biernacki and I stood facing each other in the atrium of international supermodel Renata Kovalenko's lavishly decorated Gold Coast penthouse, where we had both been invited to celebrate her son, TV actor Ezra Adelman's, thirtieth birthday, at a party funded by her husband, billionaire CEO of Knydus Technologies Paul Adelman's, endless coffers. I was here because Ezra was my best friend. Ashley was here because Ezra was her boyfriend. And because karma doesn't exist, she'd only become more beautiful since our last encounter (sixteen years ago, when she'd called me a gorilla for refusing to let her copy my homework).

"I—I don't know what you want me to say," Ashley blubbered. Her high, round cheeks were pink, and the tears that spilled from her large hazel eyes were pretty, like glistening glass droplets. Her effective zone was only about a two-meter radius, plenty wide enough to get me in trouble in the crowded atrium. In the two minutes or so since our unfortunate encounter began, Ashley had managed to transform me from Dr. Josephine Boateng, physician, influencer, and close friend and confidante of the hosts, into an unspecified angry Black woman preying on Somebody's Hapless Granddaughter.

"Why are you crying?" I asked, baffled. A distinguished older gentleman at my two o'clock huffed, having heard *I'll give you something to cry about.* I searched my vicinity for an ally, and, finding none, settled on an approaching Ezra, who had put me in this quandary to begin with. "Seriously?"

If I was seeking refuge in Ezra, I did not find it. Ashley was not Ezra's first girlfriend this year, possibly not his first this month. Handsome heirs to tech empires didn't really have to do the long-term-commitment thing. But although he'd always been kind of a garbage boyfriend, he'd also always been a pretty reliable friend.

Until today. Today, his expression was cold. I watched, stunned, as he grabbed Ashley's hand, gave it a squeeze, and used his other to dab her face with a pocket square that I knew cost more than my entire outfit. I'd rather he'd used it to smother me.

Really, though, I should have known. Ashley Biernacki was very cute, very small, and very blond. She possessed the H-bomb of white girl tears, and man, did she know how to wield them. As a kid, she'd employed her little siren's song regularly, usually after doing something unspeakably horrible to me, and many a beet-faced assistant principal had dragged me into their office in defense of it.

Judging by Ezra's expression and the heightened whispers around us, history was about to repeat itself.

"I just wanted to say hello," Ashley said.

Ezra gave her the most tender smile, then turned a hardened gaze to me. It was odd, seeing him look at me like that, like a stranger had slithered into his skin and was glaring at me through his eyes.

"Jo," he said. "Can we talk?" He tucked his now-damp pocket square back into his blazer, running a soothing hand down a shuddering Ashley's arm. "Alone?"

The corners of my mouth twitched downward. *Here we go.*

People were watching, waiting with bated breath for my reaction the way one might wait for a circus lion to roar.

But I wouldn't give them the satisfaction. I lifted my champagne flute to my lips, relaxed my shoulders, and gave Ezra what I knew was my most disarming smile.

"Of course," I said, then allowed the man who I knew was rapidly becoming my former best friend to lead me through the atrium. The crowd parted like the Red Sea around us, making way for their prince and the pariah.

Ezra led me down a quiet hallway in silence. I power walked behind him, trying hard to keep pace with his long strides in my stilettos, and marveled at the breadth of his back. When we first met, he'd been light enough for me to hold in my arms, so thin that when we embraced, I would wince against the daggers of his collarbones. That Ezra—the mop-haired one with a crooked smile and a lack of decorum, that had been the boy whose life I'd once saved. He'd looked up at me through glazed blue eyes and asked me to never leave him, and I'd whispered back, "I won't," and now, ten years later, I wondered if maybe I should have sought reciprocation, made him promise never to leave me either.

We reached our destination, the study, and Ezra held the door open for me, a jailer opening a cell door. I walked inside, skimming a hand along a bookshelf. I'd never seen any of the Adelmans use this room, and yet it smelled like them, like sunlight and open windows, sandalwood and citrus. In the center of the room was the bureau Mazarin, as pristine as it had been two years ago when Renata had spotted it in a museum and, in the most heinous display of unconscionable wealth, decided to purchase it right out of its case. I circled it, then leaned against it, facing the closed gold-trimmed ocher curtains. Six hundred thousand dollars and three hundred years of history, all under my bum. I spun the miniature globe atop it as I waited for Ezra to close the door.

The moment it clicked shut, Ezra rounded on me.

"So . . . care to explain why you're accosting my girlfriend?" he said.

"What do you mean?" My voice came out high, squeezed out from behind a reed-thin throat. "I was perfectly nice."

"Of course you were, and that's why she's crying," Ezra said flatly. He raised his hand to his hair to push it back, then, remembering that it was chock-full of product, lowered it again. "Come on, Jo, I know you think I'm moving too fast, or whatever, but you can bother me about that, not her—"

"Is that what you think this is about?" I cut him off in disbelief. "That woman. Your girlfriend. Her full name's Ashley Biernacki, right?"

"Yes," Ezra said instantly. And then, finally, he paused. "Wait. How did you know that?"

"Think, Ez," I said. "*Why* would I know that?"

I waited for understanding to hit, for his set jaw to go slack. Seeing the shock in his expression cooled my ire somewhat. After all, Ezra wouldn't do that to me. Wouldn't knowingly cozy up to the woman who had made my life hell, even if it had been over fifteen years ago. We'd spent too many cool nights under starry skies, unraveling our traumas like threads off tapestries, for him to hurt me by cavorting with one of the prominent actors in mine.

"Shit," he said. "Oh *shit*. Are you sure it's her?"

"Of course I'm sure," I said. What I'd said in response to her outstretched hand and peppy "Hi! I'm Ashley! You must be Jo!" was "You know me. You used to make my life miserable." Factual. Direct. Not particularly mean. I could have smiled more, sure, maybe shaken her hand instead of leaving it hanging limply in front of me, but I also could've upended my glass of champagne over her head. I'd been gracious, all things considered.

I told Ezra as much.

"I didn't know," he said numbly.

"Well, you not knowing didn't stop you from instantly jumping to her defense."

"What was I supposed to do?" Ezra said. "You of all people know how overwhelming Mom's parties can be, and this is Ashley's first one. And Jo, you know I would never have asked her out if I knew about your history. But it's been a long time, and I promise she's a good person now. If you got to know her, you'd probably really like her too—"

I tuned him out. *I don't care if she's Mother fucking Teresa now*, I wanted to shout. If I was honest with myself, I didn't much care that the woman Ezra was dating was a potentially much-improved Ashley Biernacki. Just that I was in this room getting admonished, while she was free to dab away her tears and garner sympathy in the atrium. Just that even now it didn't occur to Ezra that maybe he should have been defending *me*.

All of these years, I'd been silently hoping that Ezra would someday see me. That the flippant, habitual *love you*s that addended his goodbyes would gain definition, that one day it would click in his head that maybe the intimate, buried-in-each-other's-skin love he was searching for in women like Ashley was right in front of him all along. And, because I hated to think of myself as pathetic, I'd convinced myself that I wasn't hung up on him at all. That I hadn't looked elsewhere because I was *busy*. That I was currently a twenty-nine-year-old virgin who had gone on a grand total of three dates in my life because I had to focus on medical school, then because there was no time for romance in residency, and not because I was keeping myself available just in case the boy I'd been in love with for most of my adult life would wake up one morning and decide to *pick me choose me love me.*

A hand on my chin guided my face forward.

"Talk to me, Jo," Ezra said gently. "What is this really about?"

With Ezra's new frame had come new strength, a consequence of years spent crafting a TV-ready body with the assistance of personal trainers, nutritionists, and chefs. When his hands slid to my shoulders, I knew escaping his grasp would take effort. It was aggravating, being in love with someone who could see all of your secrets in your face except for the ones that mattered the most.

I closed my eyes, facing the darkness of my eyelids.

"I can't do this anymore," I whispered, more to myself than to him.

Ezra's voice was soft, raspy, a fingernail scratching along wool.

"What do you mean by that?" he said. "What do you mean by *this*?"

I gestured between us, to the too-close space, the desperation that hung thick in the air, tension that had no business existing, considering I was the only one who could feel it.

"This," I said. "Whatever this is. Whatever *we* are."

Ezra's hold slackened just enough that I could have slid out of it if I'd wanted to. But I didn't. Instead I watched the revelation settle over his face—first, through his rapidly blinking eyes, then the stuttering inhale followed by an exaggerated swallow, finally, the click and shift of his jaw, his telltale sign of discomfort that none of his acting coaches had succeeded in training out of him. I realized, suddenly, that this was it. That he knew. That I wanted him to know.

"Jo," he said quietly. "Do you . . . ?" He opened his mouth to continue, then clamped it shut, and I leaned into him, closing the distance that he'd already all but eradicated.

"Do I what?" I whispered. I realized, right then, that if Ezra finished his question, I would tell him the truth. That the fear that had held me back all these years (fear that he wouldn't feel the same; that we would have a few weeks of awkwardness in which he would pretend that I'd said nothing at all; that there would be a new, palpable distance between us, a millisecond's hesitation before he pulled me into hugs that were no longer crushing; that I would lose him slowly, and in the process lose Renata, and wake up in a world in which I could call neither of them mine) now paled in comparison to a future in which I stayed stagnant by his side and he continued to choose *Ashleys* over me.

Ezra stared down at me, shocked into stone. I watched his gaze slip down to my lips, then back up to my eyes, like he was seeing me anew, and a hope I'd once stomped out reignited in my chest.

"I . . ." he started.

Behind us, the door flew open.

"You two are always squirrelled away somewhere!" a voice said, Renata's. "Ezra, that girl you brought is weeping all over the atrium. Why don't you be a gentleman and . . ." A pause. "Oh. Am I interrupting something?"

I watched Ezra's eyes tick over my shoulder to meet his mother's, but I didn't turn around to acknowledge her, just chased down his gaze. I could sense him pulling away, leaning ever so slightly toward the door, and I felt every inch like a scab pulled early.

Ezra cleared his throat. "I have to go," he said.

"You don't have to," I said. "You're choosing to."

He rolled his bottom lip into his mouth, a confirmation, and my heart sank.

When Ezra stepped around me, around the desk, and bolted for the exit, I didn't watch him leave. *Is this the hurt I've been avoiding all these years?* I thought, as the door clicked shut. I'd expected devastation. I'd expected to feel like I was tearing apart at the seams, like I would fall to my feet and never stand up again. I'd expected the sort of heartbreak that inspired breakup anthems, screenplays, sonnets.

Instead, what I felt was a quiet, resolute grief, like I'd known all along that this would be the outcome of letting Ezra know that my feelings for him were not entirely platonic. And now that I'd exhausted the last of my what-ifs, the time had come to move on.

I had already tried many other methods of getting over Ezra—ardent denial, immersing myself in work, even physical space. But what I really needed was to quit him cold turkey. No more good-morning texts, no middle-of-the-day calls where we recounted an old misadventure for the hundredth time, no spontaneous meals, no innocent touches that my brain could interpret as something more. Just me, a carton of ice cream, and a fifth rewatch of *Love Actually*. Girls' nights out with my roommate, Dahlia, where I would actually let her play wingwoman like she'd always wanted. Maybe even a dating app, when I felt ready.

A hand settled on my shoulder.

"That certainly seemed tense," Renata said. "Are you okay?"

I turned. Renata looked down at me, her eyes wide with concern, and mine instantly welled with tears.

When I first met Renata Kovalenko, I'd found her hard to look at without staring. Her beauty was incisive, her features almost in-human in their perfection, and they'd graced editorial magazines for two decades prior to her retirement. Now her presence was as welcome and familiar as my favorite blanket. I remembered what she'd told me when we first met, at Ezra's hospital bed. *You're ours now,* she'd said, squeezing my hand. *I will not let you be a stranger.*

"It's nothing," I said. A tear escaped down my cheek, and I swore under my breath, dabbing it away with the heel of my hand. "All right, fine, it's *something*, but I'll be okay, Renata, really."

Renata's gaze turned hawkish.

"Did that boy say something to you?" she said. Her voice lowered to a harsh whisper. "I'm telling you, this acting business, it turns good men into such *pigs*. All that adulation, it's not good for their heads. We need to put him back in his place."

"It's his birthday party," I deadpanned.

"He's thirty," Renata said. "Old enough to be fully aware that this party is mostly for me."

I laughed. Renata didn't, and my heart ached with love for her.

"Seriously, Renata, there's no need. It's a bit embarrassing that I'm even weepy in the first place. That's what I get for mixing Prozac with champagne." When she didn't relent, I sighed. "I just need a minute to get myself together."

Renata glared at me, unblinking, for what felt like a full minute. Then she straightened, smoothing her hands down her dress.

"Okay," she said. "Your room upstairs is clean. Go. Take the time you need." She flexed a diminutive bicep, curling her mouth into a snarl. "And if you change your mind, give me the word. I'll have him thrown out by his underpants."

"I won't," I said. "But thank you."

"Of course," she said. Then, squeezing my shoulder, she swept the door open and disappeared into the throng, leaving me to contemplate a future without her.

CHAPTER TWO
Mal

Malcolm Waters had been described in many ways: *A dynamic new voice*, the *New York Times* had proclaimed, following the publication of his debut novel, *She Blooms at Dusk*. *Supremely gifted*, his photography professor had said. *A sweet kid*, his mother still liked to say, even though he was thirty-two and very much a man now—*Come on, Momma, Jesus. Brimming with talent, and yet completely lacking ambition*, his ex-girlfriend, Portia, had said, shortly before permanently ending their tumultuous on-again, off-again decade-long relationship.

An incredible idiot, Kieran of Kieran and Kelechi, programmer power couple and the only friends Mal got in the divorce, typed into the group chat. Seriously. How does one get invited to an Adelman party and NOT PREPARE?

Be nice, babe, Kelechi responded. Mal's just not used to being a big shot.

In Kieran's defense, it was true that Mal had not prepared for the Adelman party, which was why he'd shown up at Kieran and Kelechi's doorstep the day before with all of the formal wear he owned hanging over his shoulder and a stream of questions about which of his pieces qualified as cocktail or black tie falling off his tongue. And in Mal's defense, he had not been expecting an invitation. His connection with the Adelmans was tenuous at best; his mother had retired from Knydus a few years ago and, back when his photography studio was still operational, he'd done a few promotional shoots for their associated charity. When he received the email from his literary agent, Amelia, informing him that the Adelmans had requested his address, his first concern was that he was being sued.

Instead, he had received a personalized invitation to Ezra Adelman's birthday party from the one and only Renata Kovalenko.

Even in his discomfort, Mal could recognize the gravity of this event. The wealthiest and most important people in Chicago, all gathered in the five thousand square feet of the Adelmans' Gold Coast penthouse. He felt like he'd crawled through a closet to Narnia, and that everyone on the other side wore Dior.

Kelechi: By the way, Mal, your read receipts are on. Put away your phone and go rub elbows. Also, if you do manage to get an audience with THE Renata Kovalenko, please please pretty please get her autograph for me. Thank youuuuuuuuuuu.

I'll do my best, Mal typed dispassionately. His (Kieran's) jacket was too tight in the shoulders, and he rolled them back, dropping his head against the sculpted wood walls of the Adelman penthouse atrium. He did not want to rub elbows. If Renata hadn't personally signed his invitation with *Bravo on your beautiful novel! Would love to discuss further, xoxo*, he probably wouldn't have come to this party at all. But if he hadn't, Amelia would track him down and roast him over an open fire. (This was not an exaggeration. She'd told him as much. "With adobo seasoning.") By Amelia's calculations, Renata was going to offer to buy film rights to *She Blooms at Dusk*, and, given the newness of her production company and the depth of the Kovalenko-Adelman coffers, the offer was sure to be fuck-everybody-else huge.

As long as he didn't muck things up.

But one hour in and he'd seen neither hide nor hair of Renata. At some point, exasperated, he'd asked a group of unnaturally gorgeous women whether they'd seen the hostess, and they had tittered among themselves and said with at least an ounce of derision, "Good luck." Apparently, an audience with Renata was hard to get.

Which was how Mal found himself at the back of the room, nursing a glass of excellent Scotch, texting his friends, and trying to determine how much longer he had to stick around before Amelia would cut him some slack and allow him to make a graceful exit. He could feel his skin beginning to crawl, his discomfort coming through in his jostling legs and the whirlpool forming in his glass. Eventually, after plucking a croquette from a passing waiter's tray, he stepped away from the wall, crossed the room, and wandered out into the hall. God, when had he become so useless? Not so long ago, he'd taken pride in being able to meld into any group, anywhere, to find familiar ground among Kieran's rugby friends, in Kelechi's slam poetry groups. He'd been the king of diffusing tension. When had he lost that ability and become "spineless," as Portia had once said? Renata Kovalenko might want to make his book into a freaking movie, and he could hardly stand to stick around long enough to start the conversations that could turn that into a reality. A once-in-a-lifetime opportunity, and he was fumbling the bag.

"Get your shit together," Mal said under his breath. He remembered advice his therapist had first given him, when he'd realized that maybe his aversion to public spaces was more than run-of-the-mill introversion. *It's okay to find a space if you need it*, he'd said. *As long as you don't let yourself sink into it.*

Space. Space was certainly not lacking in this place. He'd already traversed the crowded first floor, but there was a stairwell near the back that he'd seen only a few people ascend since his arrival. He propelled himself off the back wall, then power walked down the hall.

A couple of guests were milling about upstairs, peering down on the party from a mezzanine balcony, and the reduced density made it easier for him to breathe. The hallway just beyond was lined with dark wood doors, and he lingered, waiting to see if someone would appear before letting himself into the first room on his right.

It was a bedroom, but not one that was regularly used, judging by its lack of personal effects. Mal lingered by the door for a second, feeling (knowing) that he was trespassing, considering how he would explain himself if someone were to walk in after him. But just this short moment of solitude was already doing wonders for loosening the band around his chest. He snapped the door shut. Wiped his hands down his face. Sat on the edge of the perfectly made bed and inhaled, focusing on the top of his head, his shoulders, his palms. Calm spread down his body like cool water. The image of a person materialized behind his closed eyelids, hazy but tall, intimidatingly beautiful, and he practiced flashing them a smile.

"Hi. I'm Malcolm," he said out loud, and, in his mind, the person responded. Despite appearances, they were warm, much more approachable than the guests beyond this room. They introduced themselves, expressed how much they loved his novel, and asked, *Has anyone talked to you about potentially bringing it to a screen?*

"There's some interest," he responded. "But we're still looking for the right team for it, someone who will understand the vision—"

The door opened and closed, so gently that, given a few more minutes, Mal might have dismissed the sound as a part of the scene he'd concocted in his mind. But then someone cleared their throat, and it became apparent that he'd been caught.

A woman stared at him from the closed door, her eyebrows raised high. She grasped the doorknob behind her, as if she were still deciding whether she intended to make a quick escape. But of course she was. She'd just happened upon a strange man muttering to himself in a room that was very likely off-limits. If only he could cease to exist. Better yet, if only he'd never been born.

Then, inexplicably, things got worse.

"What," the woman said, her lips barely moving in shock, "are you doing in my room?"

CHAPTER THREE

Jo

It had been some years since I'd last slept in my room in the Adelmans' Gold Coast penthouse. During my second year of medical school, the radiator in my studio burst, plunging the temperature of my already shoddily heated apartment into the low forties and coating my windows in a gray layer of frost. I'd spent a week shivering under piles of blankets before Ezra dragged me out of "that fridge" into his house and declared a guest room mine. When two weeks passed and my landlord still hadn't fixed the heat, I emptied my suitcases into the closet. Put up a whiteboard. Filled the empty bookcase with Osler and Sattar and Gray's. Renata's love for me had been fresh at the time, more a consequence of gratitude than true affection, and she showed it by leaving small trinkets by my door: boxes of chocolates, a diamond tennis bracelet, unhelpful study guides recommended to her by her out-of-touch, long-out-of-practice doctor friends.

But a man? Even for Renata, that would be a bit much.

"Um," the intruder said, jumping jaggedly to his feet. "Sorry. I—I didn't realize—"

I assessed him. Copper-brown skin gleaming under my bed-

room lights, neat finger-thick locs that fell artfully over his forehead, stubble that probably reappeared within hours of a shave.
Too broad to be one of Renata's models, too easily flustered to
be one of Ezra's actor friends. His blue velvet smoking jacket was
certainly a choice, but he filled it out nicely.

"I promise I'm not a pervert," he said, and I raised my eyebrows, not sure if I'd anticipated those words in that sequence.
He must have heard himself because he winced. "Oh god. That
is definitely something a pervert would say. But I had to say it,
you know, because there's a very short list of reasons why I could
be in your room, and I'm sure you were thinking it. So yes. Your
panties are safe, or whatever." I raised my eyebrows higher, and
he cursed under his breath. "If it helps, I really want to disappear
right now. So, um, let me get out of your space . . ."

My body moved automatically to block his path.

"Who were you talking to?" I asked. I watched his eyes flit
pleadingly to the door. "Earlier, I mean."

"No one," he said quickly. Then he dragged a hand down his
face. "But you knew that. There's no one else here. I was talking
to myself."

"You could've been on the phone," I offered, holding back a
smirk when he scowled. To think I'd come into this room to *sulk*.
This was so much more fun.

"Well, I wasn't." He sighed, shoving his hands deep into his
pockets and rocking forward on the balls of his feet. "All right,
I think I've been punished enough. Now, if you don't mind, I'd
really like to leave with at least a shred of my dignity intact—"

"Josephine," I said suddenly. I thrust out my hand, holding his
eyes in a challenge. "Most people call me Jo."

He stilled. I watched, with fascination, as a full spectrum of emotions crossed his face—bewilderment, embarrassment, curiosity, and then finally, relief.

"Malcolm," he said, taking my hand in his. "Most people call me Mal." This time, he held my gaze. From up close, I could see that his eyes were uniquely shaped: partially hooded, slightly downturned, soul-searching in a way that lent a quiet intimacy to his regard. They widened, almost imperceptibly, with recognition. "And . . . please don't be weirded out, but I think I know who you are."

I pursed my lips. I was nowhere near as famous as Ezra, who could barely get a coffee at the Intelligentsia's on his block without ending up in a Bustle article critiquing his outfit, but I was niche famous, familiar to health care workers and the kind of vaguely man-hating doomscrollers who appreciated my frank approach to sex ed and my perspectives on being a woman in medicine. People like Mal—namely, presumably straight men—were definitely not my target demographic.

"Through social media?" I said.

"Yeah," Mal said, suddenly shy. "You're Dr. Jojobee on Instagram, right? We've . . . um . . . talked before, in the DMs."

"Oh?" I said, stepping around him to sit on the edge of my bed. "What's your handle?"

He told me: Inlandwaters ("Made the account in college," he confessed, sheepish.); and I pulled out my phone, navigating to our conversation. The second I saw his profile picture, a stylized photograph of a hand crushing a juice box, heat rushed to my face.

"Oh *god*," I said, scrolling through our conversations. Most of them were likes and thumbs-ups, singular comments ("Have fun," he'd said, to a video of my roommate Dahlia and me drunkenly belting "The Boy Is Mine" by Brandy and Monica on the Ferris wheel in Navy Pier), and the occasional brief exchange on the topic of my most recent posts. But sometimes the conversations were extensive. My most viral post to date, a video in which I responded to a follower's question about how I communicated my boundaries with my sexual partners with an apparently shocking "Actually, I've never had sex," had generated a surprisingly academic hour-long conversation about virginity as a social construct. In response to my post explaining why I hadn't started a staff job after residency, he'd said, "I think it's good that you're taking some time—whether to rest or to evaluate what you want to do with your life next. We don't romanticize just existing enough in this culture," and I'd spent the rest of the afternoon lounging on the couch, encouraging him to massage away my guilt.

The mattress dipped next to me.

"Find anything good in there?" Mal said, a smile in his voice.

"I don't know if I'll call it *good*," I said, stunned, still scrolling. "Oh my god, I told you about my *mother*."

Mal laughed. Even quietly, it sounded like thunder.

"I thought you were very appropriate," he said. "And I was touched that you confided in me."

I peered at Mal out of the corner of my eye. When I first started my social media platform, Dr. Jojobee, I'd answered almost all of my messages. But when my following exploded, the expectations of parasocial relationships had floored me. Four hundred thousand people who thought they knew me and therefore owned me, who greeted me with wide smiles and open arms like old friends when they saw me in real life, who dissected my every move and threw tantrums in my comments section when I made posts criticizing behavior that they felt echoed their own.

I didn't know Mal. I hadn't even known what he looked like. His page was sparse, with only one photo from eight years ago of a significantly lankier, significantly gawkier version of himself, with a face that hadn't yet hollowed out. But he sort of knew me, and I found that immensely irritating.

"All right, Mal," I said. "You know that I'm an unemployed doctor who's never had sex and has serious mommy issues, which I think puts us on *very* unequal footing. You owe me some secrets."

"Secrets?" Mal said, considering. "I don't really have many of those."

Somehow, I believed him. There was an openness to his expression that suggested that, unlike half the attendees of this party, Mal wasn't accustomed to artifice.

"Truths, then," I offered. "No low-hanging fruit, though. The kind of truths that you wouldn't normally tell someone you just met."

"Truths," Mal repeated. "Okay. Well. I'm a writer who used to be a photographer, and I have a pretty good relationship with my parents. And I have had sex, though I'll admit it's been a while."

I nodded, trying to keep the surprise off my face. Mal had been blessed with good looks, not the kind that would inspire a double take, per se, but features that got more interesting the longer you looked at them. And there was a steadiness to his spirit that set me at ease, as if I were talking to an old friend rather than some guy who knew me from the internet and had been muttering to himself in my bedroom. In the few minutes since our interaction had begun, I'd almost forgotten about Ezra and Ashley, about Renata, about the loss I was soon to endure.

"A writer," I said. "And I'm assuming a good one, since Renata invited you."

"Ha," Mal said. Suddenly he looked shy again, as if, despite having never read a word of his work, I'd just offered him the highest praise. "Um, who knows. I don't check my ratings, and I'm only on social media to lurk, so I don't even really know how my book's being perceived."

"What's the name of your book?" I said, my finger hovering over the search bar to look it up.

Mal scratched the back of his neck nervously.

"*She Blooms at Dusk*," he said. "Came out last winter."

My jaw dropped. *She Blooms at Dusk* had topped the *New York Times* adult hardcover list for three weeks straight, and I'd seen it all over my feeds, and, more recently, on Renata's bookshelf. "Have you read this one yet, Josephine?" Renata had asked me just the other day. "It's divine. Very different. I think you'll like it. And, I think, a great potential project for En Garde."

"You're Malcolm Waters," I said. *Inlandwaters*. Of course. "Have you met Renata yet? She's obsessed with your book."

Mal ducked his head, embarrassed, and I studied his face, trying to piece him together. Most writer types were a bit self-absorbed, soaking up flattery like neglected houseplants even while they played at humility. But Mal seemed genuinely uncomfortable with my commentary, as if he'd rather I hadn't offered it at all.

"She's who I'm here to see. Just haven't been able to track her down," he confessed. He stared at the floor, a muscle in his cheek twitching. "But honestly, before you showed up, I was thinking about getting out of here. I got a bit, ah, overwhelmed."

The man I'd seen when I first entered the room had seemed nervous, his legs jostling, his hands anchored on either side of the bed. I'd watched him inhale, count down on his fingers, exhale, breathing exercises that I, being chronically serotonin-deficient myself, recognized on sight.

"Anxious?" I said, nodding sagely.

Mal glanced up at me with saucer-wide eyes.

"A little," he confessed. "I . . . don't do well with people."

"You're doing well with me, though," I said, and I watched him fight a smile, fascinated by the flash of his teeth, by the way it softened his entire face. It occurred to me, suddenly, that I thought Mal was cute. And not in the passive, fleeting way that I sometimes found men attractive, but in the way that made me want to see what other expressions he could make.

"That's . . . I'm shocked by that," he said. "I know this isn't news to you, but you're *stunning*. I'm surprised I've managed to string a sentence together."

And there it was: confirmation of mutual attraction. An idea formed in my head, rapidly taking shape as I assessed him. Smart—check. Respectful—check. Thoughtful—check. Hot—*very*. Experienced? Well, certainly more than I was, and probably willing to teach, if his insights on my posts were any indication.

A very suitable virgin slayer indeed.

Ezra Adelman didn't want me. Fine. But Malcolm Waters might, and I was very interested in seeing where that could take me.

I stood, placed a hand on Mal's, held back my satisfaction when he winced like I was hot to the touch.

"No need for flattery. I was planning to help you out anyway," I said, guiding him to his feet. "Come on. Let's go find Renata."

CHAPTER FOUR
Mal

Mal could hardly believe his luck. When the woman in gold, now known to be Josephine Boateng of @drjojobee fame, opened the door, he'd been certain that he was cursed. There was having zero game, then there was getting caught mumbling to yourself in a woman's bedroom and promising that you weren't there to steal her underwear. And yet, despite his many foibles, Jo was guiding him through the foyer, two manicured fingers hooked loosely into his, melting barriers between him and the other guests with the efficiency of a blowtorch. She had a cosmic pull, dragging people from across the room into her orbit to say hello, to kiss her on the cheek and tell her, "You look incredible tonight, Josephine. Who are you wearing?" To waggle their eyebrows and toss him knowing looks and ask, "Now, who is *this*?"

"Malcolm Waters, author of *She Blooms at Dusk*, which may sound familiar because it's been dominating the lists lately," she would say, smiling like she was unveiling a masterpiece. "He's very humble, so he won't tell you any of this, which is why I'm doing it first."

"A pleasure," he would say after their requisite oohs and aahs, marveling at how simply being perceived as hers turned him visible.

Mal knew he tended to romanticize real life. It was what made him a strong storyteller, but also what had kept him going back to his ex over and over again, despite years of evidence suggesting they were best apart. One heartfelt apology, one well-timed sunset kiss, and he would be sucked back in, spinning together the vision of a future in which Portia returned to him a changed woman and their second (third, fourth) attempt at romance could end with a happily ever after.

And right now he was romanticizing Jo. Jo, who, when she leaned in to whisper a joke in his ear, smelled like ginger spice and jasmine; Jo, who, draped in shimmery, slick gold satin, seemed to glow from the inside out, luminous as the full moon he could see peeking through the panes of the floor-to-ceiling windows. Jo, whose focus made him feel like the most important person in a room full of newscasters and TV producers, actors, models, and entrepreneurs.

He'd thought she was beautiful when she was one of the one thousand and fifty-two people he followed on Instagram. He'd thought she was charming in her messages—alternately bold and self-effacing, witty and occasionally profound, curious in the way academics so often were about exactly how people ticked. More than once during their conversations, he'd considered asking her to meet up. *We're in the same city*, he had wanted to say, *why don't we continue this conversation over coffee?* But then he'd recall that he was just one follower in her legion of four hundred thousand, and he'd remember Portia telling him that he was *much better on paper*, and the whim would pass. Besides, social media was a disguise. It was the face people chose to show the world, not the one they lived in all day.

Except Jo's face in real life was so much more. Dr. Jojobee was glamorous, aloof, and always put together, but Jo was charming, cheerful, a little silly, even. He wanted to go back upstairs and tell her all of his truths. He wanted to kiss her, if she'd like it. If the night continued to go the way it was going, he thought he might try.

"Ugh. Where is she?" Jo said, frustrated, leading him out of the atrium and into the hall. She sucked in her cheeks, annoyed, then turned and gave him a helpless look. "I'm sorry. I promised you that I'd deliver you to Renata, and I've introduced you to basically everyone but her."

"That's okay," Mal said. "I appreciate it. Lots of interesting people out there."

Jo wrinkled her nose.

"You really enjoyed listening to Boris tell me about his *gout*?" she said.

Mal laughed.

"I thought it was fascinating that an Academy Award–winning director comes to you for medical advice," he quipped.

Mal expected a laugh from her, or at the very least a pleased eye roll. But Jo's gaze had shifted to somewhere over his shoulder and had turned hard. When it slid back to his, it didn't soften.

"Your bow tie's crooked," she said, suddenly curt, and then, with a click of her heel that sounded like she intended to drive it through the floor, she stepped in close to adjust it herself.

Before Mal could fully formulate the question gestating in his mind, its answer presented itself.

"Jo," a man said, breathless. "I've been looking everywhere for you."

Mal turned and found himself the subject of intense scrutiny.

He had never seen Ezra Adelman in real life, but he managed to be more aggravatingly good-looking than he appeared in his photos, the combination of Renata Kovalenko's inhuman beauty merged with Paul Adelman's aggressive averageness to create a man Mal had once seen declared America's Bachelor Prince.

"Can we talk?" Ezra said, presumably to Jo, though his eyes hadn't left Mal's.

"I'm a bit busy," Jo said. She'd undone Mal's bow tie entirely and was retying it with the deftness of someone who'd tied a thousand bow ties before, many of them, Mal realized, possibly worn by the man who was glaring daggers at him right now. "Have to deliver this one to your mom. This is Malcolm Waters. She's trying to buy film rights to his book, and for some reason decided the best place to talk to him about it was here."

Ezra's expression cleared as cleanly as if he'd wiped it away.

"Nice to meet you," he said, in a way that suggested that *nice* was generous. Then, to Jo, "It'll just take a minute."

Jo snapped Mal's bow tie tight, then tapped it once with the tips of her fingers.

"No it won't," she said. To Mal, brightly, "Much better. Let's go."

Then she set off, stepping around Ezra like he was a fallen log in her path.

And, despite the uncertainty that churned like a whirlpool in his stomach, Mal had no choice but to follow.

"So they're definitely fucking," Kieran said, when two days after the party, Mal showed up at his place to return his borrowed suit.

"Were, maybe," Mal said, keeping his voice low. Harvey, their two-year-old, was fast asleep in the room next door. He didn't want to consider the possibility that the so-called Virgin Sex Doc had been lying about her lack of experience, not because he cared much about Jo's sexual history, but because it would mean that she had lied to him. Which, he supposed, was only marginally worse than using him to make Ezra Adelman jealous.

"Sound a little less excited about the idea, babe. Mal's clearly disappointed," Kelechi said from the couch where she lay, phone balanced on top of her pregnant belly, a candy-striped pink sock over her left residual leg. "Also, I'm, like, a thousand percent sure they are not."

"Kind of cocky, for someone with no evidence," Kieran said.

Kelechi grinned. In college, she'd earned the nickname FBI for her ability to track down the names of her friends' missed connections based on astonishingly limited information. She'd once hunted down a guy her friend had danced with in a club based on the clue "Chris from Canada." Finding info on an influencer and a guy who was actually famous was a piece of cake. With a flourish, Kelechi turned over her phone to reveal a photograph of Ezra Adelman, a few years and twenty pounds (lighter) ago, dressed in a crisp black tuxedo and escorting a smiling Jo on a red carpet. She looked incredible in a turquoise floor-length gown and a slicked-back high ponytail, and Mal felt his stomach clench at the sight of them together.

"Not sure if this helps, K," he said.

Kelechi rolled her eyes.

"Did you read the article?" she said. She cleared her throat, then started, "'Jo's my closest friend in the entire world. There's no one else I'd rather be here with tonight.'"

Kieran nodded sagely, rubbing his chin.

"Intimate, but heavy on the platonic vibes. He's definitely not claiming her," he observed. He nudged Mal, just a bit too hard, in the ribs. "I stand corrected. Maybe you do have a shot."

Mal wasn't so sure. The way Ezra had looked at him, like he wanted to drive an ice pick into his chest, was not how one generally looked at a man who was cavorting with his entirely platonic friend.

And then there was Jo. She'd shone blindingly bright for the hour or so they'd had together, but the second Ezra appeared, it was like a curtain in her eyes had snapped closed. Suddenly she was curt, her smiles unnaturally tight at the corners. They'd found Renata at the end of the hall shortly afterward, and she'd excused herself after introducing them with a quick "I'm sure you two have a lot to talk about," disappearing like a sullen Cinderella at the stroke of midnight.

Mal knew a breakup when he saw one; after all, he'd been involved in several himself. And what he had witnessed between Jo Boateng and Ezra Adelman was most certainly its aftermath.

He'd heard neither hide nor hair from Jo since. This, Mal knew, was for the best. It had been two and a half years since he'd last seen Portia, and while he'd licked most of his wounds clean, he was still wary of the sort of all-consuming, whirlwind infatuation that he'd felt with her, that he'd immediately sensed forming with Jo. The next time Mal fell for someone, he would do it slowly, ease himself in, get to know them before they surprised him with red flags he'd ignored among the sea of green.

But then, just as he gathered his resolve, his phone buzzed.

It was a notification from Instagram. Drjojobee has sent you a message.

Mal choked on his spit, and Kieran and Kelechi looked at him in alarm.

"You okay there?" Kieran said hesitantly.

Mal coughed, beating at his chest as he read the message on his screen. Then read it again.

Hey, it said. You seem to have forgotten to ask for my number. Would you like me to give it to you? Maybe over dinner?

"I think . . ." he said, clearing his throat. "She might have just asked me out."

CHAPTER FIVE

Jo

This one is for my independent girls. You've been through it. You've been gaslit, you've been drained dry, you've been told what you can and can't achieve, and you've proven everyone wrong along the way. And because you've endured, you've decided that you are strong. And I'm here to say: enough of that. Strong isn't a personality trait. It's a sign that you're neglected and not protected. It's just as much evidence of your trauma as it is of your triumph. So this year, I say, enough with strength. I'm entering my damsel era. I'm eating cake and being pretty and crying when I'm hurt, and apologizing for none of it. Won't you join me?

"Two weeks," Denise said, her voice mosquito shrill through my earbuds. "You have screened my calls for two weeks, Josephine. How am I supposed to make us money if you can't be reached?"

I rubbed my temples, flinching when I caught the edge of the motion reflected in my monitor. Respectfully, I looked like shit. It was a small mercy Denise had accepted a phone call rather than the video she typically insisted on in order to keep me honest.

"I know," I said. "I'm sorry. How mad is Tanaka?"

"Not mad yet, but they're definitely getting impatient," Denise confessed. "I bought you forty-eight more hours. But forget Tanaka. I'm mad! What the hell happened?"

Oh, Denise. Four years ago, when she'd approached me via DM to offer to manage my Dr. Jojobee influencer platform, I'd been impressed enough with her gumption to give her a try. She was unaffiliated, her agency's single-member LLC only recently incorporated, and her client list had featured only one other physician-influencer, a dermatologist-slash-fashionista who turned out to be one of Denise's old high school friends. But Denise was hungry and no-nonsense and constantly on the hunt, and I liked that about her. It meant she got me paid. Her ability to monetize my platform was the reason why I could survive without my residency salary. And critically, she minded her business and only got heated up when someone tried to sabotage it.

And right now that someone was me.

"Nothing happened. I got a little behind," I said. It was technically the truth. Nothing had happened. I'd dragged my feet because I was tired. Of twirling around in gifted dresses that overstuffed my closets; recording pithy, unrelated "inspirational" voice-overs; and selling myself to four hundred thousand onlookers when I probably should be getting off my ass and taking care of patients.

An email from my old pulmonary critical care mentor, Dr. Makinen, echoed my sentiments.

Have you considered applying to fellowship next year? You would have the full support of the department. And you wouldn't have to make your living making ticky tocks anymore.

I didn't respond to Dr. Makinen. The truth was, the concept of walking back into the hospital filled me with bottomless dread, matched only by the concept of putting together another video / photoshoot / promotional campaign for a company that wanted to take advantage of my sizable following and the letters after my name to sell people shit they didn't need. Alas, I needed to eat, and to pay rent, and I was lacking in skills that could be used outside the wards. Check, meet mate.

"Tanaka doesn't have to wait forty-eight hours," I said. "The video's done. I'm sending it to you now."

The woman in the video I played back to myself looked up at the camera coquettishly over an ornate painted teacup, the puffy periwinkle-blue tulle sleeves of her Tanaka Couture gown billowing around her like plumes of smoke. Her teeth were bright white (Crest Whitestrips; $8,000 for a video post, six-month ad rights), lips a romantic crimson (ColourPop; $3,000 for the feed), and hair plaited into passion twists that draped down her back and over the swell of her chest (-$350, because Fatou, her humorless Senegalese braider, could care less that her favorite client had a social media following nearing half a million). She was giving Black Girl Luxury. Black Girl Opulence. Black Girl with Expensive Taste.

But that was two weeks ago, and that same woman was now sitting cross-legged in her office chair and giving Black Girl in Crisis. Black Girl in Desperate Need of a Shower. Black Girl Trying Her Best to Convince Her Agent Not to Drop Her Like a Hot Rock.

I clicked "compile" on my video editing software, then dragged the finished file into Denise's and my shared drive.

"I'll check it out in a minute," Denise said, mollified. "But, my dear Dr. Miracle? This can't happen again. Seriously."

She hung up, and I leaned back in my office chair. Light streamed through my blinds, streaking across my lap in bright stripes, and I squinted at the window, marveling at the passage of time. It was almost eleven in the morning, seven hours after I'd crawled out from under the stifling heat of my comforter and onto my desk chair. I'd never been a good sleeper, and the beating my circadian rhythm had taken during the shifting schedule of residency had only made things worse. But since Ezra's party, sleep had eluded me completely. Putting my phone away hadn't helped. Melatonin didn't touch me. Even the fifty milligrams of Benadryl I'd downed last night in a moment of desperation had only bought me a few hours of fitful rest before summoning my sleep paralysis demon. (Daisy, I'd named her. She liked to ogle me from the ceiling.) At the moment, I was about one more sleepless night away from concussing myself just to give my consciousness a break.

A sharp sound, too loud to be blocked by state-of-the-art manufactured silence, forced me out of my thoughts. I popped out my earbuds, my heart ratcheting up to my throat. I was supposed to be alone. Dahlia wasn't getting back from her travel nurse contract until the twenty-eighth, and—

I checked the date on my phone. It was the twenty-ninth. *Christ.*

"When'd you get back?" I said, walking into the kitchen.

Dahlia twirled to face me, clutching a blue owl mug to her chest. Her silk floral robe was open to her navel, exposing a curling sternum tattoo and the arcs of breasts that had no business sitting so high on her chest. Even from ten feet away, I could hear pop music blasting through her headphones. She nudged them off her ear with her shoulder, placed her mug on the counter, and launched herself into my arms.

"You *stink* stink," she said lovingly, holding me tighter when, self-conscious, I tried to pull away. "And I mean that in all the ways. Left me on read for two whole days. Gave me absolutely zero intel about the Adelman shindig. *And* you smell like Fritos."

I winced. I still wasn't totally used to having my absence routinely noted by anyone other than the Adelmans, and between Dahlia and Denise, it was almost stifling. Almost. Mostly it was nice.

"Sorry," I said. "You know. Had a bit of a slump."

One thing I appreciated about Dahlia was that she never performed pity. There were no upturned eyebrows, no protracted *awww*s, no empty claims of *Well, if you need to talk about it, I'm here.* When Dahlia and I had first met, the ink on her divorce papers barely dry, the ink on her arms hardly healed, she'd made it clear that she had no intention of being the sort of woman people felt sorry for. I liked that about her, liked even more that she insisted on extending the same courtesy to me.

"You been taking your happy pills?" Dahlia asked matter-of-factly, settling onto the cushioned seat at our kitchen bar.

"Yup," I said, popping off the *p* as I dug through the cupboard for our French press.

"Okay then. Anything set it off?"

"Adelman shindig, probably," I answered simply. "You want any?" I asked, shaking a bag of coffee grounds.

"I was going to do tea today. Preserve my stomach lining." She tapped long coffin-shaped nails against our granite countertop. "Speaking of tea. Are you going to spill?"

I sighed, stirring the mixture of grounds and boiling water with a chopstick, watching the rainbow slick of oil form at the top.

"Well, for one, Ezra's dating my childhood bully," I said plainly.

Dahlia placed her mug on the counter so firmly I had to check to make sure the ceramic hadn't cracked.

"*What?*" she said, all the mirth draining from her face. Then: "Tell me everything."

So I did, amazed by how I could recount the events without batting an eye, like I'd witnessed them from afar. Ashley weeping in the atrium, Ezra marching me into the study to scold me, before dodging a very much needed, much overdue conversation about what *we* were. Finding Malcolm Waters, the surprisingly cute writer who'd holed himself up in my bedroom, and discovering that apparently, we'd been chatting for the last six years on my platform. How easily Mal had managed to help me forget my angst until the source of said angst showed up and burst our bubble. I'd been so in my feelings afterward that I'd stormed away after dropping Mal off with a particularly elusive Renata and probably looked like an enormous ass to whom he would never want to speak again. *She's kind of a bitch in real life*, I imagined him telling his friends.

"Why would you think that he thinks that?" Dahlia said when I was done. Predictably, she'd started with the juiciest tidbit, which was that I, Josephine "he's all right, I guess" Boateng, might be interested in someone other than Ezra.

"Because I was," I said plainly. I remembered how he'd looked at me when I'd left him with Renata: knowingly, like he'd expected me to disappoint him.

Dahlia shrugged.

"Maybe he likes that," she said. She blew over her tea. "Look,

I know Ezra is your friend and all that, but what would you even do if he'd told you he was secretly into you too? Do you *want* to be girlfriend number five hundred and fifty-two? Especially right after this Ashley chick?"

"Number nine," I corrected quickly, slurping my too-hot coffee through pursed lips. As predicted, Dahlia had cut right to the meat of the matter. "And no. No, I don't think so. I think I need to figure myself out first."

Romantic love, or at least what I'd seen of it, was flighty. You could love someone desperately for five years and never speak to them again for the rest of your life. It made you do stupid things, like choose your best friend's childhood bully over her in a roomful of people, or let yourself get to twenty-nine with less sexual experience than the average sixteen-year-old because you were waiting on a guy who made it clear that you were just his friend to change his mind.

Actually respecting and regarding another person for who they were, without the cascade of hormones and impingement of lust, was more long-standing. And what I wanted from the Adelmans was preservation. When, the morning after the party, Renata sent me a text reminding me that *whatever issues Ezra and I were having had nothing to do with her* and assuring me that she would even seat us at different tables at her upcoming Knydus Nest health benefit if I wanted, I'd felt overwhelming relief, like I'd been released from an obligation. It was okay that I'd responded to Ezra's litany of pleading texts (Where did you go? Did you leave? I don't want to fight. Can you talk to me, please?) with a true, simple I need space. It was okay that I'd unfollowed him on social media and put his calls on "straight to voicemail."

We were friends. When I was ready, maybe we could come back to that again. If we'd crossed any more lines, maybe recovery would have been impossible.

Dahlia had a similar revelation before, two years ago, after finalizing her divorce from her high school sweetheart, Jonathan. Jonathan had been a dreamboat of a boyfriend for a teenager: sweet, prone to grand romantic gestures, the kind of good Catholic boy that her friends in her junior praise group prayed for. But he hadn't transitioned well into adulthood. His college major in psychology was meant to become a PhD, lead to an academic career, but he'd dropped out three years in with a masters he never intended to use. While Dahlia worked her way through nursing school, he was intermittently employed, grumbling about how the world had wronged him, directing his frustration toward his wife. Eventually, he'd had an affair with a nineteen-year-old coworker at Best Buy, and Dahlia, who had spent the latter part of their marriage suppressing and remolding herself to bring back the great love of her youth, let go.

Away from her childhood home and childhood love, Dahlia had rediscovered herself. She learned that the obsessive admiration she'd occasionally had for other women was actually attraction, that the nursing job that she'd spent years pretending to feel fulfilled in was in fact destroying her spirit (and her back). So she quit her job, started taking travel nursing contracts that sent her to intensive care units around the country on her own time, started dating (*see* sobbing over) girls, and embraced her new identity as a "baby goth disaster bisexual."

"You won't die without romantic love. In fact, it's statistically more likely to kill you," she'd said after I first confided in her about my lack of experience. "But I also wish you'd put yourself out there. Your world won't stop turning without Ezra Adelman in it. Maybe it's time to move on."

And now she was sitting across from me, grinning like the Cheshire cat.

"You just had an epiphany," Dahlia observed. "And I hope it's that you should hook up with the writer."

I sputtered around my coffee.

"How did you come to that conclusion?" I said, exasperated. "Shouldn't you be telling me I need to *heal* or something?"

"Is this what you call healing?" Dahlia said, gesturing to my admittedly pitiable state. "Sitting in your apartment, half-jobless, weeping about the same guy who's been stringing you along for ten years while your coochie continues to grow cobwebs?" I winced, stung that she'd given a voice to my most critical thoughts. She tapped a nail next to my phone. "No, girl, it's time to try something different. Hit up the writer. I can tell you want to. If he doesn't respond, no harm done. It's time to get you laid."

Getting me laid was a ridiculous place to start, I thought. The first place should probably have been a shower. The second, a check-in with my therapist.

And yet. *And yet.* I thought of Mal sitting next to me on the bed, how I'd known implicitly that I could have fallen asleep at his side and he'd take off my heels and tuck me under the covers. How his top lip was ever so slightly darker than the bottom; how, for a brief second when he'd smiled, I'd wondered how he'd react if I'd caught it between my teeth. I'd liked how pliant he'd been, how easily he'd taken my hand when I offered it. I'd liked the firmness of his chest under my hand even better. *Would I?* I'd considered, already knowing that my answer was *I would.*

"No," I said, wagging the thought from my head. "No, I can't do that to Mal. He's sweet, and I'm not sure I should be trying to jump into a relationship right now. I don't want to hurt him."

"A relationship?" Dahlia said with a snort. "Be for real, woman. You said he feels safe, you find him attractive, and you're ready to jump-start your journey to find your inner goddess, or whatever. Just say, 'Hey, I would like to have sex with you, no strings attached,' and see if he's down."

"Are you sure?" I asked. "He won't feel objectified?"

"He's a guy, Jo," Dahlia said, rolling her eyes. "He'll probably think he won the lottery."

I laughed to myself. It was funny how, despite running a sex-positive platform, I hadn't considered that I could just *ask* Mal if he wanted to sleep with me. I had always been practical about sex, which was why I hadn't yet had it. Pregnancy, sexually transmitted diseases—all of those had seemed risks too great to take on a random person who would most likely prove less effective at getting me off than a good vibrator. And critically, sex required trust, and I didn't trust many people.

But I could see myself trusting Mal. Eventually. Enough to proposition him.

Five years ago, when I was but a wee innocent medical student who blushed whenever I asked my patients about their sexual histories, this suggestion would've been nuts. But I was grown now, and hungry. Picky too. It would be good to strike now, while Mal was still exciting, before he had a chance to say something stupid that would dry me out like a sponge in the Sahara.

"Okay, okay. I'll message him. But not because you bullied me into it," I added, when Dahlia's smirk turned too smug. "But because I *want* to."

My heart hammered in my chest, and I willed it to slow, reminding myself that Malcolm Waters was just a person, and unlike him, I was very good with people. I typed a message, showed it to Dahlia. "How's this?"

Dahlia took one look at the screen and cackled. "Woo boy, you're good at this," she said, fanning herself. "Send it."

So I did.

CHAPTER SIX
Mal

Mal had a thing for formidable women. He came from a long line of them: his mother, Lena Waters, had graduated summa cum laude from Caltech in computer science and had once successfully warded off sexual harassment in her workplace by smashing a keyboard over the head of a senior developer who had tried to feel her up. And he was pretty sure that his grandmother, Coretta, had murdered her abusive first husband (the formal reports said that he'd died, drunk, in a shed fire, but she liked to drop sly hints that she'd helped it along with some lighter fluid). Through stories and aged photographs, he'd learned of his great-great-grandmother Paulette, who'd bought a small ranch for her eight children in the Reconstruction era South and protected it with a shotgun half her size.

So when Portia first marched across the quad on his college campus to demand that he stop going out with Marilyn Fletcher and date her instead, he'd been so floored by the familiarity that he'd muttered, "Okay," and texted Marilyn his apologies on the spot.

And now, looking at this message from Jo, he felt like there was no world in which he could refuse.

"Yoooooo," Kelechi said, cackling, when she read the message. "Who *is* this woman? Was she like this in real life?"

Mal thought of the ease with which Jo had grabbed his hand and dragged him out of her room, how being in her presence felt like being swept up in a tornado. Terrifying. Riveting.

"Yes," he said, wiping a hand down his face to hide his grin.

"I have got to look her up," Kelechi said, and seconds later Jo's smooth alto filled the room.

"It's time for another episode of Dr. Jojo's 'Birds and the Bees,' where I answer the questions you couldn't ask in sex ed. So let's start with this one: 'My boyfriend and I have been together for six months. I was a virgin before I met him. A week ago, I started having a burning sensation when I peed, and so I went to go get tested and was positive for chlamydia. He swears that he isn't cheating. Is it possible to just get chlamydia out of nowhere?'

"Well, Jiminsprettyprincess, that's a great question. First, let's keep in mind that many sexually transmitted infections—or STIs, as you might hear them called—are silent. This means that you can be infected without symptoms for a long period of time. Here are the facts: people with penises are less likely to experience symptoms with STIs and are therefore less likely to get tested. So before you let them anywhere close to your bits without barriers, you need to—"

"Why am I getting seduced by some woman educating the masses about venereal diseases?" Kelechi said, lowering her screen in awe. "I'm in love. I think I might have to fight you for her."

Mal laughed, but Kieran was uncharacteristically quiet, looking thoughtfully at the floor.

"You good?" Mal asked, and when Kieran turned to look at him, he guessed where his friend's thoughts led. After all, he'd been Mal's roommate for years and had had a front row seat to his last relationship's recurrent meltdowns.

"You have a type," Kieran said finally, exhaling.

"Yeah?" Mal said, holding back the edge in his voice. "And what's that?"

"Hmm. Let's see. Ambitious. Assertive," Kieran said, counting off qualities on his fingers. "Toxic as fuck."

"That isn't fair," Kelechi whined, sticking out her bottom lip. She'd scrolled through multiple videos and had been snickering to herself. "Jo isn't toxic. She's a badass. Nothing like . . ." She paused, catching herself, and Mal held back a sigh.

"Nothing like Portia, yes," Mal finished. As if on cue, Kieran and Kelechi winced, and an old shame bubbled in his stomach. He'd put his friends through so much in the final act of his relationship, but he wished they could stop treating him like he would splinter at the sound of her name. He was better now. He had a book deal to show for it. A mortgage. A life that had direction. *I'm fine*, he wanted to tell them. *And even if nothing comes out of this, I'll still be fine.*

Harvey started to wail from his room and Kieran rocked himself to his feet. He looked weary, two years of sleep deprivation slackening the skin in his cheeks.

"Just be careful," Kieran said, before disappearing down the hall.

Kieran's warning bounced around Mal's head as he and Kelechi plotted how to respond to Jo's request for dinner. Kelechi insisted that he take the reins—"It's hotter if you plan it, especially if she initiated, so she knows you're really interested, you know"—which spurred a discussion about what exactly one did on a first date in one's thirties. Especially when the date in question wasn't an easily impressed college student but a grown woman with a doctorate, rich friends, and expensive taste. Google searches for "first date ideas Chicago" yielded generic results. Dinner for dinner's sake seemed a bit uninspired, and he knew he couldn't afford the kind of dining experiences the Adelmans probably treated her to on a weekly basis.

If only this were a romance novel. No one went on clumsy first dates in romance. They professed their love in the middle of vicious fights, seconds before tumbling into bed, or were driven to five-star restaurants in long limos by butlers who showed up at their place of work. They stumbled into each other repeatedly at their competing bakeries or business trips or vacations, and they never had to ask each other what they were doing, because they both obviously knew.

Eventually, Kelechi let out a squeak.

"This restaurant does cooking classes! You should do that," she declared. When he raised an eyebrow, she continued. "Less basic than just a meal, and you get to show off your skills. Plus, they have a clear start and end. If you realize you don't mesh, you can just focus on the task."

It was a brilliant idea, and Mal immediately put it into motion. He confirmed a time and a place (Friday at seven? Il Latini?) and let out a slow exhale when Jo responded immediately (See you there), before forwarding her number.

CHAPTER SEVEN

Jo

The patient lying on the bed in front of me could have been seventy or twenty-five. The skin of their hands was mottled halfway up their arms, spiderwebs of violent purples and greens and yellows creeping higher before my eyes. Next to me: my favorite nurse, Kristin.

"What do you want to do, Dr. B?" she said pleasantly.

I stared at the patient, at the flat line on their monitor. The tips of the patient's fingers had turned as black as tar. Frantic, I searched my mind for what to do next, a nonsensical flurry of mnemonics and medicalese scrolling down my vision like a credit crawl (*blood gas, pseudomonas aeruginosa, cefepime flagyl septic shock pulsus paradoxus*), until finally, I arrived at my diagnosis.

"They're already dead," I said.

Suddenly, a light flickered on, and the room was swirling with activity, anesthesiologists pushing the bed forward to place a breathing tube, a medical student losing his glasses in the yellow-stained tangle of sheets in the patient's bed as he did compressions. Dr. Makinen stood, ghoulishly tall and perfectly still, at the foot of the bed, peering at me from behind thin-rimmed glasses. I hadn't noticed him there before.

"How could you let this progress?" he said calmly, his voice preternaturally loud against the dissonance. "You call yourself a doctor?"

On the bed, the patient began to buck, their chest arching to resist the compressions, their withered hands raised toward the ceiling. Then, between one blink and the next, they were facing me.

Ezra stared at me through cloudy blue eyes. The mottling had progressed to his face, bruises blossoming up his neck like ink crawling along a wet page. A tear pooled and crested in his eye before streaking to the corner of his dry, cracked mouth.

"You left me," he croaked.

I stepped back, horrified, and then his face changed, became rounder, his hair lengthening and becoming coarse, the eye sockets widening, irises darkening to black.

My mother.

"You ruined me," she said.

My chest seized, and I scrambled backward, searching for an exit. But the scene chased after me, the room shifting to keep up like a predator as Prudence Boateng spoke.

"I was right to never love you," she said, her voice echoing in my skull like she was speaking directly into my mind, and finally, with effort, I wrenched myself awake.

I sat up, cradling my head. It was still bright outside; by the time flashing on my digital clock across the room, my attempt at a midday nap had lasted only forty-five minutes. My mother's face lingered in the darkness behind my closed eyelids. It had been thirteen years since I'd last seen her in person, and so in my mind, she'd remained forever in her late thirties, not so much older than

I was now. I wondered, not for the first time, where she was, what she was doing. Whether she was even alive.

And then I shook my head. I'd filed for emancipation at age sixteen, and in that time, Prudence Boateng had made minimal effort to establish contact. Surely she could have found me if she wanted to. I had to be one of the more prominent Josephine Boatengs in the country, and I hadn't changed my phone number from the one I'd handed her on the day I moved out of her apartment. If I was still a stranger to her, it was because Prudence wanted me to be. And if that fact still gave me grief, well, that just meant I wasn't as healed as I liked to pretend.

My pillow began to vibrate. I fished out my phone from under it.

"Hey, Dr. B," my building's doorman, Raymond, said. "You've got a package at the front desk."

I gritted my teeth, suspicious. I'd played this game before.

"Didn't realize we got personal phone calls for our packages these days," I said flatly. "Ezra send something?"

"Yup," Raymond said brightly. He was a kid, young enough that the shift work didn't wear on him, brazen enough to pull the kind of stunts an older man knew could cost him his job, like accepting bribes to guilt his tenants into picking up unwanted gifts.

Groaning, I tossed away my sheets, threw on a pair of athletic shorts, and made my way down to the lobby.

THE IRONY OF trying to get over Ezra Adelman was that I'd never wanted anything to do with him in the first place.

College may have been a place where reedy teenagers went to become capable adults, but I arrived at Gertrude B. Elion University fully grown. Unlike my roommates, I had already paid taxes, found roommates on Craigslist, worked retail, challenged my bank's overdraft fees. My admittance to a prestigious college was a golden ticket, a chance for a girl like me—poor, Black, effectively orphaned—to find stability through education. There would be no delving into dormitory drama; no house, frat, or pool parties; and certainly no boys, who would offer little more than obstacles to my goal of independence.

And then, one fated Friday night, a very drunk Ezra Adelman barreled into my dormitory room.

"What the fuck?" I'd said, holding my pillow in front of me like a weapon. Ezra didn't know me, but I knew him. Everyone at Elion University did. In our ritzy private college full of filthy rich trust-fund kids, he was the filthiest and the richest; his matriculation at Elion was hailed by an article in the local newspaper: CEO OF KNYDUS BUYS $1.3 MILLION HOME NEAR ELION UNIVERSITY CAMPUS. Adelman sightings filled the class Facebook groups, grainy shots of the handsome heir buying coffees at the library café or running across campus in the rain to make it to his next class, accompanied by heart-eye emojis. We shared a class, American Literature, and on the first day, it had taken the professor fifteen minutes to settle everyone down after Ezra had walked in.

Most of the time, I felt sorry for him, for his inability to disappear. At that moment, however, I was very pissed to find him in my room.

"What are you doing here?" I'd said when he didn't respond. "Get out!"

Ezra raised bleary eyes to me. I remembered thinking that they were jarringly blue, stark against his pale skin.

"Oh shit," he slurred, pushing his hair off his forehead. "Ellie didn't tell me she had a roommate. Sorry. I was just going to take a piss."

"There's a common bathroom!" I said. "Use that!"

Ezra shook his head, already making a turn into our bathroom. "It's occupied," he said. To my horror, he didn't close the door, and I caught the sound of his zipper being undone, our toilet seat being lifted, urine hitting the center of the bowl. When he reemerged (after washing his hands, thank goodness), he grinned up at me. "You're in my American Lit class, aren't you? I don't think we've met."

"We're not meeting now," I said, blinking away my shock; that class was forty people large. I would never have expected him to recognize me. Suddenly, I became aware of my state of undress, my thin, oversize sleeping tee, my magenta satin bonnet. He seemed to notice too, because he cocked his head to one side, regarding me more closely.

"Well, for your reference, my name's Ezra," he said. Then finally, he turned on his heel, making for the door. Before his hand closed over the handle, however, he looked at me over his shoulder and tapped his head. "I like your sleeping hat."

My pillow bounced against the closed door, and behind it, I could hear Ezra laughing.

Our interactions beyond that had been entirely out of my control. If I sat down at a library table to study, I would look up to find Ezra sliding into the seat across from me, emptying his backpack like we'd planned to meet. He invited himself to my previously lonely lunches in the cafeteria or to my quiet afternoons reading on grassy knolls on the quad and attempted to coax me into breaking into the campus observatory. When someone tried to get credit for my contributions to a discussion in American Lit, Ezra would adjust his slouch, throw up his hand, and say, insouciantly, "I think Jo just said that."

I had no choice about whether Ezra Adelman was in my life. If I closed the door on him, he would simply ram it open again.

Just as he was attempting to do now.

"I'm sorry, Dr. B, but you've got to take them," Raymond said, grinning up at me sheepishly.

"You are so annoying," I said through clenched teeth, staring at the unglazed white vase full of pristine blue hyacinths. Apology flowers, from the one person I knew pretentious enough to still communicate in Victorian era floriography. Nestled within the blossoms, a small card with Ezra's elegant handwriting in dense black ink: *I'm sorry. Talk to me please. And don't get mad at Raymond. He's a good kid making an honest living.*

"I told him to add that part," Raymond quipped, raising his phone hopefully. "Sorry, I have to send him proof of receipt. Do you mind?"

"How much did he pay you this time?" I asked, flipping him off for the picture.

"Two grand," Raymond said cheerfully.

I scowled. For someone so desperate to pretend that the twenty-four-karat-gold diamond-encrusted spoon lodged in his throat was a mere silver one, Ezra sure loved to test the limits of what his money could buy.

"Ask for more next time," I said. "The price of breaking my boundaries has got to be higher than that."

"Got it," Raymond said, not even playing at contrition. "Just promise to keep your man in the doghouse, okay? If you keep this up, I might be able to pay off my car this year."

"He is *not* my man," I hissed, storming off.

It would have been easier for me if he had been. Mourning a relationship that had only ever existed in my head was not bad-bitch behavior, and yet here I was, mooning over a man who had never really been mine. If only I'd been braver. If only, nine years ago, when I first felt this stirring in my stomach, I'd told him what it was so he could turn me down for good. I would have moved on, saved time, never caught myself in a position where drawing boundaries between us could inspire nightmares.

Balancing the vase on my hip, I opened up our text thread for what had to be the hundredth time today. Ezra had sent me messages after the party, but his most recent one, sent twelve hours ago, had replayed in my mind like a bad pop song.

Fine, Jo, I get it. You need a little space. I understand that, and I'll give it to you. But don't think that means I'm giving up. I love you. I know you love me. No matter what, we'll be okay.

I jammed the up button on the elevator, squeezing my eyes shut as I waited for it to arrive. I was so tired of Ezra's *I love you*s, so undefined that they'd become almost meaningless. "You mean like a sister?" I'd asked him once, out of frustration that I had delivered as a joke, and he'd laughed, shaken his head, and curled his pinkie finger around mine.

"Like something that doesn't exist," he'd said. "Like a part of my soul, maybe."

Suddenly, the vase in my arms felt heavy. I resisted the urge to throw it against the wall. Instead, I scrolled to a different thread, a newer one. Mal's.

Unlike Ezra, Mal was naked with his intentions. I'd asked him to get dinner, and he'd responded, minutes later, with a place, a date, and a time. When I agreed, he said: Great! It's a date, as if to confirm what he'd rightly assumed. It was refreshing, to be wanted the way Mal seemed to want me. It made me want him too.

The elevator arrived, and I typed out a text as I stepped in.

I'm going to bring your book to the date. Don't act too embarrassed when I ask you to sign it.

It took Mal approximately three seconds to respond.

Mal: Jesus. Don't do that.

Mal: In fact, don't read it at all. I don't want you walking around thinking I'm my characters or anything. I'm not nearly as suave as they are.

I like that you aren't suave, I said honestly. I was used to the kind of man who could charm a room with a smile, the kind who had a guy who could arrange out-of-season flowers in an artisanal porcelain vase on short notice. The kind of guy who could tell you he loved you while simultaneously waltzing around with the person who had once poured spoiled milk down your back in a middle school cafeteria.

I realized, suddenly, that I was furious. Not with Ezra, who had never lived in a world in which he couldn't have his cake and eat it too, but with myself. Why had I deprived myself of this, of the little thrills of a budding dalliance, of sending a text and twiddling my thumbs as I waited for a response? Why hadn't I indulged the way Ezra always had?

Mal responded, sweetly, the way he always did, with a You do? I'll lean into my awkwardness then, and I made up my mind then. I would not call Ezra back. I would not think of him at all.

Instead, I thought, as I upended the flowers, water and all, into a garbage can outside the eighteenth-floor elevators, I would open up to the world I'd closed myself off to, the one I had previously only observed from a distance.

On Friday night, at Il Latini at 7:00 p.m., I was going to seduce Malcolm Waters.

CHAPTER EIGHT

Mal

Friday came, and Mal shocked himself by not being nervous. Now that he had Jo's number, she'd suddenly become accessible. Gone were the days of shooting a response into the ether of her DMs, hoping that his messages were interesting enough to catch her eye among her legions of fans. Now, if Mal saw a compelling article in the *Post*, he could send it to Jo with the message: Have you heard about this? and she would respond with a paragraph of insight before he could provide his own. Sometimes she reached out first, like when she sent him a selfie of her holding up his novel, with a Starting this soon! And even when she sent a link to a *Fresh Prince* pop-up announced for December, with an Interested? as if she already assumed *he* would be present in her future.

As Kieran had begrudgingly noted, he had nothing to worry about. "You've got this one in the bag, honestly," he'd said. And Mal didn't worry, not really, until Jo showed up at Il Latini.

"Whoa," Mal said.

On the one hand, Josephine Boateng looked fantastic. Her braids hung down her shoulders, framing the deep-V neckline of a green blazer dress that tightened her hourglass figure to a point, which she'd matched with a pair of strappy stilettos. A gold emerald pendant nestled in her décolletage, glinting in the evening light as she walked.

On the other hand, it was not an appropriate outfit in which to make pasta.

"Hello to you too," Jo said. She looked him up and down, her expression passive. "I'm overdressed, aren't I?"

"Yes, maybe," Mal said, chagrined. He realized, too late, that he should have advised her that the dinner he'd asked her to was actually more of an activity. Strike one, and the night had barely started. "But you look amazing."

"I'm aware," Jo said, strutting ahead of him, and he swallowed, sure that he'd already messed up. Then she smiled, a rapid quirk of her lips, and he realized that she was just nervous too. "So . . . what have you planned? And will it involve sitting? Because I have maybe twenty minutes left in these before I kick them across the room."

Mal laughed helplessly.

"Oh god. No, sorry, I don't think you'll get to sit much." He thought for a moment. "Wait here."

His gym bag was still in his backseat, in it a pair of multicolored neon running shoes. He yanked off his white Air Forces, put on his backups, and jogged back to Jo with them in hand.

"Worst-case scenario, you switch into these. That okay?" he said.

Jo raised an eyebrow. "Wow. The shoes off your feet," she observed. "Why are you still single, Malcolm Waters? What am I missing?"

His cheeks warmed. "I—" he started, just as a hostess bounced to the stand and smiled at them.

"Are you here for the class?" she asked.

"Yes," Mal said. He prepared to show her his phone with their access codes, but instead held out his shoes. "No. Sorry. This. Please."

A true professional, the woman didn't let her expression waver.

"Please head to the end of the hall, past the dining area, and to your right."

They entered through a set of glass double doors into an enormous kitchen with multiple stainless steel islands. As in the photos on the website, the fixtures were crisp and modern, the room itself bright, especially compared to the dim restaurant. A few other guests had already arrived, most of them in casual clothes—T-shirts, jeans, hair up in ponytails. Behind him, he heard Jo's stiletto scrape against tile.

"I did all this for a cooking class," she said to herself. She chuckled, and the hollow sound made Mal's heart fall. "Is this to show that you're domestic? Or to test whether I am?"

Mal barely held back a wince. *Damn it, Kelechi.*

"I thought it would be nice," he said. "You know, to eat something we'd made."

"You see, I only find the pleasure in the eating part," Jo said. "I'm an awful cook, and I don't think any amount of tutelage is going to change that."

"Well, I'll take that as a challenge," a smooth, accented voice said from behind them. They whipped around at once, tilting their heads up to face an olive-skinned, bearded middle-aged man with twinkling brown eyes.

Shit. Their instructor was supposed to be someone's squat, arthritic nonna, not Italian Hugh Jackman.

"Everyone before you has failed," Jo said, looking at him from under heavy lids.

"My dear, I am not everyone," their instructor said. He clapped his hands, and everyone stood to attention. "Please, pick a station."

Mal and Jo wandered to an unclaimed station in the back. Jo draped an apron over her head, then bent to snap off her heels and slip her feet into Mal's sneakers. The instructor introduced himself as Emiliano (*Even his name is hot*, Mal thought bitterly), then announced that they would be making cacio e pepe. "So simple, even my worst cooks have managed," Emiliano said, winking at Jo.

Thankfully, even if Jo was a terrible cook, she couldn't resist a challenge. She borrowed a hair tie from a woman at the station behind them and secured her hair into a ponytail, rolled up her sleeves so they wouldn't dip into the flour. Despite her initial reticence, she seemed genuinely engrossed.

She had not, however, been joking about her lack of skill.

"Oops," Jo said. Her attempt to crack an egg open at the edge of the counter had resulted in her smashing it instead, and a sticky glob of yolk dripped onto the floor. She crouched to clean it. "It looked cooler when you did it."

They came to a tacit understanding after that. Jo read out the steps from the recipe card, measured the ingredients, and handled the unskilled labor, such as grating cheese, and Mal did the mixing, the kneading, and eventually the rolling when Jo's attempt to help led to a glob of dough getting stuck in the pasta maker.

"I don't understand how you're alive," Mal said, stunned, when Jo asked Emiliano exactly how much salt she was expected to add to the boiling water.

"I'm too pretty to cook," she said with a sideways smile. She turned the dial on the timer. "Besides, I can tell you set me up. You clearly know what you're doing."

Okay, so he'd been caught.

"My dad and I used to make pasta once a week when I was a kid," he confessed. "I was a picky eater. Would only eat vegetables if they were drenched in alfredo sauce. I can still make a pretty respectable tortellini."

"Okay, sure, that's cute. But you still attempted to deceive me," Jo said. Then she reached into her front apron pocket and produced her phone. "As your punishment, I'm going to need you to take a picture."

"Already got me doing Instagram boyfriend duties," he muttered.

Jo smiled beatifically at him, holding up a ladle that she hadn't used once. The clear incongruence between her clothing and their setting was silly but charming, like she'd stepped off a movie set and onto a cooking show.

"Is that what you want?" she said the second he'd returned her phone. "To be my boyfriend?"

Mal choked on a laugh. He'd expected to have this conversation at some point, maybe on date three, or at the very least after they'd covered such bases as where they were from or what they liked to do with their free time. Just not now, and certainly not with two minutes left on their boiling pasta.

"You . . . That is a question," he sputtered.

"Does it have an answer?" Jo asked.

Behind her impish expression, Mal could sense something else. Her stance had shifted, legs set wide, arms tense, her smile all teeth. This question, he sensed, had a wrong answer.

Thankfully, Emiliano swept by their station, slapping a meaty hand onto the counter.

"Josephine! You have left all the work to your partner. I'm ashamed! I thought you would at least try for me!"

"Emiliano, I wanted us to have something edible for dinner at the end of this—"

Mal took advantage of the time Jo was using to defend herself to drain the pasta—setting aside some of the water for the next step, of course—and think. Someone else might let a topic like this go, but Jo was like a bull, and she'd already seen red. If he'd learned anything from his last interaction with her, it was that he'd do best by being honest, not by trying to tell her what he thought she wanted to hear.

Emiliano hovered by their station, forcing Jo to crack the black peppercorns, then sauté them in a second pot. He swept away to check on other guests for only a few minutes before he was back, snatching the tongs out of Jo's hands to demonstrate how to coat the noodles with cheese without breaking them.

By the time they'd transported their finished dishes out of the kitchen and to the attached dining room, Jo's pout was in prime form.

"I was just bullied, wasn't I?" She dropped into the chair facing his and crossed her legs, smiling at a waitress as she poured them both glasses of wine. "I was bullied for thirty whole minutes, and you did nothing."

"You're so overdramatic," Mal said. Despite Jo's best attempts at sabotage, the pasta was delicious. "You did well at the end. It's not rocket science. Or *medicine*."

"Does it bother you that I don't cook?" Jo asked suddenly. "Because I don't really clean either. I hire someone to do that for me."

"That sounds nice," Mal said dryly. "And no? Why would it?"

"You don't expect it of the women you date?" Jo said. She'd lined under her eyes, and it made her stare even more predatory, like a cat waiting to pounce.

"I expect the women I date to be adults who know how to take care of themselves," Mal said carefully. "However they make it happen."

Jo hummed.

"I'll probably make more than you if I start practicing again," she continued. "Does that bother you?"

When they first met, Mal had found Jo's directness comforting. But today, it wasn't cute. It felt like he was being tested, and she was grading him in real time.

"Why are you interrogating me over dinner?" he asked, swirling a glass of wine.

"Why aren't you answering my question?" she said, doing the same.

He held her gaze, stewing, for a full minute.

"My mom was the breadwinner in my house growing up. We moved around every few years for her jobs. My dad stopped working and stayed at home full-time when I was in third grade. Whatever hang-ups you're assuming I have, I don't. I think it's great that you've got your life together. I also think it's rude to guess how much I make, but all you need to know is it was enough to support two adults in a big city a couple years back, and I'm doing better now than I was then. Oh, and I'm paying today, not because of the patriarchy, but because I want to." He placed his glass back on the table, a quiet checkmate.

Jo rolled her bottom lip into her mouth as if he'd just dropped the swooniest pickup line rather than put her in her place.

"Touché," she said. "It is a little rude. But you like that."

"I don't," Mal insisted.

Suddenly, something glanced up his leg—Jo's bare foot, gliding slowly up to the crook of his knee. His face flushed instantly, and he held his breath, unsure of where it was headed, where this was going. They were far from alone. None of the tables in this room had cloths. If any of the other attendees were paying attention, they would trace the path her leg had taken, catch the way it had stopped just at the juncture of his thigh.

"You do," Jo said confidently. She eased a bundle of noodles off her fork, then lowered it and her wandering leg all at once. "And why shouldn't I interrogate you? We're grown. I just want to know what your expectations are of"—she waved between them—"this."

The light caught her pendant, and Mal's eyes flickered to her chest at exactly the wrong time. When Mal looked up to her face again, she looked triumphant.

"I want the things most people want when they're getting to know someone," he said. "I want to spend time with you. See if we vibe . . ."

Jo laughed. "Is that what most people want?" she said. She nodded sagely, took another sip of wine, and then added, as plainly as if she were commenting on the color of his shirt, "Mostly, I want to sleep with you."

Mal choked—quite literally—on his tagliatelle.

"Are you okay, my friend?" Emiliano said, sweeping over to him, clearly ready to deliver a Heimlich. Mal shook his head vigorously, pounding on his chest and trying not to heave. Jo didn't get up from her seat, just pushed his cup of water toward him.

"You're heartless," Mal joked weakly when he finally recovered, dabbing the tears from his eyes. "I could've died, and you just sat there."

"You were protecting your airway," Jo observed, bemused. She tapped a finger next to his water, directing him to drink.

Mal took a swig, using the split second to collect his faculties. Okay, so he knew he was a good-looking guy. All that time in the gym post–cataclysmic breakup had given him a physique that got him the occasional appreciative glance. An old woman on the Red Line had told him he had a nice butt just last week. But he had never been the type to inspire primal urges. The women in his friend groups referred to him as "sweet." No one was tagging him on #mancrushmondays.

And yet, nothing in Jo's expression indicated that she was joking. If anything, her entire getup suddenly made sense, the sky-high heels, the dress that left little to the imagination, even her slight annoyance at his choice of first-date activity.

Oh my god. She'd intended to seduce him, and now she was wearing his sneakers. To think *she* was the virgin here.

"I . . ." Mal said, gaping at his half-empty plate. "I don't know what to say." He dropped his voice to a whisper, suddenly hyper-conscious that he'd be overheard, though he figured he needn't be worried—the ladies to his right had already uncorked their second bottle.

"Don't think too hard about it," Jo said. Then, coyly: "Do you not want to sleep with me?"

"Of course I do," he said, just a bit too enthusiastically. "It's just. Ah. Um."

Jo's smile became feral. "You're a writer, Mal, use your words," she said.

Mal was laid-back. It was a quality he liked about himself, that he had the capacity to take things in stride, that, at least when he was spending time with someone one-on-one, he could carry himself with ease. Even Renata Kovalenko had commented on it, ending their conversation with a *Has anyone told you that you have a gentle aura?* He could roll with the punches like the best of them, but right now he felt like he was taking a beating.

It was time to throw one himself.

"Okay, fine, since we're using words," he said, adjusting himself in his seat. "What's going on with you and Adelman?"

If Jo was taken aback by his question, she didn't show it. Instead, the corner of her lip twitched, and he realized that she was impressed.

"Of course a writer would be perceptive," she muttered, straightening in her chair.

"It's complicated," she started, then sighed and shook her head. "No, actually, it's not. Classic case of unrequited love, honestly. I have feelings for him. He doesn't have feelings for me. I'm cutting my losses and seeing what's out there."

Her honesty was bracing, and if his stomach hadn't just dropped like an anchor, he might have found it admirable. He imagined most other people would hold such information close to their chest, wait until they'd extracted what they wanted from him before sharing their motives.

"So . . . this is your attempt at a rebound?" Mal asked. He could practically hear Kieran's chiding voice in his head—*I told you: toxic.* How had he ended up in this situation, sitting across from a woman with whom he'd imagined a genuine connection, only to find out that she intended to use him as a stepping stone to recovery?

But Jo was shaking her head, no longer gleeful.

"It's not that simple," she said. "Mal. I'm twenty-nine. I've kissed *one guy* in my life, and I didn't even enjoy it. Did it because I thought I should." Mal blinked, shocked by that revelation. "But you . . . I like you. I like talking to you. I think you're interesting, and insightful, and I'm only, like, thirty pages into your book and I can already tell that you're ridiculously talented. If I wanted to sleep with just *anyone*, I would've found one of Renata's models back at the party. Or hooked up with one of Ezra's costars. I want to sleep with *you*. I just think it's only fair that you understand where I'm at first."

Suddenly, one of Jo's older posts came to mind: a clip from an Instagram Live with HuffPost, the screen split horizontally between a severe-looking white woman and Jo.

"Honestly, I find the fascination with my virginity interesting," Jo had said, somehow managing to sound both bored and biting. "I think when people see Black women, they try to categorize them as respectable or not respectable. I talk about sex, so I must be hypersexual, but I can't be hypersexual because I haven't had sex. I'm neither the Madonna nor the Whore, not the Mammy nor the Jezebel. It confuses people."

"On your platform, you encourage pleasure," the interviewer had said, after a pause to absorb Jo's first response. "Do you also encourage abstinence? Do you intend to continue practicing it?"

"I encourage being discerning about all of the things we put into or around our bodies. Sex can greatly impact both physical and emotional health." Jo paused, balancing her chin on her fist. "And I wouldn't say I practice abstinence. I'm simply aware of the risks, and I haven't met a man who is worth me taking them yet."

It occurred to Mal, then, that Jo had decided that he was such a man.

Of course he was flattered. Who wouldn't be? Jo met all manner of people, fraternized with the kind of guys that some women put on their mood boards, and the person she found most worthy of her was *him*. Still, even as he reeled, he knew that what

Jo wanted would require a level of ambiguity that he couldn't provide.

"I'm not interested in hookups," he said. "Sorry."

The stoicism that Mal had suspected was a facade cracked, and for half a second, Mal saw that he'd wounded her. But then, with a blink, it was back.

"Okay," Jo said. She gave him a smile that was almost placating, as though she felt the need to soothe him for rejecting her. "Totally understandable. Sorry if I put you off—"

"You didn't put me off," Mal interrupted. "I just don't do the casual thing. And . . ." He tested the words on the back of his tongue, then, feeling bold, said them aloud. "Specifically, I don't really want to do the casual thing with *you*. Because I like you too."

Jo's expression opened up, and he marveled at how much more she resembled the girl he'd met in the Adelmans' bedroom, the one whose sincerity had turned a lion's den into a safe space. The one he'd immediately felt comfortable spilling his heart out to, because she'd done it so easily first.

"We've talked about this before, you know. Online," Mal continued. "Virginity is just a social construct, and sex is just a physical act. You can go out to Viagra Triangle right now and find some guy who'll be willing to sleep with you, then roll over a few minutes later feeling completely unchanged and totally let down." He leaned in closer, enthralled by her focus, by how her gaze hadn't lifted from his mouth since he'd started speaking. "But . . . *wanting* someone for more than just their physicality? Wanting to hear from them, speak to them, see them, every second of the day? That feeling when their hand brushes against yours and you ask yourself if you want to hold it? That first kiss? It amplifies everything. You feel like you're on *fire*. It's transformative, in the best ways. In the *worst* ways too. That's what I want for myself. It's what I want for you too, especially since you're new to this. And if we can find that together, great. But I'm not taking anything less."

He'd tried to capture that feeling in *She Blooms at Dusk*, the tension that went beyond a physical yearning, the other person etched so far into your skin that you couldn't scratch them out. Lust that couldn't be sated with one passionate romp but needed to be addressed over and over again, every time with increasing urgency. Once upon a time, Mal had tried to be pragmatic. Feelings like those were short-lived, after all, reserved for a finite honeymoon period. Only a few lucky people could put in the work to keep a fire like that alive. His parents had managed; Mal had spent his entire childhood grimacing at their public shows of affection. Now he knew that he would take the fairy tale or nothing at all.

Across from him, Jo had gone stock-still, holding in a breath that he didn't remember watching her suck in. It should have scared him, speaking so candidly. He could never have imagined having a conversation like this, never thought he could form words like this in public, that he could look someone right in the eye as he said them. His teenage self was kicking him—*A beautiful woman throws herself at you, and you turn her down?*—but he felt comfortable in his resolution. Jo herself had requested his difficult truths. Here he was, delivering them. If she decided to walk away and find someone else, that would be fine. He had a second book to write, after all. He could go back to his monastic life, the one in which he spent his days staring at his computer screen, bothering his chosen family, and seeking out endorphins at the gym. It was a good life, a respectable one—

"Okay," Jo said suddenly. She blinked, rolled her lips into her mouth. "Okay. Yes. Yes, I guess I want that too."

Mal grinned, victorious.

"Great," he said. "So you'll let me date you?"

Jo laughed. It was a full-bodied sound, rich, reminiscent of poured honey and smooth jazz in the mornings.

"I'll let you date me," she agreed.

CHAPTER NINE

Jo

It was foolish of me to underestimate Mal. I'd identified him as complex, and yet I'd tried to proposition him with a simple arrangement, as if he were just some guy. No. This was not my run-of-the-mill, self-satisfied straight-male creative. I couldn't manipulate him by appealing to his ego or set him off-kilter with disarming questions aimed at his intentions. When I'd said, "Well, I'm not planning on seeing anyone else. Are you?," he'd answered unflinchingly, "Great. Me neither." When I asked him why, he'd smirked, and informed me that he was "lazy" and "tended to fix-ate." There were easier questions too, about where he was from ("Missouri City, just outside of Houston, but my family moved around a lot."), when and why he'd moved to Chicago ("Three years ago, because my ex-girlfriend's family is from here."), how he felt having his work out on display for the world to see for the first time ("Terrified, most of the time. Like all the inner work-ings of my mind are just out there for people to dissect. Like they'll assume the wrong things about who I am because of it.").

People normally fit neatly into the boilerplates I developed for them in my mind. A man like Mal—handsome, well built, intelligent—was supposed to expect adulation. His humility was supposed to be a cellophane-thin facade meant to make him seem more noble, and his "honesty" was supposed to be a farce, his truths selected to depict himself alternately as a hero or a victim, depending on the circumstance. When I told him that I had feelings for Ezra, he was supposed to either be offended that I expected him to take up another man's discarded goods, or delight in the prospect of screwing a girl who could have screwed America's Boyfriend.

He was not supposed to turn me down because he wanted to get to know me better, then make good on that declaration by actually asking me questions about my life.

"I know you're taking a break right now, but do you think you'll ever go back to medicine?" Mal asked, after I recounted a story from residency that I remembered as hilarious but, in retrospect, was probably traumatic.

We'd lingered at the restaurant a little later than the other guests, leaving only when Emiliano loudly announced that he would be retiring for the night. It being a temperate Friday night, every twentysomething with a functional liver had spilled out onto the streets, which meant I had a twenty-minute wait for my Uber. Mal, ever the gentleman, offered to drop me off at home, but I declined, and he refused to leave ahead of me. I gave him back his sneakers, and we settled on the bench outside the restaurant, watching cars whiz by and listening to clubgoers in Y2K-chic argue about which bar would have the strongest drinks.

I winced, waiting for the judgment that invariably accompanied this question—the insinuation that I was wasting my degree, that I owed society a debt that I had yet to pay back, that it was deceitful to call myself a physician when I'd never practiced independently—before remembering that Mal had offered his opinion on this before, and that it had been gracious.

"I think so," I said slowly. "I just keep waking up every day hoping I'll finally be ready to restart. I've got a few recruiters in my inbox right now. And one of my old attendings . . . he really wants me to come back and do additional training. But I haven't been able to get myself to respond to any of them. I'm still exhausted, somehow."

Mal nodded. His expression was perfectly neutral, neither critical nor supportive.

"Do you miss it?" he asked.

I pondered his question. "I miss a lot about it," I confessed. "My primary care patients, especially. I had to transfer their care to an intern when I graduated. She still sends me updates sometimes. Things like, 'Ms. X got her surgery! Mr. Y wanted me to tell you he quit smoking!'"

"You're smiling," Mal noted, smiling too. "Makes me think you actually enjoyed it."

"Yes, well, I actually *like* medicine," I said.

Even the intensive care unit, like Dr. Makinen noted, had once called to me. The high of snatching a person from the jaws of death, using nothing but my understanding of their body and the skills in my hands, had been unmatched. Knowing that I wasn't just useful, but pivotal, *necessary*, in the course of an entire family's life.

But the rest of it? Acting as a stewardess for society's ills? Hearing my colleagues who'd grown up with two doctor parents refer to poor patients as "not wanting to help themselves" when they showed up in our Emergency Rooms worse for wear? Spending my days off duking it out with insurance companies who refused to cover vital prescriptions and procedures? The endless stream of paperwork and messages and phone calls from desperate patients whose questions I couldn't answer and ailments I couldn't cure, their need for help necessarily superseding my own for sleep? The rush of repressed memories that consumed me the second I got rest, the way the horrors I had witnessed always managed to reconstitute, months later, in my nightmares?

"So much of medicine isn't taking care of people," I continued. "It's being pushed past all of your human limitations and still being expected to overfunction, to be empathetic and kind and make zero mistakes on two hours of sleep and a diet of ginger ale and peanut butter cups. It's knowing that you can do everything within your power to help your patients, but that it'll change nothing, because outside of the hospital no one gives a shit about them. It's having to answer to people who care more about a bottom line or their own egos than they do people. And besides that, the money isn't always as good as people think, especially in primary care—"

I clamped my mouth shut, suddenly ashamed to be caught mid-vent, more ashamed of what I was going to say next. It was all well and good to claim that I was just tired or burned-out or ethically conflicted. But that I was greedy?

Next to me, Mal's silence was expectant. I realized that he was waiting for me to continue, that, unlike the many who'd inquired about my hiatus before, he was more invested in hearing my response than he was in crafting his own.

"Are you worried that I'll judge you for talking about money?" Mal prompted after a moment.

"Most people would," I said, stretching my legs out on the sidewalk in front of us, studying the way the headlights of passing cars reflected off my shins. "Doctors get paid well compared to the general population. No one wants to hear me complain about a six-figure salary, even if it comes at great expense. Really, I'm not supposed to care about the money at all. Being a physician is a calling, or whatever."

"Is it?" Mal said. He shifted closer, his shoulder bumping into mine, and when I turned to him, his expression was gentle. "It doesn't have to be. It can just be a job."

I winced. "See, that's why I'm confused," I said quietly, "because calling it a *job* doesn't feel right either."

A crowd of college students ambled by us on the sidewalk. One of them stumbled, giggling, into her friend's back, and they held on to each other, as if their four tangled legs could better keep them steady on their feet. Mal cleared his throat, his gaze following the students as they crossed the street.

"You know, I've always heard the saying that life is short. And I used to interpret that to mean that I had to figure myself out as fast as possible. That I didn't have time to waste. That if I wasn't careful, my clock would run out before I could make something of myself." Someone drove by blasting Bad Bunny, and Mal waited for them to pass before continuing. "But now I think it means that I should try to live authentically. To be true to myself whenever possible, to be okay with the fact that what is true for me might change over time. And I think . . . to get there, I have to know myself, know what I want, know what I'm working toward.

"Like—here's a question for you: When you imagine a world without limits, without bills, without duty and expectations, what do you see yourself doing?"

A breeze blew by, and I shivered, watching Mal's face in profile, trying to learn it.

"You go first," I said.

Mal turned to me fully, his features outlined in a soft yellow glow from the streetlamps.

"I would keep writing," he said. "But I'd be more nomadic. Write a book in a villa in Bali, then the next on the coast of Spain. And . . . I'd pick up my camera again. Go to thrift stores and get stuff to create sets. Shoot more places, more people, just for the love of it." He nudged me, gently, in my side. "Your turn."

I stiffened. Even though I'd asked for a head start, I still wasn't sure if I had an answer.

"I don't know," I confessed in a small voice after a few long seconds.

"Jo," Mal said, stunned, "you have, like, three hundred thousand followers—"

"Four hundred and ten," I corrected.

"Okay, four hundred and ten," Mal clarified, rolling his eyes. "Four hundred and ten thousand followers. How do you get to that without an agenda?"

Because dreams, I wanted to say, *are a luxury*. When you were sure you could eat, sure you had a place to sleep, when you knew that your place in the world was secure, you could have dreams. And maybe I had access to them now, but, like my tendency to add water to empty bottles of dish soap, pragmatism was a habit I'd yet to break.

"I needed money," I said truthfully. "I worked through undergrad. Got a full ride to med school, but on matriculation, they make you sign a document saying you won't get any other jobs. I didn't have a car, and they wanted me to do some rotations on other campuses. Rent within walking distance of the hospital was out of control. All of the study materials cost hundreds of dollars, and none of that was factored into my living stipend. One of my upperclassmen was making five hundred dollars a post promoting Sleepytime tea on her blog, and it seemed like a good gig, so I tried it out. As it turns out, I'm very good at being exactly who people want me to be, so I blew up. And now here we are."

I folded my arms around myself, suddenly cold. I could feel Mal's gaze on me, his pity. He'd grown up differently than me, with two loving parents and a financial safety net sturdy enough that he could pursue an artistic career without the pressure of providing for himself. I wondered how he saw me now, if the quick glimpse I'd given him of the person who existed behind the glitz and glamour of my platform and of my friends in high places had lost me my luster.

"You know, my friend Kelechi is obsessed with you," Mal said. "She just discovered your page last week, and she's watched basically all of your content. Was just telling me that she wished she'd had your page as a teenager. That you take a lot of shame out of difficult topics."

I blinked up at Mal, but his focus had drifted to the bodega across the street, his face perfectly placid as he spoke.

"I've been following you for years. In that time, my dad's been diagnosed with high blood pressure. My mom has sleep apnea. I've had about a hundred sore throats. And when I had questions about why the minute clinic didn't give me antibiotics, or my dad wanted to know why he had to take meds when he felt fine, I could go to your page and find an explanation that made sense. And you were always humble about it. Talked about things in a way that helped me understand, or at least gave me a place to start. You aren't going to convince me that all of that was a fluke. That you aren't at least a bit passionate about it. If it was just about the money, you wouldn't bother putting in the effort. You would just, I don't know, do what everyone else is doing, and sell yourself. Post pics of your face, or your body."

"I do a little bit of that too," I said.

Mal looked directly at me. Under the shroud of night, his eyes were dark.

"Oh, I know," he said.

I shivered, and this time, it wasn't from the cold.

"Social media is how most people get their information," I said, ignoring the stammering in my chest, the way it felt like I was losing hold of invisible reins. "I like that I can teach people through it. I feel like I might be doing something . . . good. Filling in gaps in medical knowledge. Meeting people where they are. So in a world without limits, I'd probably keep doing that, but make it bigger. Create courses, maybe. I don't know. I haven't thought about it like you have."

Mal nodded, satisfied.

"There's a lot of value in that," he said. "And honestly? You're probably closer to it than you think. You already have the platform. And clearly, the charisma. The sky's the limit for you. You can go anywhere you want to. You just have to point to your destination on the map."

I bit back a smile. Mal sounded so earnest, so matter-of-fact, that I couldn't help but believe him.

"You know there's no need to butter me up, right?" I reminded him. "I'm the one trying to get in your pants."

Mal laughed, then placed his hand over mine and squeezed. His hand was large, its hold as firm as it was familiar.

"I know that too," he said. "And I'm not trying to butter you up. I've just admired you for a while and wanted to make sure you knew."

The temperature had cooled to a crisp sixty degrees, but my body buzzed with warmth. Not from the wine we'd drunk earlier, or even from embarrassment, but from the balmy sensation that came with being properly perceived.

"Thank you," I said.

"For what?" Mal said. "I didn't do anything."

I chewed on my inner cheek. *For listening,* I wanted to say. *For seeing me, even before we met, even when I was just one of a hundred physician-influencers and you a picture of a crushed juice box, but especially now that we're both flesh and blood.*

"For imparting your wisdom," I said instead. "You *are* wiser than I expected, you know. Considering all of *this*."

I gestured down his muscular frame—which looked even better outside of a suit jacket—and Mal ducked his head as if to hide his face from view.

"Just because you think I'm cute doesn't mean I can't have important things to say," he grumbled.

"I mostly think you're greedy," I teased, delighted by his sheepishness. "Your inner monologue is supposed to be all *protein, macros, gains,* not sage life advice . . ."

"Come on, now you're just being mean—"

"It's okay, Malcolm, you can talk to me about your max reps or whatever. I speak gym bro—"

I was interrupted by a ding: a notification from my rideshare, informing me that my driver would be arriving any second.

"My Uber's almost here," I said, still laughing. "So if you're going to kiss me, you should probably do it now."

Mal chuckled, shaking his head, then bounced to his feet. A true gentleman, he held out a hand, and I took it, cataloging the fizzy sensation that rose up in my throat as he helped me up. Then, holding my gaze, he pressed soft, lingering lips to my knuckles.

I wobbled in my heels, shocked by how easily he'd stolen my upper hand.

"That's not what I meant," I managed.

Mal smiled. "I know," he said, just as my driver pulled in front of the restaurant. His thumb swept over my knuckles, and I thought of what he'd said earlier, how a touch like this could be better than sex. Then, after confirming the identity of my driver, he opened the back door. "Have a good night, Jo."

CHAPTER TEN
Mal

A week before Portia graced him with a formal goodbye, Mal returned from a trip to Missouri City to visit his parents to find that his girlfriend had disappeared. Her side of the closet cleared, her endless pomades and lotions and conditioners gone from the bathroom, her phone going straight to voicemail and then disconnecting altogether. Her existence in his life scrubbed so thoroughly that, for the first few days, he'd thought he might have just imagined the past ten years of their life together. The only evidence of his new reality was a note written on a Post-it and left on the coffee table. *I'm sorry. I'm a coward. I can't do this anymore.* He'd picked it up so many times that the paper grew waterlogged with his sweat. Portia had left him before, but usually explosively, impulsively. Within hours she was back at their door, begging for another chance that he invariably gave.

This time was different. This time, when she left, it was for good.

Portia's biggest complaint had been his lack of focus. To Portia, the time Mal spent tinkering with the story he'd started before they met ought to have gone into networking, scheduling more shoots, amassing more clients. If only she'd stuck around for six months longer. She would have seen him sell his "waste of time" to a major publisher. If she'd given him two years after that, she would have watched him settle at a long conference table in a glass high-rise with the CEO of a production company, her executive producer, and (over a video call) his literary agent to discuss adapting his "waste of time" for the screen. To think said CEO was Renata Kovalenko, whom Portia had only ever seen staring back at her through the pages of an editorial magazine and had once dubbed the "most beautiful human on earth."

To think that he was doing all of this while surreptitiously messaging a different woman about a potential photoshoot under the guise of taking notes.

The subject is a bit unorthodox, Jo qualified. So before I tell you what it is, you have to say you'll do the shoot for me.

Suspicious, but I'm intrigued, so sure, Mal typed back, just as Amelia asked whether En Garde envisioned *Dusk* as more of a film or a limited series.

I'll take that as a yes. Let me send you the brief.

"We want to make sure we give this project enough breathing room to do it justice," Renata's executive producer, Rudy, a man with impeccable posture and an even better fashion sense, was saying. "So definitely more of a limited series."

"Unless you have your heart set on a film," Renata interjected. It took Mal a few seconds to understand that she was waiting for his response.

"Um . . ." he said, looking from Renata to Rudy, then at his laptop screen at Amelia, whose eyes were narrowed ever so slightly. "I don't think I mind. Whatever you guys think is best."

A message from Jo appeared on his screen: a photograph. Mal's eyes widened, and he resisted the impulse to slap his laptop shut.

"Everything all right?" Rudy asked, peering over his thin-framed glasses to give Mal a look.

"Yes," Mal said a bit too quickly. "Sorry. I just can't believe we're having this conversation at all, actually. Just need to shake myself off."

Another message appeared on his screen, this time a private one from Amelia: Dude, you are so distracted.

"There's no need to be nervous," Renata said from the head of the table. Ironic, Mal thought, considering she'd probably been leaving people tongue-tied for most of her life. "We're celebrating your work."

"I'll try not to be," Mal said. The image Jo had sent him was seared into his brain. It was just so . . . *big*. Unwieldy, really. The moment attention shifted away from him, he opened up her message again, staring at the image of the ten-inch curved vibrator that Jo had sent him.

Read the brief and let me know what you think, she said.

The brief was short: the company, Heavenly Vibes, wanted a professional-quality video, a carousel of photographs, and six months of ad rights of Jo *interacting with* their newest product. In a separate tab, Mal looked up the company, then quickly clicked out when a video of a woman, um, *testing* a product popped up on his page.

I don't think I'm the best person to do this, Mal confessed. I've done boudoir photography before, but I think this is out of my comfort zone.

Oh my. Where is your mind going? Jo typed back. You really are a pervert.

Amelia and Rudy were starting to talk money.

"I'll be honest. We're getting a lot of interest right now," Amelia was saying. "When can we expect you to be ready with an offer?"

Mal closed his messenger app, forcing himself to pay attention. He fielded questions about the cast—the main character, Iris, was a young Black woman with albinism, and it was important to Mal that they found an actress with the same condition—and tried to stem his excitement when Rudy announced that they would be in contact within a week with the paperwork.

"Wonderful," Renata said, standing. Then, smoothing down the front of her dress, added, "Well, this is when I must kick you all out. My son is bringing me lunch and will be here any minute."

Rudy stood as well, waving to Amelia on his laptop screen.

"You don't have to tell me twice," he said. "I hear the Knydus employee lunch today is Persian. I'm going to run down to the cafeteria before the line becomes atrocious." He extended his hand for Mal to shake. "Looking forward to working with you very soon."

Then he grinned, as if he fully understood the presumptuousness of his statement, and marched out the door. Leaving Mal alone with Renata.

With Amelia and Rudy present, Renata had seemed almost human. Now, without them, he found himself caught in her inquisitive stare, wondering how one could be blessed with cheekbones so sharp. He muttered an *excuse me* under his breath, shoveling his laptop into his bag.

"Thank you for giving us a chance, Malcolm," Renata said, and Mal looked up at her, astonished.

"Giving *you* a chance," he repeated, dumbfounded. "No, no, thank *you*. I . . . honestly can't even believe that I'm here right now."

Renata's smile dimmed.

"Stop saying that," she said. "You deserve to be here. I read your book from cover to cover, all in one night. I'm not surprised that you have multiple offers, and likely from all sorts of reputable companies. En Garde is new. We're not based in LA with the rest of the hotshots. As you can see, we don't even have our own physical location—I'm mooching off my husband's office space right now. *She Blooms at Dusk* will be our first major project. You are the one investing in us, not vice versa. And you better start acting like it."

Thoroughly admonished, Mal stood straight. Up until this point, he'd seen Renata as larger than life, a living statue of sorts. Right now, however, she reminded him of his mom.

"Got it," he said. "Sorry."

"Stop apologizing too," she said, pointing at him. "One of the first things I learned when I came to this country was that I needed to be audacious. The second was to never apologize for anything that wasn't clearly my fault." She walked over to her desk in the far corner of the room and settled into her white leather chair, and Mal followed, sensing that their conversation wasn't quite over. "I thought Josephine would've taught you that by now."

Mal sputtered. Yes, Jo had been the one to hand him off to Renata, but she'd made it clear that they'd just met at Ezra's birthday party. How did she—

"Jo told me about your date," Renata provided, smiling at him knowingly. "Don't worry. She said you were a perfect gentleman."

"Ha. Thank goodness," Mal said. His attention snagged on a sole framed photograph on Renata's desk: a picture of her, Jo, and Ezra, several years younger, judging by the roundness of Jo's face and Ezra's shaggy hair, dressed to the nines, with their arms around each other. Paul Adelman, her husband, was notably absent. When he looked back at Renata, she was regarding him carefully.

"She's special, you know," Renata said. "An exceptionally strong, exceptionally brilliant young woman. Fiery. If she decides to love you, she does it with her whole heart." She propped her head on the heel of her hand, and Mal swallowed under the intensity of her assessment. "Make sure to earn her, Malcolm. It won't interfere with our business if you don't, but it would make me very happy."

"I—" Mal started, his face warm, but another voice from the doorway cut him off.

"You've seen Jo, then."

Mal turned to find one Ezra Adelman standing behind him. In casual dress, he perfectly encapsulated the small-town-pretty-boy aesthetic, his artfully tousled hair perfectly ruffleable, porcelain skin unblemished. Mal hadn't watched any of Ezra's shows, but he'd once caught an episode of *One True Kiss*, the popular teen rom-com in which Ezra played Zachary, a simple and happy-go-lucky baseball player vying for the affection of the nerdy-hot female lead. Mal couldn't imagine a person further from his character. He wasn't sure he'd ever seen Ezra smile—which, he supposed, might be his fault.

I have feelings for Ezra. He doesn't have feelings for me, Jo had said. If only she knew how dead wrong she was.

"Jo?" Mal said. "Yeah, I've seen her."

Ezra nodded to himself, placing a delicious-smelling paper bag onto the table.

"How is she?" he asked.

"You still aren't talking? Jo and I just caught up the other day,"

Renata said, surprised. She'd hustled back to the table and had pulled a takeout box and a pair of chopsticks from the bag. Mal wasn't sure what was more surprising, the fact that Renata Kovalenko willingly consumed carbs, or that she would speak so candidly in front of him.

"Nope," Ezra said, not elaborating further.

"She's fine. Great, actually," Mal said. He held back the urge to exaggerate, to tell him exactly how *fine* she had looked that night.

But Ezra nodded, looking wistful.

"Glad to hear it," he said. "I worry about her, is all. She's tough, but sometimes she struggles, and . . ." He looked at his mom, then back at Mal, the corner of his lip curling up. "Sorry, I didn't realize we had a guest, or I would have ordered more food."

That, Mal thought, was the most polite *get the fuck out* I have ever heard.

"No worries, I was just about to leave," he said, throwing his backpack on. He nodded to Ezra, then to Renata, who was watching the exchange with barely contained amusement. "Thank you again for your time, Renata."

"Anytime," Renata said, raising her chopsticks in salute, and Mal deemed now the time to go.

CHAPTER ELEVEN

Jo

[IMAGE DESCRIPTION] *A dark-skinned Black woman with long box braids stands in front of a French window, facing away from the camera. She is backlit. The light catches the curves of her cheek, her shoulder, an uncreased forehead. You can't see her face, but you can tell that there is a solemnity to her expression.*

[CAPTION] Being alone, to me, is different than being lonely. I've been alone for a long time, and there's a lot of freedom in that. Freedom to do what I want when I want, freedom to be selfish, freedom to always choose me. But if I'm honest with myself, there's also fear. Fear of change. Fear of letting someone close. And lately, I've been asking myself—am I choosing myself out of fear? Because I'm afraid of choosing someone else? Afraid of giving them the power to hurt me?

[Comments]
beyoncesgivenchydress: Speak your truth, Dr. Jojo! I'm alone a lot myself, but I'm only lonely on occasion. Sometimes I really

do wonder if fear is what's keeping me from doing something about it. But then I meet men . . . and I get over it lol

iamnursemegofficial: 🔥🔥🔥

exquisitetaste: Honestly girl, I never felt more lonely than when I was with my ex husband. The grass isn't greener.

h0tnb0thered69: hi I'm so horny right now visit my profile if you want to see more 😉

palomaortizauthor: I had this epiphany two years ago, and a few months later I met the love of my life. I was really closed off before him.

enlightenedone1357: oh so you're alone now? This is what's wrong with you bitter ass bitches. U spend all that time talking smack about men and then when you get old and your value declines you start crying about being alone. I hope your feminism keeps you warm at night

beyoncesgivenchydress: lol this comment has 'no bitches' written all over it

enlightenedone1357: jokes on you, i get my pick of women

beyoncesgivenchydress: your waifu pillows don't count

Malcolm Waters: yo is your latest post about me?
I snickered, then sent Mal a YouTube link to "You're So Vain"

by Carly Simon. He responded with a laugh emoji, and a Fair, followed by Are you on your way? Parking's pretty rough right now.

Already here, I replied. I'd arrived at Lincoln Park Zoo thirty
minutes early, in part because I was nervous, but largely because I
had nowhere else to be. Once Mal got over his assumption that I
was asking him to shoot soft-core porn ("What else was I supposed
to think?" he'd said later, when we met at a coffee shop to plan
the shoot), we'd gotten deep into brainstorming ideas for how to
sell the world's most conspicuous vibrator in a fun "safe for work"
fashion. We ran through multiple motifs—Mal suggested emu-
lating vintage vibrator ads, which mostly featured women with
sky-high beehives smiling vacantly as they pressed their phallic
"beauty aides" against their cheeks, an idea we quickly discarded
once we discovered that the Tantra eclipsed half my face—until,
exasperated, I made a joke about how I could probably saddle the
thing up and ride it into town. Mal's face had gone dead serious.

"That's it," he said. "That's perfect."

Which was how I ended up waiting at a bench outside the
Lincoln Park Zoo Endangered Species Carousel in a voluminous
pink dress, marveling at how much the seal steed already resembled a gigantic dildo preproduction. Luckily, it being a Tuesday,
the zoo wasn't very busy, and the red-bearded carousel attendant
agreed to give us a little time on the carousel in exchange for a
sneaky forty-dollar tip.

I scrolled through my email. Denise had forwarded me a
handful of campaign offers, most of them from hair gummy
companies hoping I'd be willing to sully my MD with their
snake oil for a good price. And there was another, again, from
Dr. Makinen.

Josephine,

I just met a young woman during training who also does the social media thing. I've been informed that maybe the ticky tocks have more value than I initially assumed. So please take this as an apology for my dismissive tone in the last email.

On a more serious note, please let me know if you are still considering a fellowship in Pulmonary Critical Care. I really think you'd be an excellent addition to our field, and I would be happy to aid your application in any way.

Sincerely,
Mikael Makinen, MD

I bit down on my cheek, warring between annoyance, because why wouldn't he accept that I wanted to be left alone, and delight, because Dr. Makinen still thought I was so good at my job that he wouldn't allow me to escape it.

Not that he had a choice. Once upon a time, I'd been a machine of a resident, on the wards earlier than everyone else, gone later, shrewd, on top of my patients. Good at procedures. Before graduation, I'd probably appeared hypercompetent to people like Dr. Makinen.

But it had been an illusion. It hadn't been strength or talent that fueled me, but constant, crippling fear that I would miss something, do something wrong, hurt someone irreparably. The second they handed me my diploma, the anxiety that had held me together like Elmer's glue melted away.

Posting a video of myself riding a man-size dildo might scar a few soccer moms, but they would be much more likely to recover than a patient.

I got a text. Mal.

Just parked. Walking over. Which dress did you pick again? Mystical Woodland Fairy or Tavern Wench?

I smiled to myself, then typed back: Woodland Fairy. But make her a little edgy, you know? I'm wearing one of those leather harnesses over it. In pink, of course.

Mal: Oooooooo. Very chic. Very Gen Z. I approve

Jo: Well, just in case you don't, I brought a backup. And obviously a dress change

Mal: Ah, of course. You must be prepared for everything.

Mal: I think I see you. Though to be fair, I think it would be hard not to.

I rocked to my feet, fluffing out the layers of tulle and waving Mal my way. From afar, I could tell he'd come prepared, with a softbox in hand and an enormous backpack I assumed held all of his gear bouncing off his shoulders. He returned my wave, hustling faster, and I held back a smile. There was something so pure about Mal, something precious that I wanted to preserve.

"Not going to lie, I think this dress is a bit conspicuous for a woodland fairy," Mal said when he skidded to a stop in front of me. He was dressed today in joggers and a very slutty black compression shirt that outlined the curves of forearms into biceps into shoulders into a chest that looked like it would serve very nicely as a pillow. Feeling wicked, I tugged at his hem.

"Rich coming from you," I said. "You've got all your goods on display."

"My goods?" Mal repeated, confused.

I smoothed a hand down the curve of his chest until it was cupped in my palm, then watched for a reaction. Mal had refused to sleep with me, refused to touch me much at all, really, and his reservations were as annoying as they were thrilling. Because I could always see in Mal's eyes that he was holding back. That there was a beast lurking behind that adorable sweet-boy exterior, and it was my job to coax it out. That eventually, his legendary control would snap.

Mal didn't disappoint: his eyes darkened, nostrils flared. I squeezed, and he clasped my wrist.

"Jo," he said in a low, warning growl.

"Mal," I said gleefully.

He peeled my hand away, turning toward the carousel.

"Come on," he said. "Your deadline is in three days, and we only have half an hour until closing. You'll have time to tease me later." He bent forward, unzipping his backpack and producing a camera. "Go. Get on."

"Yes, sir," I said, and then, gathering my skirts about me, clambered onto my seal steed. Mal waved to the carousel attendant to keep the carousel stationary, then took a few test shots.

"This is going to work. This is *really* going to work," he said excitedly, adjusting his settings. "You've got a good eye for composition, don't you? Like the photo in your post this morning. You took that yourself, right?"

I shrugged. Early in my influencer career, I'd gotten handy with a tripod, a Canon point-and-shoot, and a self-timer. On a social media feed full of filtered phone shots, strong photographs stood out.

"Might be the whole regularly-spending-time-with-an-international-supermodel thing," I said. "Who, by the way, I heard you met up with not too long ago."

Mal's face instantly went blank. Renata had informed me that she'd met with Mal's team to discuss *Dusk*, but he had neglected to mention it himself.

"Yeah, I did," Mal said. He busied himself by repositioning his softbox, then unfolding a diffuser. "She's . . . a force to be reckoned with."

"Renata's wonderful," I said, smiling. "And she didn't tell me to tell you this, but I promise you, Mal, if you sell to her, you'll be in good hands."

Even with his head ducked, I could see that Mal's eyebrows were knitted together.

"You're really close to them," he said. "To both of them."

My smile tightened. It was clear who the other counterpart of *them* was.

"Yes," I said simply. "Very."

Mal nodded, pensive. If I was honest with myself, I was surprised it had taken so long for Ezra to come up again. We'd skirted around him like a sink of dirty dishes—difficult, considering how much Ezra hated being ignored. Mal was quick on the uptake: I had a room in the Adelmans' home, an obviously special relationship with Renata, a discernibly complicated one with her son. I wondered what Mal assumed about us—that I was a scorned ex whom Ezra's mother could never let go, or perhaps a dedicated groupie who, after years of perseverance, was eventually accepted into the Adelman fold. If he'd looked us up, he might have seen pictures of me and the Adelmans chumming it up going back a decade, and maybe that would confuse him more.

I doubted he would arrive at the truth, that once upon a time, I'd saved Ezra's life, and that they had decided to love me ever since.

"I saw Ezra that day," Mal said. "He asked about you. Wanted to know if you were okay."

The corner of my mouth twitched. "And what did you tell him?"

"That you were." He took another picture, still framing the shot. "Are you?"

I laughed, but it sounded bitter even to my own ears.

"For the most part," I said. My heart was racing, my brain doing silly things, trying to picture exactly how Ezra had looked when he asked, if his forehead had creased when he heard that I was out with Mal, texting with Renata, living a whole life without him.

"He's jealous, you know," Mal said. He was giving me a strange look from the base of the carousel, one part amused, one part suspicious. "Clearly wants to launch me into the sun."

"He's like that with everyone I get close to. Took him like six months to get used to my roommate," I confessed. "It doesn't mean anything. Promise."

Mal hummed, unconvinced, then scrolled through his photos. "Okay, this looks good," he said, changing the subject. Then, brightly: "You ready for the real thing?"

I tossed my braids over my shoulder, praying my body language conveyed more ease than I felt. It was just like Ezra to get under my skin, even when he was nowhere in sight.

"Of course," I said.

WHEN WE WERE nineteen, Ezra taught me how to swim.

We were fresh off the tragedy of his near demise, though the time we'd spent fused at the hip afterward had felt condensed, a lifetime squashed into one hundred and thirty-seven days. I rolled awake to Ezra's texts telling me good morning, fell asleep to his scratchy voice proclaiming his hatred of Cheever or his father's questionable politics over my speakerphone, and so when he invited me on his family's annual trip to the Maldives, I wasn't surprised. By that time I had already recognized that such gestures came not out of generosity but out of avarice, that Ezra wanted nothing more than to swallow me whole, absorb me into his side like an anglerfish. And I was fine with that, elated with it, really, prepped and marinated myself to make me more palatable for him. We had faced death together. Facing life seemed so easy in comparison.

But then he started talking about what we would be doing. Snorkeling. Deep-sea dives. The crevasse between us that I could normally ignore widened to a canyon. Being able to swim was a given for students at Elion University, who'd had private tutors, where I'd had an underfunded library, backyard pools with a deep end, where mine had been inflatable. It had seemed just another way to demonstrate our incompatibility.

"I just want to stay on the beach," I said. Then: "I don't want to get my hair wet." It had taken hours of needling for me to admit the truth. "Ez, I can't swim."

Soon after that, we were at Elion's Olympic-size pool, Ezra's hands gripping my hips to hoist them higher in aqua blue water eerily close to the color of his eyes. I savored our closeness then, the slickness of his bicep when I grabbed hold of it for purchase, how easily the greed I sensed in his voice extended to his hands in this place.

But a few weeks into our lessons, someone posted a video of us to the Facebook group Overseen at Elion: Ezra Adelman Catches Jungle Fever. Hundreds of comments and reactions amassed, most of them detailing all the reasons why I wasn't hot enough to breathe his air.

I didn't mind them. I was used to rhetoric on how worthless I was, and I knew how to deflect. Ezra did not. Anything short of adulation terrified him. I wasn't surprised when, a few days after the post went live, he hooked up with a stunning sophomore named Amanda Alkins to ward off allegations.

I *was* surprised when he invited her to the Maldives. A few weeks later, all of us hopped on a plane—the Adelmans, Amanda, and me, the family pet. Their room was next to mine, and even before my years reading up on sexual health, I'd known her squealing was more porn star approximation than true pleasure. On the day of the snorkeling expedition, I feigned a stomach bug. Ezra hadn't come looking for me.

Years later, he apologized. *I was such an ass back then*, he said. *It would be an honor to be thought of as yours.* Which was why whenever we hit a red carpet together, he made sure to tell every interviewer who shoved a mic into his face that we were "just friends."

"You good?" Mal asked, his voice snapping me back to the present.

I shook my head, watching the image of Ezra's wet, focused face fade from my mind's eye. Mal looked up at me sheepishly from the tiles at the base of the carousel, his expression one part amusement, one part concern, and zero parts irritation.

"I'm good," I said. I scooted up higher in a saddle made for toddler-size butts and loosened my hold on the pole. "Sorry. I promise I'm usually better at this."

"Yes, yes, on account of regularly hanging out with an international supermodel, I know," Mal said, offering me a sly smile. "But seriously, let me know if you want to take a break."

"We don't have time for a break," I said. "They're closing soon, and besides, if any kids show up, we'll have to set up again." I waved to the carousel attendant, who gave us a thumbs-up. "Come on. Let's try again."

Mal circled me slowly for a few more minutes, and I forced myself to laugh, kicking my legs to send my sheer pink skirts into the air. Then he straightened, lowering his camera.

"It's bad," I said.

"It's not bad," Mal said unconvincingly.

"No. I can tell from your face that it's bad." I rubbed my temples. "I'm sorry. I don't normally get in my head like this."

"I get it," Mal said. "You don't have to turn into Tyra Banks, you know. You just have to look happy. Well, not just happy." He waggled his brows. "*Orgasmic.*"

Laughter burst out of my chest.

"Orgasmic? You sure you want that?" I contorted my face into a grimace, rolling my eyes backward, and Mal laughed with me. It wasn't all that funny, but it gave me a good jumping-off point for the joy I was supposed to be portraying. I hooked into the sound of his laughter and prolonged it, let my body loosen naturally and my head tilt back ever so slightly. Made myself fluid.

"That's more like it," Mal said, triumphant.

"Great to hear that I've redeemed myself," I said. I peered toward the carousel entrance; a beleaguered woman in a wide-brimmed hat and a bald man had approached with their kids. "You got what you need? I think our time is up."

Mal craned his neck. The red-bearded carousel attendant

waved at him, slicing into the air in a universal *you're cut off* sym-
bol, and Mal responded with a good-natured wave back.

"Ah, well," he said, capping his lens. "I'm not mad at it."

"Yeah, should probably let an actual kid use this thing, huh,"
I said, making to slide off the seal. Before I could dismount,
my sandal slid off with me, and I cursed; the laces, which had
been wrapped around my leg to the knee, had loosened and now
flopped in a sad tangle around my left ankle. "Oh no. Did that
mess up the shot?"

"Oooh, let me check," Mal said. He took a moment to dial
through his gallery, then gave me a thumbs-up. "Nope, we're
good."

"Thank goodness."

I eased myself to my feet, wobbling as my heel slid out of the
shoe entirely. I'd chosen these particular gladiators for their short,
comfortable block heel, but today, they were failing me spectacularly. The little boy at the entrance was tugging his mother's hand
as he picked out his steed, and I sighed, pulling aside layers of
tulle to right myself before Red Beard could set the carousel spinning.

A hand on my elbow stopped me in my tracks.

"Wait," Mal said, and then, without a second's hesitation, he
dropped to his knees and hoisted my foot onto his thigh.

"Whoa," I said, so shocked by his touch that I nearly snatched
my leg away. "What are you—"

"Relax," Mal said. "I don't want you to fall."

Blood rushed to my head. A hypocrite, I opened my mouth to
complain, then clamped it shut again. If Mal noticed my mortifi-
cation, he didn't show it, busying himself by winding the laces up
my calf with alarming efficiency, his fingers barely ghosting over

my skin as he worked. From my vantage point, he was nothing but compacted curls, broad shoulders, careful veined hands. The carousel music sounded distant and distorted behind my ringing ears, like I'd dunked my head underwater, and a silly, girlish thought came to my head: *This is what Cinderella must've felt like.*

Good lord. Why should I give a shit about Ezra Adelman when I had fine-ass Malcolm Waters on his knees in front of me right now?

"Where'd you learn this move?" I said, trying to keep my voice even as he skimmed past the sensitive skin at the back of my knee.

Mal tilted his head up to look at me, a self-satisfied twinkle in his eye.

"Nowhere," he said. "This is just good old-fashioned chivalry." He pressed a knot into my shin with his thumb, pulled the bow tight. When he was done, he cradled my calf in his palm, admiring his handiwork, and I felt a frisson of *something*, maybe pleasure, maybe anticipation, crawl up my skin.

"Good to hear it hasn't died," I managed. It came out husky, a strained whisper that would have embarrassed me if I weren't so distracted by his touch.

Mal unfurled himself, shoulders rising and rolling back to give way to chest and a face that landed closer than I had expected. His eyes seemed unfocused, faraway, and it took me a split second to realize that it was because he was staring at my mouth.

All this time, a small part of me had wondered if I was deluding myself, that I was in fact alone in my lust. If Mal's unshakable discipline was actually a consequence of not *really* being attracted to me, that in the time he'd taken to get to know me he'd decided that my boorishness outweighed my beauty. But now he'd revealed himself, closed the space between us without realizing it. All I had to do was tilt my head and—

A hand smoothed up my neck, steadying me.

"I really want to kiss you," Mal said, his breath wafting soft and warm over my lips. "Just wondering if it's a bad idea."

Kissing me sounded like a *splendid* idea. Possibly the best one Mal'd had since we met.

"Why would it be a bad idea?" I asked, shocked by the whine in my voice, its pleading edge.

Mal laughed, a huff of a sound that only made his hesitation that much more frustrating.

"Because . . ." he said slowly. "I don't want you to be thinking about anyone else when I do it."

I felt a pang of guilt, as acute as an arrow to my chest. Of course Mal was perceptive. Of course he'd seen the way I'd drifted into my memories the second he brought up Ezra. Maybe that had been a test of my readiness, and I had failed.

But I didn't want to dwell on that, not when it could cost me this moment.

I closed the space between us, pressing my lips to his unmoving ones. Mal exhaled, trembling, and, encouraged, I kissed him again, and then suddenly his arms were tight around my waist, his body crushing me into him, his mouth opening to mine.

My mind went blissfully blank. I forgot that we were standing on a carousel, that there was a family staring at us in horror, that the zoo was closing in fifteen minutes, and that we might get stuck by the lion enclosure if we didn't hustle. All I knew was fire and fingertips, Mal pressing hard into my ribs like he wanted to leave a mark, his mouth clashing against mine like we were trying

to steal each other's air. The hard meat of his thigh pressed between my legs, the exquisite friction we created together. *Shit.* The
last time I'd been kissed, by Sean Peterson, a rising R&B crooner
who'd asked me out after performing at one of Renata's galas, I'd
concluded that kissing was sort of sloppy and maybe overrated.
But when Mal's tongue slid against mine, the feeling that skittered down my body was the opposite of disgust. Suddenly I was
frustrated by his hands, by the way they hadn't wavered from my
waist, by the fact that Mal wasn't touching me more, kissing me
harder.

When Mal pulled away—maybe five seconds later, maybe five
minutes—his eyes were wild. They darted across my face, dropping from my half-lidded gaze to my swollen lips, dipping briefly
to the swells of my breasts in my corseted top. I watched, in real
time, as he regained reason.

"Um," he said. "Sorry, I—"

I opened my mouth, ready to tell him that there was no need to
apologize, that actually, kissing him had been better than I'd
imagined, that I'd like to do it again, for longer, in a place with
fewer prying eyes, but then a scream that wasn't mine rent the air.

"Oh my god! Help!"

My body stilled, then chilled. Reflexively, I pushed past Mal,
my gaze zeroing in on the scene at the base of the carousel.

Two kids under ten. The woman in the wide-brimmed hat,
wailing, holding up the bald man by his armpits.

His eyes had rolled to the back of his head.

I gathered the layers of my skirts into my fists and ran.

CHAPTER TWELVE
Jo

My first year of residency, I was paired with a burned-out third-year resident who spent most of the day with his feet up, watching football while I drowned under endless pages and phone calls. Most of the time I found him obnoxious and unhelpful. But whenever disaster struck and a patient we'd previously thought stable suddenly declined, he would appear in the room with a plan in place and tools in hand before I could think to call him for help.

"How do you *always* know when they're about to crash?" I asked, exasperated, after the third time he'd come to the rescue.

"It's the old Sick, Not Sick spidey-sense," he said. "I promise. The whole point of residency is to help you grow one too."

The man who had collapsed in front of the zoo entrances was *sick*, and not I-walked-around-all-day-in-the-hot-sun-without-eating-or-drinking sick, but maybe-about-to-die sick. I dropped to my knees in front of the family, slapping two fingers over his carotid before remembering to introduce myself.

"Hi. I'm Dr. Boateng," I said. His pulse was thready. His breaths shallow. "Sir? Sir? Can you hear me?" When he didn't respond, I looked up at the woman. "Can you please tell me what happened?"

"Y-you're a doctor?" the woman sputtered, looking me over, and I barely held back from rolling my eyes because *really*? Was now the time for her to be having the revelation that *young Black women in fluffy pink skirts can be doctors too*?

"Yes," I said. The man still wasn't responding, and I rubbed my knuckles firmly against his sternum. Nothing. *Shit.* Suddenly I was aware of his children, small, mopheaded, but old enough to understand that something was amiss. Moving automatically, I eased the man out of the woman's hold to lay him on the cobblestones.

"What happened right before this? Did he complain of anything? Chest pain? Back pain? Shortness of breath?"

The woman started to shake, overwhelmed by my barrage of questions.

"Nothing, nothing," she said. "A little aching in his leg. But he was fine. I promise, he was fine, oh my god, Craig—"

"Call 911 right now," I told her, and she obeyed, whipping out her cell phone. I surveyed my surroundings for onlookers. Most people kept walking past like nothing was happening, but a few had stopped to stare. Too many others had their phones out, recording the incident in front of them instead of offering aid. I turned back to the carousel, where I'd left Mal, to find him nowhere in sight. Bewildered, I whipped around, searching for him . . . and then jumped when I found him kneeling next to me, hovering just within my blind spot.

"How can I help?" Mal said. His hands were folded expectantly on his lap, clenched, to keep them from shaking.

"Stay put," I said.

I pointed to a group of women who were staring down at the scene and whispering among themselves. "You. Go get a defibrillator. It should say AED on it. Ask the staff for help if you're having trouble."

To the carousel attendant: "The zoo has got to have a paramedics unit, right? Can you call—"

The thrumming under my fingers stilled altogether, and dread coiled in my stomach. I moved to the man's chest, placed one hand on top of the other, and began compressions.

The woman screamed again, the sound sharp as a spike through my eardrum. Someone took the phone from her and was speaking to the dispatcher—"Yes, we're in Lincoln Park Zoo, between the Lion and Primate Houses, man collapsed"—but I focused on my work. The last time I'd done chest compressions was a year ago, in a controlled hospital environment with medications, a swarm of nurses swirling around me and a stony-faced critical care fellow at the foot of the hospital bed barking out orders. This time I was alone amongst chaos. I focused on the force of my compressions, the rhythm (to Lady Gaga's "Poker Face"), the sensation of my knees scraping against the cobblestones. *You're not doing it right if it isn't a workout*, our Advanced Cardiac Life Support instructor had said when we were practicing on rubber dummies. *If you feel something crunch underneath you, keep going.*

"Mal," I huffed, screening out everyone else around me to focus on the one person I knew I could count on. "I'm going to get tired soon. I'll need you to tag me out."

"Yes," Mal said, already shuffling to the other side.

I walked him through the compressions—"Deeper than you think. Pick a song to go with, 'Stayin' Alive' by the Bee Gees is good. No, you don't have to stop to give him a breath like in the movies"—and he listened attentively, and when the girls finally showed up with the AED, I swapped out with him.

It took what felt like an eternity for an ambulance to come. I corralled a ragtag team of onlookers: a gray-haired, wiry man who took over communicating with the 911 dispatchers when Craig's partner could no longer stand to, a woman who identified herself as a physical therapist who queued up behind Mal to go next on compressions. When the sirens finally wailed in our ears, I breathed out a sigh of relief.

"Story sounds like a pulmonary embolism," I told one of the paramedics, after we finally stabilized him enough to strap him to the gurney. "Leg aching, then suddenly went down. Partner says otherwise asymptomatic. Probably four rounds of compressions before we finally got ROSC. PEA the whole time, so I didn't shock him."

The paramedic nodded, jotting down everything on a notepad. His partners had successfully intubated Craig, and I watched them load him into the van, feeling both relief and a cold sense of dread.

"You in the field?" he observed.

"Yeah," I said. "I'm a doctor. Internal medicine."

"Well, good thing you were here," he said. "Probably saved him."

I shrugged. My tulle skirts were stuck to my legs and my knees were raw from scraping against the ground. For months after my graduation, I'd dreaded the inevitable emergency, a flight attendant asking if there were any doctors aboard a plane, a bee-stung child with a rapidly closing throat collapsing at my feet, and now the time had come and the experience had been just as awful as I'd expected.

There was some fanfare after that, the gray-haired man hailing a cab for Craig's family, a round of applause after the ambulance peeled away. The same people who had stared ghoulishly as we pumped Craig's chest suddenly rushed forward to thank me, and I gave them the same requisite smiles that I gave followers who recognized me from my social media, feeling my facial muscles slacken as the minutes ticked by.

I was tired.

A gentle hand landed on my lower back.

"I think we need to get going now," Mal said, cutting off a woman who had just asked for my name.

Mal guided me out of the throng, moving quickly, considering the equipment on his back. I followed, exhausted but grateful. His presence had been a comfort, the way my coresidents had been during codes in the hospital.

We didn't stop until we were a couple of blocks away in a part of Lincoln Park that didn't know that I'd just led a resuscitation effort. Then and only then did Mal drop onto a bench.

"Fuck," he said, dropping his head into his hands. Then: "Is that guy going to be okay?"

I surveyed him. He was appropriately shaken, but surprisingly steady.

"Maybe," I said again. "But he's where he needs to be, at least."

Mal nodded rapidly, not looking at me, then reached out and squeezed my hand. He looked ashen, his face still shining with a layer of sweat.

"And what about you?" he said.

I chuckled. "I should definitely be asking you that," I said. "This isn't my first time at the rodeo."

Mal nodded, understanding. "I guess I knew that objectively.

But seeing it?" He inhaled sharply, then flashed me a shy smile. "You were *incredible*, Jo. But shit. Is that what you used to do every day?"

"Not every day," I confessed. I tilted my head. "You did great too."

Mal shook his head, laughing nervously. Then, arms swinging, he stood.

"Sure. Thanks. *Jesus.*" He tilted his head back, let out a slow, whistling breath. Then: "There's a Jeni's right there. We might have just saved a man's life. Want to get ice cream?"

CHAPTER THIRTEEN

Mal

Three days had passed since the carousel-photoshoot-turned-real-life-emergency, and Mal could not stop thinking about what it felt like to crush a man's ribs.

"Should I stop?" he'd asked Jo when he felt the first pop: cartilage disengaging from bone, bone digging into lung.

"No," she'd said, not looking away from the AED the girls had brought, not lifting her two fingers from the fallen man's neck.

Later, when they were eating their ice cream (his butter pecan, hers strawberry cheesecake, both in dipped waffle cones), he asked her about it, and she'd said, "Sometimes you have to hurt people to help them."

"That's hard-core," Kieran said, impressed. "Are you okay, man? Because that would mess me up a little bit."

They sat on the rooftop of Kieran and Kelechi's apartment, looking out over the Chicago skyline from under wide umbrellas. Harvey sat on the wood floor, wearing a bright orange sun hat that cast him in a puddle of shade and plastering himself with the reusable stickers that Mal had brought as a gift.

"I think," Mal said. In truth, the experience hadn't been traumatizing so much as it had been galvanizing, in that it had turned his crush on Josephine Boateng into something of an obsession. He could hardly go two hours without recounting the image of her on the carousel, her hazy, half-lidded eyes, the way she arched into him as they kissed, then leapt away to help the fallen man. Her skirts had floated behind her like a pink moth's wings, and he recalled being both bewildered and captivated by her. One-sided trauma bonding? *Or*, Mal thought bitterly, *me up to my usual bullshit?*

"That explains her CPR video today," Kelechi said, snapping him back into the present. She cocked her head toward him. "Mally-wag, I think your phone is ringing."

It was. Mal reached into his pocket, stemming his disappointment when he realized that the caller was not Jo, Girl of His Dreams, but Amelia, Woman Who Made Them Come True.

"En Garde put in an offer," Amelia said.

Mal sat bolt upright.

Intrigued, Kieran and Kelechi leaned forward, and Mal put his phone on speaker, holding a finger to his lips to keep his friends quiet. Harvey, who did not yet understand such cues, threw his hands down on the floor with a frustrated "BAH!"

"Hi, yes, good," Mal said, biting back a laugh. "What is it?"

Amelia told him, and all three of their jaws dropped in unison.

"One hundred grand for an option?" Mal repeated, shocked.

"And a *million* if it gets made. Which it will," Amelia said smugly.

Mal slumped in his chair. His two-book deal with his publisher had been "major," which had equated to three hundred thousand dollars suddenly appearing in his bank account one day. Between the foreign deals and this, his life was never going to be the same. Across from him, Kelechi was doing a silent, joyous dance.

Amelia wasted no time bringing him back to Earth.

"Which brings me to my next point. Malcolm, you need to get on social media."

Mal groaned.

"This again," he muttered, taking the turn in conversation as his sign to make their call private. Standing, he paced along the roof, squinting out into the bright midday sky. Amelia had badgered him about cultivating a presence on social media from the day that they'd signed together, and all this time, Mal had resisted. It was bad enough to be perceived by people who saw him in real life. But by complete strangers who'd read his work? No. He wanted to be like the authors he'd admired in his youth, unreachable except by fan mail, knowable only by the words they left on the page.

But the world was changing. The art and the artist were now inextricably intertwined into a brand that at times was more sensational than the work itself. Eventually, Mal knew, he would have to get with the times. Amelia seemed to think that *eventually* was *now*.

"Yes, this again," Amelia said. "We're going to announce the deal soon. You're already in the public eye. And, not to give you a big head, but you're *cute*. They pay more attention to you when you're cute. When that headshot goes live on Deadline, I want people to be curious, and they need a way to channel that curiosity."

The way she'd said it, so matter-of-factly, reminded him of Jo. When Jo told Mal he was handsome, she stated it as fact, in the same no-nonsense, nonnegotiable way in which she might have given a diagnosis. He'd started seeing himself in the mirror a little differently as a consequence, assessing his own interactions with others through the lens of a handsome man. Suddenly, the young man at Starbucks who snuck him a free cake pop wasn't just being friendly, and the girl at the farmers' market with the sunflower dress who'd made conversation with him in the bread-guy line wasn't just a chatty person. Mal had entered his most recent relationship at a time when his baby face still rendered him a bit awkward-looking, and the knowledge that he was now good-looking enough to garner the appreciation of one of the most beautiful women he'd ever met was disorienting.

Without warning, another memory of Jo sprang to mind, this time of them seated on the bench outside Il Latini. She'd cast aside the brash persona she had donned for much of the evening, and what was left was a woman he examined like a jewel, fascinated by her many facets. She was at turns vulnerable and guarded, easygoing and intense, and he wasn't always sure whether his overwhelming attraction to her was just a consequence of an in-dependent desire to be deemed worthy by her. But then she'd cocked her head to take him in, her eyes sweeping over his body like he was the third course to their meal, and he found him-self entranced by the glistening pillow of her lower lip. He had guessed, correctly, that it would be as plush as the rest of her, that she'd taste a little sweet, like the cherry-colored gloss he'd watched her apply minutes earlier—

"It doesn't have to be extensive," Amelia was saying. "Just updates. News. Answer readers' comments every now and then. Maybe even advertise events, when you get around to doing them."

Mal shook himself. *Chill.*

"I'll think about it," he said. Kissing Jo had been a mistake precisely for this reason; not even the news that he'd just won the equivalent of a jackpot could distract him from the memory of it.

But then, Amelia asked him the one question that could slap him out of his stupor.

"Also. How's the proposal for number two coming along?"

Mal flinched like she'd just upended a bucket of ice over his head.

The truth: number two was not coming along, a problem, considering he'd been paid for two books. *She Blooms at Dusk* had been the story of his heart for years, a book written in stops and starts and finished in a few fevered weeks after he was dumped. Mal had tried to tap into the same creative space that had given him the story of Iris, the young woman with albinism who ran an apothecary with only nighttime hours, and Louis, the foreign flower merchant who loved her, but nothing was sticking.

Maureen, his editor, had sent no less than five kindly worded emails with some variation of Whenever you're ready, I'd love to discuss your ideas for book two! To which he'd responded, vaguely, Soon! or I'd love to! or Sure thing!

It was time to fess up.

"It isn't coming along, unfortunately," he said. "Honestly, Amelia, I'm stuck."

There was silence on the other end, but Mal could practically hear Amelia thinking.

"All right. Homework: I need you to put something on paper by the end of the month. I don't care if it's rough. I'm going to call you, and we will smooth it out. Oh, and I'll expect you to at *least* have an Instagram by then, or I'll be very disappointed. Okay?"

"Wouldn't want that," Mal said dryly. They talked for a little while longer about some of the details of the offer from En Garde, and when they finally hung up, Mal released an existential sigh. What had Renata said, that he needed to be audacious? He'd found that audacity when he finished *She Blooms at Dusk* and decided to submit it to agents. Had it when Amelia called him to offer representation and he'd told her that he wanted to make "real money off this thing." Had it three days ago when he decided, against all reason, to kiss Josephine Boateng on a carousel.

Not that it hadn't been a good kiss. If he were honest with himself, it had been exceptional, the kind he could get addicted to, if he allowed it. And if he were the sort of person who could separate the physical from the emotional, who could imagine himself fucking her without relishing holding her close afterward, then perhaps it would have been a fine choice.

But Mal wasn't stupid. He'd read enough books to know who got the girl between the millionaire-playboy childhood friend and the down-to-earth, comparatively normal second lead. He knew what his ascribed role was in this narrative—to force millionaire playboy's eyes open, so that he could see that the girl who'd never left his side was the one he should have loved all along. And yes, the female lead would be conflicted. She'd genuinely like the second lead. He would make her bolder, help her understand her worth, provide arms for her to cry in when said millionaire playboy hooked up with someone else or lashed out at her in his confusion. But in the end, he was not the one she chose.

The moment they broke apart at the carousel, Mal had remembered that. He'd recalled how Ezra's voice had cracked just a little when he'd said her name, how he'd asked how she was in earnest rather than to showboat. How Mal knew next to nothing about Jo outside of what she shared on social media, how Ezra had years of history and baggage and memories to call upon. How, the second Jo realized that Ezra was in love with her too, she'd be gone, wisping through his fingers like mist.

Mal had spent the last two and a half years building himself back from nothing. He was tired of heartbreak. And yet here he was, rushing headlong into another one, all while he ought to be directing his energy into doing his *job*.

"Why the long face?" Kieran said when Mal headed back to their table. "Didn't you just make a bucket of money?"

If Kieran could follow the path of Mal's thoughts, he would probably have slapped him upside the head. Before Mal could fess up, thankfully, Kelechi came to his rescue.

"Weren't you listening? His agent wants him to become an *influencer*." She scooped Harvey onto her lap, who promptly planted a sticker of a heart onto the tip of her nose.

"I just don't know where to start," Mal said, collapsing back onto the bench.

"What do you mean?" Kelechi said. Her eyes were fixed on her son, removing the stickers that papered his arms and cheeks like mosaic tiles, but her smile, he sensed, was for him. "Aren't you dating an expert? Hit her up. She'll probably be down to help out."

So much for stepping on the brakes. At Kelechi's suggestion, Mal felt a surge of excitement, then alarm.

"I don't want her to feel like I'm just using her," he started, and Kelechi snorted, waving him off.

"You're thinking too hard," she said. "She already set this as a precedent when she asked you to help with her photoshoot. It gives you a reason to see each other again that's not a big production." She tilted her head, eyes shining. "Besides, Mally-wag, I'm pretty sure she'll be down. She obviously likes you."

Mal resisted the urge to ask *Do you really think so?*, sure that it would make him sound like more of a sop than he felt. Instead, he waited another thirty minutes before excusing himself from the hangout and then texted Jo the second he stepped into the elevator.

I figured out how you can pay me back for the Tantra shoot.

Jo responded immediately. Oh? she said. Do tell. And when he did, she responded, This will be fun. What are you up to right now?

TWO HOURS LATER, Mal settled at a stone table in the public park where Jo had asked to meet. At her suggestion, he'd brought one of his cameras, an old point-and-shoot he hadn't dusted off since shuttering the doors of his photography studio, and an extra shirt, a short-sleeved button-down he could easily layer over his T-shirt. It was a perfect Chicago summer day, one of the first that didn't carry the chill of "sprinter" in its gusts, and children and dogs tumbled across the grass together, their overtired parents looking on from benches and blankets.

As a kid, Mal had a habit of constructing stories about people he'd never met, filling them in like color within lines based on the way they carried their bodies, their clothes, the wear in their hands. The man sitting at the street corner peddling essential oils didn't talk to his ex-wife anymore and had been dodging child support for the last decade, but occasionally snuck cash to his kids in crumpled white envelopes. The teenage boys who sat in the grass a few yards away from him, passing a giant 7-Eleven cup between them and snickering, had broken into one of their parents' liquor cabinets this afternoon and stolen half a handle of vodka, refilling the bottle with water in the hopes their subterfuge would go unnoticed—

"You're early."

Mal looked up and fought back the idiotic smile he knew was already unfurling on his face.

"So are you," he said, standing to greet her. "Thanks for agreeing to help me out."

Jo cocked her head, a silent *you're welcome*. She'd traded her
braids out for flat twists into a low ponytail, and her natural hair
shrouded her face like a cloud, rounding her cheeks and making
her look much younger. Her dress, loose, off-shoulder, linen, and
baby blue, helped bolster the illusion.

"These are for you," she said, handing him a large white paper bag.

Raising an eyebrow, Mal looked inside to find a box of four
cupcakes.

"They're from Magnolia's. I don't know what flavors you like,
so I just had them give me the four most popular."

Mal looked up at her, moved. He couldn't remember the last
time someone brought him cupcakes for anything other than his
birthday.

"Why?" he said, then, realizing that he sounded ungrateful,
added, "Not that you need to have a reason, but . . ."

Jo cut him off. "Didn't you get big news today?" When Mal
blinked at her, she sighed. "An offer? From En Garde?"

"You know?" Mal said, owlishly.

"Of course I know. Renata told me Rudy was going to send it
out this morning," Jo said. "Congratulations."

Mal's face warmed as he set the bag on the table. "Thank you,"
he said.

Jo's grin turned impish. "Where's my reward?" she said. When
Mal gave her a puzzled look, she squeezed her eyes shut and
pushed out her lips.

Mal laughed, then leaned forward and pressed a soft peck on
her lips.

To his amusement, Jo seemed shocked that he'd complied. She
looked up at him with wide eyes, raising a hand to her mouth
when he settled back onto his stone seat.

"You actually did it," she said, voice high with wonder, folding onto the chair across from him. "Is this how it works now? I ask for a kiss, and you just give it to me?"

"You're a menace," Mal deadpanned.

"I'll take that as a compliment," Jo said. Then her playfulness cooled. "I have to say, I'm surprised that you want advice on how to build a social media brand. Doesn't seem like it'd be your thing."

"It's not," Mal confessed, wiping a hand down his face. He explained his reasoning—namely, that he was being strong-armed into creating one by his agent—and to his relief, Jo didn't brush him off. He remembered then that, as natural as it looked, her brand too had been formed out of necessity rather than a desire for quasi celebrity. When he was done, Jo looked pensive.

"You know, everyone and their mom wants an influencer side hustle, but most people fail because they lack direction. My goal, as you know, was to make money, so I needed to grow a following as fast as I could without feeling like I was pandering or violating my ethics, but also without requiring too much time, because I was still in med school and I had to study. I had to make my followers interested in *me* and *my thoughts*, so that they would be more likely to accept what I could easily give," she said. "So, Mal. Having heard that, my question for you is—what do you hope to achieve with your platform?"

"I want to sell books," Mal said plainly.

"You're already selling books," Jo countered.

"Sustainably, I mean," Mal explained. His gaze skittered to a beleaguered mother in a drenched sundress who was trying, and failing, to convince her child to put away his water gun. "Up until now, I've been riding on luck. I was lucky to find my agent. Lucky she found an editor who believed in my work. Lucky that the right people picked up my book at the right time. *She Blooms at Dusk* got good marketing, sure, but it also went viral a week after its release, and that's probably part of why it did as well as it did. But that was just luck too; I had no hand in it. I know having my own platform might not move the needle, but if there's a chance that it can, I want to take advantage of that. I'm down to do whatever is within my power to make sure I can really make this my *career*."

Jo leaned forward on her elbows, squinting as if to better make him out, and Mal swallowed, nervous that he'd said the wrong thing. Whenever he'd proposed writing to Portia, even as a side hustle, she had scoffed. *How are you supposed to provide for a family with that*, she'd said. *Starving between projects, all for a dream.* But Mal was determined not to starve, determined to stay relevant until the second he decided, of his own volition, to lower his pen. But what if Jo thought he was foolhardy too? By confessing his concerns about the stability of his career, had he reminded her that she still had another option, someone who would never worry about money?

"Fine. I'll help you," Jo said, cutting off his train of thought. "But on two conditions."

Condition number one, that Mal use his photography to help her generate her own content, was easy enough to agree to. Condition number two . . .

"I need you to stop saying it's luck that got you where you are," Jo said. "I've read *She Blooms at Dusk*. It's been a long time since I've been so absorbed in a story. You're *talented*, Mal. Claim it."

Blood rushed to Mal's ears, drowning out the sounds of the park. He felt like a child again, beaming under the praise of the third-grade teacher he'd told his mother he was going to marry.

"I didn't realize you finished it," he managed, unable to meet her eyes.

"Of course I did," Jo said. "And if getting a following means that you think you'll be able to keep writing more like it, I'm happy to support that mission." Before he could melt further onto the table, she slapped it like a gavel. "All right. Let's see what you've got."

After that, they went right to business. Jo had opinions about everything—from his username ("Malcolm J. Waters, just like on your book cover. No, don't add any cutesy numbers or letters; you're a professional.") to his profile picture ("Why can't I just use my headshot?" he'd whined, to which she informed him that he looked "dead in the eyes."). He couldn't populate his feed all at once; instead, "to take advantage of the algorithm," she advised him to schedule a series of posts that dropped approximately forty-eight hours apart. There needed to be *aesthetic cohesion* ("Let's use colors from your book cover. Those gorgeous blues, pinks, and oranges."). Mal learned a lot of things: first, that this social media thing was significantly more deliberate than he'd previously thought; second, that despite her insistence that she was only in the business of "influencing" for the money, Jo took pride in her expertise. He watched her, bemused and a little nervous, as she dialed through the small gallery of self-portraits on his camera, her frown deepening with every flick of her thumb.

"When did you take these?" she said. "You don't even look like this anymore."

Mal peered at the screen.

"A year ago?" he said. He could understand what she meant; his locs were shorter then, and he'd put on considerably more bulk. Then there was his body language—stiff, uncomfortable, like he hardly believed that he was worthy of being documented.

Jo released an all-suffering sigh.

"All right. Well, there's nothing in there good enough for a pro-file pic, let alone a post." She tapped her fingers against the table, thinking. Then, abruptly, she sat up. "Hold on. I've got an idea. Play along with me for a minute."

Mal inclined his head to give her permission, and Jo responded with a series of increasingly bizarre instructions: "Take a cupcake. Take a bite. Keep your mouth open for a sec . . . not that open. Flatten your tongue a little. Dip your nose in the frosting, just do it, I swear it's cute. Put your arm on the table, yes, perfect," all the while taking a flurry of photographs. When she was done, she reviewed her handiwork, then handed Mal back his camera with a smug smile.

"I'm not going to lie," Mal said, wiping the frosting off his nose. "That was a little weird."

"Okay, but look at the pictures first before you make a judg-ment," Jo said, like there was no doubt in her mind that he would find them satisfactory.

Mal wished he had a spoonful of her confidence. Here she was, handing a camera back to a professional photographer without even an iota of self-consciousness. When the tables were turned and it was him doing her job, his hands on a man's chest, the only thing more horrifying than his proximity to death was his fear that he would do something wrong and lose her respect.

But as he scrolled through the pictures, Mal understood. It was clear that Jo wasn't technically skilled; a few of her shots were out of focus, and he would have chosen to frame the photo differ-ently, maybe adjusted the white balance some. What Jo could do, however, was craft a story.

Photography and writing, in his mind, were sisters: in one, he guided interpretation through framing, focus, and lighting, in the other, through words. In Mal's confusion, he had looked up at Jo with a wide but earnest expression, like a puppy who, having been given an incomprehensible command, attempts to please their owner by trialing every one he knows. The smearing of frosting on his nose could have been an accident, or it could be suggestion, a coy *This one's a messy eater*, and juxtaposed with the flex of his forearm on the table, created an image that Mal recognized immediately for what it was: a *pinup*. Or more accurately . . .

"Is this a thirst trap?" he said, incredulous.

Jo laughed, delighted at having been found out.

"Someone understands the female gaze," she said. "Look. They'll make a great introductory post. Post, like, four of the pictures. And for your caption, you say: 'Hi, this is Malcolm Waters, author of *She Blooms at Dusk*, finally getting on social media and having a cupcake to celebrate.' Insert self-deprecating joke—be like, 'I'm not that interesting, so you get what you get'—and tell them what you'll be talking to them about. Writing. Photography. Magical realism. Whatever you're into. Done."

His anxiety positioned as humility. His awkwardness, vulnerability. The concept she constructed was true to him, and yet he could never have come up with it himself.

"You're good at this," Mal said.

"We're not done," she declared, standing. "We still need a profile pic."

Mal had wondered why she'd asked him to bring another shirt. Now he understood that it was for smoke and mirrors; to obfuscate the fact that he was generating multiple posts in one day. They walked, seemingly without direction, across the park and down the street, Jo pausing at murals and by cute storefronts to take short videos of him walking "for filler, just in case." It pleased him how seriously she'd taken his request. He remembered what Renata had said about her, that when she loved, she did so with her whole heart. If this was how she treated him, a guy she probably liked but mostly wanted to sleep with, he imagined what it was like to be loved by her. He imagined that, once earned, her love would be pure, unmarred by anxiety and misunderstanding, the kind in which she only saw him for his best self, and he worked tirelessly to make her image of him reality.

Their knuckles brushed, and Mal reached for her hand, swallowing back the fizzing in his chest when she took it. Already images were flickering through his mind like frames in an old film reel: Jo walking with him hand in hand on various streets and in various states of dress, a ring flashing on her finger, then the bar of a stroller under her hand, a smile on her face that he knew was just for him. *So much for holding yourself back,* Mal thought wryly. What would Jo say, if she could witness what was going on in his head? Would she laugh? Would she tell him to dial it back—*I just agreed to date you like two weeks ago*—or would she like the fact that he was already hers, that already he could hardly imagine himself with anyone else?

Just as he was mustering up the courage to ask her if he could take her out again, Jo skidded to a stop. The momentum of their joined hands made him stagger, and Mal released her, turning to her in a question.

"Bookstore," she explained, pointing to the sign above their heads stating "Palmisano Park Books."

Mal's face fell.

Part of the unwritten duties of an aspiring career author was that Mal frequent independent bookstores. He was to go to the checkout counter, introduce himself as an author, then give out his full name and the title of his novel, all while curious customers looked on. Afterward, he would have to endure questions about what his book was about, at which point he would conveniently forget the thirty-second elevator pitch he and Amelia had practiced, or worse, he wouldn't be questioned at all and be forced to purchase the nearest book that looked interesting just to allow himself a graceful exit.

"Um, I'd rather not," he said, feeling queasy.

Jo tilted her head in a question, her hand already on the door handle.

"Why not?" she asked. "I think it'd be good to get a picture of you and your book in a store. And I'm sure they'd appreciate if you signed a few copies for them."

"They might not have any," Mal countered, praying she would drop it.

"Well, you won't know that if you don't ask," Jo said. She narrowed her eyes. "Didn't you tell me you wanted to sell books? Won't this help you do just that?"

It *would*. Mal knew from the various local author group chats he'd been invited to that his colleagues often made a point to network with booksellers and generated hundreds of copies of sales as a consequence. Jo seemed to know too, by the way she was regarding him with something akin to frustration. It was a little too close to how Portia had looked at him too, when he'd been shy about giving out the studio business card.

"No one has ever given me anything just because," Jo said after a moment. "I've always had to reach for it myself." She pulled the door open just enough for the bell to ring, not dropping his gaze. "I'm going inside to look. You can stay out here if you want."

Mal grabbed the door before Jo could disappear behind it. At the smell of fresh paper and coffee grounds, saliva gathered in his mouth, his heart racing so quickly that he had to squeeze a fist to calm it. As a child, small, cozy bookstores like this one had been a haven to him, but now they felt like a stage, a place where he was expected to perform and always floundered.

He felt a tug at the hem of his shirt—Jo, her fingers pinching the fabric to drag him to the front desk. A middle-aged woman with a blunt-cut bob stood behind it and smiled at them as they approached, and Mal realized there was no going back.

"Hi," Jo said brightly. "I'm wondering if you have a book in stock. *She Blooms at Dusk*?"

As expected, no recognition flashed over the woman's face.

"Let me see," she said. Mal gulped down air as she typed the title into her computer, then clucked her tongue. "I'm sorry. Unfortunately, it looks like we don't have it in stock. It looks like it's a fantasy-romance? We have a few other titles in the genre, if you'd like to see—"

"No need," Jo said, and then to his horror, waved to him. "I'm just here with the author, Malcolm Waters. He's local."

The bookseller gave Mal a perfectly polite smile, like she wanted this interaction to end as much as he did. He waved lamely, then realizing that it was strange to wave at someone who was right in front of you, lowered his hand.

"Nice to meet you," the bookseller said. "Well, please come back in a couple of weeks. It would be lovely to have you sign stock. And don't be a stranger—we love local authors!"

"Sure thing," Mal said.

To his relief, Jo didn't make him stick around to take more photos. Instead, after less than a minute of small talk with the bookseller about some admittedly adorable enamel pins she had up for sale, she cocked her head for the exit.

"That wasn't so bad, was it?" Jo said once they were outside.

Mal sighed mightily. He wasn't sure whether to be upset with her for forcing him into that interaction or grateful that she'd initiated it. When he was honest with himself, it *hadn't* been too bad. He'd been too focused on Jo to notice the other customers, and the bookseller had seemed genuine enough in her interest that he didn't feel like a bumbling fool. Most importantly, the entire exchange had lasted two minutes at most, a finite interaction. Mal realized that all along he'd probably been the reason his bookstore escapades always felt excruciating; he spent too much time hemming and hawing before revealing his intentions. The Celtic knot his stomach had coiled itself into was already unwinding.

"Well, I survived," he allowed.

"Exactly," Jo said, one hand on a hip. Her lips were pursed into a frown, but her eyes were narrow with laughter. "You survived. You'll survive again."

She was talking about visiting the bookstore, but Mal couldn't help but think that her words were more apt than she knew. After Portia left him, Mal had felt like he was dying. But he hadn't. And thank goodness for that, because the future without her that he'd feared so much was brighter than he could have ever imagined.

"Sure, fine, I'm alive," he allowed. "But you owe me for putting me through that. We have to do something I actually like now."

Jo responded to his brazenness by taking his hand. "All right," she said. "Lead the way."

Posted: 1 month ago

[IMAGE DESCRIPTION] *Four images posted in a carousel. Image 1: A woman in a pink taffeta dress poses in front of a carousel, tossing her hair playfully. Image 2: The same woman, laughing, bumps plastic cups filled with bubble tea with an unseen companion. Image 3: The woman, dressed in loose-fitting jeans and a tight-fitting shirt, poses in front of an arcade machine. She blows smoke from a neon orange gun while the screen behind her reads Game Over in pixelated font. Image 4: A selfie of two women—one a dark-skinned Black woman with rhinestones placed at the corners of her eyes, the other a tan-skinned Asian woman with similar rhinestones placed above her eyebrows—under a black light. Their arms are around each other, and they are laughing.*

[CAPTION] During my three years of internal medicine residency, I often felt guilty for having fun. When I wasn't in the hospital, I put myself under a lot of pressure to read, study, do research, prepare for boards. Rest felt wasteful, even if it was necessary. Nowadays, I am doing my best to live my life authentically, to reach for human connection as much as I do achievement. What are you doing to refill your tank?

Photo credit: @malcolmjwaters

@therealezraadelman and 62,392 people liked this.

Posted: 21 days ago
[VIDEO DESCRIPTION]: *A woman holds up three different intrauterine devices. She describes reasons why patients may choose one over the other. At the end, an image appears of a brand-name intrauterine device, which she presents as the most recent addition to the lineup.*

[CAPTION]: #Contraception has many functions outside of preventing pregnancy. My IUD gives me freedom from monthly periods and their side effects so that I can get shit done. Scroll through the slides to check out available options! #iud #ad

@therealezraadelman and 12,340 people liked this.

Posted: 18 days ago
[IMAGE DESCRIPTION] *A woman and a man sit next to each other at a table in front of a filled bookshelf. The man holds up a book. They are both smiling.*

[CAPTION] Thank you to everyone who tuned in to my Instagram Live for my chat with Malcolm Waters, New York Times bestselling author of my favorite read of 2023, She Blooms at Dusk! Missed the conversation or want to meet the author in person? Follow him @malcolmjwaters for updates on upcoming events and appearances!

@beyoncesgivenchydress and 22,328 people liked this.

"So I've been replaced, huh," Dahlia said, after she asked if I wanted to get dinner with her and I informed her that I already had plans with Mal. "Would never have pegged you for the kind of girl who gets a man and ditches her friends."

I stuck my tongue out at her, responding to Mal's I'll be there in ten minutes with an I'll head downstairs. Both Mal and I worked from home with no set hours, and so it was easy to get together and getting harder to justify being apart. The day he asked me to help him with his social media page, we'd stayed together until ten at night, wandering first from the bookstore to his favorite farmers' market to a surprise summer street festival a few blocks away, before eventually settling in his apartment, where, to my chagrin, I passed out on his couch. He'd driven me home and asked, with uncharacteristic boldness, if he could see me again the next day. I'd said yes, and since then we fell into a routine: days that started with *good morning* texts, afternoons at coffee shops or bubble tea spots or park benches where Mal attempted to write his proposal for his second book and I dug through offers to collaborate with brands and emails from recruiters asking if I was interested in working at hospitals in "sunny West Virginia." Evenings were spent checking out various Chicagoland events, typically initiated by Mal sending me a link and a text with Interested? and me responding with a brief Let's do it. He'd even

joined me last week to go dress shopping for Renata's upcoming
health benefit, under the pretense that he needed to check out a
nearby photography equipment outlet to buy a new lens.

"As if you don't abandon me all the time," I said to Dahlia,
counting off the evidence on my fingers. "Let's see. Two weeks in
Nebraska for locums. That weekend you left me to hang out with
that dirty climber guy you'd just met off Hinge in the Indiana
Dunes. Then four days in New York hanging out with your nurse
friends. And that's just in the last two months—"

"Okay, fine, touché, bitch," Dahlia said. "Have fun with your
man, I guess. You'll definitely have a better time with him than
getting arepas with me and discussing why Ezra Adelman is liking all of your posts."

Ezra's three-million-large following meant that he couldn't in-
teract with my posts without doing the social media equivalent of
blasting an air horn. Of course Dahlia had noticed. A lot of my
followers had too, and the comments section was peppered with
the occasional Do you know that Ezra Adelman follows you, girl?
To which a seasoned follower would respond, They're friends irl,
old news, and a snoopier one would stir the pot further with a
Then why doesn't she follow him back?

I was careful not to respond to any of the speculation, even
when it happened in real life.

"That hardly requires a discussion," I said. "Ezra just wants me
to notice him."

Dahlia grinned, a cat with a mouse under her paw. "Is it working?" she asked.

I shrugged. Mal had done an excellent job of forcing Ezra to the
back of my mind, and I was sure Ez could sense it, that this was
his way of clawing back into relevance without explicitly breaking

any of my stated boundaries. And I would be lying if seeing his name didn't give my heart a jolt. But then I could settle into the new memories I was making with Mal, kisses that always ended just a little too soon, intentions so pure and plain that I never wasted time questioning them. My therapist, Rochelle, thought all of this was a good thing. *I'm proud of you for being open*, she'd said during our last session. *Even if this doesn't work out, you've learned so much. You can live without Ezra. You can love someone who isn't Ezra.*

Progress. More than I'd managed in years, at least. All thanks to the sweet man whose genial smile I could already see stretching across his face even from several paces away.

Mal rolled his window down, throwing his head and arm out. "I hope you don't mind me saying, miss, but you're looking thicker than a bowl of grits," he said, licking his lips in mockery of a guy who'd catcalled me outside a pharmacy we'd stopped by last week.

I rolled my eyes, grinning in spite of myself, and watched his light up with delight.

"You were a little too good at that," I said, walking around his car to the passenger side.

It was hard not to draw parallels between Mal and Ezra. With others they couldn't be more different; Mal was reserved, preferring to stay cloistered within his small circle of friends, where Ezra made a point to be seen by as many people as possible. But with me? When we were alone? Ezra probably would reach for my hand across the console, like Mal was doing now. He probably would also roll down the window just an inch to let the air in, then lower the volume of his music to better hear me discuss the brand partnership I was considering. Like Mal, he would've probed me for details, asked how I intended to tie the project to a

hot topic in health care, what I would be asking Denise to negoti-
ate for in the contract. When Mal and I reached our destination,
he stepped to the counter first, recounted my order, and slapped
his credit card on the reader before I could even consider offering
to pay, just as Ezra had done a thousand times before him.

But after dinner, Ezra had never taken my hand to walk down
a hedge-lined street, had never kissed the laugh off my lips when I
poked fun at the tiny giraffes on his shirt. Had never pulled back
to cradle my face in his hands and say, "Just because you're pretty
doesn't mean you get to be an asshole."

"But being an asshole is so fun," I said, leaning in closer in
invitation. I dropped my gaze to his lips, a silent *kiss me again* that
I hoped he might heed.

The corners of Mal's eyes creased with affection, and then his
hands dropped, once more, to his sides.

I tried to hide my disappointment. Mal's chaste gestures were
nice, sure, but what I wanted was to be handled the way he had at
the carousel, with recklessness and fiery abandon. That was why
we were dating in the first place, right? So we could inject a little
emotion into the inevitable fucking? But Mal seemed insistent on
treating me like a long-term girlfriend.

Except I wasn't Mal's long-term girlfriend. And unlike Ezra,
whose habit of dating Russian models kept me from getting my
hopes up, Mal's earnestness was dangerous. Too good to be true.
Too pure to be sustainable. Sure, right now, while I was a con-
quest, something to be earned, his interest was genuine. But what
would happen when he caught me? When the chase was over and
he had me in his grasp, when he'd lodged himself into my perfectly balanced life, would he steal away my hard-won independence? Would he do the same as the boyfriends and husbands of

the countless women who cried to me in my DMs because of the STDs they gave them or the children they didn't support or the emotional and physical abuse they forced them to endure?

Would letting myself fall for the first guy I properly dated be naive, a silly mistake made by a grown woman who *would* have known better, had she an iota of experience?

A hand brushed against the small of my back. "You still with me?" Mal asked.

I blinked, reorienting myself. "Yes, sorry," I said. "You wanted to head to Millennium Park?"

"I know it wasn't part of our plan, but there's a free concert tonight for the summer music series . . ."

"Oh," I said, processing his request in real time.

"If you have to head home soon, though, that's also cool. I know I've been monopolizing you lately, but I don't know." He shrugged, tucked his hands into his pockets. "I guess I'm not ready to say goodbye just yet."

Nah. Men this sweet didn't come with that face. *Or* that cuppable ass.

"I don't have anything else to do," I confessed, feeling the heat rise to my face in spite of myself.

We walked back to his car and piled in. Mal pulled out his phone to navigate, then winced. Five missed calls, all from his "Momma." He'd put a heart next to her name in his contacts. Cute.

"You can call her back," I said, relieving him of his visible internal struggle.

"Sorry," he said. "I'll be quick. Just want to make sure it isn't an emergency."

It clearly was not an emergency, judging by the loud "Malcolm,

I know I raised you better than to not pick up your mother's calls"
that I could hear through the receiver.

Mal wiped a hand down his face.

"Sorry, Momma," he said. "I'm guessing by your tone that no
one's died."

"Is that the only time I have permission to call?" Momma Waters said. "Your dad is here too. Say hi—"

"Hey, Dad, um, I promise I'll call you later, but I'm a bit busy
right now—"

"What could you possibly be busy with—*oooooooh*. Are you
out with the girl you told us about? What was her name again,
Russ?"

"Dr. Josephine Bo-ah-teng," a sonorous voice responded. "Isn't
that right, son?"

Mal glanced at me with the helpless look of a man who has
accepted his fate.

"Yeah, that's right," he said. "Look, I'll be home later tonight,
I'll call you then—"

His phone buzzed in his hand. His parents were requesting a
video call.

"Just let us see you," Momma Waters said. "God knows how
long it's been since I've seen your face."

"Momma . . ." Mal started in protest.

"It's okay," I said, bemused. "You can pick up."

Mal swallowed an inaudible sigh, then held out his phone and
hit "accept."

A man and a woman filled the screen, staggered behind each
other and grinning with mischief. Their faces were unreasonably
close to the camera. Mal's parents.

"There you are!" Momma Waters said. She wore red lipstick

and pearl earrings, presumably while lounging around the house. "Where's Josephine? I want to say hi to her too!"

Defeated, Mal tilted the screen toward me.

Instantly, I could see the family resemblance—Mal's features were a perfect intermediate of theirs, his skin a blend of his father's caramel and his mother's deep umber, his nose and lips containing elements from both. Only his eyes were distinct, snatched clean off his daddy's face. Unbidden, I thought of my own mother. Her hand on my chin, examining my face for any evidence of the father I never knew. Her smug satisfaction when she could find none. How, when I was young and starved for her approval, I'd mistaken it for affection.

"Nice to meet you, Mr. and Mrs. Waters," I said, feeling, to my surprise, a bit shy.

"Lena and Russell, please. And it's lovely to meet you too, Josephine," Momma Waters said. Then, with a wink: "Hopefully, someday, in person."

Mal snatched the phone back.

"That's enough," he said. "I'm hanging up."

"She's a beautiful young lady, son, good job—" Russell started, but Mal, true to his word, jabbed a finger on the screen to end the call.

We sat in stunned silence for a long, protracted second. Then Mal dropped his forehead onto his steering wheel.

"I am so sorry about that," he said, plugging in our destination on his phone and snapping it into the mount on his dashboard.

"Don't be. That was sweet," I said. "They love you."

I'd hoped to sound unaffected, but Mal sensed my tension all the same. He snapped back to look at me, biting the hollow of his cheek.

"I remember you saying that . . . you don't really talk to your parents," he said hesitantly. "Is that still . . . accurate?"

I nodded. "Got emancipated at sixteen," I explained. "I've talked to my mother once since then. Which is fine. She never really wanted a relationship."

I waited for him to gasp, to say *wow*, or to call me *strong* or something equally asinine.

Instead, Mal fell back into his seat, released a slow breath. Then: "Did she . . . hurt you?"

I stared down at my lap, swallowing down my panic. The turn in conversation took me by surprise, so far from the safe shores of our typical banter.

"Sorry," Mal said. "I shouldn't have asked that—"

"Not often," I provided. "She beat me when I was younger, but at some point, she stopped, and somehow that was worse. Like she no longer really cared. I mean, she kept the fridge stocked enough for two, covered the basic necessities, but it was clear from early on that I was on my own. I learned how to take care of myself pretty quick. But I turned out okay, so—"

"You were a child," Mal interrupted. Then he turned to me, sorrow and something like anger creasing a furrow in between his brows. "Jesus, Jo. I'm sorry. You shouldn't have had to go through that. You should have been cherished. You should have been protected—"

I cut him off, wrapping my arms around myself to stop the tears that still, after all these years, threatened to sprout at a mention of this topic.

"It's okay, seriously." I gave him a hopeful smile that did nothing to ease his expression. "I have Renata now. She's a better mother than I could've ever asked for. And . . . I think it's sweet that your parents love on you as much as they do. Even if they are a bit extra about it."

At last, a snort.

"More than a bit," Mal said, and I used that as an opportunity to change the subject.

"So you've been telling them about me, then?" I teased.

My feint worked masterfully. Mal gave me a queasy look, then started the car.

"We're not talking about this," he said.

"Oh, so we can discuss my childhood trauma, but asking why you're out here giving your parents my whole government name is off-limits—"

Mal turned up the radio to full blast, drowning out my cackles, and then we were on our way. We parked, and he procured a pair of beach towels from his trunk—"I was hoping I hadn't taken these out"—and we sprawled out on the lawn of Millennium Park, listening to live jazz as the sky darkened. Dusk brought a chill with it, and when I shivered Mal pulled me backward into his chest, draping himself around me for warmth. Our arms stacked against each other, and I looked down at the layers we made, my skin reflecting streaks of violet light, his absorbing them. A girl sitting a few paces away stopped to tell us we were "a cute couple," then offered to take a picture, and when she handed Mal back his camera I felt a strange surge of gratitude, glad that she had captured the moment, like it was a memory to which I might someday want to return.

"Thank you for confiding in me, earlier," he said into my hair, during a sonorous saxophone solo. "I know it wasn't easy for you."

"It was nothing," I said, following the path of his veins down to the tendons in his hands.

"It wasn't," Mal said. "But I appreciated you letting me know you a little better, all the same."

Shit shit *shit*. What happened to *having fun*? What happened to *no strings attached*, like Dahlia had suggested? Instead I was walking right into Mal's web.

When the concert ended, we walked back to the parking garage in silence that would've been comfortable if not for the thoughts buzzing through my mind.

"I still don't want to say goodbye," Mal confessed when we reached his car. I knew that he meant it in the most innocent possible way, and it irked me as much as it thrilled.

"Then don't say goodbye," I said, meeting his eyes in a challenge. "Then take me home with you instead."

I half expected Mal to resist. Minus his singular lapse of control at the carousel weeks before, he'd done an excellent job of exercising very unnecessary restraint. But then instead, his smile tightened, shadows deepening the hollows of his cheeks and casting darkness under his brow, and I felt the air between us crackle.

"You sure that's what you want?" he said, his voice lowering to a rasp. "I'm not sure if I can be held accountable for what I might do to you if I do."

"You mean in a sexy way, not in a murder way, right?" I joked, stepping closer to eradicate the space between us.

Mal sighed melodramatically, but he didn't pull away. "Of course, though, you'll have to just take my word for it."

"Then I'll forgive you," I said, shoving my hand into his back pocket.

Turning Mal on was like flicking on a switch; one second he was gentle, his touch overly respectful, and in the next he pulsed with desire, his body flattening mine against the passenger door of the car as his hand looped around the back of my neck to direct my face to his. I closed my eyes expectantly, but instead of the clash of mouths, I felt the glide of his nose against my cheek, skimming, featherlight, past the angle of my jaw. The innocuous touch ran down my body like a lightning strike, and I gritted my teeth, frustrated.

"You're not going to kiss me?" I whispered.

This close, Mal's face was a study in cubism, his deep chestnut eyes overlapping, his chagrined smile repeating twice. Then, finally, slowly, he pulled my bottom lip into his mouth.

I opened to him, winding my arms around his waist as he tilted my head to his. My body felt compressed, molding into the dips and divots of his. The only thing better than the taste of victory—vanilla mint, like the lip balm he favored—was the head rush that came with it. God, I wanted this man. I wanted his hand up my skirt and his mouth on my neck, wanted him to hike my legs around his waist and take me right here in this garage. Wanted to hear our breaths echo against the concrete, the squeal of our hands sliding against glass—

Mal wrenched himself away. I stared, breathless, as he guided my still-pliant body away from the passenger door, opened it, and directed me inside. His drop into his own seat was graceless, his expression strangely stoic, a muscle in his cheek as tight as a cord. We drove in clinical silence, tension thick as clouds in the small space, and I watched the flex of his hand around the steering wheel, the skin pulling tight on his knuckles. When he slid into his parking spot in front of his condominium, his movements were methodical, shifting the car into park, pulling his key from the ignition, stepping out, opening my door. He walked ahead, leading me up the stairs to his apartment, then stepped aside to let me in.

I'd been in Mal's apartment twice before, and both times I'd left decidedly not deflowered. But today felt different. The air felt charged as Mal stalked behind me, flicking on lights one by one, and I swallowed, suddenly feeling less like a sexy lioness and more like cornered prey. My heart racing, I sat down on his couch, listening to the sound of glass clinking in Mal's cabinet, ice grinding in a fridge. There was a flyer on the table: Mal's updated headshot on a brightly colored background, announcing his upcoming event at Em-Dash Books. I picked it up just as a pair of legs appeared in front of me.

"I wouldn't have done something like this if it weren't for you, you know," Mal said. He turned to place two glasses of water onto his coffee table coasters, then took the flyer out of my hands.

"A bookstore event?" I said. "Of course you would've."

"No, I wouldn't," Mal said. "Before that day, when we went to Palmisano Park, I hadn't been in a bookstore since *Dusk*'s launch party. But I passed by Em-Dash Books and I remembered what you'd said. That if I wanted something, I had to reach for it." He swallowed jaggedly, then propped a knee onto the couch next to me, caging me between his arms. "And so I did."

"That's great," I started. "I'm not surprised they wanted to do an event with you. They were probably so excited to—"

"Even now," Mal said. "You're doing it now."

I bit my lips, confused. "Doing what?"

I watched Mal's brow furrow: a writer, searching for words. When he chose them, he delivered them with care, like he wanted them to be petal-thin, to land softly.

But then he spoke, and I felt them like a bludgeon.

"Seeing me," he said. "You see me, Jo."

You see me, Jo.

I'd heard those words before, from a different man, in a different place, at a different time. The memory was still crisp: me, eighteen years old, sitting at a booth in the Sheridan Student Center, across from a boy who had just unilaterally declared himself my best friend.

"Your only friend," Ezra clarified.

"I think you're mistaking my disinterest for affection," I said, trying to flip nonchalantly through my biology textbook even while my heart pounded in my chest. It had been hard to be cool around Ezra, and not just because of his stupid too-blue eyes that, at the moment, were too black, or the grin that cracked over his face, unfolding from the corners of his mouth like I'd coaxed it out. But me and him? We weren't possible, in any capacity. Not even in the way he was proposing. "I don't want to be your friend."

"Why not?" Ezra said, pouting.

I had a list of reasons, and I didn't hold back. The girls (many of whom wanted my head on a pike). The parties (so legendary that I, despite having never been invited, heard about them every other week). The drugs.

"You're literally high right now," I said. "I'm not getting caught up in your bullshit."

Ezra's grin turned feral. "How did you know?" he said conspiratorially.

I'd recently taken up a job as a campus paramedic, a service that paid a whopping thirty dollars an hour for four-hour shifts three days a week. During our orientation, we learned how to look for the signs of intoxication. To search for clammy skin, bloodshot sclera, racing pulses. To always check the eyes.

"Your pupils," I said simply. "They're super dilated right now. It's kind of creepy, honestly. You look like a wolf."

Ezra laughed. "All the better to see you with," he growled. Then he flopped onto the table, peering up at me with a gaze I could only describe as soupy. "But you're proving my point. You're the only one who's even noticed. You do see me, Jojo."

"Don't call me that," I said, stamping out the thrill in my chest at his stupid nickname, at his stupid pretty face. "And no. I don't. All I see is a brat who doesn't even know how good he has it, burning up his brain cells so that people will pay attention to him."

The fight that we had after that had been something of Elion legend. I'd meant to wound Ezra, and I'd succeeded spectacularly ("At least I'm capable of fun," he'd spat, "not always scraping to survive like a creature.") and for months afterward, students I'd never met would approach me on my way to class to ask if I was really the one who'd cursed out Ezra Adelman in the middle of the SSC. But a year later, when I asked him why, of all the kids at Elion University, some who would have given their pinkie toe to be his friend, he'd chosen me, he repeated the sentiment.

"You made me feel like I could do anything, if I just tried hard enough," Ezra had said. "Like I would get roles because I was smart and could be good at my job, not just because my parents knew someone who knew someone. And you were so hard to impress, so I was constantly trying to impress you. And I got better as a consequence."

And now here was Mal, saying the same.

"You see me as the best version of myself," Mal continued. "And it makes me want to become that. Not just for me. But for you. Because, as ridiculous as it sounds, I want you to be proud of me." He ducked his head helplessly. "I don't know, Jo. I really like what we have now. I don't want to mess things up."

"You think sleeping with me will mess things up?" I asked.

"Maybe," he said. "I'm not good at being . . . nonchalant. And, you know"—he smiled sheepishly, stroking my chin with his thumb—"I want this to be special for you."

Today, I thought, had been special. Lying in Mal's warm embrace under a color-streaked sky, listening to jazz on a cooling summer evening, even the surprise phone call with his parents. I'd experienced so many new sensations, all in one day.

I told him as much. Then, because I couldn't help it: "Unless what you're really concerned about is your performance."

Mal drew back just enough to laugh. Then, without preamble, he pulled me to his chest, and in a clean, practiced swoop, flipped me onto his lap.

"Oh," he said, "you don't have to worry about that."

TWO MONTHS AGO, when I showed up at Il Latini for Mal's and my first date, I had come prepared. Dahlia and I had picked out a showstopping lingerie set ("Because if you're going to do this, you should do it, feel me?" she'd said). I'd trimmed, sugared, and plucked every errant hair on my body, doused myself in the most inoffensive perfume I owned, and spent an hour in front of my vanity beating my face into submission . . . all for Malcolm Waters to take me to a cooking class and kiss my hand.

Today, the only makeup I wore was a clear lip gloss and a bit of concealer; I couldn't remember the last time I'd shaved my pits, and my lingerie was composed of anti–chub rub bike shorts, an old thong that had *Cutie Pie* in peeling white vinyl on the crotch, and an industrial-grade strapless bra with four rows of clasps and memory foam cups.

"Gorgeous," Mal muttered, one hand palming my ass, the other hooking around the back of my neck to keep me close. He kissed like a man dying of thirst and I was an oasis, like he'd been plotting where to touch and grab and hold from the second we met.

No wonder Dahlia enjoyed fucking so much. If this was what I'd been missing out on, I had a lot of catching up to do.

And tonight, I was certain that Mal would be down for some fucking, if the length that had formed in his pants was any indication. He rocked against me, letting me ride the hard ridge of him through his jeans, the room growing balmy with our mounting lust. His hands reached into my bike shorts, skating blunt nails along the backs of my thighs, and I cried out as a lightning bolt of sensation coursed into my center. Mal had only been touching me for five minutes, and I was already desperate for him, something deep inside of me pulsing, hungry, eager to be filled.

Feeling bold, I grabbed for the hem of Mal's T-shirt, and he didn't hesitate, chucking it off and giving me barely a second to appreciate the work of art that was his body—those tawny, broad shoulders, the deliciously powerful arms—before helping me out of my dress. Then he paused, holding me firm to him while his eyes roved greedily over my skin.

I'd never assigned much value to the aesthetics of my body. When I was young, I'd heard nothing positive about it—my dark skin deemed me *burned toast, a roach, a shadow*, my fleshy thighs *thunderous*, and so I became more preoccupied with its utility, grateful that it could stand during my long shifts, stay awake for twenty-eight-hour calls. It was only when I started posting as Dr. Jojobee that I started to factor in its appeal. The Ghanaian hips that Ashley Biernacki had once declared needed a Wide Load sign now got me envy, BBL accusations, and the occasional brand collaboration.

And this. It got me this: Mal regarding my body like it was something he'd dreamed up, his calloused hands following a reverent trail up and down my sides. Silently, I reached behind me, undoing the clasps of my bra one by one until it fell, useless, onto my lap. Mal's eyes darkened instantly, and I felt his stare like I did his hands.

"You are so fucking sexy," he muttered, almost more to himself than to me. He palmed my breasts, weighing them in each hand, circling my nipples with his thumbs. Then he leaned forward, sucked one into his mouth, and released it with an indecent *smack*. "You know that, Jo?"

If I had been of sound mind, I would have told him, *Yes, but in a clinical way, the way that I know to start a statin when someone's LDL is above 190*, and certainly not the way he was making me feel now, like I was barely real, like I was something to be worshipped. But my forebrain had long ago vacated the premises, and so instead I moaned, pushed into him, whimpered against the friction. Mal's head fell back against the sofa, his hips rising to meet mine. He kissed me hard, our mouths colliding, then suddenly pulled away.

"That's enough," he said haggardly.

"What . . . ?" I started, ready to launch a complaint, but then, to my complete shock, he hoisted me, shrieking, into his arms.

Mal smirked, tossing me higher in his arms like I were a sack of potatoes. Then, with a deft foot, he guided his bedroom door open and kicked it shut behind us.

THE REPORTER AT HuffPost sent a message over my website's contact form just minutes after the video that would label me as the "Virgin Sex Doc" surpassed ten million views. Over our video call, she looked prim, her brown hair tied into a lacquered bun, matte plum lipstick perfectly even.

"How can you give advice on sex if you've never had it?" she asked.

"The same way I can tell someone how to manage their diabetes," I responded. "By reading the literature."

"SHIT," MAL SAID, grasping the sheets as though they would ground him. His grip on my head tightened, caught between not wanting to let me out of his sight and keeping his eyes from rolling back. "You sure you haven't done this before?"

I smiled around him, watching him wince as I lapped at his head with the flat of my tongue.

"I have a doctorate, Mal," I said. "Is it really surprising that I've done a little research?"

Any potential retorts were cut off when I tried out a move I'd read about in Paul Joannides's *Guide to Getting It On*, which had been an exceptional resource, if I did say so myself. And effective, judging by the way Mal's hips were rocking off the bed. First attempt at fellatio, and I'd give the experience a solid seven out of ten. A bit rough on the jaw, sure, and there had been that brief snafu when I'd grazed him with my lower teeth, but overall, good. I was already feeling new, exciting sensations, like the rush of want that flooded my body when he lowered his pants and unveiled himself to me, the way my mouth watered with a Pavlovian need to have him in it. The satisfaction of watching Mal struggle beneath me, his chest heaving, his skin glistening, his core tense from the effort of keeping himself from thrusting down my throat.

Sublime. Nothing I had ever conjured in my mind could compare.

I was pretty sure that when Mal threw me onto the bed, he'd intended to get to me first. But he should have known that there was zero chance that he was going to get away with *carrying me* into his bedroom without getting his dick sucked. Virgin I may be, but I was still a grown woman, and I knew that that type of behavior had to be rewarded. Besides, now that Mal had finally given me access, I had a laundry list of tests to run. How long would I last riding him before my thighs cramped? Would I enjoy being eaten out? Doggy was supposedly good for G-spot stimulation, but how was I going to convince this very nice man to go face down ass up with me on the first encounter? I swallowed him down, and he quivered, his grip on my hair tightening.

"Stop stop stop stop," Mal hissed, reflexively pulling my head back. I released him with a pop, and he dragged me up his body to kiss me, catching his breath. When we pulled back, he smiled brokenly, bowing his forehead against mine.

"Is that what you spend your time doing when you're alone?

Reading dirty books and taking notes?" he asked. His voice had become husky, low. "Touching yourself?"

"Sometimes," I confessed.

Mal grunted, then, in a quick motion, flipped me under him and slotted himself in between my knees.

"Show me," he said.

His gaze was direct, unblinking, and for the first time, I felt shy. It hit me, suddenly, that I was naked, all of the bumps and crevasses I'd taught myself and my followers to love suddenly on full display. I guided my hand in between my legs, turning away as if to hide, but Mal's firm hand on my chin guided me back, his eyes jumping greedily from my face to my moving fingers. I watched him too, the ardency of his arousal feeding mine. Silently, Mal brought a hand to my lips, requesting entry. I gave it, sucking his fingers into my mouth and watching as something wild flickered across his face.

"You nervous?" he asked softly, trailing his wet fingers down to join mine.

I laughed, breathless. "A little," I confessed.

He nodded, serious as sin. "Don't be," he said. "I got you."

Then he slid down my body, lifting my thighs onto his shoulders.

"Wait, Mal—" I started, alarmed, but I didn't have time to be shy, to warn him that I might be sweaty from our evening running around the city, to wonder if I should have found an excuse to run into the bathroom for a quick rinse before things got hot and heavy, because his mouth was already on me.

Holy shit. I should have suspected that Malcolm "acts of service" Waters would be a cunnilingus connoisseur. This was not a man who considered eating pussy a chore, or a means to an end.

No. For Mal, it was very clearly a privilege. Right now, I was a delicacy, and Mal the starving man on a desert island presented with a feast that he dived into face-first with no hands. Over the rush of blood in my ears, I could hear him talking, muffled *fucks* and *you taste so good*s that I could feel against my lips, and I threw an arm over my eyes, overwhelmed, oversensitized. My hips roved against him restlessly, the ache in the pit of my belly becoming a yearning. I could feel the pressure inside me building like a pot about to whistle, and I arched out of his reach, desperate for a break, only to be yanked back down onto the bed.

"Where do you think you're going?" he crooned, pinning me in place.

"Please," I whimpered, delirious. I was throbbing, squeezing, the space where Mal wasn't aching with the urge to have him in it.

"Please what?" Mal teased, lifting my legs higher to give himself better access. He sucked my clit into his mouth, and I cried out, too far gone to be embarrassed by the naked longing in my voice. "Come on, Jo, use your words."

Damn. I should have suspected that Mal could throw down from the second he kissed me at the carousel. That had not been a kiss from a man who stumbled over his words and got flustered when I poked fun at his old-man Instagram. Clearly I had been had. Hopefully, I would be had again. Repeatedly.

"Put it in," I whimpered.

Mal hummed.

"Put what in?" he asked. He slid two fingers inside of me, curling them in a beckoning motion. "My fingers?"

"No," I said, arching against pleasure that still, somehow, was not enough. "No, Mal, you know what I want—"

"No I don't," Mal teased. "Maybe . . . my tongue?" He slid that inside of me next, and I sucked in a stuttering breath.

"Your dick, you asshole," I managed finally. Then, just in case he decided to punish my impertinence by prolonging my misery: "Put your dick in me. Please."

Mal nodded sagely, then finally released me, wiping off his mouth with the back of his hand and rocking back on his heels to reach into his nightstand. I watched, entranced, as he tore a condom wrapper with his teeth and rolled it on. Looming over me like this, his dick seemed huge, bobbing like it had a mind of its own. I remembered how heavy it had felt on my tongue, how substantial it felt rocking between my legs, and, for the first time since we'd started this, my anticipation was laced with a ribbon of fear.

Mal caught me watching, then lowered himself to me, kissing me sweetly.

"We can stop here, you know," he said. "Or do something different. Just tell me what you want, and I'll give it to you." His eyes were burning coals in the dimly lit room. "Anything."

His consideration set me aflame, my skin tingling with every part of me that he had touched.

"I want this," I said, angling my hips for him.

Mal smiled like I'd given him a gift. Then, pressing his mouth to mine, he slowly, carefully, eased into me.

Even with all my education, I expected pain, tearing, something to signify that the label that I'd held for twenty-nine years had been ripped away. But instead, there was pressure and pleasure, an indescribable fullness. Mal's firm body against mine, his slow, sighing exhale into the side of my neck.

"You good?" he said, trembling with restraint.

I smiled, then pressed a heel into his ass to egg him on.

"*Move*, Mal," I begged, and Mal grunted, then hooked my legs over his arms for leverage. I let him take charge, gasping against the sensation of him driving into me over and over again, watching the shift of his expressions in the dimly lit room, his lips parting as he gasped for air.

"I can't believe—" he started, brokenly. "You're so beautiful."

"You too," I said, tilting my hips up to take more of him in. Mal's jaw tightened, something dark passing over his eyes, and then, without warning, he pulled out, flipped me onto my stomach, and drove back into me in a smooth, purposeful motion. I let out a sound that was somewhere between a gasp and a cry, stunned by the feeling of him so deep inside of me, the pulsing pleasure of being stretched to my limit. Behind me, Mal was a force, his grip on my waist almost painfully tight, the echoing slap of my ass against his hips so obscene that I could hardly believe that we were creating it.

"Fuck, Jo," Mal groaned, and I realized just how delectable my name sounded falling off his lips like this, like he was losing control and I was the reason why. "*Fuck*. You feel so good."

I opened my mouth to respond but found that I couldn't. My voice had been stolen by someone else, some wild, wanton woman who produced the kind of melodramatic moans that I'd once considered theater. *No way could it feel that good*, I had once nitpicked, only to discover now that *yes* ("Yes, yes, *yes!*") it could.

Suddenly, there was heat: Mal's chest a furnace against my back, his hand slipping between my legs, the pad of his finger worrying at my clit just as his mouth closed over my shoulder. He let out a final, ragged groan—my name, repeated like a mantra as he pushed into me in short, final ruts.

All at once, my body seized. My orgasm crashed over me in waves, pleasure starting in my center and rippling to my curling toes, to fingers that clenched around sheets. God, I'd come before, but never like this, never from such unconscionable heights. My vision blurred, then came back in Technicolor, and finally, sapped, I collapsed forward onto the mattress.

Mal came down with me.

"Good?" he asked after a minute, having transformed from sexpot back to golden retriever. His weight on top of mine was crushing but comfortable, and I looped an arm around his neck, using the last of my energy to pat him on the cheek.

"Good," I managed.

And then, with an ease that I thought impossible for someone who constantly chased sleep, I promptly passed out.

CHAPTER SIXTEEN
Mal

Mal awoke, for the first time in over two years, to another person in his bed. Light poured into his bedroom from its single window, bleaching his pale blue sheets almost white and bathing his delightfully curvy bedfellow in an almost angelic light. He blinked himself back into awareness, watching her face. Asleep, with all of her ferocity locked away, Jo's features were actually cute: her button nose pairing well with her full, round lips, high cheeks, and long curling eyelashes. She would be mad about her hair when she woke up—they'd fallen asleep far too suddenly to remember bonnets or satin pillowcases—but he'd never seen a sight more beautiful than this. Josephine Boateng, naked and sated, in his bed.

"I think I'm in love with you, you know," he said softly.

Jo hummed, not opening her eyes.

"Good morning to you too," she said. She reached for him blindly, then, finding his arm, dragged him back under the covers. He kissed her, sure she could feel his heart thundering through his chest, and she opened her eyes, forcing him to watch as she licked her palm and reached between them. She stroked him with slow, languid movements, her grip already sure; then, after clumsily slipping on a condom, turned to her side and guided him into her. She was warm, tight, wet, and he found himself too close too soon, the sight of her body rocking against his in broad daylight too stimulating for any hope of longevity. When they were done, reveling in the aftershocks, Jo kissed him deep and slow, morning breath be damned.

"I really, really like you," Jo said. Her voice sounded ragged, stripped of its usual bravado. "I just think . . . I probably shouldn't be saying the word *love* yet."

Mal nodded, fighting to keep his expression even. He'd known that Jo didn't quite feel the same, but hearing it out loud stung. All things considered, she'd reacted very well to him dropping the *L* bomb; there had been no snickering, no queasily delivered *thank yousss*, and, by the way, she was still tucked into his arms, no haste to leave his bed. Also, the sex. That she'd initiated. That had to bode well for him, right?

"It's okay," Mal said. "I wasn't expecting you to say it back. Just wanted to let you know where I was at."

Jo nodded slowly, then blinked away, and he was shocked to see that her eyes had welled with tears.

"Whoa," he said. "Please don't cry. I'll be fine—"

"No, no, I know," Jo said, rubbing at her eyes with the heel of her hand. "It's silly. But. Um. No one's ever told me they loved me before. At least, not in the way you mean."

"Never?" Mal said. He couldn't imagine that a woman like Jo didn't have a hundred suitors, a thousand guys who would be willing to fight to the death to swap places with him right now. "You don't think that, maybe, someone's felt this way before but wasn't able to tell you?"

Jo's laughter was a single bark.

"No way. I've only been hot for five years or so. Boys used to ask me out as a *joke*." She paused. "Wow. I feel like we've talked about *everything*, but somehow I've neglected to ask you about your dating life. Let me guess. Trail of broken hearts left in your wake?"

Mal rolled onto his back, propping his head up onto a pillow.

"I had some fun in college," he confessed. "But, um, not really, no. One long-term relationship. Nothing else outside of that."

Jo draped an arm over his chest, tracing the sparse hairs.

"One long-term relationship," she repeated, mimicking his gruff tone. He felt rather than saw her smirk against his skin. "There's a four-word story if I've ever heard one. It's giving: 'Baby shoes, never worn.'"

Mal cracked a smile that was half grimace. It disappointed him some that his bitterness was still so conspicuous, like he should have been a little closer to apathy by now.

"Yeah, well, it's not nearly as tragic as that," he said, half a lie.

Jo propped herself up on one arm, and Mal realized, with some annoyance, that he was going to spend his first morning after with Josephine Boateng talking about his ex.

"How long were you together?" she asked.

"Ten years," he said, predicting Jo's gasp and preemptively answering her next question. "Broke up two and a half years ago."

"Ten years," Jo repeated. She sounded, to his relief, curious rather than put off. She drew something around his nipple with her pointer finger: A star? "Why'd you split? Grew apart?"

Mal scoffed. "Nah," he said. "It was kind of a unilateral decision. I came home after a trip, and she'd moved out."

Just as he'd expected, the amusement fell from Jo's face like a candle being blown out.

"Oh," she said simply, and Mal swallowed. The last thing he wanted Jo to feel for him was pity, especially not now, on the legs of his blundered confession. But when she spoke again, it wasn't pity he heard, but something like envy.

"I don't think I could do that," she said. "Fall in love again, if someone I loved did that to me."

The words themselves were chiding, as if she were chastising him for expressing his feelings too soon, but she said it like she was in awe of him, like she found his capacity to still love something to be admired.

"It's not something I actively chose to do," Mal said, feeling his face warm. "It just happened."

"That can't be true," Jo said. "It didn't just slam into you like a ton of bricks—like, *Wow, I think I love this woman*. It had to be a decision, right?"

That's exactly what happened, Mal thought. Jo had grabbed hold of his hand in that bedroom at the Adelmans' and he'd felt himself sink like he'd stepped into quicksand. That had been natural. Only his resistance afterward, his attempts to slow himself down, had required intention.

"It wasn't conscious, Jo," he said.

"It is for me," Jo said quietly. She tucked herself farther under the covers. "You're very brave, is all I'm saying."

This, from the woman who had looked him dead in the eye and told him that she intended to sleep with him on the first date. From the woman who spoke her mind so clearly that she transformed him into someone who could do the same, if only in her presence. He told her as much, and she snorted.

"That's not me being brave. That's me being careful. You can tell a lot about a person by how they react to someone's truth.

Talk to them straight, without all the social niceties, and they'll let you know sooner rather than later if they're someone you can trust."

Mal started, looking down at her with renewed understanding. Suddenly, his early interactions with Jo made sense. How she'd behaved during their first date, coming after him with rapid-fire questions, how he had once felt like their conversations weren't conversations exactly, but oral examinations. The small sense of triumph he felt when he realized he'd provided the answers she sought. Even the way she seemed with him lately: less intense, more playful, like once he'd stepped over her defenses, she'd let him closer to her real self.

"But you trust me?" Mal said, wanting to hear her confirmation.

From this vantage point, Jo's eyes were round, shining.

"As much as I possibly can," she said. "More than I should, if I'm being real."

"More than you should?" Mal echoed.

Jo sat up, and he worked very hard to focus on her eyes and not the full, swaying breasts she'd brought back into view.

"Do you want me to be honest?" she asked. "Or do you want me to be nice?"

The fact that there was a choice to be had shook him, but his answer was obvious.

"Honest," he said. "Always."

Jo didn't look away, but her gaze sharpened, and he could sense that he was walking into another test.

"The first thing I wondered when you told me you loved me was whether it was a trap," she said. Mal winced, but she pressed on. "That maybe you were love bombing me and going to turn into a monster the second I got comfortable, or that you're currently trying to replicate what you had with your ex and will drop me once you realize I'm not her. At best, that you're just saying things because the vibe felt right and you're happy to get laid."

Her words burned like a fire iron against his chest. All this while, Mal had thought that Jo assumed the best of him, only to find that it was the opposite, that actually she assessed him through the most uncharitable light possible.

"That's . . . I'm sorry that's how you feel," he said. "But that doesn't sound like me at all."

Jo turned his head back to her by his chin. "You're hurt," she said.

"A little," he admitted.

She ducked her gaze, but she didn't apologize, nor did she take back her words.

"For what it's worth, I assume the worst of everyone. And most of the time, I'm right."

"Did that go for Ezra too?"

The second the words left his mouth, Mal wished he could snatch them back. Even to his own ears, they sounded petty, and he wondered if by uttering them out loud he'd set himself back.

But Jo didn't look upset. Instead, she snorted with amusement.

"At first? Definitely," she said. "But he's had time to prove me wrong. And he has, a thousand times over."

Then why aren't you fucking him instead?

Mal squeezed his eyes shut, banishing the thought before it could crystallize into a feeling. He felt raw, flayed, and also a bit sticky, and his discomfort was making him vicious. He needed clarity, the sort he could find in a cold shower.

"I'm going to clean up," he announced.

Jo had the nerve to look embarrassed, as if she'd had no hand in his mess.

"Of course," she said. "I'll go after you, if that's okay."

Mal snorted a confirmation, then tossed the sheets aside and clambered out of bed. It had been so long since he'd slid out of bed with a new partner in it that he forgot what it felt like to have eyes trailing after him. His last first time, he'd had roommates, and he hadn't stayed naked long, tugging on boxers and a shirt before waddling to the communal bathroom. And he was pretty sure Portia had huddled under the covers and pretended to be asleep, not trailed his every move like Jo was doing right now. Ordinarily, her naked admiration would have made him flush, but now all of his energy felt frenetic. There was rejecting him because she didn't feel the same way, and then there was not believing him at all. He'd rather she'd laughed at him, instead of this. Instead of telling him that what he felt for her *wasn't real*.

Suddenly, a memory came to Mal, of Yves, his therapist, peering at him over round rimmed glasses.

"We're doing an exercise today, where we try to step into another person's shoes. A practice in empathy, so to speak," he said. "And I want us to start with Portia."

Mal remembered this session well, even though it was one of dozens, a single point in the extensive timeline of work he'd done to rebuild himself. It was not his first appointment, but one of his earlier ones, attended at a time when Mal was still skeptical about this whole therapy thing, and even more skeptical of the thin, bespectacled Haitian man sitting cross-legged in front of him. Yves preferred to keep his clinic space sparse and depersonalized, so there had been no photographs of family, and the only artwork on his wall was so nondescript that it gave no clues about his personal tastes—watercolor sailboats and thinly rendered flowers that Mal suspected had come with the frames. But on this day Mal had walked in to see a vibrant print of six children gathered behind a seventh, whose arms were spread wide, as if to protect them from an unseen threat.

"Bisa Butler. *The Safety Patrol*. She had a great exhibition at the Art Institute recently," Yves said, following the path of his stare. "So. What do you think was the greatest source of Portia's frustration in your relationship?"

"I don't really understand what the point of this is," Mal snapped. "Portia wanted me to be some big hotshot. She wanted spreads in magazines and partnerships with major brands. She thought I should want the same things. I didn't. She left. End of."

But the question had lingered in his mind, sticking to him like a burr, until, against Yves's advice, he convinced Portia to meet and asked her his question directly. Portia had answered succinctly, with a hard gaze and a tight smile: "You never gave me the space to figure out me. I was too busy trying to figure out you."

And even though it hurt, Mal understood. He understood that Portia pushed them to take on more clients because she'd come from a working-class family in which fourteen-hour days and six-day workweeks were the norm rather than the exception. That she grew frustrated when he missed opportunities to network because those networks had not been available to her growing up. That ten years into their relationship, she'd looked back at her life and realized that she was living it for a man, just like her auntie Elaine, who'd given up a future as an accountant to have four kids and clean house for a husband who picked the craps table over her in the end. Mal had known Portia's history. He should have realized that self-determination was important to her, shouldn't have let her yoke herself to his talent just because a photography business had made sense when they were first trying to make it out of college. He should have tried to look beyond his hurt and *listened to her*.

He wasn't going to make the same mistake again.

Mal let go of the doorknob, turned around, and marched back to Jo's side, then dropped onto the bed next to her.

"I'm not running away," he said. "I'm going to go shower, and then I'm going to make breakfast, and then we're going to continue this conversation. Cool?"

The look Jo gave him was indiscernible, her hands clenching and unclenching around blankets like a kitten kneading biscuits.

"Cool," she said.

Jo BRUSHED HER teeth with his toothbrush, showered with his products ("Good arsenal you've got," she said. "I was kind of worried I'd be walking in to three-in-one shampoo and the sad remnants of an Irish Spring situation."), sipped his coffee at his kitchen bar while wearing his T-shirt and basketball shorts and watching him flip pancakes over his gas stove. She'd emerged from the bedroom shortly after he'd finished in the shower, her expression pensive. He tried to play Yves's empathy game and step into her shoes. Josephine Boateng, who'd been abandoned by her parents at a young age, who learned early on that the only person worth relying on was herself. Who, despite the cosmopolitan big-city-girl image she projected online, was sort of a hermit. Who trusted people so little that she struggled to accept love when it was offered.

"I think that one's ready," Jo said, appearing by his shoulder to point to the pancake that was beginning to smoke.

Mal cursed, then flipped it over.

"That one can be mine," he said. "Almost done."

Jo stretched, bouncing to the tips of her toes, and it took a Herculean effort not to ogle. She was beautiful dolled up, of course, but he thought he preferred her like this, her face wiped clean and skin shining, padding about braless in one of his favorite graphic tees.

"It smells incredible," she said, leaning against the counter. "Is this a thing for you? You try to impress me with your cooking?"

Mal laughed, bumping her aside with his hip so he could get sausages from the oven.

"If you're impressed by pancakes and pasta, then I'm going to blow you away someday," he said, laughing. He cocked his head toward the dining table. "Go sit."

Jo obeyed, but only after badgering him into letting her set it. It occurred to him, as they gathered around the table, that this was the first time in years he'd had breakfast at home with someone else. Even more since it was someone he could say he loved.

"It's not that I don't believe in love," Jo clarified around a mouthful of fluffy buttermilk pancake. "It's that I think it's very temporary. The majority of the time, it doesn't have much staying power."

"Okay," Mal said, propping his chin on one hand. "Explain."

"All right," she said. "Divorce rates. Fifty percent of first marriages end in divorce—"

"Which means that fifty percent of couples stay together forever," Mal continued, waving a hand dismissively.

"Not necessarily because of love," Jo said. "People stay together who shouldn't all the time. For the kids, or because they like the societal benefits that come with being married, or because of financial situations. You catch my drift."

"So let's be generous and say three-quarters of the people who stay married shouldn't. That still leaves millions of happy couples, still together, still obsessed with each other." Mal popped a grape into his mouth. "My parents, for example, are disgusting. You saw them. It's like Gomez and Morticia in the Waters house."

"Well, that just means you're biased, because what I've got is my sperm donor ditching my mom the moment he found out she was pregnant, and Paul Adelman's potato-looking ass getting caught on TMZ sleeping around on his literal supermodel wife," Jo said, and Mal held back a grin, realizing that his ploy to use being open about his own history to get her to share her own was successful. "Okay, fine, I guess I'm biased too. But I guess what I don't understand is . . . why we have to even declare things. I like you, I enjoy your company, and I've just discovered that I really, really like having sex with you. I've already told you I'm not planning on seeing someone else. So why even bring love into it?"

"Because I want to," Mal said, bewildered by the question. "Because I think there's freedom in being in love."

"Freedom?" Jo repeated, skeptical.

"Yes," Mal said. "In trusting someone with your whole heart. In not having to put on airs, or to pretend to be someone you aren't, because they accept you as you are."

Jo scowled, dunking a chunk of pancake into a pool of syrup. She wasn't incapable of love; he knew that. If anything, he suspected it came easily to her. Renata had said it herself—that when Jo "decides to love you, she does it with her whole heart." And he'd felt that from her, that day when she'd dragged him to the front desk at a bookstore, her unabashed enjoyment of his company. The feeling that Jo genuinely, selflessly wanted him to be happy.

"That's a very privileged take on the subject," she said. She chewed, swallowed, pointed at him with her fork. "Because I think the opposite. I think, for women especially, that love is usually a prison."

Mal recoiled. His mind flashed back to two years before, standing in an eerie, sanitized version of his living room: throw pillows gone, candles cleared off end tables, a bookshelf half-empty. Portia's scribbled words on a Post-it note—*I can't do this anymore*—as if loving him had become a burden too great to bear.

"Did you know that men are six times more likely to leave their female partners after they get a devastating diagnosis?" she continued. "Go to a hospital sometime. Take a look at the patients. The men? They either have no one or there's a woman by their side, arthritic, with medical problems of her own, working hard to maintain an income for the house while cooking for the guy, cleaning him, giving him his meds. Being his night nurse and his momma all at once. The women? It's their daughters. The men they made them with are nowhere in sight, and even when they're around, half of what they do is try to tell you about their issues or complain about how she doesn't put out anymore." She looked at Mal, tired, her arms crossed tightly around her waist as if to protect herself from him. "You might think love is unconditional because you've been loved unconditionally. But from everything I've seen, for a woman to be loved, she has to serve a purpose. She has to look good on your arm, but not too good or she's a slut. She has to be sensual but puritan, needs to work or she's a gold digger, but not more than her man or she's a harpy. She can't gain weight, or she'll have let herself go, and if she has your children, she has to prioritize them over herself at every turn or she's a bad mother. She has to be strong, the backbone of the family, an extension of a man instead of his partner. If she defies any of these terms, most people won't blame a man for telling the world that his love for her has dried up."

Jo took a deep breath, her gaze focusing on him.

"Mal," she said. "I'm the happiest I've been in a long time right now. I'm not going to lie and say that some of that hasn't come from being with you." Before he could delight in that information, she continued. "But I'm scared. Scared that once I let you in, I'll no longer get to be the main character in my life. Scared that you'll start expecting that of me once my novelty has run out. Is that a good enough answer?"

Mal took a deep breath, then chased it with a chug of coffee so big that it hurt his chest on the way down. He understood what she was describing because he had once done something close. He'd been too afraid to look inward and address his own fault lines, too content to hand over the reins of his life to a woman who loved him and then grew bitter when she turned them in a direction he didn't want. But he wasn't that person anymore. He was doing the work to never become him again.

"I get it, Jo, I really do," he said. "What you're describing is a pattern of behavior that you've observed and lived through. I'm not going to pretend that nothing you've said is valid, or that I haven't been guilty of some of it. And I don't deny that society enables us to behave in the ways you describe. But I'm one person, Jo. Give me a little agency. Judge me for me." He reached for her, gently uncurling her arm from its hold around her waist. "You don't have to trust me fully right now, but I hope you can eventually. And I want you to decide whether I'm worthy of your trust based on *my* actions, not all the shit other people are doing and have done. Okay?"

For a slow, torturous second, Mal thought Jo was going to cry again. She swallowed, looked away, tucked her lips in the way people did when they were holding back tears.

But then she clasped his arm back tight, as if he were pulling her off the edge of a cliff and onto stable ground.

"You sound like my therapist, getting after me for my 'defense mechanisms,'" Jo said. Then she laughed. "But damn. You're right. I'll try. But I'm a harsh judge, okay? And I will let you know when you start slipping up."

"I'm good with feedback," Mal said, grinning. Negotiating his own trustworthiness shouldn't have made him this giddy. But the realization that he *could* have hard conversations, and that they could feel productive, gave him hope. Jo smiled back, bashful, and he tugged her chair closer to him, catching one of her legs between his.

Across the room, a high-pitched tinkling punctuated the air.

"Hold on," Jo said, whipping around to find it. She followed the sound to the couches, to their pile of carelessly discarded clothes, then, with a cheerful "A-ha!" found her phone inside the pocket of her bike shorts.

Mal cleared the table as she spoke, feeling rejuvenated. With Jo, things were going to be different. He wouldn't make the same mistakes he'd made last time. This time, he'd check in, and Jo would be comfortable with those check-ins, and maybe someday she would look him in the eye and say those words (*I love you too*), and they would be all the sweeter because he would know he'd earned them. And after that, well, maybe days like this could become more regular. Maybe Jo would start moving her things over, her face masks and skin serums filling in the empty spaces in his bathroom cabinet, her clothes filling a drawer—

"Hey," Jo said. She'd appeared behind him in the kitchen, her tote bag slung over her shoulder, shoes on, expression suddenly somber. "Um . . . sorry, but I've got to head out."

The domestic picture he was painting in his head blotted out.

"So soon?" Mal said, then realizing that he'd sounded disappointed, tried again. "I mean, yeah. Of course. It's almost ten. I've kept you long enough—"

Jo cocked her head to the side, pursing her lips to hold back a smile that didn't reach her eyes. Then she stepped forward, bouncing to her tiptoes to kiss him gently on the cheek.

"It's not you," she assured him. "It's just, ah, I spoke of the devil, and she emerged." When Mal blinked at her in confusion, she clarified, "My mom just called, and I need to go be in my feelings about it."

"*Oh,*" Mal said. He had so many questions, but all of them seemed inappropriate. "Oh shit. Are you okay? No, sorry, there's no way that you are—"

"Relax, Mal, it's not a big deal," Jo said, already headed for the door. She turned back, gave him a small smile. "I had a great time. I'll see you later."

"Yeah," Mal said. "I'll call you."

"Sure," Jo said. The door snapped shut behind her, and he listened to her steps echo down his hall, down his staircase.

The next day, when Mal tried to make good on his promise, her line had been disconnected.

CHAPTER SEVENTEEN
Jo

I knew from a very young age that my mother didn't love me because she told me so herself. She'd been drunk, sprawled out on our ratty sofa with a leg propped up on its arm, an unstrapped heel hanging from her foot, her usual post-Saturday-night-party position. I—being ten years old and already accustomed to taking care of myself—had asked for ten dollars and her signature on a permission slip for a school trip to the history museum. She'd looked me dead in the eyes, released a long-suffering sigh, and said, "I think I'm broken. I was supposed to love you by now."

"That's horrifying," Ezra said, sputtering, when I'd told him. We'd been lying on his bed in his house on campus, my feet braced against his headboard, his crossed by my head.

I disagreed. If anything, by telling me outright that she didn't love me, Prudence Boateng had given me clarity. She'd spared me the torment of disappointment, assured me that I was, in fact, alone in the world, and as a result, I'd behaved accordingly. From that moment on, I signed my own permission slips. Told my teachers never to expect my mother for their scheduled parent-teacher conferences and made excuses so that they wouldn't call Child Protective Services. Worked odd jobs, cooked my own meals, managed my own schedule, and made myself as unobstructive a roommate as possible so that I could continue to have a roof over my head. The second I turned sixteen, I moved out and filed for emancipation. As expected, my mother didn't show up for my hearing to contest.

What she had not successfully eradicated, however, was hope.

Because no matter how much I tried to convince myself that Prudence Boateng meant nothing to me, that the relationship I had with Renata was enough, there was still a part of me that hoped. *Maybe she struggled with depression too*, I thought. *Maybe she was young and overwhelmed and was forced into motherhood against her will. Maybe she didn't know how to mother a child but might know how to befriend an adult.*

And then one day, Prudence called.

I'd just been pictured in a *Marie Claire* magazine article alongside Renata at an event for New York Fashion Week. Ezra was out in LA shooting a pilot for a series that never made it off the ground, and Paul had long established himself as too busy to make it to Renata's little parties, and so she had asked me to be her plus-one. We had a fabulous time shopping for my outfit and an even more fabulous time cutting up on the dance floor, and when an unfamiliar number flashed across my screen the next morning, I'd been too giddy and exhausted to think twice before picking up.

"I see you've made friends in high places," Prudence had said, skipping even a perfunctory attempt at small talk. "Look, I was wondering if you could ask them if—"

I'd felt like I'd been dropped into a wind tunnel. Her voice sounded just as I remembered it, a clipped, resonant tenor, an American accent layered over the Ghanaian one like paint-on plaster. But instead of apologies, I heard demands. Instead of contrition, I heard derision.

Stunned, I hung up, increased my therapy sessions to bi-weekly, and tried, with limited success, to piece my self-esteem back together.

And now, five years later, Prudence was calling again, and this time she didn't even bother to say hello.

"I need help, Josephine," she said. "I know you don't want to hear from me. But I did one good thing by bringing you onto this earth, and—"

I hung up before she could say another word, unsure if I could hold myself together. Suddenly, Mal's living room felt too bright, the sun shining through his windows searing hot. Haphazardly, I slapped two fingers to my pulse at my neck, following the second hand on the analog clock hanging on the wall across from me. *One two three four five six seven eight nine. Sixty divided by six seconds is ten. Nine times ten is ninety, regular rate, regular rhythm, physiologic.* I inhaled through my nose, let the breath round my belly, hollowed it with a slow exhale through my mouth.

In the kitchen, I could hear the clang of dishes hitting the sink, Mal humming contentedly as he ran them under water. Some people, I thought, were born good, and Mal was one of them. Others were rotten.

I wasn't quite sure what category I fell under yet.

"Hey," I said to his broad back. "Um . . . sorry, but I've got to head out."

Mal whipped around, surprise rounding out his face, and I felt a pull in my chest, knowing that if he asked me to stay, I might like to cry in his arms. They would be good arms to cry into, bigger than Ezra's, warmer than Renata's, his scent spicier, his hold necessarily closer. The arms of a man who was *in love* with me.

But Mal was respectful, and not at all selfish, and granted me the space that I had requested without fanfare. So instead, I cried in the backseat of my Uber.

"Ummm, you good, girl?" my driver, a woman with cherry-red locs named Kayla, who I suspected might have recognized me, said.

"Yeah, thanks," I said. It was an obvious lie, given the mess I'd made of my face, but Kayla, who was making three dollars and twenty-two cents to cart me from Bronzeville to Lincoln Park, didn't seem in the mood to play therapist. That was just as well. I was busy emailing the person I paid to help me process my Big Feelings, and oh, was I going to get my money's worth.

Dear Rochelle, I typed to my therapist.

> *Sorry for the long disappearance! Busy busy! Anyway, wondered if you had any availabilities this week for an appointment.*

> *Thank you,*
> *Josephine Boateng*

I received a response instantly.

> *I am currently out of the country from July 14 until July 23, and will have limited access to my email and phone. I appreciate your patience. If you are in crisis and need to*

*speak to a mental health professional immediately, please
call the office phone number and dial 8 to reach the on-call
team. Otherwise, I will return your message when I return.*

*Thank you for your patience,
Rochelle Washington*

Damn. There was being abandoned by your mother, and there
was being abandoned by your therapist while she drank mai tais
on a beach in Malta. (Not that Rochelle going on vacation constituted abandonment. Rochelle, bless her, needed a vacation more
than the best of us.)

Luckily, I had the next best thing: Dahlia.

"You *whore*," Dahlia shouted from her bedroom, after I opened
the door to our apartment. She leaped into the living room, her
bangles clashing against each other musically, short black A-line
dress swishing around her thighs. It was ten thirty in the morning, and she already looked ready for a night out. "I saw the most
ridiculous couple at the Audi dealership yesterday, and I came
home all ready to make fun of them with you—seriously, nothing
against sugar babies, but this guy looked like he'd just stepped out
of the crypt and the girl was definitely serving barely legal—and
come to find that not only are you *nowhere to be found*, but you're
not even answering your texts! And at first I freaked out, but then
I checked your location and there you were, in Bronzeville, probably getting dicked down and . . . *oh*."

Oh meaning that I looked worse than I thought. The downside
of having lusciously melanated sun-soaking skin was that I could
hardly ever get away with crying without leaving salt tracks on my
cheeks, and the picture always made me more pitiable, like I was a

child walking around sticky-faced after a meltdown. I rubbed my cheeks, and Dahlia sighed mightily, taking my bag and guiding me to our sofa by my wrists.

"Do we have to kill him?" she said, stonily.

"No." I laughed.

"Okay, then was it *bad*?" she said, looking even more horri-fied. "God, I hope you don't feel like I pressured you into this. I usually have a good read on these things, I'm so sorry if I led you astray—"

"You didn't lead me astray," I assured her. It was moments like this when I really appreciated Dahlia; if I'd answered in the af-firmative, she would have climbed mountains to avenge me. "And you know better than anyone that you didn't pressure me into anything. I'm a grown woman and I made grown woman deci-sions, none of which I regret."

"Then what happened? Is sweet Writer Boy into some freaky shit? Like, does he like to make girls cry or something?"

"My mother called," I interrupted, before Dahlia's imagination could get any more colorful.

Shitty mothers were something Dahlia and I shared; mine ab-sent, hers oppressive, both of us now without contact. Most of the time, I considered myself lucky—my mother had so little inter-est in me that the daily chance of her reaching out was close to zero—but Dahlia's was constantly hacking at her defenses, writing diatribes about her on Facebook, convincing bewildered cousins to lend her their phones so she could chastise Dahlia for "living an ungodly lifestyle" and "abandoning her own mother when she only wanted the best for you." Dahlia had blocked her on email, text, and all her social media outlets (including LinkedIn), but every three months or so, Dahlia would waltz through the door with a bottle of wine and a Jewel-Osco cookie cake and I would know that Cecilia Cortes had successfully slithered through another crack.

But today was a first for us, because this time it was *my* mother who had made an appearance.

"Oh wow," Dahlia said. "What did she want?"

"Probably money," I said with a shrug. "Don't know for sure. She started with the whole at-least-I-didn't-abort-you-when-I-had-the-chance schtick, so I hung up before I could hear more."

"Good girl, enforcing your boundaries," Dahlia said. She squeezed my hand. "And don't you dare feel guilty about it either."

I shrugged. Not feeling guilty was easier said than done. The little girl who had once held out her report card to her mother, hoping that she would hear more than a *that's nice*, had never quite gone away, and a part of me wondered what would have happened if I had lingered on the phone longer. But Prudence had never let me dwell for long in my delusions that she wanted to reform our relationship. What she wanted had never been *me*.

"All right, that's it," Dahlia said. Ever energetic, she launched herself off the couch and back into her room, then reappeared seconds later with a purse slung over her shoulder and her key fob spinning around a finger. "Get changed. We're going for a ride."

ONCE I WAS suitably dressed, Dahlia led me to the parking garage, opened the passenger door to her brand-new, tags-still-on Audi coupe, and set the map in her console to take us to the AT&T service store.

"It's beautiful, girl," I said, admiring the sleek dashboard. "Damn."

"Listen, you've got to get into travel medicine," she said. "Sure, you've got to go live in bumfuck for a few weeks, and the work is tough . . . but the pay? The check is fat for us nurses, so I can't imagine what they're giving doctors."

"Maybe," I said, noncommittal. I had about a hundred emails from recruiters from small towns across America, offering five-figure paychecks for ten-day hospitalist contracts in desperately underserved areas, that I'd yet to respond to. It felt wrong, to turn my nose up at the very money I'd busted my ass in school to someday earn, but I still wasn't ready to go back. *One crisis at a time*, I reminded myself. "I'm proud of you."

Dahlia beamed. When we first met, online of all places, I'd been impressed by how free she'd seemed in her posts, how untethered she was by traditional concepts of *professionalism*. Her perspectives as a nurse in the intensive care unit gave me insight into aspects of health care administration I'd largely been shielded from as a resident physician, and her quippy skits on patient care regularly made me belly laugh through my shifts. When she went dark, during what I later found out was her tumultuous divorce, I reached out to ask whether she was okay. Dahlia had responded truthfully. She needed a place to stay, and fast, the kind of charity she'd never thought she'd have to ask of a stranger.

Offering her my spare bedroom while she got back on her feet had seemed foolhardy at first. But when Dahlia had shown up on my doorstep, with a brand-new platinum-blond buzz cut, septum piercing, and the beginnings of a sleeve tattoo that she definitely hadn't had a month before, I'd sensed that I'd made one of the better decisions of my life.

And now here she was, being hot, paying her rent on time, and speeding down Lake Shore in the impractical, sexy car of her dreams. Talk about a come up.

"Proud of you too," Dahlia said.

I scoffed. "For what?" The last time I'd done anything worth her pride was graduate residency, and even that had not come easy.

"You know. For following through on what you said in that one post." She turned to me for just long enough to wink. "For no longer moving in fear."

I snorted, but I thought about what she meant as we walked into the AT&T store, as I switched out the phone number I'd had since I was sixteen for a new one with a Wisconsin area code because, per the clerk, they were out of 312s, and finally, as we sat down at the nearby semi-classy bar/restaurant for a brunch I definitely didn't need. When our waiter swept by to take our drink orders, Dahlia managed to convince me to split a blood orange mimosa pitcher, and I was forced to also conquer my fear of day drinking.

"I had a big breakfast, so I'm not really hungry," I told Dahlia as we looked over the menu.

"Thought you didn't really eat breakfast," Dahlia started, then dropped her menu in realization. "Hold up. Did Writer Boy *make* you *breakfast*?"

I giggled, feeling light-headed with bashfulness and bubbly. Long gone were the bad feelings about my deadbeat mother; I'd thrown them away alongside my old number. Girl talk was so much more *fun*.

"He did," I said, tucking my lips into my teeth. "A full meal. With pancakes. And he made them from *scratch*."

"From *what*? You mean . . . like, not from a box? No Krusteaz? Bisquick? Aunt Jemima? Are you sure he didn't just add egg and milk and call it a day?"

"I'm sure," I said. "Like, there was baking powder involved.

And buttermilk." I settled a hand on my chin, reminiscing. "They were *divine*."

Scowling, Dahlia poured herself another mimosa and downed it in three gulps.

"I guess God really does have his favorites," she grumbled. Then she added wickedly, "Ugh. I just *know* he talked you through it."

Suddenly, I was back in Mal's bed again, dusk dyeing his white walls blue. The high points of his cheeks flushed and shining, dark eyes half-lidded, body pressed hot and slick into mine. *Just tell me what you want, and I'll give it to you*, he'd said, and I hadn't known what to ask for, because, in that moment, I had wanted it all. Everything he had.

"That good, huh," Dahlia said, catching my faraway stare.

"Honestly . . . yeah." I clenched my thighs, feeling the ghost of him between them. "I didn't even know it could *be* like that."

"Wow. You're sprung," Dahlia said. "But, more importantly, sounds like he is too."

I winced, all of my latent horniness passing like it had been blown away.

"He's a bit more than sprung, I fear," I confessed. When Dahlia raised her eyebrows in a question, I told her what he'd whispered to me the next morning when he thought I was still sleeping.

Dahlia's mouth rounded into an O.

"Oh my," she said after a moment. Then: "How do you feel about that?"

I gave her a knowing look, and she returned it, and then we both erupted into helpless giggles. I knew Dahlia understood, because she was just like me. Both of us battle worn, reveling in our hard-won independence. Both of us, as she'd said, as I'd said before her, used to moving in fear.

Dahlia wagged her head, her shoulders still shaking, then raised her glass.

"Go ahead, Writer Boy, put your whole heart out there," she said. "And for you! Cheers to new beginnings. And being brave. And not letting our exes kill our inner goddesses."

"I don't have an ex," I said, probably for the third time this week.

"Didn't Ezra Adelman pay our doorman thousands of dollars just to ensure you picked up your apology bouquet?" Dahlia said flippantly. "I don't care if you weren't sleeping together. That man is your ex."

"Yes, but . . ." I sighed, already exhausted by the turn of conversation.

But before I could redirect it, a glass shattered at the bar.

Instinctively, the sparse brunch crowd in the restaurant whipped toward the sound, then lingered when they found the source: a pretty blonde with Farrah Fawcett hair who'd managed to spill the contents of an electric blue cocktail down her ivory sheath dress. She stood, still as a Banana Republic mannequin, in the middle of her mess, staring down at an expanding splotch on her chest as if she were unsure how it got there.

I stared too. Even when a waiter rushed to sweep up the shattered glass, the woman didn't move, only jolting back to life after he tapped her on the shoulder. She laughed sheepishly, accepting his offered bundle of napkins, and stumbled back to her seat with the jointless fluidity of someone who was totally, gloriously plastered.

"Oh Jesus," Dahlia observed. "Someone's having a rough morning."

I watched the woman hoist herself back onto her stool. One of her falsies had lifted off the corner of her eye, and she peeled it off and attempted to stick it on the bartender's forehead, and at that point I sighed mightily and made a decision.

"I know her," I said.

I didn't like Ashley Biernacki, but I liked the predatory way the guy a seat over was sizing her up a lot less. I kicked back my chair with my heel and made my stand.

CHAPTER EIGHTEEN

Jo

Ashley Biernacki didn't recognize me at first, though, in this state, I suspected she might not have recognized her own mother. I planted myself in the chair next to her, rested my chin in my palm, and waited to be noticed. Ashley leaned over the bar, gesticulating to a bartender who was pointedly ignoring her.

"Excuse me," Ashley said, not giving up. "Excuse me, I need another drink? I spilled mine?"

"Ashley," I said firmly when it became clear I might be waiting awhile.

Ashley blinked up at me. Now that I was sitting next to her, I could see that her eyes were glassy with something more than just alcohol.

"Oh Jesus Christ," she said blearily. "I've had too much to drink, and now I'm seeing things." She reached out suddenly, and I dodged, wincing when the tip of her sticky finger brushed my cheek. "Weird. I was just thinking about you, and now you're here."

I swung around to make eye contact with Dahlia, who gave me a wide-armed gesture that I translated to mean *What the fuck?* as

she stood. I shrugged, then turned back to Ashley, who was staring very intensely at me.

"You need to go home," I informed her. "Did you come here
with anyone?"

Ashley dissolved into a fit of giggles.

"Come with anyone? That, my dear Josephine, is the entire
point," she said. She leaned in conspiratorially, bathing me in
breath that smelled strongly of rum, then in a stage whisper said,
"I don't think that's going to happen, though. I'm a bit of a mess."

"That's an understatement," I muttered. I made a point not to
ask her why she was hoping to pick up a random man in a bar
before noon; what went on between her and Ezra was none of my
business. What mattered to me was that she got home. "Do you
have your phone? Can I call someone to pick you up?"

"Sure," Ashley said, handing over her phone. Then, inexplicably, her eyes filled with tears. "It's the least I could do."

I definitely wasn't going to ask what she meant by that. This
version of Ashley Biernacki's tears was defanged, too red-nosed
and snotty to get me in trouble, but they still made me skittish;
I didn't care to stick around for long enough to be made into her
aggressor again. Thankfully, her phone still recognized her face. I
tapped into her contacts.

"Oh my god, she's crying," Dahlia, who had materialized behind me, said. She placed one hand on Ashley's back to rub it in
soothing circles and braced the other on the back of my stool.
"So . . . who's this?"

"My childhood bully," I deadpanned. Dahlia's jaw dropped. To
Ashley: "Where do you live? Is there anyone you want me to call?"

Ashley wiped her face with a napkin, smearing her mascara
around her eyes.

"I deserve that," she said in lieu of an answer. "I was so mean to you. Why was I so mean to you? You're so nice. And you got soooo pretty. Eventually. Like an angel." Her lower lip wobbled. "You know he calls you that, right? His *angel*."

I snapped my fingers in Ashley's face. "Focus, girl. What is your address?"

But Ashley was too far gone, her sobs transforming into absent-minded giggles. Exasperated, I made eye contact with the bartender, who was shaking up a cocktail and pointing with her eyes toward the door.

Shit.

The knot in my throat felt like one of the vegetable pills Renata had once tried to get me on in medical school, but what else was there to do? I scrolled to *E* in her contacts, found Ezra's name, and tapped "call."

The phone rang four times. My heart had settled after my brief exchange with my mother, but it was off to the races again in anticipation of one with Ezra. I rehearsed what I would say in my head. *Keep it to the point*, I thought. *No small talk. Just a location, a time, and then hand Ashley over like bitter divorcés exchanging their kid on a Saturday morning.* And, best case, Ezra wouldn't pick up at all, and I could say that I'd tried my best, throw Ashley into an Uber with a twenty-dollar bill folded into her palm and whatever showed up as "home" in her map app set as her destination, then send her on her way.

"Hello?" Ezra said. "Look, Ashley—"

I'd almost forgotten what Ezra sounded like, the thirty-pack-year smoker rasp of his voice that had always added an edge to his boyish charm. I'd heard that voice almost every day, on voice notes he recorded for me when he was shooting overseas, snickering next to me during one of his dad's self-important speeches at a company release, through my television, professing love to an actress I knew he couldn't stand.

It had been easy, in his absence, to say that I was over Ezra. But if that were true, why had hearing him say *her* name make my throat constrict?

"Ashley is currently completely trashed and alone at Early Bird in West Loop," I said. "Can you please come pick her up? I don't know where she lives, and right now, neither does she."

Ezra didn't say anything for a moment, and I steeled myself at the potency of his pause.

". . . Jo?" he finally said. "Jo, what are you—"

"Don't worry about what I'm doing," I said quickly. "And come get your girl."

I waited for Ezra to fight me. It was his usual way, to respond to my boundaries with petulance. In retrospect, it was amazing how often I'd let him walk all over me. Now that he finally had me on the line, he'd probably use Ashley as a hostage to keep me talking—

"Okay. I'm coming. Don't go anywhere."

He hung up.

I smiled queasily to myself. Of course Ezra was coming right away. Of course he hadn't missed me enough to fight to keep me on the phone, to bring me back into his life. This was Ashley we were talking about. He'd already chosen her before. And me? Once more, I'd managed to convince myself that I was stronger than I really was. That by shutting Ezra out, creating distance between us, I was giving myself space to heal from a decade of pining. But a few seconds on the phone with him had called my bluff. What I'd really wanted, all along, was to hurt him with my absence.

Pathetic.

My vision cleared, and I looked up to find Dahlia staring at me with round eyes. She was a smart girl, and I realized that she'd probably put two and two together.

"You okay?" she asked. My eyes darted to her hand, still on a now-slumped Ashley's back, and something ugly surged inside me, not quite hatred, not quite envy, but the slimy, familiar feeling of knowing that, even after all this time, I was not quite enough.

"I'm fine," I said sharply. "Ezra's coming to pick her up."

Ashley perked up suddenly. "Ezra?" she said. I recognized her despondence; I'd seen it on the faces of Ezra's girlfriends before. "Noooo. Don't call Ezra. He hates me."

"He doesn't hate you," I said plainly.

"No, no, he does," Ashley insisted. "Because I wasn't nice to you. His most precious person in the world. No way was I ever gonna compete with that." She sighed with her entire body, sagging onto the counter. "Karma's a bitch, I guess. I finally find a guy who's rich, hot, and not a douchebag, and he's in love with Jungle Jo." She paused. "I can't believe I used to call you that. That was hella racist."

"See?" Dahlia said. "Even your ex's ex thinks I'm right."

"Do you know how many of Ezra's girlfriends have said that?" I said, frustrated. "Ezra isn't in love with me. Ashley's just feeling insecure right now. And *drunk*."

Dahlia gave me a devilish look. "Lots to unpack here, huh," she said, snickering.

"The understatement of the century," I said. Ashley hiccupped, a single, errant tear trailing down her face, and for a moment, I felt sorry for her.

Not enough, however, to oversee her nap.

"Is she snoring?" Dahlia said.

"Yup," I said.

"You want to make yourself scarce until he shows up? I can watch her," she offered. I opened my mouth to refuse, and she held up a finger, tutting me. "Don't consider this altruistic. I'm just conning you into getting the bill." Her smile flickered. "I'm kidding, by the way. That was a joke. Obviously I'll split—"

I laughed, touched by Dahlia's offer.

"No, no, I'm the one who got us into this. I got it."

"Okay, but I got you next time," Dahlia said with a wink. "Try to flag someone down. It's getting busy."

I did. I was unsuccessful. In the last thirty minutes, the tables at Early Bird had filled with real brunch aficionados. From our table, the bar was in clear view, and I sat and watched, looking up hopefully at every passing waiter and busboy, a voyeur in my own story. The scene in front of me played out like a clip from *One True Kiss*. The woman with the buzz-cut blond hair and sleeve tattoo is eye-catching, but a side character, hanging on to the hot, blubbering, blond female lead. She tips a glass into the female lead's mouth, dabs it when water dribbles down her chin. Then the door to the restaurant opens, and a man enters. He's tall and strikingly good-looking, even dressed as he is in a Batman graphic T-shirt and heathered gray sweatpants. Even before he approaches the blonde, it's clear that he is her counterpart. His hand delves into his hair in exasperation, but the viewers know that the movement is intentional, that it will lift his shirt just enough to reveal the crisp V of his hips, and he hands a credit card to the bartender, settling her tab. But then he turns. Looks right through the screen. The fourth wall shatters, and suddenly the man is walking forward, jaw clenched, a hundred thousand teenage girls' dreams coming true before their eyes, because all along he was coming for *them*—

"You're still here," Ezra said, like he expected me to be gone.

Then he pulled up a chair.

CHAPTER NINETEEN
Mal

"Who do we have here?" Kieran said from his doorway, hands on his hips, bags under his eyes. With Kelechi's due date three months away, he'd been working overtime to get his team of software developers to the end of a project before he disappeared for his six-week paternity leave. Chasing after his toddler was not helping. "You decide you bit off more than you could chew, fraternizing with these celebrities, and now, the moment they stop paying you attention, you come crawling back to us normal people."

Mal rolled his eyes just as a pair of small feet pattered across the wood floor.

"Uncle Mal!" Harvey shouted, holding out his arms to be picked up. Mal chuckled, placing the plastic bag full of apology beer on the floor before bending to lift the kid into his arms. It had been only a few weeks since he'd last visited, but Harvey was already heavier, his annunciation clearer (last time, he'd been "Uncuh Mah"). Nothing like small children, he thought, to clue you in on how long you'd been neglecting your friends. As usual, Kieran's ribbing had a kernel of truth to it: he really had disappeared once things with Jo had gotten serious, and also equally true that he'd come crawling back to them the second things got rocky.

Not that he would describe his inability to reach Jo as *rocky*. Surely there was a reason why her number no longer worked. Maybe her phone had died (doubtful, as she'd updated her Insta-gram story today with a video of her roommate doing a shimmy in front of a mimosa). Maybe she needed a little space after their admittedly intense conversation (worrisome, but he would have found a way to be okay with it).

"Or maybe she ghosted you," Kieran said at the door when Mal presented these possibilities.

"Boo!" Harvey said. Then he erupted into a peal of giggles, delighted by his own joke.

"Sound a little less gleeful about it, maybe?" Mal said, making a face for Harvey that made him laugh even harder. Mal wasn't an idiot. He knew that this was the most likely scenario: that Jo had gotten exactly what she'd wanted out of him and, freaked out by his premature use of the *L* word, disappeared in a cloud of jasmine-scented smoke.

"You think I'm *glad* to be right?" Kieran said. "Nah. I'm sorry things didn't work out. You handling it okay?"

Mal shrugged. Mostly he felt numb. It had been two days since he'd tried to call Jo and been answered by three long, grating beeps and a robotic voice informing him that "The number you have called is not available." He'd tried to send a text, only to get a red exclamation mark and a Not delivered notification. His DM felt about as effective as a glass bottle pitched into an ocean; she had yet to even read it.

Mal's initial drop into despondence had been precipitous, a lot of moping around his bedroom and staring longingly at the photo a girl had taken of them at the Summer Concert Series at Millennium Park. But now, two days later, he could be objective. Dating wasn't the straightforward game it had been in college. There were mind games now. A talking phase, which might give way to a hooking up phase, which may or may not lead to exclusivity, which wasn't even the same as a relationship anymore. Nothing was predictable; a girl could text you every day for three months and then stop responding altogether when you tell her that you love her. And a girl like Jo, whose DMs were probably overflowing with six-pack abs and celebrity dick pics? Maybe she'd just been humoring him all along. Maybe he'd never really stood a chance.

"Is that Mally-wag?" Kelechi shouted from the other room. He twisted around fast enough to catch her cane turning the corner before she did. "Are you here to drink away your sorrows? If you are, can I please smell your beer?"

"I did bring libations, yes," Mal said, pushing past Kieran to let himself inside, Harvey still balanced on his hip. "Not planning to drink, though. I need to be productive." Then, to Kelechi, who had long ago proven herself his best brainstorming buddy, "I need to borrow your brain today."

"Ooh, yay, are we finally working on number two?" Kelechi said, gesturing to Kieran to pick up Mal's bag. When he did, she tore an IPA from the six-pack, turning it around in her hand with longing in her eyes. "I know this baby is going to be a rebel. She's got me craving *beer*, of all things."

She snapped the can open, then handed it over to Kieran, her expression grave. Kieran obeyed automatically, taking a quick swig before giving it back to his wife. She inhaled deeply, then, satisfied, gave Mal a sideways hug to get around the kid in his arms and the one in her stomach.

"I, for one, would like to entertain the possibility that this is all one big misunderstanding," she said. "It's a bit too early to catastrophize, don't you think?"

This too Mal had considered, but that didn't change the fact that Jo had become a central thread in the fabric of his life. They talked so often, and so consistently, that this change, if only for a few days, felt like a paradigm shift.

"Here you go again, being reasonable," Kieran said in feigned disgust, carting the remaining beers to the fridge. "Giving people the benefit of the doubt. Yuck."

"Yuck!" Harvey echoed. "Mommy, that's yucky!"

Kelechi kissed her baby's cheek and rolled her eyes at her husband. "Okay, bet. If three days go by and you still haven't heard anything from Jo, I'll handle Harvey on the day of Mal's event so you two can have a boys' night and cry about it together," she said. "If I'm right, though, I get to go."

"Oh, that's a deal I'll take, easy," Kieran said. "You see, I'm not blinded by my parasocial relationship with this girl, so I can be objective."

Kelechi stuck her tongue out at her husband, then lumbered to the couches, gesturing for Mal to follow. Mal acquiesced, handing a fussy Harvey back to his dad.

When he thought too hard about it, seeing Kieran and Kelechi as parents freaked him out. He still remembered when Kelechi was the cute Nigerian girl in the suite next door to him in college with a highlighter-pink prosthetic leg and a life-size DIY cutout of Sokka from *Avatar: The Last Airbender*, and Kieran his foul-mouthed half-white, half-Chinese roommate, who sometimes forgot to wash his Rugby jerseys and let Mal eat half the dumplings out of his mother's care packages. When they first started hooking up, Mal had privately thought they would never work.

But he'd been wrong. The living embodiment of them "working out" was toddling around his playpen, pushing a toy ambulance. Mal still remembered when Kieran first evoked his son's eventual existence, with a long-suffering sigh, a backward collapse onto his twin XL mattress, and a casual "my kids are going to be so fucking mixed."

Unbidden, an image of a different child flashed into Mal's mind: toddling around his living room with nut-brown skin somewhere between Jo's deep ocher and his sandalwood, giving him her impish smile with his Cupid's bow mouth.

"You'll have this someday too, if you want it," Kelechi said, interrupting the course of his thoughts.

Mal tore his gaze away from Harvey, embarrassed by the longing he assumed had been apparent on his face.

"Get out of my head, K," he said.

"Never," Kelechi said. "But I'm just saying. If not with Jo, definitely with someone else. You're a good man, Mal. Always have been." She scooted up higher on the arm of her couch, then spared him further humiliation by changing the subject. "Anyway, yes, you said you wanted to be productive."

"Yes. Please." Amelia had given him less than a week to come up with a list of potential plotlines to pitch to his editor, and he knew that if he tried to kick the can any farther down the road, she might try to stuff him into it. Back in college, when his writing was more of the embarrassing thing he did in his own time and told almost no one about, he'd spent hours sinking into Kelechi's fuchsia sofa, throwing around ideas for stories he would never write and letting her tease them apart. *But why would the hot vampiress go for the dorky self-insert photographer?* she would say, and he'd be back at the drawing board, making the vampiress a little less femme fatale and a bit more "girl next door who happens to have an appetite for blood," and the dorky photographer a little less, well, *him*, and a bit more "distinct protagonist with qualities a woman might want aside from being the hero." She'd helped him hone his niche of epic romance in a small setting of a slightly fantastical world, forcing him to define the traces of magic he liked to interlace in his narratives over and over again until he could almost feel them swirling around his skin.

Idea number one: Man and woman have torrid affair. Man's ailing and scorned wife, a witch in hiding, curses all their future incarnations to fall helplessly in love, and for that love to end in tragedy.

"How would the future incarnations even know they were in love before?" Kelechi asked. "Do they keep their memories from their past lives?" And when Mal said that yes, perhaps they would, she argued, "If they know it'll end in terrible tragedy, then why even bother to get to know each other?" To which Mal had no response and tabled the thought.

Idea number two: Man falls in love with mysterious foreign woman. She agrees to marry him, but with a catch—her culture practices polyandry, and she has another husband already in her home country. The man agrees to split time with his wife with this unknown man, and for half the year she would spirit away, like a migratory bird, then return with the change of the seasons to be with him—

Kelechi snickered.

"What?" Mal said.

"Are you down so bad that you're willing to share her with Adelman?" she asked. "Because that's what this is giving."

Mal sputtered back his response. "What?" he said. "No. Never."

Now that he'd held Jo close, the thought of the man she'd confessed she had *feelings for* ever doing the same inspired a howling fury that he couldn't examine too closely for fear of getting sucked too far into it. But even if Kelechi was off, she'd scratched right at the surface of his greatest worry. It would be one thing if he could no longer reach Josephine Boateng because she'd run out of his arms, but another thing entirely if she'd fallen right into Ezra's.

Ezra, who per her own admission, had already earned her trust.

"Oof, hit a sore spot," Kelechi said gently. "Look, Mal. You're clearly preoccupied. Maybe take a break. Detox. We can do this later."

Mal shook his head, his hands hovering over his keyboard. Writing had always been his escape. He'd buried himself in it before and come up with gold. And besides, he had deadlines. The event at Em-Dash. A career that required his attention.

"No," he said. "No, let's do this now."

CHAPTER TWENTY

Jo

It had taken three days for Ezra to be weaned off the ventilator. Before my first day at Elion University's campus, I had sworn to myself that I would never let a boy derail my studies. But for those three days, I didn't go to class, didn't study for my looming midterms, just sat at Ezra's bedside, the numb, silent girl who haunted his hospital room like a ghost while international supermodel/entrepreneur Renata Kovalenko wept beside me.

For three days, I had watched the stilting, artificial rise and fall of his chest, thinking about how, when I first found him, it had been so eerily still. Breathing wasn't something I'd noticed before this. But now I watched for it in everyone, taking note of the subtle expansion of ribs beneath the scrubs of the respiratory therapist who suctioned out Ezra's secretions, the slight rise of shoulders of the nurse looking over her IV pumps.

The doctors tried to be optimistic. *He's young*, they'd said. *He'll pull through.* But they also said that he'd been "down" for a long time. That his brain might not have gotten enough oxygen, and that even though he seemed to follow simple commands like "wiggle your toes," "squeeze my hand," they couldn't be sure what he would do with more complex ones. If he would be able to talk, walk, *act* again. So when, on the fourth day, the team stopped by his room to announce that they were going to pull his breathing tube, I grasped Renata's hand and led her out into the hallway.

"He's still in there," I assured her.

Renata nodded, tears trailing down her face. She cut an imposing figure against the hospital's wheat-colored walls, her jutting hip bones, angular cheeks, and arched nose a study in geometry, and it struck me that, despite her incredible looks and absurdly wealthy husband, her employees and her millions, she was alone. That the only person here to share in her horror was me, a surly, poorly dressed teenager her son knew from class, who was alone too.

When we walked back into the room, Ezra was watching for us. He gave his mother a chagrined wave, like he was greeting her after a weekend road trip, and she launched herself, sobbing, into his arms.

I watched them, knowing that my part in this had ended. I had three days of lectures to catch up on, an email to send to my Chemistry TA begging to make up my missed lab. A life that I was still yet to build. Quietly, I crept for the door.

"Jo, wait," a voice croaked behind me. Ezra, peeking out from over his mother's shoulder, his skin pale, the circles under his eyes dark, his gaze clear and direct. "Stay. Please."

Then, he extended his hand, and without missing a beat, Renata did too.

I understood, in that moment, that they were offering me

something that I'd never had. I understood, too, that I might never be able to give it back.

"I won't," I promised.

It HAD BEEN weeks since I'd last seen Ezra, and in that time, he'd let his facial hair grow. I'd never seen him with more than a five-o'clock shadow, but today he was rocking more week-old scruff, and it had a strange effect on his appearance, making him less billionaire playboy and more front man of an indie rock band. It didn't suit him, but that didn't stop him from being more beautiful than I remembered.

"Long time no see," he said.

I could feel eyes settling on our table, snapping to Ezra like magnets to metal. Probably trying to place him, wondering where they'd seen him before, or perhaps just checking him out. People like Renata and Ezra could hardly escape notice, but today, Ezra didn't seem to care. His focus was homed on me.

"Yeah," I said weakly.

It hadn't been that long since Ezra and I had last sat in a restaurant like this, stuffing our faces with the carbs he'd deprived himself of while shooting shirtless scenes for *One True Kiss*, before heading to our next stop: a concert we'd seen advertised on a streetlamp, a secret magic show in the basement of a bar, an overpriced speakeasy where I would try the cocktails and he would make fun of my expressions while sipping a club soda. Afterward, we would hobble back home to his Gold Coast apartment and, after forcing me to chug his mom's weird electrolyte water, collapse on either side of his California king. I'd wake up before him, like I always did, and draw a mustache on his face with washable marker, and he would enact his own revenge by wearing it the next morning to brunch, twirling the corner like a cartoon villain while reading through the menu.

And yet now, he felt like a stranger.

"Did you change your number?" Ezra said. "I tried to call you, but it said the line was disconnected."

"Maybe," I said. "Or maybe I just blocked you."

Ezra didn't take the bait.

"Did something happen?" he asked. Then: "Did your mom call?"

I winced. "Yes," I said.

"Are you okay?" His voice was gentle, its natural rasp turning his question into a whisper.

"Fine," I said. "Can't say the same for your girl, though."

Ezra looked over his shoulder at Ashley, who was staring at him longingly from the bar.

"She's not my girl," he corrected. "We broke up. At my birthday party, actually."

I could tell he expected to see a reaction from me, and internally, I was having one. The problem was that I couldn't quite figure out what it *was*. Just a few hours ago, I'd told Mal that love was a conscious choice. But there had been nothing intentional about my free fall for Ezra. It had taken years for me to label the stirring in my chest for what it was, and I'd come to it kicking and screaming, cycling through denial and anger because no way was I stupid enough to develop real, actual, nonfraternal feelings for Ezra Adelman.

And yet, in these few short months, those feelings had already changed into something unrecognizable.

"I hope you didn't dump her on my account," I said, trying to sort through the mess of my emotions. "Obviously I would've been uncomfortable if you'd stayed together at first, but if you really felt like she was the one, I wouldn't want to be in the way."

Ezra gave me an incredulous look, and what remained of his composure shattered on the spot.

"You wouldn't want to be in the— Jo, you've been avoiding me for *three months*. You didn't pick up my calls or answer my texts. You unfollowed me on social media. You asked my mom to put you at a different table at the benefit—"

"I didn't ask," I interjected. "Renata thought that it might have been uncomfortable for us to be sitting together and offered to make a switch—"

"You cut me out," Ezra finished. "Out of nowhere, like I meant nothing to you."

I'd never done well with seeing Ezra in distress. It was like I'd seen him burn through his lifetime's worth of suffering in a few short weeks, and I needed to shield him from more. Even now, I had to hold myself back from reaching across the table and placing a comforting hand on that shaking fist.

"That's not true," I said. *That was the problem*, I almost added. *You meant too much.* When Mal held my hands and told me he was determined to earn my trust, I'd experienced what it meant to be desperately wanted, to have a man anchor me in his gaze and tell me that he was going to do whatever he needed to prove to me that he loved me. When I was busy being Ezra's loyal hand, the best I could hope for was a kiss on the cheek before he went running back to his model of the week.

"You sure?" Ezra said. "Because you seem perfectly content to keep living a life without me in it. Seems like I'm the only one here having a hard time."

"I figured you'd find someone else to keep you occupied," I said truthfully.

"You're not replaceable to me, Jo," Ezra said.

I didn't say anything to that, which in itself said too much. We sat in silence for a long time, long enough for a waitress to swing by hopefully to ask Ezra what he'd like to order. Ezra shook his head without even turning to look at her, then wiped his hands down his face.

"Look. I didn't mean to ambush you. I swear I was planning to leave you alone, grab Ashley and run, but then I saw you sitting here and I . . ." He sighed, dropped his head into his hands. "I'm sorry. I screwed up that night. I knew I screwed up the moment I walked out of that library. And I just want a chance to try to make it right. So can we talk about what happened? Please."

What happened, I almost said, *can't be explained in one sentence.* It had been a thousand tiny heartbreaks over ten years: honoring his then girlfriend Becca Holiday when he won the People's Choice Award for Best Male TV Actor when I was the one who'd run his lines with him in the middle of my oncology rotation, sternly correcting every interviewer who insinuated that I was his girlfriend, taking women he'd known for two weeks to events that he promised to sneak me into and expecting to be forgiven with a simple "I'm sorry, she just assumed we would be going together and I couldn't disappoint her."

I'd suppressed these memories, but at their resurgence, I felt my throat tighten.

"You're still pretending you don't know," I said. "Even now."

"Know what?" Ezra said.

I scratched a line down the table, feeling the grit of the wood grain against my nail.

"That I was in love with you," I said.

You've honed your craft, I thought. If I hadn't been searching his face for a reaction, I might have missed his wince. But then something in his expression changed, a twist at the corner of his mouth, a slow, pained swallow.

I knew Ezra's face. I'd studied it under different sources of light, seen him delirious with joy and sad and angry and high out of his mind, and I could most certainly make out disappointment.

"Was?" he said softly.

I recoiled, astonished. His reaction, his displeasure—they were incongruent with the man who had run out of a room at the first hint that I was going to confess. Across from me, Ezra hadn't looked away from me, his lips tucked into a line, waiting for me to speak.

I opened my mouth to say something—*What do you mean by that? Did you know all along? Are you so greedy that you want things to go back to the way they were, with me pining away in your number two slot?*—when suddenly I was engulfed in a coconut-lime scent.

"I hate to interrupt," Dahlia said, "but the bartender wants Ashley out of here. We should probably get the check . . ."

Ezra's features convulsed, then settled into the polite, neutral expression he always used with my roommate.

"Right," he said. He turned in his seat, smiled good-naturedly at a passing waiter, who zipped to his side immediately, busy restaurant be damned, and hit us with a "How can I help you?" Ezra handed him his black card. Then to me: "When am I seeing you again?"

I swallowed down air, still reeling. "At the benefit?" I said. "Probably?"

"You don't have time for me before that?" Ezra asked, his expression unreadable. When I shook my head (*I need a little more time than a week to sort through this mindfuck.*), he grunted his displeasure.

Luckily I was saved again, this time by the waiter, who zipped back to Ezra's side like he was attached to a string. Ezra scrawled his tip onto the receipt, barely breaking his eye contact with me, and the waiter, who'd been waiting over his shoulder, looked like he was about to faint.

"Fine," Ezra said to me, handing back the check presenter. "We'll talk then. Don't let my mom monopolize you."

"Thanks for paying," I said.

"Of course," Ezra said. His gaze was heavy on me as I stood. It was this singular focus that had made him so popular on the screen, how he managed to make the female lead look like she was the only woman in the world worthy of his notice. It was strange, to feel that intensity directed at me. "I'm going to assume that means we can sit at the same table?"

I laughed in spite of myself, too stunned to react otherwise.

"Sure," I allowed.

CHAPTER TWENTY-ONE

Mal

Mal found himself at the front desk of Paws and Peace, the two-story complex that showed up in Google Maps when he'd typed "animal shelter near me" into the search bar. Impulsivity was not his style—he'd once visited an REI store four times before deciding on a smartwatch—but technically, this wasn't an impulse decision. He'd been considering adopting a pet since moving into his own place. Mal simply hadn't woken up this morning expecting to get one *today*.

He also hadn't expected to be ghosted by a girl immediately after he'd slept with her, so in the grand scheme of things, this was pretty mundane.

A gray-haired woman with giant paw-print earrings and a rainbow tie-dye apron over a red shirt greeted him at the front desk and barraged him with questions to which he seemed to always have the right answer. He was looking for a cat, yes, a senior cat would do just fine. Yes, he lived alone and would not be adopting with a roommate. Yes, he'd had a cat growing up.

"Would you be interested in fostering?" the woman asked

brightly. Her name tag read *Cindy* in blocky, handwritten letters. "Or, if you'd like to adopt today, that would be great!"

The way Mal's social anxiety was set up, there was no way he was leaving here empty-handed.

"Maybe let me meet them first before I decide?" Mal said quickly, then, because perhaps that had been too terse: "If that's okay with you."

If Cindy was offended, she didn't show it. Instead, she led him into the shelter, opening the door with a flourish. It being a Wednesday afternoon, there were only a few people wandering inside, most of them wearing the shelter's fire-engine-red shirts. Mal pointedly avoided eye contact with the dogs, who, as if sensing that he could provide a potential escape, all began wagging their tails vigorously as he and his guide walked past them to the "Kitty Korner."

The Kitty Korner was expansive, its white walls outfitted with shelves and slings from which several cats lazed. Several others padded across the floors, playing with toys, scratching at posts, kicking furiously in their litter boxes. A flat-faced orange fellow rubbed against Mal's legs, then skirted away when he bent down to pet him.

The sight was nostalgic. When he was five, he begged his parents for a puppy, only for them to compromise on a cat instead. He'd gone to the shelter and met Choux and Roux, two rambunctious paired siblings who tumbled all over the floor and eventually into his lap. His parents tried to steer him toward other options, but he'd been set on not splitting up the brothers, and so the puppy he'd initially requested became two kittens. Choux and Roux lived pampered lives in his parents' house before passing a week apart while Mal was away at college. His parents had waited until he was done with finals to tell him, and when he'd found out, he'd spent an entire day sobbing in a blanket cocoon in his top bunk. Kieran, unsure of how else to show support, had showered his desk with his favorite snacks.

"Everything all right?" Cindy asked.

Mal shook himself back into the present. He'd gotten lost in thought, and he suspected his expression had looked inappropriately morose for a guy in a room full of kittens.

"Yes, absolutely," he said. He gestured at a fluffy bicolor tabby who was cleaning herself vigorously on top of a cat tower. "I had a cat who looked just like that one, is all."

Cindy nodded, understanding.

"They never really leave you, do they?" she said. "All right then, I'll let you look around. All the cats here are available for adoption." She pointed to a scruffy tortoiseshell in the corner. "Except Lola over there. I wouldn't try to pet her. She's still quite feral."

Mal thanked Cindy, then began his rounds. Most of the cats paid him no mind, but the tabby approached him, sniffing his hand when offered, darting around his legs when he dropped into a squat. She really did look a lot like Roux. He scratched her head, and she arched into his touch before abruptly breaking away to clean herself.

"Rude," he said, shaking his head in self-directed disbelief.

He'd taken down good notes during his brainstorming session with Kelechi, but he was still struggling to condense his thoughts into a coherent proposal. He'd spent too much time updating his Instagram (now boasting, to his astonishment, over five thousand followers) and decidedly *not* writing or even, at the very least, preparing for his event at Em-Dash Books.

Thirty minutes, Mal told himself. *You have thirty minutes to fall in love with one of these beasts, and if it doesn't happen, you are going to go home and stop procrastinating.* To keep himself honest, he pulled out his phone to set a timer.

A notification for two missed calls thirty minutes apart and a text, all from the same unfamiliar number, flashed across his screen.

Hey, the text said. This is Jo. I changed my number. Update my contact.

Mal's knees buckled. He should have been embarrassed by the extent of his relief, and probably more pissed that she'd left him on read for three days before reaching out. He called Jo back, biting down on his cheek when she picked up on the first ring.

"There you are," Jo answered. "I was beginning to think you'd gotten tired of me."

The nerve, Mal thought, pinching the bridge of his nose between two fingers.

"I had no way of knowing it was you. Tried to call a few days ago, and your phone was disconnected." Having finished bathing herself, the Roux look-alike peered intently up at him, then bumped her head against his knuckles.

"Oh dear," Jo said, "did you think I blocked you?"

She phrased it like a joke, but today, Mal didn't feel like laughing.

"Yeah," he said stiffly. "I did, actually."

"Oh," Jo said. She sounded muted, and Mal regretted his honesty instantly. How completely uncool. *She's not your girlfriend*, he reminded himself. *She doesn't owe you a prompt response.*

But then: "Sorry," Jo said. "My mom calling put me in a weird place." She laughed nervously. "I should've hit you up right after

I changed my number. I realize in retrospect how shitty that was, considering the topic of our conversation beforehand."

"It was pretty shitty," Mal allowed, but already he was thawing, placated by her apology. "But it's okay. You got caught up. I get it."

"Do you?" Jo said. "You don't have to. You can be a little mad at me. I left you on read for forty-eight hours."

"Seventy-two," Mal corrected.

"Oh my goodness, seventy-two! Straight to jail!" she exclaimed. Then she laughed. "So, what have you been getting up to in these seventy-two hours?"

Mal opened his mouth to respond—*Absolutely failing at writing my proposal, updating my socials, staring at the ceiling, trying to convince myself that you didn't block me because you think I'm trash in bed*—but Roux 2 beat him to it with an indignant meow. He'd stopped petting her, and she'd taken it personally. He snorted.

"Did that sound just come out of you?" Jo said, giggling.

"No, no. It's a cat," Mal said, laughing along with her. "I'm at a shelter. I finally lost my mind today and decided to get one." Roux 2 nudged him again. "Even though she'll probably destroy all of my furniture."

"She?" Jo said. "You picked one already?"

Roux 2 looked up at him as if to ask the same. Her haughtiness was made even more hilarious by the fact that she was slightly cross-eyed.

"To be fair, I have no idea if she's a girl. Figure cats don't really care much about gender," Mal said. As if she agreed, Roux 2 began to purr. "I think she'll be pretty upset if I leave her here."

"What are you going to name her?" Jo asked.

Mal thought about it. He'd been curating a list of potential pet names since college, and most of them related to his creative activities. When he was still a photographer, he'd thought of names like Flash and Bokeh, and now that he was writing full-time, the list had been dominated by literary devices and punctuation marks: Grawlix, Phrop, Hyphenator . . .

"Ampersand," he said.

Jo didn't say anything for a moment. When she spoke again, there was a smile in her voice.

"You are so very adorable, did you know that?" she said. "Which is interesting, because you're also very sexy. How do you manage to strike that balance, Malcolm Waters?"

Mal scoffed. He was glad she couldn't see him now, his chin tucked into his chest, his ears burning so fiercely that they felt like they were glowing.

"You think buttering me up is going to make up for how you did me these last couple days?" he teased.

"No, but I've got a few ideas on how to make it up to you next time I see you," Jo said lasciviously. "Which is . . . when again?"

As soon as possible, Mal wanted to say. *Right now. Today.* All the answers he could think of sounded overeager. Mal looked down at Ampersand, who chirped at him as if to say, *Be brave.*

"I'll be home in a couple hours," he said. "Want to come over? Meet my new cat?"

"Is that a euphemism?" Jo asked coyly. "The new 'Netflix and chill'?"

"Only if you want it to be," Mal said. "But really, I was thinking maybe we could go out. Walk to the lake. Go on a proper date. I'm supposed to be courting you, remember?"

Jo laughed, and Mal warmed, feeling, finally, settled. The moment he hung up, he'd be texting the group chat to let Kelechi know that she'd won their bet.

"Of course," Jo said. "Be there soon."

"OH wow," Jo said as she padded through Mal's living room a few hours later, observing the changes he had already made to accommodate its newest occupant: toys, wands, a robot litter box tucked behind his monstera plant. She stopped at the half-assembled cat tower that Mal had set up next to his desk and flicked the swinging mouse toy as Mal affixed the final platform at its top. "This cat hasn't even been here a full day and is already spoiled rotten."

"Just giving her the life she deserves," Mal huffed. Ampersand curled around his feet in appreciation, then froze, affronted, when she spotted Jo. "She'll warm up eventually, probably."

Seeing Jo in his apartment again after spending the past three days certain that she wanted nothing to do with him was surreal. He'd opened the door to Jo wearing an orange maxi dress that made her look like the tiger lilies growing in his neighbor's garden and a chagrined smile. Whatever anxieties he'd had that she was still in fact disinterested in him were eased when Jo greeted him by winding her arms around his waist. "Hi," she had said breathlessly, then stepped back and folded her hands behind her back like a child waiting to be chastised, and after all of that he'd sighed mightily and thrown open the door to let her in.

He should have been disgusted with himself, at how badly he still wanted her. The moment Mal shut the door behind her, he turned into a lecher, his eyes locking to the swish and sway of her round hips in the airy fabric of her sundress. He wondered how she'd react if he tucked his hand under the slit at its side. If he grasped a hold of the thigh that peeked through the fabric, raised that skirt higher and higher until her ass was spilling out into his palm. She'd play coy, probably, or maybe swat at him playfully, but she would want him too, drop her head back against his shoulder as he peeled away her underwear, plunged his fingers into the heat of her—

"Oh my god, she's cross-eyed," Jo exclaimed, knocking Mal out of his fantasy. She dropped into a squat—the reverberations of the motion certainly not helping to sanctify his thoughts—and held out a hand to a very apprehensive Ampersand. Ampersand curved away, then, having reconsidered her initial judgment, rubbed her haunches against Jo's knee. "And *very* comfortable already. Congratulations, Daddy. What sparked this?"

If Jo knew what calling him *daddy* was doing to him right now, she might rethink it.

"Procrastination," Mal admitted, wandering into the kitchen to finish packing for their date. "I have the event at Em-Dash the day after tomorrow. Got a proposal due Friday. So, naturally, I felt like now was the time to make a big life change."

Jo laughed. "Hold on, am I part of the procrastination plan?" she said, catching right on. "Did you just invite me out to distract you from your work?"

"No regrets," Mal said. Finished, he hoisted the insulated bag onto his back. "You ready to go?"

Jo and Ampersand cocked their heads at him simultaneously, and Mal wished he could whip out his phone to take a picture.

"What's all that for?" she asked, rocking to her feet.

"You'll see," he said.

Mal's apartment was a ten-minute walk from the lakefront. It was part of why he'd moved there after he and Portia split; he started most days with a run down the lakeshore path and ended several more clearing his mind looking over the expanse of crystalline waters. He'd gotten so used to walking this path to the pier alone that it felt strange to do so with someone by his side. Mal and Jo walked in comfortable silence on the trails along the lake. It being a gorgeous day, most of the city had spilled out onto the grassy hills, parents chasing after kids, kids chasing after dogs, college students lying on their stomachs and flipping through books, families grilling burgers over the firepits. A crew of shirtless men in cargo shorts blasted reggaeton from speakers mounted on their bicycles and cheered when an elderly man danced along from his hammock. Even the pier was occupied, mostly by teenagers daring each other to dive off the docks into the calm waters below. They reached the end, and Mal laid out a blanket.

"Romantic," Jo observed.

"Kind of the point," Mal said, unzipping his cooler and assembling its contents before them: a thin wooden cutting board, jarred honey, small bricks of cheese, prosciutto, olives, a bowl of cherries. Then, finally, a pair of personal bottles of rosé.

"This is quite a spread," Jo said, in a way that could have been either appreciative or critical. She pulled out her phone to take a photo, rolling her lips into her mouth, and Mal realized, suddenly, that what he'd often read as disapproval on her face was actually astonishment.

"Not to be creepy or anything," he explained, "but you had a video a while back, where someone asked you what your ideal date was, and you said . . ."

"A picnic," she finished for him.

"Yeah," he said. Under her probing gaze, he felt shy, like he was admitting to something he shouldn't. "What did you say? You didn't want Doritos and Jimmy John's. You wanted something that was just as pretty as it was good to eat, with items you wouldn't normally get, you know, so it felt special, and so I tried to do that. The lady at the cheese counter said this cheddar paired well with this prosciutto, so—"

His words were cut off by Jo's lips, her hands hooking under his jaw to open his mouth to hers. She tasted vaguely of spearmint, and her kiss was declarative, as much a statement as it was a show of affection. Its force knocked him off-balance, and he fell backward on the heels of his hands to support himself, knocking over the bowl of olives in the process.

"Sorry," Jo said, pulling back abruptly. "I'm sorry, I just . . ."

"No," Mal said, flustered. "Jesus. Don't apologize. Please kiss me whenever you want."

In response, Jo leaned forward again, angling her body carefully over his effortfully arranged spread. This time her lips were soft, their press almost hesitant, and when he placed a hand under her chin to guide her closer, he realized her skin was damp.

"You're crying," Mal observed. He filed this as another thing he knew about Josephine Boateng, that despite her stony exterior, she was quick to tears.

"I know. I can't help it," Jo said, sniffling through a smile. She settled back onto her haunches, then popped a cherry into her mouth. "I cry at everything. Movies, TV shows. I was a hot mess during residency. Couldn't make it through a family meeting without losing my cool. It's annoying."

Mal wiped a tear from the corner of her eye with his thumb, then draped an arm over her shoulders and gathered her into his side. She molded into him easily, and he marveled at how sweetly she nestled into him, her heat becoming his, their scents inter-mixing.

"I'm sure they appreciated that," Mal said. "Seeing their doctor cry for them."

"Sometimes," Jo said with a laugh that was almost a whine. "Sometimes it pissed them off. Like I was making their loss about me."

Mal nodded, understanding. Then: "So why are you crying now?"

"Because you're wonderful," she said simply.

Mal chuckled nervously. "I'm not," he began, but Jo shook her head.

"No, no, but you *are*," she insisted. "Like, look at you. You just set me up a picnic. You listen for what I want even when I don't tell you directly. You definitely should be working on your proposal right now, but you're here with me instead." She nestled farther into him, turning until her voice was muffled into his arm. "I think I might adore you, Malcolm Waters."

"But . . ." Mal provided, already knowing that it was too early to revel in her words.

"But I'm scared," Jo finished.

Mal opened his mouth, then closed it, swiveling to face the water. It was nearing sunset, just as he'd planned, the clouds streaked with pink and purple, the sunlight spilling over the lake like a popped yolk. Frustration burned a hole in his chest. He knew that Jo's trust wasn't something he would magically get, that there was no fixed number of romantic gestures and sweet words that would eventually help her realize that he was safe. When they first met, he had seen Jo as a blazing star, someone who shone relentlessly regardless of circumstance or surround-ings. Now he recognized that as fantasy. Jo was human, and a little broken, and the pessimistic worldview she'd built was in-formed by experiences that he would be remiss to diminish. There was no reason for her to believe that he had no ulterior motives, even if he knew that he'd put together this picnic just to make her smile. She would have to decide for herself.

"I can't fix that for you, you know," he said, after a moment. "I can't chase away that fear. You just have to believe that I'm not going anywhere."

Jo nodded, dabbing her face with a napkin. Then she steeled herself and reached for his hand.

"I know," she said. "But that isn't what I mean. I'm not scared of you anymore, Mal. I'm scared *for* you."

A breeze blew by, uncommonly brisk for the time of year. Across the water, Mal could hear children screaming.

"I need to tell you something," she said.

"Yes," Mal said. He could feel his pulse jumping in his neck, his body preparing itself for a blow.

And with a slow, shaking breath, Jo gave it.

"I saw Ezra the other day."

Mal let his next breath round out his belly, then pushed it out in a slow, controlled exhale. *Be cool*, he thought, even as howling filled his ears.

"Oh," he managed, not sounding cool at all.

"Yeah," Jo said.

"So, uh . . ." he started, clearing his throat. "How did that meeting come about? Did you reach out?"

"No, actually," Jo said. "Coincidence. His ex got trashed at a restaurant I was in."

Jo told Mal, then, how just minutes before she found him in her bedroom at the Adelmans' the day they first met, she'd learned that Ezra was unknowingly dating her childhood bully, Ashley, then knowingly took Ashley's side when she made a scene at his party. How Jo had found that same bully making a mess of herself at a bar the morning after her and Mal's night together, and how, in a show of apparent benevolence, Jo had called Ezra to pick Ashley up.

"It wasn't because I wanted to see him again," Jo insisted. "I just didn't know what else to do."

Serendipity was just fate for the unromantic, Mal thought. He imagined Ezra walking into the restaurant, a red string of fate tightening and resonating between him and Jo.

"Okay," he said steadily. "And what did you feel, when you saw him again?"

Jo extricated herself from under his arm slowly, and the loss of contact told him her answer before she could say it.

"I . . . don't know," she said. "Not what I used to feel. But not nothing either."

Logically, Mal knew that Jo was just being honest, and that he appreciated honesty. Jo would never feed him just what he wanted to hear, and her transparency was one of the things that drew him to her in the first place. But emotionally, hearing her answer with anything other than apathy strummed a chord of misery in him.

Jo seemed to sense his despondence. "Not the way I feel about you," she tried, putting a hand over his.

Her attempt at comfort came too late; he was already spiraling. If Jo had loved Ezra Adelman once, it would not be hard for her to find that feeling again. And Mal had met Ezra, had felt him size him up. That was a man who didn't intend to lose the same woman twice.

"Is that why you didn't reach out after you changed your number?" he asked, willing his voice to be steady. "Because you were with him? Because you weren't sure about *us*?"

Jo's smile fell to her feet. Mal heard it drop like a bell toll.

"It wasn't just that," she said softly.

"But it *was*, a little bit," Mal said.

When Jo didn't respond, Mal turned away. His body had kicked right into a fight-or-flight response, and he felt dizzy with adrenaline, the muscles in his calves tensing and relaxing as they dangled over the edge of the pier. He picked up a cherry, pitched it into the lake, and somehow the fact that it bobbed in the water instead of sinking underneath frustrated him more.

"I understand that things are complicated," he said, "but I'm not going to wait forever. At some point, you'll have to choose."

He didn't need to look at her to tell that she'd frozen in place.

"I know that," she said eventually.

Mal smiled, more to himself than to anyone else. The old Mal, the one Portia had left behind, would have taken a year and a half to recover. He would've holed himself up in his apartment, shut the blinds, and become one with his carpet.

This new one was capable of snapping back.

"Good," Mal said.

CHAPTER TWENTY-TWO

Jo

Paul Adelman was of the belief that there was nothing in the world that money couldn't buy, and forgiveness was no exception. The bigger his transgression, the more ostentatious the gift, and over the twenty-eight years of their marriage, Renata Kovalenko had accrued villas in balmy locales; historical diamonds with names like the Heart of the East, which she loaned out to museums; and, on occasion, seed funding for what her husband termed her "pet projects." The day after an exposé in *US Weekly* dropped, detailing the Knydus CEO's scandalous weekend in LA with a twenty-two-year-old reality TV bombshell, he presented Renata with the gift of her dreams: fifty million dollars and the staff to kickstart a film studio. *Imagine yourself sitting in the theater. The lights dim, and then, there on the screen: En Garde*, he'd told her, dropping a binder of mock-ups of her logo over the splayed pages of the magazine.

Renata took the money. She'd understood when they were married that Paul was not a man who let opportunity for either business or pleasure pass him by. Once upon a time, she had admired that about him, and now she found that she could tolerate it, when the price was right. Still, the night after Boris Finnegan solemnly handed her the fresh-off-the-press printing, she'd wandered into her expansive bar, hunted down a bottle of horilka, and knocked it back straight.

"Want more for yourself than this, Josephine," she'd slurred when I found her hours later, slumped like a felled angel at her kitchen table next to a half-empty bottle of Nemiroff.

I stared, stunned that a woman so full of fervor could let someone snuff her out.

"I don't understand why you don't leave him," I said.

Renata snorted, then lifted her head back to look at me through bleary eyes.

"Paul is a great man, but he is not a good one," she said. "When you love a great man, you understand that that love can't be just yours. Men like him will love other people too."

I refused to accept that as an answer. Before we had ever met, I'd seen Renata's face staring back at me from magazine covers, billboards, and, later, television shows. She commanded attention in every room she existed in, even when she wasn't physically present. To me, Renata was not just a woman but a monument. Her husband, in contrast, was just some guy. Sure, he was a guy with a multimillion-dollar company, but after meeting him and his ilk, I'd been convinced that even that wasn't impressive—anyone with enough ancestral wealth, a deficient supply of scruples, and a dragon's hoard of audacity could make it big.

"You're great too," I'd said, but I knew that any more would be overstepping my boundaries. Paul Adelman was a ghost in his own home. His interactions with his own son were stiff and stilted; with his wife, strained; with me, nonexistent. He could disappear in a puff of smoke overnight and his household would operate as it always had, probably not noting his absence until the next time they had to make a public appearance. What Paul Adelman was doing—humiliating his wife, dragging her honor through the streets—was not *love*. It was selfishness. It was cruelty.

Ezra had been away for a shoot on the day the article about his father's affair dropped, but he booked a flight home the next day. By that time Renata was back in her normal state, the only sign of her hangover the extra-large cup of coffee she carried into her office that morning. When Ezra tried to ask how she was doing, she said primly, "Come now, we both know how your father is," before opining about a meeting she had had with a producer about being a judge on a reboot of *America's Next Top Model*. But when Ezra asked me, I didn't mince words. We debriefed in his room, the only place safe from prying eyes and curious ears, and I watched his face tense with anger.

"That man is the greediest motherfucker alive," he said of his father. "If I had the honor of being loved by someone like my mom, I would never even think of letting them go, let alone disrespecting them like this."

I stilled beside him, noting two things at once. First: that Ezra hadn't yet met a woman he wanted to hold on to, not even his girlfriend at the time, with whom I'd thought he was head over heels in love. The second: that this also included me.

"Those are some high standards," I said. "Your mom is literally one in a billion. Does a woman like *the* Renata Kovalenko even exist?"

Ezra shrugged, but his expression was no less fiery. "You exist," he said.

I snorted, rolled my eyes, forced my heart rate to slow. *He didn't mean it like that*, I thought, as he steamrolled ahead, vent-ing about the man who was more his benefactor than his father. *He never means it like that.*

But what about now? I thought, staring at Ezra's revived text thread. What did he mean now that he knew how I had once felt about him?

Ezra: I want to see you.

Ezra: I know I agreed to wait till the benefit. But I'll be honest with you, I don't see the point. It can be quick. Coffee? Or I can just come by your place? Just like old times.

Ezra: You look amazing today, by the way. Hope you and Dahlia are having a good night.

"Uh-oh, what is that face?" Dahlia said, leaning out of her seat to snatch a salmon maki off the rotary sushi belt. Her social media platform had recently shifted focus from health care to lifestyle, and she'd initiated the transition by visiting little-known Chicago restaurants and posting reviews. After a few of her posts went viral, she'd started getting offers for comped meals in exchange for promotion. "I can't believe you're not making them pay you," I'd complained, but as a former poor kid, I knew better than to turn down free food.

Not that the meal didn't come with a price. Instead of money, I paid my way through my services as Dahlia's camerawoman and collaborator. In true Boateng-Cortes fashion, we'd shown up fabulously overdressed: Dahlia in a tight black mock-neck dress that showed off her tattoos and lace-up booties that showed off her calves, me in a white baby doll dress and clunky Mary Janes that lent me four inches of height and gave my legs the illusion of length. Of course we'd taken pictures for the Gram. I kept it cute with the caption: health care heroes 😇 😈

Within two minutes of posting, Ezra had commented from

his official account: gorgeous ♡. My followers immediately fell into a tizzy: @beyoncesgivenchydress had already commented: NOT ONE TRUE KISS' ZACHARY THIRSTING ON OUR GIRL DR. JOJO!!!! 🔥🔥🔥🔥🔥🔥🔥🔥🔥

"Wait, do that again," I told Dahlia. "I got a text. It messed up the shot."

Dahlia gave me a knowing look but acquiesced, this time grabbing a spider roll from the rotating belts. I sat up straighter, zooming in to capture its textures, then panned over to Dahlia, who mimed snatching it in her chopsticks excitedly. The second I lowered my phone, she lowered her smile.

"It's Ezra, isn't it?" she asked.

"Yup," I admitted.

"Told you," she said. I threw a kick under the table that she dodged. Then she held out her hands for my phone. "Let me see."

I handed it over, and Dahlia scrolled through Ezra's messages, her eyebrows rising higher as she went.

Ever since I lifted the embargo on communication between me and Ezra, he'd been coming on strong. Where he'd always sort of skirted the line between amorous and platonic intent, now he was crossing it boldly and unabashedly. He'd sent me apology hyacinths before, but yesterday's delivery had been vibrant red camellias. ("I negotiated my terms and got five grand this time! Thanks for the advice, Dr. B," Raymond said gleefully before taking his delivery confirmation picture.) Dahlia and I had looked up the meaning together and found words like *passion, desire, romantic love*. And then there were the photos Dahlia was seeing now, sent this morning, of Ezra looking very dapper in a navy suit, with the shirt unbuttoned just enough to show the dip of his clavicle, and another of him in a sheer, bejeweled black button-down and leather pants that made him look like he'd just walked off the set of a vampire movie. Underneath, his pretense: What do you think I should do? Play it safe? Or have some fun?

Or, he sent a few seconds later, you could send me what you're wearing and we can try to match.

No wonder all his girls folded so easily. I'd only ever received Ezra's charms at half power. Now that he'd pulled them out full force, the emotional equilibrium I'd built had been upset. Twenty-year-old Josephine would have been thrilled. Twenty-nine-year-old Josephine was bewildered. I'd gotten used to a clumsier, more earnest approach, to sincerity and directness. To a guy who could tell me he loved me without flinching or talking around it, then promise to wait for me to catch up.

Except I'd only known Mal for three months to Ezra's ten years. Except in those three months, Ezra Adelman might have actually woken up and seen me in a new light. Except if my suspicions were correct, and Ezra, who I knew would never screw me over, had feelings for me, I might regret not giving him a chance.

"God*damn*," Dahlia said, zooming in at the hint of abs visible through the mesh. "Don't know if I realized that Adelman was built like this. Sheesh."

"Yes, yes, he's irritatingly hot," I said, groaning. "You know, maybe I should respond to Dr. Makinen. Medicine was traumatizing, but at least I wouldn't be bothering myself about *boys*."

This time it was Dahlia who threw a kick, and unlike mine, hers landed squarely on my shin.

"Nuh-uh. You've spent enough of your life hiding behind the hospital. It's high time you *do* bother yourself about boys," she said. "And just FYI, I veto Ezra's request to 'come over.' I do not trust that man in our home. He's going to eat you alive."

Suddenly I remembered the last time I had been consumed—
Mal's hot breath against my ear, his hand holding my jaw as he
plowed into me, *You like that?* whispered into my ear. I buried
my face in my hands, flustered. Yesterday on the pier, when Mal
asked me whether I'd avoided calling him because I was confused
about Ezra, I'd answered truthfully and watched his heart break
before my eyes. We nibbled at his spread for a little while after that,
watching the sun dive below the horizon, and when we packed up
to leave, he didn't hug me, didn't kiss me, didn't invite me home.
Instead, he'd held on to the straps of his cooler backpack in tight
fists, smiled at my shoulder, and said he would *see me around*.

I'd hurt him and hated every second of it. When I told Dahlia
this, her jaw dropped.

"This man asked you what you felt when you saw Ezra again
and you said *not nothing*?" she repeated, aghast.

"Yes? Because it's the truth?" I said, confused.

One, I thought that Mal deserved to know. It was his right
to decide whether what I could offer him was enough. What he
deserved was a person who could love him wholly, who could
trust him with her whole heart, who wasn't so messed up inside
that when he told her he loved her she couldn't say it back, even
though she suspected she might feel the same.

Dahlia's hand covered mine. When I looked up at her face, her
expression was grave. I groaned.

"I thought we didn't do pity," I said.

"Just this once, I think I should be allowed," Dahlia said. "Jo.
Speaking as your friend. Writer Boy has been *good for you*. He's
patient and sweet, not afraid of loving on you, and, more importantly, you are obviously so very into him."

This too was true. When I first saw Malcolm Waters in my

bedroom at the Adelmans', I hadn't imagined that I would ache for him. I'd thought he was pleasant to look at, yes, and shockingly sincere, but I'd imagined him as a short-lived bit of fun, an experiment of sorts. I'd wanted to experience Mal the way Ezra experienced his many paramours, with just enough depth that I could enjoy myself without putting myself in harm's way. One toe in the pool.

But Mal had pulled me under the surface. The worst part was that he'd warned me that this was his intention. *You feel like you're on fire*, he'd said, of the kind of desire he intended to inspire. And here I was now, burning to ash, terrified to bring him down with me.

It was different from what I felt for Ezra. *More.* And yet.

"He knows what he's getting into," Dahlia continued. "You told him straight up, from the beginning, about Ezra. There was no need to reiterate it."

"Of course there's a need," I said. I thought of Renata lying across her kitchen island, then imagined Mal doing the same, his locs splayed around him, Ampersand crying at his feet. "I don't want to deceive him."

"Oh my god, you're not listening," Dahlia said, frustrated. "Jo, I am trying to tell you that you are *scaring the hoes*."

With timing I could only describe as immaculate, a waiter appeared at Dahlia's side.

"Can I get anything for you two?" he asked, just barely holding back a smirk. He, like all the other waiters at this restaurant, was egregiously pretty, his feminine features contrasting with the jagged tattoos that covered his hands down to the knuckles. I imagined he overheard all sorts of commentary from the tables he waited, and that much of it was about him.

"Yeah, um . . . Daniel," Dahlia said, squinting to better read his name tag. "Can I get your opinion on something not food related?"

Daniel flipped pink hair out of his eyes and gave us a crooked grin. "Sure, why not," he said.

"Say you're really into a girl. A baddie. One who looks like this." Dahlia pointed to me with her chopsticks, and I sputtered, trying and failing to keep my bubble tea in my mouth.

"I'm following," Daniel said, ticking his eyes over me in appreciation.

"Say she's into you too. But you've got competition. Some other guy—and this one is a catch: think the hot CEO guy in a K-drama. And the kicker! She's kind of into him too."

"Oh dang," Daniel said. "So I'm trapped in a classic love triangle trope."

"Exactly," Dahlia said. "And everything is going well, but whenever y'all are together, she brings him up. Basically reminding you that not only does he exist, but that she's not sure if she's picking you or him. What do you do?"

Daniel tucked his hands into the pockets of the apron tied around his waist, considering. Then he straightened, looked from me to Dahlia and back again.

"I mean? If she's bad, then I kind of expect her to have a roster," he said. "And if I'm really into her, then I'll just have to love on her better than the other guys until they get dropped."

"And if, after a while, she's still unsure?" Dahlia pressed. "Still talking about the other dude?"

Daniel shrugged. "Then I'll have to get over it, won't I?" he said. "Plenty of fish in the sea. Maybe someone else will bite."

"Exactly," Dahlia said, then, after sucking through her straw. "Okay, for real now, can I please have an order of gyoza?"

Laughing, Daniel swept back into the kitchen to fulfill her order, and Dahlia turned to me, smug.

"You're the worst," I groaned, but she and Daniel had successfully struck fear into my heart. Perhaps out of arrogance, I'd assumed that Mal would wait for me. That he'd give me the space to process the mess of my feelings, that he would be satisfied enough with the sex and the dates and the intimacy, that he would be okay with forgoing my love until I was ready to give it.

"I'm okay with being the bad guy if it means I stop you from doing something you regret," Dahlia continued. "What I'll say is this: Mal has done more to make you happy in the last three months than Ezra has managed in the years I've known you. If things go south with Mal, Ezra will still be your friend and you'll be back at your status quo. But if you go chasing after Ezra, you *will* lose Mal. Will you be able to handle that?"

I imagined it. Waking up in the morning to no continuation of the conversations we'd had the night before. No more of Mal's bashful smiles, no more hesitant kisses that turned hungry a second in. Never speaking to Mal ever again, knowing that we were *so close* to something good.

"No," I allowed, my throat tightening at the thought. "No, I don't think I could."

"Then do something about it," Dahlia said. "Look. I get that you're scared. Ez? He's the devil you know. And Mal might still be a bit of a mystery. Things are great now, but you don't know what he'll become later, and you're worried you'll blame yourself for taking the shot if things go south."

"Yes," I said, struck by the accuracy of her assessment. "Yes, exactly, that's it."

Dahlia nodded. "I get that, I really do. But Jo. Every single time I've taken a chance at love, I haven't regretted it. Yeah, sure, I might end up having a hard time after things don't work out, but eventually, I wake up, and always to a world that was bigger than it was before."

"You don't regret Jonathan?" I asked, invoking her ex-husband, the year of hell that had come at the hands of someone who'd once vowed to love her through all trials and tribulations, only to reveal himself as the source of them.

Dahlia smiled wistfully, as if she were recalling a sweet memory.

"No," she said. "I don't."

"But he made your life miserable," I said, stunned by her answer. "You were functionally homeless, Dahlia, what—"

"Make no mistake, I hope that man gets a paper cut every day for the rest of his life," she said. "But I don't regret marrying him because I don't regret the person I am *now*." She sighed, popped an edamame bean into her mouth. "Leaving him was the hardest thing I've ever done. No one supported me. But because of that experience, I can live freely now. I might never have come to terms with my sexuality. Definitely wouldn't have covered myself with all these doodles." She snickered, holding out her decorated forearms. "And my approach to dating is so different now, so much clearer. I don't get lost in the what-ifs anymore. I'm not planning a future with every person I meet. I just focus on what I want in the moment. I let myself *live*."

It was moments like this one when I remembered that, despite appearances, Dahlia was almost six years older than me, with the experience that came with it. I squeezed my eyes shut, then pulled out my phone. I could feel Mal's arms around me again, feel the warmth of him against my back, the rumble of his voice against the hollow of my neck. How, that day, sitting on the grass in Millenium Park, I'd asked myself what it would feel like to be nestled in the comfort of his hold every day. Imagining what it would be like to free-fall.

"What are you doing?" Dahlia said.

I ignored her, gathering my nerve, and called Mal. The phone rang once, twice, thrice, and I tapped my foot, violently overcome by a need to act, to undo the damage I'd already wrought.

Just when I thought it would go to voicemail, he picked up.

"Hey, Jo," Mal started, his voice obstructed by a din. "Sorry, I'm a bit—" Another voice, high, feminine, interrupted him, and Mal cleared his throat. "Yeah, I know, honey, one second . . ." He sighed, then said to me, "I'll call you back later."

Then he hung up.

Stunned, I looked down at my phone until I saw the time. *Shit.* It was almost five. Mal's event at Em-Dash Books for *She Blooms at Dusk* was starting any minute now. My annoyance at myself for losing track of the time was the only thing that overshadowed the raging curiosity at hearing him address another woman as *honey.*

"That was a very one-sided conversation," Dahlia observed, watching as I stood up and gathered my purse.

"Do you need any more footage?" I asked Dahlia.

"Other than what you already showed me?" Dahlia said. "Nah. I think I'll be set."

"Great," I said, waving Daniel over to our table to announce our departure. "Because I need a ride."

CHAPTER TWENTY-THREE

Mal

Mal's first event as a published author had been subpar. He'd hosted it, at his mother's behest, at a local Barnes & Noble, who set him up with a small table in the corner of the fiction section and provided twelve books, of which he sold nine, most to family members. Despite rehearsing with Amelia, he'd fumbled when a customer, who was shopping in the section and stopped to listen out of curiosity, asked him what his book was about. A girl in the front row kept picking her nose and wiping it on the cushion seat, which distracted him so thoroughly that he misspelled a reader's name during his brief signing. Afterward, his dad had clapped him on the shoulder, told him he was proud of him, and emphasized that he needed to "learn to make better eye contact."

And then, magically, things fell in line. Paloma Padovani, pop star turned cultural curator, read *Dusk* and named it one of her favorite novels of all time. A famous book blogger described it as "a Studio Ghibli movie with spice," and before he knew it, *Dusk* was going viral. Every other day Kelechi sent him videos, many of them with hundreds of thousands of views, of readers celebrating the world he had created. After that, it was off to the races—features in the *Washington Post* and *New York Times*, the starred reviews he'd received from *Kirkus* and *Publishers Weekly* suddenly prominently displayed on billboards and internet ads that his marketing team initially told him they didn't have the budget to fund. Even the video he posted on his newly made Instagram explaining his novel's synopsis had gone viral the next day—mostly, to his chagrin, due to readers being shocked by his appearance. (As if I needed another reason to be obsessed, @lisapayne340 commented, to which @realhotgirlsheet responded, FR??? Why he look that? Come home babe, our children miss you.)

It should not have surprised him that his first in-person event since his disastrous launch would be more successful. But it was the extent of the success that shook him. The crowd was mixed gender ("Unusual," Hani, the blue-haired bookseller who was running the event, observed.), an apparent side effect of Mal being the rare Black man successfully writing love stories since the late Eric Jerome Dickey. And it was packed, people filling every corner of the bookstore's floor, visitors wedged between bookshelves and spilling out into the street just to see him.

He searched the sea of faces for the one he wanted to see the most, and tried to ignore the lump that formed in his throat when he couldn't find it. The moment he'd gotten home after the picnic, he'd regretted how he'd handled his conversation with Jo. He'd been too wounded, felt too cast aside, to really articulate his feelings properly, and prayed that she'd heard a plea rather than a threat. What he should have said: *I'm jealous. I'm worried. I feel like I don't have the history with you that Ezra does, and that you going back to him is inevitable. I want to hear you tell me that it's not. And when you're finally ready to choose, I want you to choose me.*

But then five o'clock came, and most of the gathered guests were seated, and Jo was nowhere to be found.

"She'll come," Kelechi had assured him. She was in her wheelchair today, settled in a place of honor in the front row.

"You ready to start?" Hani asked, tapping the microphone to test it. "There's a big crowd here, so we'll be efficient with signing—"

Mal's phone screen lit up. The woman of the hour.

"One second, let me pick this up really quick," he said, smiling queasily at the crowd of expectant faces.

"Hey—" Jo started, and just hearing her voice when her face wasn't here to accompany it made his heart sink. Next to him, Hani was getting impatient.

"I'm sorry, Malcolm, but I think in the interest of time we need to start *now*."

"Yeah, I know, Hani," Mal said, just a little irritated. Then, to Jo: "I'll call you back later."

He felt bad for hanging up and putting his phone on Do Not Disturb, but he would make good on his promise afterward. He'd call her, and maybe they would discuss expectations, define themselves a little more beyond the exclusivity they'd agreed on during their first date.

But for now, he had to give a performance.

The event itself went well. For the next hour, Mal put on his bravest face and answered the questions Hani and the Em-Dash staff had put together to the best of his ability. He fumbled a few sentences, talked too fast sometimes, caught himself going off on a tangent about how he'd fashioned the disorganized mess of Iris's apothecary off the bedroom in *Howl's Moving Castle*, and somehow the awkwardness that had left his first audience bored enraptured his current one. Kelechi tossed him a thumbs-up. He remembered what Amelia had told him when *Dusk* first came out: "Don't worry too much right now, Malcolm. You'll find your readers eventually."

When it came time for audience questions, ten people filed into an orderly queue in front of his table. Mal felt like a king of a court, taking time aside to listen to the concerns of his vassals, all starstruck, some of them carrying tote bags and handmade pins with references to *Dusk*. He thanked each of them.

"This is a dream come true for me, really," he said, overtaken by emotion. "If you told me last year that this would be my life now, I would have said you were joshing me. So thank you all."

Amongst the ensuing *awwww*s, Mal didn't hear the door to the bookstore swing open. A woman approached the mic, dressed in a shimmering violet dress not unlike the one *Dusk*'s main character, Iris, wore on the day her love interest, Louis, found her fishing in the stream by her house.

"Hi, I'm Juliet, and I'm going to ask the question that we're all thinking," she said, giving him a wicked smile that, in retrospect, should have served as a warning. "Are you single?"

Heat rose immediately to Mal's face, and he felt the entire room focus in on him like sharks. Suddenly he noticed the number of phones in the audience, raised high to get the best angle, to capture his answer for posterity.

"I'm not . . . available," he said hesitantly.

"But you are *single*," the woman said, undeterred, and he was about to attempt to redirect the conversation when suddenly, a woman in white cut in front of him and snatched the microphone out of his hands.

"No, he most certainly is not," Josephine Boateng said, her voice echoing mightily through the small bookstore. "He's mine."

Fuck. Mal should not have found Jo's righteous indignation or the way she'd cut in the middle of the line and commandeered his microphone sexy. But there was something thrilling about the way Jo had just claimed him, so assuredly, with cameras rolling, that felt like exactly what he'd needed from her all along. And then there was how she looked, dressed in a white baby doll dress that skimmed around the flesh of her thighs, hair plaited into a long braid that swung like a whip down her back. She held a bouquet of flowers the color of sunset and, giving him a crooked smile, handed them to him.

Mal took them, shell-shocked. In *She Blooms at Dusk*, Louis, the male lead, lamented that by nature of being both a florist and a man in their quaint, superstitious mountain town, he was fated to forever give flowers but never receive them. But on their first meeting, Iris had given him a cluster of blossoms as vibrant as the setting sun.

The audience burst into a roar of giggles, applause, and wolf whistles. Juliet lifted her hands, accepting defeat.

"Sorry, sis, just shooting my shot," she said good-naturedly, then made her way back to her seat.

The event was somewhat in disarray after that. Not because of Jo, who, having said her piece, leaned against a bookshelf at the back of the room. Nor really because of the attendants, who turned the topic of conversation appropriately back to his novel. But because Mal was a mess. Blood had vacated his brain entirely. When a reader asked about why he'd decided to include real-world commentary about isolation and persecution in the narrative, he gave some half-baked response about how it had just felt right, while imagining propping Jo's legs on his shoulders. And when someone asked whether the villagers were right about

Iris having intentionally poisoned the town magistrate who had been disturbing her business, he shrugged, too busy thinking of biting down on the lip Jo had just sucked into her mouth. Hani, realizing that she had lost her author for good, cut the Q&A short and started the line for the signing. In the front row, Kelechi was barely keeping the glee off her face.

"Okay, so that was true live entertainment," Kelechi said, joining the signing line just to give him a hug. "You did so good. Proud of you, Mally-wag."

"Thanks," Mal said. He'd known his face would hurt from smiling politely all evening, but it was outright aching because he couldn't keep his smile from stretching across his whole face.

"And you're also down sooooo bad," Kelechi said. She looked behind her conspiratorially. "No wonder. She's that nineties it-girl Nia Long fine. And that flowers move . . . *Sheesh.*" She rubbed her belly. "Even baby Noelle is getting shivers. I should go meet her."

Mal laughed, then sucked in his cheeks to give his aching face a break.

"You should," he said. "She's nicer than she looks."

It took nearly two hours for Mal to finish signing books, during which he spent much too much time peeking out around the swell of the crowd to catch sight of Jo. As it thinned, he found her, her chair angled to face Kelechi's, both of them snickering so hard that their heads nearly knocked together. A warm sense of pride bubbled in his chest. Kelechi and Portia had never really gotten along—Kelechi thought Portia too frigid, Portia thought Kelechi too flighty—but Jo slotted in next to his friend like she'd known her forever. When Mal reached the end of the line, they sidled up to him together.

"How dare you not let me know that you were dating my long-lost African sister," Kelechi said, standing to give Mal a kiss on the cheek. Then, she leaned in close to Jo, whispering something in her ear that made her smile turn somber. Jo nodded, and Kelechi squeezed her shoulder, then turned back to Mal. "All right. I'm heading out. Your parents are blowing up my phone, by the way. I sent them pictures."

Then she was gone, leaving Mal, Jo, and a beleaguered Hani carrying away chairs. Mal bent to help, and she waved him away.

"You're our esteemed guest," Hani said, balancing two chairs under each arm. She looked over to Jo, grinning knowingly. "Enjoy your night."

Hani disappeared into the back room, leaving Mal and Jo alone in the dimly lit bookstore. The silence between them felt potent, full to the point of bursting.

Jo broke it first, rocking back on her platforms.

"Sorry I was late," she said. "You were phenomenal. Didn't feel like someone who isn't 'good with people' at all."

"Yeah?" Mal said, grinning.

Jo pursed her lips. "Yeah," she said. "I think you made every person here feel special."

"Not too special, I hope." He stepped closer; reflexively, she stepped back, steadying herself with a hand against a shelf behind her. "Thank you for the flowers. Nice nod to *Dusk*."

In response, Jo reached around him for the bouquet on his signing table, snapped off an orange daisy, and tucked it behind his ear.

"I'm a fan, remember?" she said. Her fingers lingered on the side of his face, brushing ever so softly against his cheek.

"How could I forget?" Mal said.

Jo blinked away, and Mal studied her, fascinated by her shyness. Just hours before, this same woman had snatched a microphone out of his hands to lay claim to him, and not too long before that, she'd saved a man's life with the efficiency of a soldier. Maybe when they first met, he would have thought that sort of boldness was just in her nature. But Jo wasn't driven by impulse. She moved with intention.

He realized then that Ezra Adelman didn't matter. He could try all he wanted. When it came down to who could love her harder, Mal would not be beat.

"So I'm yours, huh," he said, tilting her chin up to him.

"If that's okay with you," she said softly.

"It is," Mal said, "but only if you promise to be mine too."

Jo bit back a shy smile, finally meeting his eyes. "If I'm not too late," she said. "If you still want me."

Mal dropped his forehead against Jo's, stifling a snort. He'd wanted her since the moment he'd perceived her. Since the second she'd taken his hand to shake.

"Always," he said, and when he kissed her, it felt like breaking through a finish line, like diving into the deep end and coming up for the first gulp of air.

CHAPTER TWENTY-FOUR

Jo

I awoke the next day, for the second time, in Malcolm Waters's bed, except this time I felt like I'd been put through the Olympic Trials. Which, in my defense, was not far from the truth. Apparently, sweet Malcolm Waters had been holding back, and now that I'd given him the all clear to take whatever he wanted from me, he'd revealed himself for the beast I'd always suspected him to be. I'd been pressed, folded, twisted, and tossed around like pretzel dough all night. In the best way. I wasn't even sure I had any endorphins left to release.

"You up?" he said, pressing soft, playful kisses to my shoulder.

"Mmm," I managed, and Mal took that as a yes, diving under the covers and down my stomach. When he reached his destination, he nipped at my inner thigh, and I threw off the sheets to watch. I liked seeing the full expanse of him: the broad back that tapered to a slim waist, his round, firm shoulders, the crown of his lowered head. It made his teasing all the more potent, to see the self-satisfied glint that appeared in his eyes right before he touched me. And when he finally did, his warm breath becoming a wet, probing tongue—*my god*.

"You're so happy," I said when I came down from my high a few minutes later to find Mal grinning stupidly up at me from between my legs.

"Of course I'm happy," he said. "You're here with me."

I rolled my eyes, trying to pretend that he hadn't already won me over. Not that Mal wasn't aware. He flopped onto his side, his grin no less soppy, and pulled me into his chest.

"Okay, I've got an item on the agenda," he informed me. "I'm tired of telling people that I'm 'seeing someone.' Was hoping to just call you my girlfriend. Is that cool with you?"

My stomach lurched.

"That's fine," I said in a small voice. Mal tipped my face to his, raising an eyebrow at my lack of enthusiasm, and I huffed. "Just . . . I might not be so good at the girlfriend thing right off the bat. So you'll have to be patient with me."

"What do you mean?" Mal asked, his tone neutral: not accusatory or angry, but curious.

I buried my face into his chest, embarrassed. My followers might have interpreted my videos on "consent" and "maintaining healthy boundaries" as relationship advice, but I had no experience whatsoever in relationships. Mostly I'd gotten tired of seeing young women who'd been pressured to forgo condoms by men who promised they were "clean" show up in my clinic with gonorrhea. (Mal, bless him, had offered me his negative test results during our first night together, a gesture I found oddly romantic.)

And besides that, being somewhat responsible for Mal's emotional well-being when my own was so tenuous was terrifying. I could probably be a halfway decent girlfriend when I was well. But when I wasn't? When darkness infiltrated my thoughts, and it took all of my energy just to remember to eat, drink, and shower?

Mal had already experienced my depression-triggered disappearing acts twice, and both episodes had hurt him. Could our relationship withstand more? The version of Jo that Mal loved was confident, honest, comfortable in her skin. Someone who made him want to be stronger. Someone he wanted to impress. But what if he met the other version: the one who barely believed she had a right to exist?

"I'm used to doing my own thing, I guess? Not really checking in with anyone?" I said, a half-truth. "Like, when I changed my number. A good girlfriend would have called you right away, right? I didn't really think about that. I just fell right into a slump. And . . . I don't know. There's a lot of etiquette I don't get. Do we have to see each other every day? Text all the time?"

How long can I disappear for before you'll be done with me? Twenty-four hours? Thirty-six?

"It's not prescriptive. We just do what comes naturally, like we have been," Mal said, kissing my hair. "What's important is that we're considerate of each other. That we communicate. Keep each other in the loop."

I hummed, apprehensive, but didn't object. Mal had made me greedy and therefore selfish. I knew he had fallen for a facade, but I couldn't bear to push him away for long enough for him to notice. It felt too good to be in his arms.

"I'll try," I said, closing my eyes. But then I remembered something, and the corner of my mouth twitched. "Here's something I should probably tell you, then. I'll be seeing Ezra at the health benefit this weekend."

To his credit, Mal didn't wince. Instead, he pulled me farther into him, and I would not have noticed the tension in his arms if I hadn't felt them bulge around me.

"I figured he'd be there. His mom's running the event," he said. I closed my eyes in the safe space his body had created around me.

"I agreed to talk to him there," I confessed.

"Hmm," Mal said noncommittally. "About what?"

"Boundaries," I said. I had a decent idea what was going to happen when I saw Ezra again. I would tell him that there was no need to force things. That, in telling him that I had once had feelings for him, I hadn't intended to declare that we could only be in each other's lives in a romantic capacity. I'd needed space to "find myself," so to speak, and now that I'd accomplished that, there was no reason not to return to how things were. (Mostly. Sharing beds was pretty out of the question now that I was somebody's girlfriend.)

When I told Mal this, he snorted.

"Wow," he said. "You really are clueless."

"What do you mean by that?" I said, pushing away just a little to make sure he could see my scowl.

Mal kissed the space between my eyebrows, smoothing out the furrow.

"Nothing," he said. "Just that I trust you."

We languished for a little while longer. I would have been content to spend the rest of the day in bed with Mal, being intermittently ravished, but I had a hair appointment in the afternoon, and if I was even two minutes late, Fatou would let someone else into her braiding chair. Mal offered to drop me off at home, and when we pulled up in front of my building's sea-glass green entrance, I mourned our imminent farewell. I sighed my way through my braiding appointment, not even getting annoyed when Fatou took a forty-five-minute break to pick up Chinese food.

Liking someone is scary, I told Dahlia as Fatou flicked through the channels on a television that likely hadn't been replaced since the '90s. Because why am I smiling at myself like a dodo bird while this lady yanks out my hair follicles?

It's that tru luv, Dahlia responded. You better make me a flower girl at the wedding.

With all the plucking, pruning, and preening I did over the next twenty-four hours, I certainly felt like a bride. It had taken me until medical school to realize that beauty by and large came out of a box, one that I built for myself back when I had nothing to my name but a paltry stipend and a vintage iPhone. My overnight transformation from a generous six to a humble eight had been like something from the movies: all it had taken was a little eyebrow threading, some falsies, the right sew-in weave, and judiciously applied makeup to turn me into someone worth looking at.

"You're going to let Adelman see you like that?" Dahlia said, admiring me from her doorframe as I struggled to put on my heels.

"Ezra's seen me in about a million dresses," I said. Though, to be fair, this dress was different: red as sin, backless, figure-skimming. The kind of dress that would have made my old female attendings pull me aside for a lecture on professionalism. I'd bought it weeks ago, when I was still trying to hype myself up as a Hot Girl Who Was Totally Capable of Seducing a Certain Withholding Writer. "Shit. My ride's here."

"Wait wait wait," Dahlia said, whipping out her phone. "Are you an influencer or not? Let's get some evidence that you look good for the Gram."

Laughing, I spun for her, falling quickly into three or four practiced poses.

"I really have to go," I said when she started to push for a fifth.

"Fine," Dahlia said. "Have fun! And don't let Ezra mow you over!"

"I won't."

I blew her a kiss, and then flew out the door.

Operation Don't Let Ezra Mow You Over started out as a success. Ezra had texted me earlier to suggest we share a ride: I was on his way, after all, and Harold, Renata's driver, had been asking about me anyway. But I'd turned him down. The concept of spending twenty minutes trapped in an enclosed space with an Ezra who was clearly on the hunt was too obvious of a trap. He knew where all of my buttons were, and I knew that he would spend the entire journey pushing them.

I arrived at the venue with my heart in my throat. The Knydus Nest annual health benefit regularly raised upward of $5 million for an underfunded disease of interest (this year, sickle cell anemia). Without an association with the Adelmans, I could never have afforded a ticket. When I reached the grand doors of the entrance, a man in all black opened them to let me in, another escorted me up the stairs to the event.

Renata wasn't a big fan of red carpets outside of film premieres, so the Knydus Nest carpet was a rich velveteen blue that ended outside the open heavy doors that led to the ballroom. I stepped into line behind a dashing older couple, my fingers sneaking to my neck to check my thundering pulse. *It'll be fine*, I told myself, as I waited for my turn in front of the expansive Knydus Nest logo. *It's just a conversation. You and Ezra have had a thousand of them. And a lot of them have been harder than this.*

The older couple walked into the ballroom, and suddenly, it was my turn under the spotlight. I stepped into place, waving hello at Felipe, one of Renata's go-to photographers.

"Beautiful dress, Josephine," he responded, snapping away. "Let's get a few more—"

Suddenly, a hand fell on the small of my back. I recoiled, ready to smack my assailant with my clutch, but when I looked up it was to a familiar set of smiling eyes.

"Hey," Ezra said casually.

"When did you get here?" I said. Clean-shaven, hair artfully tousled, and dressed elegantly in a navy-blue suit that turned his eyes cerulean, Ezra looked his part as the prince of the party. He grinned wolfishly, then gently nudged me into position like he hadn't just crashed my solo shoot. My smile faltered, but Felipe didn't seem to notice. The flashes intensified; photographers who'd been less interested in faceless donors and niche influencer types like myself were suddenly engaged by the arrival of a real celebrity.

"What are you doing?" I hissed through my smile.

"What do you mean?" Ezra teased. "I'm getting my picture taken."

We'd taken photos like this together a thousand times on a hundred random carpets: for benefits and retirement parties, premieres and award shows. But this time, something was different. Maybe it was the placement of Ezra's hands, just a touch too low on my waist, just a touch too firm to feel like an accident, or the angling of his body into me, the heat of his front radiating into my bare back.

"Is Josephine your date tonight, Ezra?" Felipe asked, stepping closer to get his perfect shot.

Ezra laughed, his touch on my back becoming a squeeze. Then, before I could comprehend what was happening, he pulled me against him fully, wrapping his arms around me from behind.

"I don't know," he said, his voice a rasp at the corner of my jaw. "You ask her."

Heat rushed to my face, and I tore myself out of his hold, fighting back my fury as I stormed off the carpet. Felipe had definitely gotten that shot, and it was just juicy enough that I knew he wouldn't be able to resist sharing it. God, what if Mal saw it before I could explain? I unsnapped my purse, pulling out my phone to furiously text him: If you see a photo anywhere of Ezra hugged up on me, no, I did not want him to do that.

I didn't have to look behind me to know that Ezra had followed.

"Who are you texting?" he asked.

I glared up at him. "My boyfriend," I informed him, tapping "send." Mal responded instantly with: Next time he does something you don't want, punch him. I'll bail you out. "I've got to do damage control for that stunt you pulled back there."

"Your boyfriend," Ezra repeated. He tilted his head to the side, like he would perceive me better from an angle. "Is it the writer guy? Mom just bought rights to his book?"

"Yup," I said, walking across the decadently decorated room toward the seating chart, Ezra trailing me like a shadow. As promised, Renata had put us back at the same table, but she'd also added Boris on as a buffer. Brilliant woman.

"Do you like him?" Ezra asked.

"Obviously," I said, then softer, "very much."

Ezra nodded sagely. Then: "Is he better-looking than me?"

I scowled. "Stop that," I said.

"Stop what," he said.

"*Flirting* with me," I said. "You want to talk? Talk to me straight. Without all the fluff."

Ezra's smile dropped like I'd scraped it off.

"Sorry," he said, waving away a waitress when she approached us with a tray of hors d'ouevres. "I just— You didn't mind . . . before."

The room was beginning to fill, guests in floor-length gowns and tuxedos crowding around the seating chart. The noise they created (clacks of heels against marble tile, boisterous greetings from people who had last seen one another at the previous year's event, all layered on top of an orchestral rendition of Mariah Carey's "We Belong Together") was giving me a headache.

"I always minded," I confessed.

"I didn't know," Ezra said softly.

I swallowed against a tight throat, knowing that he was telling the truth. Our friendship had been full of boundary blurring, and as much as I blamed Ezra for walking the line, I'd walked it alongside him. Whenever he reached for my hand, I'd held it. I'd let him fall asleep on my shoulder, agreed to be his interim plus-one in his short, rare periods of singlehood, fell asleep in his bed. When he told me he loved me, most times I said it back. And truthfully, I'd liked our closeness. Encouraged it. It was only recently that it had become unbearable.

"Let's sit," Ezra said.

We were early, our table unoccupied. It was close to the raised stage, across from an ornate podium, kitty-corner from the string quintet. Ever the gentleman, Ezra pulled out a chair for me, then turned his to face mine and dropped gracelessly into it.

"Do you remember when we first met?" he said, bracing himself on his knees.

"You mean, when you broke into my dorm room?" I said with a snort.

Ezra smiled wistfully.

"First of all, I didn't 'break in.' I was given a key," he said. "And no, actually. It was in American Lit. The third day of class. I asked to borrow a pen. Do you remember?"

"No, honestly," I said. Those first few days on Elion's campus were a blur. I'd been too preoccupied with getting a job outside of work-study to pay attention to any of my classmates.

"I know you don't," Ezra said. "And that was the beauty of it. It wasn't that you didn't know who I was, it was that you didn't care. You didn't try to make useless conversation or attempt to ingratiate yourself to me. You even made me give it back at the end of class."

"I used those really nice gel pens in American Lit," I said with a small smile. I remembered them; they'd cost seven dollars for the pack, my sole splurge during college move-in shopping. I told Ezra, and he laughed.

"You remember the pens but not me, huh," he said. "But honestly . . . that tracks. You were refreshing. It felt like the first time I was being judged for who I was, and you decided that who I was was kind of a little shit." Ezra grinned, like my less-than-charitable initial opinion of him had been a blessing. "Remember when we had that huge fight in the SSC? Because I called you my friend and you basically told me I was delusional?"

"You *were* delusional," I said. "But you weren't a little shit. You were pretty great."

Even then, I'd known that it had been fear that had caused me to keep Ezra at arm's length when we first met, not dislike. People like Ezra got do-overs; first, second, third chances; sympathetic letters from parents proclaiming his *potential*; people like me weren't supposed to be at institutions like Elion in the first place.

I'd seen his self-destructive behaviors and thought of myself getting crushed in their aftermath. But I'd also seen his spirit. Ezra was kind to me, surprisingly sensitive. It had frustrated me, how he never seemed to hear the noise that followed him like a swarm of hornets, how insistent he was that we lived in a world where things like class and race and gender didn't matter. He'd invited me into his family, into his home, into his heart.

"I *was* a little shit," Ezra said quietly. "I still am, sometimes. But I'm a little shit who misses you." He leaned in closer, his expression earnest. "Jo. You're my best friend, and you saved my life. I'm not willing to accept you not being in it. So I want you to tell me all the ways that I've hurt you so that I can make sure I never do any of them again. And if that means I start by cooling off on the flirting, I can do that."

I sniffed to hold back the tears that were forming in the backs of my eyes. There wasn't anything to say, because truthfully, Ezra hadn't done anything *wrong*. It had all been about my own perception of us. I had wanted him to look at me and me alone, to be the most important person in his life no matter who else was in it.

But now that I had Mal, I understood. Because what I felt for Mal was different from anything I'd ever felt for Ezra. It was comforting and safe in similar ways, yes, but it was also passionate, searing. I wanted to touch Mal in ways and places I'd never wanted to touch Ezra, wanted to be held by him, but I also wanted to fight with him over the type of granite we wanted for our countertops, wanted to sit proudly in the front row of his book events, wanted to bring him steaming cups of tea in the dead of the night when he was typing feverishly toward a deadline. When I thought of Ezra, I thought of our past. With Mal, I saw our future.

Maybe that was how Ezra had felt about Ashley, about every one of his eight ex-girlfriends. Maybe I'd minimized his relationships with them because I'd assumed they could never compare to the one he had with me. Maybe Ezra had just wanted to experience multiple kinds of love, just as I did now. Maybe I had been wrong to condemn him for that.

"I'm sorry," I said. "I . . . This wasn't your fault. This was about *me* and figuring out my own shit. You didn't do anything—"

A hand clapped me on the shoulder, cutting me off midsentence. I turned to find Boris Finnegan grinning down at me like he'd just been handed his third Emmy. I sucked back my tears, rearranging my face into what I hoped was an inviting smile.

"Dr. Boateng, as I live and breathe! You look beautiful as always," he said, then to Ezra: "Hello, Ezra."

"Make it less obvious which one of us is your favorite, why don't you, Boris," Ezra said good-naturedly, and we both stood to greet him, understanding that our time alone was over for now. As the table's occupants arrived, Ezra and I split, making all the requisite small talk—or, in the unfortunate case of Boris's recently drained buttock abscess, very *big* talk—until the lights in the room dimmed. Then, when everyone shuffled back into their chairs, Ezra stepped in close, pulling me in by my elbow.

"Check your phone," he said. And then, with a genial smile, he took his seat.

RENATA KOVALENKO KNEW how to put on a show. She graced the stage in a baby-blue Jenny Packham gown, her hair fashioned into a low chignon that showcased the giant sapphire on her chest like a talisman. The speeches were short and to the point, the singular boring academic who stepped forward to accept the gala's donations ushered offstage after only three minutes to make way for the live band.

I paid attention to none of it. I was trying my hardest not to crack up at Ezra Adelman's less-than-charitable live commentary. The thin, raven-haired woman who accepted the Knydus Nest award for the biggest donation in a pink feathered dress looked kind of like a flamingo. The sixteen-year-old son of a hedge fund manager who was seated at our table thinks he's being subtle about staring at Boris's girlfriend's tits. Even his own mother was not spared: Somebody's soul is trapped inside that rock around her neck, I swear.

Jo: You're being an ass. Stop it.

Ezra: What was that? I have a cute ass?

Ezra: Oh. Sorry. Am I flirting again?

Jo: Yes. But I'll let it slide. Just this once. Because you're learning.

Ezra: I don't know if I can get away with once. You know this is just how I communicate.

Jo: Yes, yes, you only speak Fuckboianese.

Ezra: Excuse you. What I speak is clearly Wastemanian. It's a different dialect. Don't be insensitive, Jo.

"You're a disaster," I responded out loud, when the night's program concluded and the dance floor opened up. The live band started the night off with a poppy rendition of Earth, Wind & Fire's "September," and half of our table, their nerves lubricated by an hour of sipping at wineglasses that were magically refilled by the overattentive staff, made for the dance floor.

"Still remember the words?" Ezra asked, getting to his feet.

I laughed. "Some of them," I said. "The chorus, probably."

"Good enough," Ezra said, then held out his elbow for me to

take. I hooked my arm through his, and together, we made our way to the dance floor.

Back in college, I'd told Ezra that I didn't know much popular music, a consequence of a childhood spent listening only to my local library's outdated cassette tapes, my mother's gospel music, and my bus driver's chosen radio station. In response, Ezra gave me homework. For an entire semester, I was to stop by his house after work to study party jams. I memorized lyrics to songs by artists ranging from Queen to Lil' Kim, learned that I was meant to belt Backstreet Boys' "I Want It That Way" with feeling but shout Journey's "Don't Stop Believin'" tonelessly and at the top of my lungs. Perfection was not required, but general intelligibility was, and so Ezra ended all of his lessons with a practicum by blasting the songs through his state-of-the-art speaker system and stopping the music right before the chorus hit. Neither of us could sing, and neither of us could really dance either, but at the end of the night we would invariably try, serenading each other with mostly correct renditions of the songs we'd studied while flailing and spinning all over his kitchen.

Ezra had changed so much since then, but none of his trainers had succeeded in teaching him rhythm. ("I was never meant to be a triple threat," he once joked.) When his poorly executed two-step became an even worse body roll, I had to cover my mouth to hold back a guffaw.

"If all your fans realized this is what you looked like dancing, they would get the ick immediately," I said.

"No, they wouldn't," Ezra said, transitioning to a much more temperate fist pump. "They'd probably find it endearing, same as you."

I did find it endearing. I found the way he tilted his head back to belt out the chorus, and how he threw an arm around Boris's shoulders as they jumped to "Shout," even more so. We danced our way through "Hey Ya," then twirled to "Total Eclipse of the Heart," kicked our feet to Pharrell's "Happy," and I realized how much I'd missed this. Missed him. I couldn't remember the last time I'd cut loose and had fun, but I could almost guarantee it had been a night like this, with Ezra. He'd always been good for me like that, capable of cracking me open and drawing me out. I'd grown up too early, Ezra too late, and we pulled each other toward a comfortable middle.

I wished Mal was here too. He didn't like crowds the way Ezra did, but he'd probably enjoy the food, the clothes, the spectacle. I could imagine him staring up at the ornate tiled ceiling, making note of details I didn't notice, like the trim on the tablecloths or the interesting husk in the flamingo woman's voice. Maybe I'd be able to draw him out too, drag him to the dance floor. When the band transitioned to a slow song, like they did now, with a loud "All my couples, get out on the floor," he would probably pull me close, sway with me, tell me how beautiful I looked and what he planned to do about it when we got home.

But he wasn't here, and so when the lead singer stepped close to the mic, crooning out the first lines of Nat King Cole's "Unforgettable," I made for our table.

"I'm getting water," I told Ezra. I'd left my clutch hanging off the back of my chair, and I popped it open, fishing out my phone to check in on my boyfriend.

In the hour or so I'd spent cutting up on the dance floor, my phone had blown up. I had some messages from the usual suspects: Mal informing me that Dahlia had posted a picture of me in her story and requesting to talk afterward ("You look incredible," he said. "Have fun, try not to catch a case, and call me tomorrow, please?"), Dahlia telling me something very similar but with ten more fire emojis, and one text from Renata, sent after she left the stage, insisting that she had intended to find me tonight but had been pulled into an urgent call by Rudy.

More peculiar, however, were the five missed calls from Denise.

"What's up?" Ezra asked. I hadn't realized that he'd followed me. He drained a glass of water in one gulp, shaking a lock of damp hair off his forehead.

"My agent is desperately trying to reach me," I said evenly, though I felt like I'd just stepped through a trapdoor. "Which is weird, because it's almost 11:00 p.m. on a Saturday."

"That is weird," Ezra echoed. He knew better than anyone that a late-night call from your representation hardly constituted good news; the last time he'd gotten one, it was to inform him that one of his exes was threatening to leak his nudes.

"I'll be back," I said, throwing my clutch under my arm and hightailing it for the exit. The music reverberated through my body, pounding in my head alongside my heart. Had Denise finally gotten tired of me? Had her Saturday evening nightcap given her the courage to drop me, her most elusive client? I was stupid to have not gotten a clinical job. The influencer life was inconsistent even for those who were fully committed, and I clearly was not, and I had always known that when it came to money, I couldn't afford to take risks. My savings would tide me over for two months, maybe three, if I budgeted appropriately, and I could always find a different agent, reach for my own contacts—

I was so lost in my thoughts that I didn't hear Ezra's footsteps behind me.

"You're spiraling, Jo," he said, turning me by my shoulders to face him. He pulled me into an alcove under the grand stairwell, tucking me out of sight. "We don't know what's happening yet, and whatever it is, we'll manage it. Easy. Breathe."

I followed his direction, taking a deep breath in, blowing it out.

"Okay, okay," I managed, shivering. It didn't matter how many times Ezra watched me lose my cool; I always felt naked afterward, like a bird with its feathers plucked out. "I . . . should call her back. You should get back in there. Have fun."

"And leave you out here to have the world's most glamorous panic attack?" Ezra teased. "No way. I'm staying right here."

I blew out a huff of air. "Fine," I said.

And then I called Denise back.

"I'm so sorry, Jo," Denise said. "I was just looking over my inbox, and I missed it. I'll be more diligent in the future. Again, I'm so sorry—"

"It's okay, Denise," I said numbly. I stared down at the email she'd forwarded me, five days after she'd received it. I heard her apologies echoing as though from a distance, like she was shouting at me from a faraway shore instead of through my speakerphone. I didn't even notice when she hung up, too hypnotized by the email I was reading on my screen.

Dear Ms. Denise Gardner,

I apologize for multiple emails. I received your contact from Dr. Josephine Boateng's website. It is imperative that we reach her for urgent matters regarding her mother, Ms. Prudence Boateng, who is currently admitted to

the Cardiac Intensive Care Unit at Featherstone General
Hospital. Please have her call me back at my personal cell
phone, listed below, or provide an alternate form of contact.
Please be advised that I am on night shifts and will be
available from 7pm to 9am daily.

    Best,
    Sahar Hosseini, MD

I read the email, reread it, tried to internalize what I'd read, failed to compute.

"Fuck," Ezra said, vocalizing my thoughts.

"There you two are!" a musical voice rang out. "And together again! I take it this means that you've made up. Thank god, I was starting to get worried—"

"Mom," Ezra said sharply, but he was too late; at the sound of Renata's voice, the tears I'd been trying to hold back dripped down my face. I watched the shimmering hem of her dress enter my field of vision as I tried to wipe them away with the heel of my hand.

"What's going on?" Renata asked accusatorily. Even without lifting my head, I could imagine that she was glaring at her son. He sighed.

"Don't look at me like that. This is bigger than me, for once," he said. "Her mom's in the hospital."

A hand lifted my chin, and I found myself suddenly at eye level with a frowning Renata. She didn't say a word, just surveyed my face for what felt like one long minute, then snatched Ezra's pocket square out and, taking care to avoid my carefully applied eye shadow, dabbed away my tears.

"Which one?" Renata asked me, all business.

"Featherstone," I managed, as the pieces of information began to connect in my mind. I knew Featherstone. I'd rotated there as a medical student. It was a nice hospital in the southwest suburbs, and far from the shabby one-bedroom apartment in Joliet where I'd grown up.

"What do you want to do?" Renata asked.

"I don't know," I said. I'd spent so much time in therapy trying to elucidate what exactly I wanted from my mother and accepting that I might never get it. It had been thirteen years since I'd last seen her, and in that time she had only attempted to make contact twice. When she called me two weeks ago, had it been to tell me that she was unwell? *I need help*, she'd said, and I'd assumed that she needed rent money or bail or something else you ask only of family and never pay back and had been furious. *You were never my safety net*, I wanted to respond. *Why should I be yours?*

But if she was dying? Would I feel differently then?

Renata dropped my chin, and suddenly I was reminded of the day that I moved out of her Gold Coast penthouse. She'd helped me with my apartment search, curling her lips at every walk-up within my budget and trying, unsuccessfully, to convince me to let her help fund something more suitable. When I informed her that I'd signed a lease and would be out of her hair within the month, she'd feigned indifference. Congratulated me ("That's lovely, Josephine, just make sure they don't have a pest problem, mice are just awful to get rid of.") and went back to discussing the week's meal plans with her chef. But as Ezra and I were packing my last box into her driver's car, she followed us to the first floor with tears in her eyes.

"I hope you don't feel like we pushed you out," she'd said. "You can stay for as long as you need to, you know." And when I convinced her that moving was my choice, she'd insisted, "If you ever need to come back, for whatever reason, just say the word. This room will always be yours."

True to her word, Renata had left my bedroom untouched. The only thing I'd ever found in it that was out of place was Mal.

My mother didn't seem to notice when I moved out. I did so gradually, splitting rent in a three-bedroom house with two of my coworkers at the sandwich shop where I worked, and when a month passed and she still hadn't bothered to call to ask after me, I filed for emancipation. Up until the day I stood face-to-face with the judge, I expected her to show up. Protest, even just a little bit. She didn't. She never had.

And yet.

"Don't live your life with regrets," Renata said now. "If you don't go, you might ask yourself what if for the rest of your life." She reached into her clutch for her phone, sent off a message. "Harold will drive you."

I blinked away tears. Renata was right. If I didn't go and see for myself what had become of my mother, it would haunt me forever.

"Thank you," I said. "Really."

"Anytime," Renata said. She gave me a cool smile and a kiss on the cheek. "Now go."

CHAPTER TWENTY-FIVE
Mal

[VIDEO DESCRIPTION] *A man sits behind a table at a bookstore with mic in hand. Off-screen, a voice asks him whether he is single. He looks uncomfortable but flattered and is about to answer when a woman in a short white dress sweeps in front of him and takes the mic from his hands. She gives him a bouquet of flowers.*

[CAPTION] Sorry, folks. Our favorite irl book boyfriend is off the market. @malcolmjwaters, thank you for writing my favorite read of the year. RIP to your DMs.

[Comments]
21stcenturygworl7: ugh stop he can still be my boyfriend in my head

theheartbreakprince: omg look at his face when he takes the flowers!!! Does anyone know who the girl is?

Reemareads: It's @drjojobee! I really like her account actually, she seems really cool

Lanaharman: well I thought she was very inappropriate. There were better ways to handle that question than interrupt the event like she did.

Reemareads: @lanaharman lol he isn't going to choose you sis

The coffee shop where Mal had settled was the perfect place to get work done. It was featured in exactly zero "Best Places to Work in Chicago" lists, meaning he could actually find a table with an outlet, and had a menu that stretched beyond overpriced espresso, including sandwiches he could eat for lunch and pastries he could nibble on when he craved something sweet. He arrived early, right at opening, and put his phone on Do Not Disturb, lest he get distracted by the group chat.

Despite ideal conditions, however, Mal had written approximately three sentences of his proposal in as many hours. Instead, he'd spent his time refreshing his feed, and specifically, rewatching videos from his Em-Dash event. He'd been tagged in five so far, all capturing the same scene from slightly different angles, each one revealing different details: the shift of his own expression from awe to adoration when Jo swept in front of him, the fierce, fiery look in her eyes when she faced off the crowd, how it softened when she turned to give him his flowers. It was one thing to remember the moment, but quite another to see it happen from an outsider's perspective. No wonder Kelechi had teased him so mercilessly. *Don't go making Harvey a cousin tonight,* she'd texted him after she'd made it home from the event.

That promise had been harder to keep. Two and a half years of abstinence and several years before that of good but perfunctory sex had cooled his libido some, but having Jo in his bed had brought it back full force. A flicker of a memory of the night before came into his mind, Jo writhing above him, her bra strap hanging off one shoulder and exposing the dark circle of her areola, her eyes glinting under his dimmed ceiling lights. His name falling from those luscious lips, the flash of tongue as she bit down to hold back moans he wanted so desperately to hear. *Fuck.* Mal crossed his legs under the table, willing the blood back to his brain.

As if on cue, his phone vibrated on his desk. Amelia.

Wincing, Mal picked up.

"I'm working on it right now," he started. "I'll get it to you by the end of today—"

"No need to lie to me. I'm not calling about your proposal," Amelia said.

Then she told him what she *was* calling about, and Mal almost slid out of his chair.

"One more time?" Mal asked, catching himself on the table edge.

"The *Lana Porter Show*? You've heard of it, right?"

Had he *heard* of it? Lana Porter's honeyed smile had been gracing televisions for as long as Mal could remember, her talk show a staple on daytime television. Mal had grown up watching Lana Porter interview everyone from basketball players to former presidents on her eponymous television show and imagined himself sitting in her famed green armchair, talking to her like an old friend.

According to Amelia, his wildest dream was soon to become a reality.

"They had a last-minute cancellation for today's author spotlight, and they want to see if you can sub in," she said. "It's virtual. Today. At four o'clock."

"So in two hours," Mal said numbly.

"Yes. But it's short. Just eight minutes," Amelia said. "You can do it, right?"

Mal laughed so loudly that the girl sitting across from him threw him side-eye.

"Yeah," he said, then more firmly, "Yes, of course."

Ever efficient, Amelia sent him a Zoom invite for a last-minute media training session, an email with tips for how to create his video call setup, and a blurb about Lana Porter's show, as if he hadn't spent his mornings at his grandma's house watching her over bowls of cereal. He drove a little too fast back home, thinking of how to set up his station. He still had a decent lighting rig from his photography days, though at four o'clock maybe natural light would be sufficient. There was a well-stocked bookshelf in his living room; if he shifted his desk in front of it, he could have a suitable backdrop. And then there was Ampersand, who had taken to yowling furiously every time he tried to deny her access to him, and well, who didn't enjoy a kitty cameo?

Then, before Mal could fully comprehend what was happening, he was logging on to a video environment through a link Amelia had sent him, then talking to a producer in the virtual backstage room who checked his microphone, gave him suggestions for his lighting, and quickly ran through potential questions.

He was still reeling from the novelty when Lana Porter appeared on his screen. She looked exactly as he remembered her, her golden skin tight over her temples, signature honey-blond curls bouncing against her shoulders. She smiled at him with great white teeth.

"Lovely to meet you, Malcolm," she said. She blinked at someone off-screen. "Are you ready?"

Not really, he wanted to say, but it wouldn't have mattered anyway. He was in too deep now. Lana didn't wait for his answer, just held up a finger, and then, suddenly, they were live.

"I think you'll all be excited to meet our next guest," Lana said. "Malcolm Waters's debut novel, *She Blooms at Dusk*, has been described as a 'revival of the epic romance,' and was recently optioned for film by En Garde Productions. Malcolm, it's so great to meet you."

"The pleasure's all mine," he said. The lighting he'd rigged in front of his laptop softened and blurred his skin, and he hoped it hid the pinpricks of sweat that he could feel forming on his forehead.

"You've said in past interviews that you like to think of *Dusk* as a love story," Lana said. "What motivated you to write about love?"

Mal inhaled. Questions like this, about his craft, he could handle. He forced himself to relax. To make himself charming. He gave a half-true answer about growing up feeling as though, as a man, he wasn't supposed to aspire to or be concerned about love, and how writing *Dusk* allowed him to explore those emotions. Lana made a comment about the quiet, cozy thread of magic interlaced throughout the novel, and Mal explained that he wanted its setting to feel like a fairy tale: "Like I could start off with *a very long time ago in a land far, far away* and it would feel right."

Eight minutes passed by at the speed of light. Lana ended the segment with a gracious smile, a thank-you, and a "quick question": "So, Malcolm, are you writing about love from experience? The ladies want to know."

"Ha," Mal said, caught off guard.

Before he could respond, a third window opened, and there it was again, the video from Em-Dash. Jo facing off Lana's live audience with a steely *He's mine*, then handing him a bouquet. His awed, enamored expression, which served as answer enough. Mal laughed, because there was nothing else he could do in the face of his shock.

"This clip from a book signing you did recently is making waves online, and I think we can all see why!" As if on cue, her audience erupted in whistles. "It seems you're living out your own romance!"

Mal's smile stretched tensely across his face. "Yeah," he said. "Um. She's incredible. So."

Lana placed a hand on her heart, and a litany of *aaaww*s followed.

"You heard it here, folks. *She Blooms at Dusk* is out now, wherever books are sold. Pour yourself a cup of hot tea, find a blanket, and enjoy."

And then, just like that, it was over.

"You did great," Amelia assured him, beaming, after the segment was done. "Very charming. I think you'll win over Lana's audience for sure."

"Yeah?" he said. He felt unsettled. Lana was known for skirting the edges of her guests' comfort zones, and today she'd done just that. He needed to tell Jo, except she was currently at the benefit having a very critical conversation with Ezra Adelman and he didn't want to add to her plate. Besides, she would probably be thrilled to be featured on Lana Porter's show, if only briefly. Likely be delighted that he'd been invited on in the first place. He would never have said yes to something like this before her influence. When Jo wanted something, she seized it, and now he was doing the same. After all, once-in-a-lifetime opportunities were exactly that: they came once.

The burst of productivity Mal fostered after this revelation could've been bottled and sold. His empty page became ten filled ones. He worked so diligently and for so long that he forgot to eat dinner, forgot to use the bathroom, forgot to turn on a light after the sun set and shrouded his room in darkness. His few breaks were short—reading a text from Jo (about Ezra, who predictably was not behaving himself), a five-minute call with Kieran and Kelechi debriefing his interview. He would probably have kept working until dawn if Jo hadn't called.

"Hey," Mal said, picking up on the first ring. It had felt wrong to text her that he'd just been on the *Lana Porter Show*, but now that he had her on the line, he couldn't wait to spill the beans. "You headed home?"

"No, actually," Jo said. Her voice sounded restricted, nasal, like she'd been crying, and Mal's smile dropped. "Um, I'm headed to the hospital."

"What?" Mal said, immediately making to stand. "What happened? Are you okay? Which hospital are you headed to—"

"Sorry, sorry, I didn't think about how that would sound. I'm fine," Jo said. "Um. It's my mother. I just found out she's admitted at Featherstone and . . . I'm going to see her. Just wanted you to know, in case I'm . . . a little weird after."

"Oh," Mal said, stunned. "Oh shit."

"Yeah," Jo said numbly.

"Do you want me to come?" Mal said. He searched for Featherstone on Google Maps. "I can drive over."

"No," Jo said. "It's okay, I—"

A voice interrupted her, familiar, raspy.

"I think that's the entrance," Ezra said in the background.

"Okay," Jo said. Then, to Mal: "I'm fine for tonight. But maybe come see me tomorrow? And bring ice cream? I think I'll need it."

"Will do," Mal said. "Do you want strawberry cheesecake again? Or something new?"

"You remembered," Jo said, sounding, despite everything, just a bit pleased.

"I try." There was a heartbeat of silence between them, potent, like they both were deciding what to say next. But what was there to say to this, aside from *Sorry I'm not there*?

"I have to go," Jo said, breaking it. "I'll see you tomorrow?"

When she hung up, Mal slouched in his chair and wondered how it was possible for him to be more relieved that Jo was not alone than he was jealous that he was not the one beside her.

CHAPTER TWENTY-SIX

Jo

You didn't have to come with me, really," I told Ezra, when we arrived at the lobby of Featherstone General. I looked out of place enough in my floor-length gown, but with a six-foot-two, TV-handsome Prince Eric look-alike trailing behind me, I had no chance at blending in. When we approached the hospital registration desk, the woman behind it took one look at Ezra and gaped.

"I know this is strange, but has anyone ever told you that you look like an actor?" she asked him as we checked in.

"No," Ezra said, reaching for a mask from across her desk. When we made it up the elevators to the fourth floor, where my mother was apparently admitted, he looked down at me. "I'm not going anywhere, so stop saying that."

"Okay," I said.

I didn't have the energy nor the desire to fight. In truth, I was glad Ezra was here. His presence made the experience less surreal. With Ezra walking down the long hospital halls by my side, I couldn't pretend that this was all a dream. My mother really was on this hospital floor, only yards and minutes away. I really was going from an opulent ballroom to her sickbed within an hour. Dr. Hosseini had filled me in on her condition during the drive up to Featherstone, and I'd found myself slipping back into the skin that I'd worn as a resident, the one that allowed me to take a step back and see my patients as cases and not people. When Dr. Hosseini told me that my mother had initially come in with a "myocardial infarction" and was "in cardiogenic shock," I'd questioned her like she was my intern, asking her things like whether she'd required mechanical support and what inotropes they'd put her on. When she told me about the blood clot that had formed in her heart and shot into her brain, about the neurology procedure to extract it that had not succeeded in bringing back her voice, I asked questions about whether they could safely start blood thinners.

"I know this must be hard for you," Dr. Hosseini had said, attempting to interject some humanity into my interrogation. I could hear the pity in her voice, and, even knowing it was appropriate, I resented it. *Don't try to guess what I'm feeling*, I wanted to snap, but instead I apologized for my truancy and told her that I would see her soon.

It had been five years since I'd last come to Featherstone, but muscle memory guided me to the locked double doors of the cardiac intensive care unit. I hit the intercom, gave my name, then stepped back as the doors opened for us. It being after midnight, the hospital lights were dimmed. The memories of my old ICU night shifts hit me like a wave: the churning in my stomach as I awaited pages, the way my ears were attuned to the cranks and beeps and honks of the various ventilators and dialysis machines and BiPAP units distributed throughout the floor. A nurse shivered at her station, wrapped in a blanket I imagined she snuck from the warmer, while another carted an armful of supplies into a patient's room. She gave Ezra and me a curious look.

"Who're you here for?" she asked.

"Boateng," I said. "Room 4016?"

"Ah! Karen's her nurse, but she's on break right now. I'll take you," she said, taking off in a direction. She looked back at us, her eyes narrowing, and I saw, in real time, as a gear clicked into place in her head.

"I'm Whitney, by the way. And um . . . I'm so sorry to ask this. But by any chance, are you Dr. Jojobee?"

I winced. I'd been so preoccupied by my thoughts that I'd forgotten that young women in health care were my target demographic.

"Yes," I said flatly, hoping my tone would invite no further speculation.

"Oh, cool. Um . . . I follow you. I really like all the things you have to say about working in health care. Also that you're, like, so girlie while doing it." Whitney's cheeks reddened, and she ducked her head, embarrassed. "Anyway, I'm really sorry you're here right now. But I just had to let you know that I think what you're doing is really important." We arrived in front of 4016, and she bit back a smile. "I'll page the team, let them know you're here."

"Thank you, Whitney," I managed, unexpectedly moved.

"It's no problem," Whitney said, then scampered away.

"That was cute," Ezra said when she was out of sight.

I nodded, staring at the silver door handle before me. Every hospital I'd been to had the same wood laminate doors, the same steel handle that I'd nudge open with my hips and elbows when my hands were too full of supplies or notes or ultrasound machine. To think that my mother was behind this door, that all I had to do was push, and she would be there.

The knot in my throat pulled tight. I could feel the ghosts of old anxieties creeping into my head, long-resolved insecurities. I'd been rejected by Prudence so many times as a child that I'd grown numb to her indifference, but now, as an adult, I felt raw, nervous. What if she didn't actually want to see me again? What if Dr. Hosseini had only called me because I was her next of kin, her living adult child and therefore her legal surrogate decision maker, and because chasing me down was simpler than assigning a legal guardian? What if I opened the door and Prudence pushed me out?

Ezra reached for my hand to squeeze.

"You don't have to go in if you don't want to," he said. "It's not too late to walk away."

I shook my head. No. I'd come this far. I had to see this through.

"I'll do it," I said softly. "I just need a minute."

But I was denied even that, because in the next second, the door opened from the inside, and a man slid out.

I could tell he was Ghanaian from one glance. Stout and square-jawed, with a bald head that folded on itself in the back, he looked like a stereotypical Ghanaian uncle, though I was quite sure we had never met. By the way he was staring at me, like he'd known me my whole life, I wondered if I was wrong. I'd met so few of my relatives, and Prudence hadn't exactly had many friends—

"You must be Josephine," the man said, and I watched, stunned, as he lowered his wire-framed glasses to wipe away tears. "Excuse me. But you look just like her."

FOR ALL OF her faults, Prudence Boateng had never brought a man into our home.

"Do not open your legs for any man," she'd told me. "Give

them something one time, and the next time, they will think they can take. And who knows what they will leave you with after."

It was one of the only times she'd ever troubled herself to advise me. The other first gen kids complained that their parents were always trying to dictate their lives, but Prudence had always seemed to regard me more like a small, unwelcome guest that she was forced to harbor. We rarely spoke outside of her directives: clean the bathroom, do the laundry, wash the plates.

But that day was special. Hours earlier, I'd lowered my pants in the bathroom during third period science to find them soaked in dark, sticky discharge. I had known my period was coming soon; I was thirteen, after all, and a cover-to-cover read of my library's copy of *Girl's Body Book* had provided me with the baseline knowledge of the wonders of puberty. When I informed Prudence that evening, it was not to celebrate my development so much as it was to warn her that she would now need to consider me when stocking up on her menstrual products.

But instead of grumbling about having to spend more money on me, Prudence imparted her wisdom: Do not listen to men. Do not trust them. They will say anything to get between your legs, and you can get pregnant now. Don't let one ruin your life (the thinly veiled implication: like you ruined mine).

And yet, so many years later, here I was, speaking to a man who called himself my mother's partner.

His name was Kweku. He was a CPA. He and Prudence had met at church eight years ago, and they shared a small three-bedroom home in Bolingbrook.

I took in the new information numbly.

"The doctors said they had a hard time reaching you," Kweku said. He had a gentle manner of speaking, soothing, like a voice

actor for the sleep meditation podcasts I often listened to at night.
He gave Ezra and me a look over. "I suppose they must have only
just succeeded."

"Yes," I said, suddenly incapable of speaking more than one
word at a time.

"Thank you for coming," Kweku said. Then: "What do you
know?"

"Heart attack, then stroke," I said plainly. "Was really sick at
first, getting better now."

Kweku nodded solemnly. I wondered what his story was. How
he fell for my mother. What he knew about me, her prodigal
daughter.

He told me none of this. Instead, he said something even more
mystifying.

"Thank you," he said. "She didn't think you would come, but
she prayed that you might. Every day, she prayed. Until she . . ."
He cleared his throat, choking on his new reality.

"Until she couldn't," I finished, and Kweku gave me a bleary
look.

"She was proud of you," he said.

I winced. "Well, she had a strange way of showing it," I said.

Kweku didn't respond to that. Instead, abruptly, he turned to
Ezra.

"I was going to the vending machine. Come. Let me get you a
drink," he said, clapping him on the shoulder. When Ezra didn't
budge, he added, gently, "Give them a little time alone."

Ezra's eyes flickered to me in a question that I couldn't answer.
Then he sagged, nodded, and they walked away, leaving me alone
at the door.

Now or never. I pushed down on the handle with the heel of my hand, sure that beyond the door I would find a vortex, a black hole, a glitch in space.

THE FIRST THING I noticed about my mother's hospital room was that it was nice. She'd scored a corner bed, which bought her not only solitude but also tall windows that probably let in a lot of light in the daytime. The couch against the back wall was covered in plush, colorful blankets: Kweku's station, I assumed. The IV pumps next to her bed whirred, and I scanned over them. She was still on a few drips, but judging by the low doses, they were close to weaning her off them. I looked up at her monitor, took note of her heart rate (ninety-three, normal sinus rhythm), blood pressure (low, but serviceable), the waveform of her pulse oximeter (shockingly good).

Don't just look at the data, I could hear my old senior resident saying in my head. *Look at the patient.*

I looked down at the bed to find my reflection staring back. When I was young, I'd dreamed of someday looking like my mother, of inheriting her long, curling eyelashes and round, high cheeks. Even ill, she looked well cared for, her skin greased and smelling of cocoa butter, her lips smooth and uncracked. I could see myself in the reflection of her large, wet eyes: her mirror image.

She lifted a hand, reaching for me.

I felt the gesture like a bludgeon to my chest, memories pummeling at the levy of my hardened heart. How many times had I reached out to her just like this? How often had I begged for her affection, or at least her recognition, only to be met with disdain, to be told that I wasn't wanted? That by existing, I'd ruined her? I tore my gaze away to face her monitors, heading back to safe shores of data. Data didn't lie. The data said that she was on the mend. That she'd had a brush with death, but that it hadn't caught her, and wouldn't, at least not today. By hanging up on her and changing my number, I hadn't left her to die.

A soft coo interrupted my thoughts, and it took me a moment to realize that it had come from my mother. The hand she'd extended still hovered, shaking, in the air, and when I looked at her face, she stared back with resolve.

"It's ironic, isn't it?" I said to her, my nails digging into the side of her bed. "All this time, I've wanted to actually speak to you. Every time you called, I thought, maybe this is it. We'll finally have a real conversation, and I can gain some understanding. And now you can't even give me that."

Broca's aphasia, I knew, affected the left frontal cortex. Patients with it have no problem understanding language but struggle to produce it. I could see the effect my words had on her, but when Prudence opened her mouth to respond, the words were lost to her. She searched for them, grunting and groaning, her tongue twisting uselessly in her mouth, before, finally, she gave up. A tear leaked out from the corner of her eye, and she kicked the foot of her bed, frustrated.

I watched her.

"You may never get an apology from your mother," my therapist, Rochelle, had said during one of our first sessions. "And that's okay. You can't control who she is, or what she does. But you can control yourself. So I want you to use your imagination. I want you to not think of her as your mother, but as your contemporary. Who was she? What ailed her? What and how did she survive? Find closure within yourself."

Prudence Boateng was a single mother in a foreign land, with no papers, keeping a household afloat by scrubbing other people's toilets, caring for other people's children. The man who'd left me with her was nowhere to be found, his existence a blight, the child he created only a reminder of the damage he'd wrought. And now she was in a hospital bed, her heart weakened, her brain damaged, her voice stolen. She should have been easy for me to empathize with. I'd lectured many an intern on showing grace to patients just like her.

And yet.

"I'm loved, you know," I told her. "I found a family. One of them is out there right now, waiting on me. And a partner too. A man who tells me he loves me and shows it too." Her monitor began to beep, and my gaze reflexively jumped to it: her heart rate, easing into the low one hundreds. Fast, but a normal rhythm. *Physiologic.* "Do you get it? I didn't need you in the end. I did just fine on my own."

Prudence's eyes turned glassy. I could tell I'd hurt her, and I was glad for it.

"G-guh," she tried. Then she cleared her throat, the corners of her mouth turning up into a small smile. "*Good.*"

The levy broke.

My hand moved on its own to clasp hers, tears streaming down her face, even more coming down mine. She said it again and again and again, her small body wracked with sobs, her grip on me so tight that she kinked her IV tubing and her pump began to beep. "Good," she said, and then later, with much effort: "Sorry." Once, when I released her hand to find tissues, she reached out for me in alarm and added, "Please."

I sat with her, sobbing, for hours. Karen came in, quietly checked her vitals and found me a chair. Dr. Hosseini dropped by to give me an update, and we talked softly at my mother's bedside about her impending transfer out of the intensive care unit and the input from the neurology team. Outside, the sky lightened from pitch black to a soft, periwinkle blue, and I held her hand all the while, marveling at how, despite our similarities, it was so much smaller than mine.

Eventually, Prudence drifted off to sleep. I let her go, knowing that she would be woken soon for a full day of tests.

I found Ezra and Kweku in the waiting room, napping on the sofas. They looked a strange pair—Ezra's long legs stretched across the tile floor, Kweku's short ones crossed on his lap. I touched Ezra, very lightly, on the arm, and he jolted awake.

"Hey," I said. Next to him, Kweku stirred and stretched. "Sorry I was gone so long."

Ezra yawned, then smiled at me through his mask.

"It's no problem," he said. "You ready to go? I can tell Harold to circle back for us."

"Please," I said.

I exchanged emails with Kweku and offered my help with choosing Prudence's eventual rehabilitation center. Before we left, he hugged me and then Ezra, and the sincerity in his hold would have brought me to tears if I had any left.

When Ezra and I finally made it outside the hospital lobby to wait for Harold, the sun was cresting the horizon. I was no stranger to all-nighters, but Ezra hadn't done a medical residency, and I could feel him lagging behind me.

"I ruined your night," I said when he caught up.

Ezra rolled his eyes. "You didn't ruin anything. I took a nap in the waiting room. I'm good," he said. He paused, and I could sense he wanted to say something else. "You know. The last time I was in an intensive care unit, I think I was the one in the bed."

I gasped, stepping around him to get a better look at his face.

I hadn't considered that Ezra might have found today's trip traumatic, a reminder of his own brush with death.

"I'm so sorry, Ez," I confessed. "Was this too much? Are you okay?"

Ezra rubbed his temples, shaking his head.

"You're something else," he said. "How are you asking me if *I'm* okay right now? After everything you've gone through today?"

"Well, are you?" I said, and he laughed.

"Of course I am," he said. "What about you? Are you seriously going to figure out rehab stuff for your mom with Kweku? I feel like you did your part already by showing up. Why do more?"

I rolled my bottom lip into my mouth. It had long lost its layer of lipstick, but I'd replaced it with Mal's lip balm in my bag, and his vanilla mint taste was vaguely comforting. I couldn't wait for my bed, for Mal to join me in it. Maybe we would talk about today, or maybe we wouldn't. By the time mark on his most recent text (Let me know when you want me over. Thinking of you.) sent at 1:32 this morning, he had had a late night too. We could probably both use the nap.

"Right now? Because it feels right," I said, folding my arms around myself. "So I'll keep helping out until it doesn't."

It was really that simple, at the end of the day. When I put aside my old hurts, when I looked at Prudence as who she might be now instead of who she'd been when I was a child, I realized that I wanted to know her. See if she'd been transformed by love, the way I had.

Ezra looked down at me through his straight, dark lashes, his expression made more unreadable by the mask covering the lower half of his face.

"You're ridiculous," he said, but before I could lodge a com-

plaint, he draped his arms over my shoulders. "And compassionate. And kind. The strongest person I know. And, as messed up as
it might be for me to say this right now, I'm glad I got to be here
for you today."

He sounded so earnest that I had to blink away, disarmed by
this serious, sincere Ezra.

"Yeah? Well, you're heavy," I said, but I didn't push him away.
"And I'm glad you're with me too. I missed you."

Ezra huffed, then pulled me fully against him. I hugged him
back, feeling many things at once: relief, exhaustion, hope. Ezra
and I had been through so much together, and now we had this
under our belt too. As always, we would be okay.

Neither of us spoke for a moment, listening to the whirr of
stalling engines as they pulled in front of the hospital, the mating
calls of early morning songbirds.

Ezra was the one to break our silence.

"Don't push me away again, Jo," he said. "I won't be respectful
about it next time. I'll show up outside your apartment with a
boombox. Playing baby-come-back songs at top volume and pissing off all your neighbors."

"Acht acht," I teased. "You're flirting again. Don't play with
me unless you mean it, Ez."

I expected him to laugh. We'd just made another inside joke
for ourselves, after all, taken a habit of his that had once hurt me
and neutralized it.

But he didn't. Instead, Ezra pulled back, lowered his mask. His
hold on my shoulders tightened, and I examined his face, taking
apart the minutiae of his expressions. The jump in his left cheek
meant nerves. His lowered chin meant determination.

"And what if I do?" he said.

CHAPTER TWENTY-SEVEN
Jo

When Ezra returned to college the semester after his month-long stint in rehab, all of Elion University blew up with speculation. Some people thought he'd flunked out, citing his tendency to party hard. Others thought this impossible—He's actually really smart, someone commented in my dorm's group chat, in response to another person's declaration that His daddy would never allow this place to kick him out.

Ezra could've cared less. With his new lease on life, he narrowed his focus to three things: his studies, his dreams, and me. We did everything together: went to the concerts on campus, stood for long hours to snag tickets for our favorite up-and-coming comedians. Ezra liked to try out new restaurants, and so dragged me to different spots around the city after class. I couldn't afford anything outside of my cafeteria meal plan, and so, as a rule, he always paid. But without fail, every time we asked for the check, our waiter would come back with two.

Eventually, Ezra got fed up.

"She's beautiful, isn't she?" he said, glaring up at the pretty brunette who had just handed us separate receipts.

Our waitress chuckled nervously, blinking down at me in a way that communicated that beautiful was a stretch. Ezra didn't smile back.

"Yes?" she said, like it was a trick question.

"Is that why you don't think we're together? Because you don't think I'm good enough for her?" Ezra said, reaching across the table to grab my hand to drive home his point. When the waitress gaped back at him, he turned away from her, running his thumb lovingly across my knuckles. "I'm paying. One check."

Ezra had held my hand many times before. But this time felt different, the swatch of skin he brushed turning hypersensitive, burning like he'd set it aflame. His stare was piercing, unrelenting, and for the first time I wondered if I was missing something. *Boys don't look at girls they don't have feelings for like that, right?* I thought. *They don't plead with their eyes; they don't tremble when they touch you.* But then the next week Ezra hooked up with the hot goth girl in his Improvisation and Performance class, and I was reminded, once more, of my place.

"Stop it," I said now to an Ezra several years older, several years wiser, an Ezra who, after our conversation yesterday, definitely should have known better. "I told you how I felt about you, Ez, so why are you still messing with me?"

"Because I'm not messing with you," he said. "Because I've been so scared of losing you that I was in denial about how I feel about you. Because you keep using past tense, and I wish you'd use present."

My mind was whirring. I wanted to clap my hands over Ezra's mouth, stop him from saying what I feared was coming next. What I had wanted to hear him say for most of my adult life. I could feel his hands settle on the sides of my face, guiding me to look at him, but I resisted, too frustrated and sad and confused to meet his eyes. Ashley had tried to tell me, drunk, at the bar, and I'd refused to take her seriously. *His most precious person.*

"Jo, please. Look at me," Ezra said, and, unbidden, my gaze finally dragged to his. "I love you. I've probably always loved you. Maybe since the day you gave me that pen. Or when you threw that pillow at my head. I don't know exactly. But I do know that the moment you came into my life, it became beautiful again. I didn't want to screw things up. I couldn't stand the thought of losing you. So I looked elsewhere. Convinced myself I could feel the same way about someone else. It never worked out, of course, because they were never you." He laughed, a soft huff of sound. "I knew you were bound to find someone else someday. I mean. Look at you. And I want to be happy for you. But after today? Having you back again? Remembering that life is too fucking short for regrets? I'm sorry. I can't let you go. So tell me you forgive me, and that I still have a shot. That you can love me too, again."

"You won't have to let me go," I said, and he lowered his forehead against mine, his hold becoming desperate. "I'll always be your friend, Ez."

Ezra's nose brushed against mine, his breath wafting against my lips. If I gave him even the slightest inclination that I might want him to kiss me, I knew that he would. I could tell how badly he wanted to.

"I don't want to be your friend," he whispered.

And I didn't want Ezra to kiss me, which was strange, considering how badly I'd wanted it once. I shook my head, fighting back against the new crop of tears that threatened to spill down my cheeks.

"I can't. You know I can't."

"Why not?" Ezra said. His voice was ragged now, and the sound of it, choked, stung. "Because of the writer? I can wait. He'll mess up eventually, or you'll get tired of him, but the two of us, we're different. We'll—"

"I don't want him to mess up, and I don't want to get tired of him," I said, squeezing my eyes shut. Why did he have to tell me this now? Why did he have to wait until I was falling for someone else? "Ezra, I'm so sorry. You're too late."

Ezra exhaled in a slow rattle. Then, abruptly, he pushed me into his chest with a hand against the back of my head, wrapping his arms around me like he would like nothing more than to wedge us together. In the darkness of his embrace, I could feel his heart thundering, pounding with a pain that I'd felt a hundred times but was more potent now that he was feeling it too.

"Don't say that," he whispered. "Don't—"

A camera shutter went off.

"Oh shit," an unfamiliar voice said. "Oh hey, you're Ezra Adelman, right? From *One True Kiss*?"

Ezra cursed under his breath, then, without looking at me, released me. I'd forgotten that we were outside, in a public place, that nurses and doctors and techs and patients were walking around us to get inside. That Ezra was no longer just the good-looking son of Renata Kovalenko and Paul Adelman, but famous in his own right.

"Give me your phone," he snarled, stalking the reedy young man who was stuffing his phone into his pocket and rapidly plotting his escape. "What the hell's wrong with you, taking pictures of people without their consent—"

"Ez," I said, alarmed, but other phones were coming out now, onlookers who, recognizing that something monumental might be happening in front of them even if they didn't understand what, were now snapping and recording. If they caught Ezra accosting this kid, they could spin it however they wanted. I could see the headlines now: One True Kiss *Actor Ezra Adelman Assaults Honors Student Over Photographs.* "Ez, no! Let's go!"

As if on cue, Harold pulled up in a black Lincoln Town Car. Before he could make a scene, I grabbed Ezra by the elbow and dragged him backward, practically shoving him inside the car before throwing myself in next to him. It wasn't until I'd yanked the door shut and Harold had sped out onto the highway that the enormity of what had just happened fell fully onto my shoulders.

Ezra loved me, and I no longer loved him. My mission to get over him had been a riotous success.

So why did I feel like absolute shit?

Harold dropped me off at home first. I would have considered this a blessing, except it meant that I was the one who had to say goodbye.

"I'll talk to you later," I tried.

Ezra didn't respond. He'd spent the entire car ride hunched toward the window, sleeping or more likely stewing, and I stepped out of the car, my stomach twisting with unease. The air felt dense, like the sky before a storm.

It didn't take long for the clouds to burst.

I jolted awake from a four-hour deep sleep to my phone pulsing on my nightstand. My first thought: *Mal's here.* My second: *Ezra got some sleep in and wants to hash things out.*

I couldn't have been more wrong. What I had instead were forty-three new emails.

This was odd. My Dr. Jojo email wasn't public; and most inquiries had to go through an intense Denise filter before landing in my inbox. I tapped the first one, with the subject line: Dear Dr. Jojo, from a parsons@protonmail.com, then reared back.

You dumb black bitch. To think that such a good man loved you and you spat in his face. How dare you, you ungrateful whore.

The words hit me like a kick to the chest. I sat up, scrolling through emails and finding litanies of How dare you, you evil cunt and racial slurs, rape threats, death threats, and combinations of the three.

Two thoughts occurred to me suddenly: (1) *The kid who'd recorded us at the hospital might not have been just a fan, but bona fide paparazzi*; and (2) *Holy shit, I've been doxxed.*

Hands shaking, I checked my Instagram. My follower count had exploded—five hundred and forty-five thousand from four hundred and twenty thousand—my notifications a mess. My Instagram was drowned in messages not unlike the ones in my email box. The photo Dahlia and I had taken before Mal's book event the launching pad: See, it's definitely her.

"What the hell is going on?" I said out loud. I called out Dahlia's name to no response, and then sent her a text: When will you be home? Shit is going down and I need you.

Dahlia texted back immediately. Oh my god, oh no. Are you okay? Sorry I didn't tell you. Picked up an overnight shift in the burbs, are you good?

I was not good; in fact, I was quite certain that I was one more death threat away from a panic attack. But there was no time to communicate that because my phone was ringing again.

It was Denise. Just the person I needed to talk to. I picked up immediately.

"Hello, Dr. Miracle," she said, sounding pleased as punch. "Just what have you gotten yourself into?"

"I don't know," I said around a closing throat. She's not even that cute, a commenter said. "I was hoping you could tell me."

"Check your texts," Denise said.

I did. Denise had sent me a post from Goss, the premier website for all things celebrity drama. The videos were blurry, presented side by side: Me, not even six hours before, wrapped in Ezra's embrace—from an outside perspective, we looked a lot more intimate than I remembered, my hands clutching his suit jacket from behind, his tucked under my jaw, our faces so close that we could have been kissing. After that, Mal's signing just days before, me snatching his microphone and declaring him mine. Finally, a video of Mal, with a woman who looked alarmingly like *the* Lana Porter, smiling shyly and admitting that he was in love.

The title, She Takes Two: Rising Star of ONE TRUE KISS and Knydus Heir Left Heartbroken by Two-Timing Self-Proclaimed Sex Doc, only further outlined how deeply fucked I was.

"For what it's worth, I think this is great," Denise said. "It was time we broke you out to a wider audience. Don't get me wrong, I think the health care community is great, but if we're thinking big, scandals are sometimes nice. Yesterday, most everyone in Hollywood had no idea who Josephine Boateng was. By the end of this next twenty-four hours, a lot of them will."

"Me being labeled a harlot who is cheating on their Golden Boy is a good thing?" I said in disbelief. Another email.

You weren't good enough for him anyway, you ugly slut.

"Not to downplay how you must be feeling right now," Denise said, meaning she intended to do just that, "but all press is good press."

"Only if you're a Kardashian," I said. My head was spinning. If this had dropped even a day ago, I would have called Ezra. Demanded he clear up the misunderstanding. Make him do what he'd always done: call me his closest friend in the whole world, his sister, go on and on about the importance of platonic love. But what could I tell him now, now that I knew he felt differently? Now that he was hurting?

"Honestly, I think this is a great opportunity," Denise said. "You've been hinting in your more recent posts that you're open to dating. And now that you are, you're only going for the crème de la crème. And even then, you still have standards. You aren't a woman who is easily impressed by money and good looks, and definitely not by a man who's openly friend-zoned you for the last decade. You want to sample the field, and you're starting off with this handsome author guy. It's consistent with the brand, and—"

I felt sick. How long had I been doing this, strategizing ways to turn my most personal thoughts and experiences into content, mining bastardized versions of my trauma for likes and brand deals? Ezra had told me he loved me, and now Denise was telling me I should throw that in his face to rescue myself, and, for a split second, I'd imagined the post. It would be a carousel of photos, the first of me artfully splayed on my couch with my phone tucked between my shoulder and ear, laughing at no one in particular, looking joyful and unbothered in a gifted Ankara lounge set. The next few photos would be screenshots of the hate mail I'd received, blurring only the vowels in the slurs. My caption would allude to the gossip without referencing it directly, instead choosing to focus on the difficulties of being a visibly Black woman in a public arena, of having my personal life out there for others to pick apart as if I hadn't spent years offering it up on a platter.

It would be perfect. It would invite what Denise would probably call the "best kind of trouble."

It exhausted me, just thinking of it.

"No," I said.

"Oh, that's okay," Denise said with a soft chuckle. "I know I'm getting ahead of myself. We don't have to bring up your dating history at all, if you'd prefer not to. We can also use this as a way to bring in Ezra's fanbase, describe yourself unequivocally as his friend. You were at the hospital, right? Did you go see your mother? If you don't mind discussing that, it would be a beautiful way to celebrate your friendship. It helps rehab his whole playboy image too, a win-win—"

My hands trembled on my lap, my vision blurring and coalescing. I could feel my heart thundering in my temples, a steady, rapid throbbing. I slapped a hand over my chest, counting the beats—*One two three four five six seven eight nine ten eleven, over six seconds. Eleven times ten is one ten, regular, probably sinus tach, physiologic.*—until the thundering in my ears quieted and my racing heart slowed.

This was too much. All of this. Seeing Ezra, going back to a hospital, seeing my mother, breaking Ezra's heart. And now, this. The deluge of comments, reminding me that after all I'd done to justify myself, my existence was still a blight.

"You're not listening to me," I said.

Denise sucked in a soft breath. I could almost hear the wheels screeching to a halt in her mind.

"Okay. I'm listening," she said after a moment, in the calm, doting voice she might use for a class of kindergartners. "You don't want to go through with this. You need a break. I get that."

"I don't think you do," I said. I inhaled. "I'm quitting, Denise. I quit. I'm not doing this anymore."

"Okay, now, let's not get dramatic," Denise said hurriedly. "I know this is bad right now. Just give it a few days to blow over. You'll be fine—"

If Denise had more to say, I didn't hear it. My thumb moved to hang up before I could think of the consequences, and I tucked myself under my covers. My eyelids felt heavy, swollen, and I closed them, a small, familiar part of me wishing I would never have to open them again.

CHAPTER TWENTY-EIGHT
Mal

Strawberry cheesecake ice cream obtained, he texted Jo. When do you want me to head over?

Jo didn't respond. After the first three hours, he thought, *Well, she was probably out late last night.* After the next forty-eight, he thought, *She saw Adelman in real life, fell back in love, and now wants nothing to do with me.* It wasn't until he received a text from Amelia requesting a video call that he understood that something more troublesome was at play.

"I've gotten twelve requests to interview you today, and none of them are about your book," Amelia said once they were done with formalities. "Can you fill me in on what's going on with you and a certain Josephine Boateng?"

Dread curdled in his stomach.

"You know Jo?" he said.

A dimple appeared in Amelia's chin. "You'd be hard-pressed to find someone who doesn't know her right now," she said. She peered at him from over her teal tortoiseshell Warby Parkers. "You have no idea what I'm talking about right now, do you?"

"None," Mal confirmed.

The chat box dinged with new messages: links to articles from Goss, *Insider*, *Marie Claire*, the *New York Post*. He clicked the first link. Scrolled through. Found a photograph from his event at Em-Dash staring back at him. Next to him, a photograph of Jo from a premiere, a straight bang hanging in front of her face, looking like a color-swapped Jessica Rabbit in a formfitting emerald sweetheart-neckline gown. And next to that, one of Ezra Adelman in a cream sweater with his sleeves rolled up, looking very much the part of an American heartthrob. The title: Who Doesn't Want a Billionaire?

"What is this?" Mal said out loud. He skimmed through the article as quickly as possible, picking up the pertinent claims: People thought Ezra and Jo may have been transitioned from "just friends" to "something more"—already a travesty, because surely she wasn't good enough—but also that Jo was simultaneously seeing Mal, making her an ungrateful seductress too. Ezra was positioned as a hapless rising star, the nepotism baby who was talented in his own right, who'd elevated her at every step.

And Mal? He was a sexy lamp. A talented one, but collateral damage all the same.

When he turned back to Amelia, she looked contrite.

"I'm sorry," she said. "I didn't think about how this might hurt you—"

"They're friends," Mal said, even though a small voice whispered in the back of his mind: *I knew it.* "They've been friends for a long time. I don't know what angle these people are taking, but they've got it wrong."

"I think they got at least a few things right," Amelia said. She shared her screen, highlighted a paragraph: Malcolm Waters is no one to snub your nose at. A Renaissance man himself, his New York

Times bestselling debut novel, She Blooms at Dusk, was recently featured on Lana Porter's long-running talk show. Another window showed the Google search history for his name, a graph that resembled a cliff. "We got eight thousand sales yesterday alone. I know you don't check your Instagram, but you're blowing up. People are very curious about what kind of man could compete with Adelman Junior." She smiled, as if Mal was supposed to be pleased by the positive reception. "You know that I hate this kind of stuff as much as the next guy, but you know what they say about a little bit of controversy. It sells."

Some part of him grasped that she thought this "little bit of controversy," as she put it, was a boon. But overlaying it, he could see Jo, her face wet with tears, her body curled into a fetal position in the middle of her bed.

"So," Amelia said. "Would you be interested in doing an interview or two? I think it could be a good idea. Just turn the conversation more to your work. We can coach you through it; knowing how and when to pivot is a skill—"

"With all due respect," Mal interrupted, "I need a little time to process all of this."

Amelia clamped her mouth shut.

"Of course," she said. "Oh, and I saw that you sent me your proposal. I'll take a look at it. We can touch base later this week."

Mal nodded, but he knew it was impossible to think of anything other than Jo after that. She wasn't answering her phone, and he quickly discovered that he had no way of reaching her. He checked her Instagram, but she'd locked down her DMs and turned off her comments. Her website's contact page had been taken down, her blog password-protected. He sent her roommate, Dahlia, a direct message on social media, but a few hours had passed without a response. The only person he could think to reach out to was Ezra himself, and Mal suspected he wouldn't be too keen on talking to "the other man."

What Mal did know was where Jo lived.

"You can't just give me a name," the young man with a patchy beard who worked the front desk of Jo's high-rise said. He gave Mal a look that could cut glass. "You need to give me a unit number. Otherwise, I could be letting a stalker upstairs, and that would make me pretty bad at my job, wouldn't it?"

Mal clutched the edge of the counter and did his best not to curse him out. He'd driven to Lincoln Park right after his call with Amelia, in the worst of Chicago rush hour, and had spent the entire forty-minute drive convincing himself that showing up at Jo's place uninvited wasn't an absolutely batshit thing to do. His already frayed nerves were now shot to shit. He didn't need this shrimpy little kid confirming his inner fears out loud.

"Can you at least try to call her?" Mal said, using all his remaining energy to stay cordial. "That's what people normally do, right?"

"We value security a little more than normal places, sir," the doorman said, but he picked up the phone and dialed. Mal heard it ring once, twice, three times, then go to voicemail. "Sorry. Looks like she's not available. Maybe try to get her yourself and I can send you up."

Gritting his teeth, Mal pulled out his phone, scrolled to Jo's name, hit dial. It was a fruitless exercise; he'd already called three times today to no avail. To no one's surprise, the call went straight to voicemail.

"Can you at least tell me if you've seen her?" he asked, desperate. "I just . . . need to know if she's okay."

Something in the doorman's face shifted, a relaxation of his expression from hostility to something like pity.

"I'm going to be honest with you, man," he said. "I haven't seen her down here in a couple days."

"Oh," Mal said, even as terror gripped him. He'd only read a few of the articles, and none of them had been particularly gracious. "Okay. Well. Um. If you do see her, can you tell her that Malcolm stopped by?"

The doorman nodded, and Mal turned to the door, accepting defeat.

"Did you say Malcolm?" a high-pitched voice said from behind him. "As in, Waters?"

Mal whipped around. He was quite sure he'd never met the small Asian woman standing in front of him, but he was equally certain that he knew who she was. With her buzzed bleach-blond hair, vampire-black lipstick, and the ends of a fine-line tattoo roping up her neck, Dahlia Cortes would have been hard to miss.

"Yeah," he said cautiously. "And, let me guess . . . Dahlia?"

"I am she," she said. "Do you have a minute? I think we share a common interest."

"Absolutely," Mal said.

DAHLIA ANSWERED MAL'S next few questions without needing to hear them: *Yes, Jo's still alive; no, I don't think she's okay; yes, I think she needs help; no, I don't know how exactly to help her.* She'd been on her way to the grocery store but insisted that they go to a coffee shop instead, which quickly changed to talking in the apartment's business center when Mal brought up that maybe being seen publicly with another woman might make things worse for Jo. Mal sat on one of the leather stools as Dahlia smacked a dusty old Keurig machine awake.

"Thanks for stopping by," she said, turning around at the counter as the Keurig sputtered and spit. "Seriously. I appreciate it. She will too, once she comes around."

"Have you seen her?" Mal said.

"Briefly," Dahlia said. "I picked up a couple shifts in the ICU over the weekend, but I saw her right before she left for the benefit. I assume she spent the night before with you, after your book signing?" Mal nodded, warmth rising to his cheeks. "I saw her for like two seconds a couple of days ago. She grabbed something out of the pantry. I knew something was up, like, I'd seen some of the early stuff on social media, but the *Post* article wasn't out yet, so I figured we'd talk about it later, but now—"

"The *Post* article?" Mal interrupted. "What's special about that one?"

Dahlia's face fell. "Oh honey," she said, then: "Let me send you the link."

She did, giving him permission to save her number to his phone. This one, unlike the articles before, seemed to be focused particularly on Ezra's mother, Renata Kovalenko, and read like the workings of a journalist who had been waiting for an opportunity to strike rather than a bedraggled intern scraping social media for controversy.

It is 1993, and Renata Kovalenko is walking the runway for Chanel's Spring/Summer collection. She holds her own amongst excellent company—Naomi Campbell is only a few paces behind her in an iconic pink princess/

punk set that remains in the American cultural consciousness to this day—but she isn't yet a star. That will come
later, after her seven-year-long affair with tech mogul
Paul Adelman culminates in a multimillion-dollar wedding and the launch of her short-lived fashion line, Syla.
At the time, however, Kovalenko is known most widely
as a homewrecker. Her son, Ezra Adelman, is born in
1991, two years before Paul Adelman's divorce from his
first wife, Katherine Listroph, is finalized. Renata herself
shows no shame for the circumstances of her marriage.
"We fell in love," she tells the *New York Sun* that same
year. "What is so wrong about that?"

It's a perspective that makes her infamous for a time,
but Renata is careful to avoid negative press after that. In
the fashion world, she's known as easygoing and fun-
loving, a personality she lets shine during her four-season
stint as a judge on *Project Runway*. Her relatable persona
helps to distract from her husband's gaffes. That is, until May of 2009, when Paul Adelman is caught on video
verbally accosting and eventually slapping one of his employees, then twenty-seven-year-old software engineer
Aaron Jackson, at the afterparty for the release of Knydus'
2010 Odyssey Operating System.

The assault is a PR nightmare. Knydus Engineering,
like many tech giants, has a diversity problem—less than
2% of its new hires identify as Black. The slap confirms
what many pundits have postulated—that Knydus Engineering does not respect Black talent . . . or people. The
effect is immediate and enormous: Knydus Engineering
stock plummets 13% overnight.

Only six months later, nineteen-year-old Ghanaian American Elion University student Josephine Boateng enters the Adelmans' circle. Even at her young age, she is even-tempered and polite, homely, and the first in her family to go to college. She is also, conveniently, the same complexion as Mr. Jackson.

It is not uncommon for celebrities to have less-famous friends, but less common for said friends to be folded into their brand. We first see Josephine at the 2010 Knydus Chicago Children's Ball on the arm of one Ezra Adelman. She appears again, just weeks later, in photographs of the family in the Maldives, and after that quite frequently as the younger Adelman's de facto plus-one. In interviews, Ezra calls her his "best friend in the entire world," Renata, "a remarkable young lady" and, on multiple occasions, refers to her as her "daughter."

Josephine fades from view for a few years, presumably to pursue her medical training, at Chicago's lauded James B. Herrick School of Medicine. On her popular social media platform, collectively called Dr. Jojobee, she discusses topics that "patients are afraid to ask." She also often divulges information about her own path into medicine and asserts that, without her full-ride scholarship, she would "never have been able to afford a medical education." She encourages premedical students from low socioeconomic backgrounds to "keep [your] head down, work hard. Go to office hours. Time for leisure will come later."

What she fails to divulge is from whence her scholarship came.

In 2012, the year before Josephine's matriculation to medical school, En Garde makes an uncharacteristically large donation to the order of $4 million to James B. Herrick School of Medicine.

"Our scholarship programs are by and large funded by the generous donations of individuals who prefer to remain anonymous," William Laurier, the Dean of Students at Herrick School of Medicine, states. "It's not atypical for them to specify a group of students they would like to support. However, donations cannot be directed toward particular students. To maintain the integrity of our selection process, they also in no way affect our admissions decisions."

It's an assertion that would be more plausible if the Adelman family had a habit of supporting higher education. As it stands, the donation to Herrick remains the only significant contribution that Nest, Knydus' charity branch, has made to an undergraduate or graduate institution. Herrick School of Medicine has a 3.9% acceptance rate, one of the lowest in the country. Josephine Boateng is admitted with a 3.7 GPA, significantly lower than the class average.

The Adelman family immediately sees a return on their investment. In 2012, Josephine Boateng posts to her popular Instagram a video of Renata Kovalenko helping take down her braids. It goes viral, with viewers commenting on both Renata's deftness and her cultural competence. She is, per several commenters, "invited to the cookout," a term meant to imply inclusion into the Black community.

Within three years, Knydus Engineering successfully rebrands itself as a great valuer of diversity. *Forbes* magazine recognizes the company as one of the "Ten Best Places for Black Programmers to Work." Knydus Engineering hires Amancia Patterson, a Jamaican American wunderkind whose résumé includes executive positions at Dell and Hulu, as chief operating officer; she appears on the *Lana Porter Show* months later to talk about her experience as the "only Black woman at the table." Aaron Jackson settles with Paul Adelman to the tune of $700,000, and his public assault is forgotten.

Which begs the question: By associating their family with a poor young Black woman, did Renata Kovalenko pull off the most successful PR move in recent history? Did Josephine Boateng reject America's Most Eligible Bachelor, or did she simply renege on a decade-long agreement to be the Black Best Friend to a family that gave her the financial backings to pursue her dreams?

At the end of the article was a photograph: a young, round-faced Jo standing between Renata and Ezra, Ezra's arm around her waist, Renata's over her shoulders. Mal stared at it for a long time before recognizing it as the picture Renata had framed on her desk. He felt like someone had knocked the breath out of him. The article had managed to do worse than all the previous ones had; stripped Jo of her agency, denied her efforts, presented her as someone willing to sell her likeness to a corporate devil. In it, she wasn't so much a duplicitous succubus as she was a creature of ambition.

"Wow. You really do care about her," Dahlia observed when

he looked up from his screen. She leaned back against the coffee counter with folded arms, looking down at him from under thick falsies. "I'll be honest, when she told me you confessed your love after the first hit, I was worried you might just be messing with her. But you seem pretty sincere."

Mal couldn't muster the energy to be embarrassed.

"Of course," Mal said. He dropped his head into his hands. "What about you? You're her roommate. I've had a few of those in my day, and I don't think any one of them would drop everything to plan an intervention for me."

Dahlia quirked an eyebrow, then knocked back her coffee like a shot and pulled out the stool across from him.

"Touché," she said. "Honestly, I probably like her more than she likes me." She sighed, dropping heavily onto the stool. "We met online, you know. I was in the middle of a nasty divorce. At the last minute, my ex-husband pulled money out of his ass for a lawyer and started asking for alimony and . . . all of a sudden I didn't have money for rent, let alone to move. Would you know that that woman just *sent* it to me?" She laughed mirthlessly. "Didn't even flinch. Didn't even tell me she was going to do it. Just wired me $5K, no questions asked, and when I tried to refuse, she told me 'not to be dramatic.' 'Do you want to keep living with that piece of shit?' she'd said. I didn't. It was done. A week later I was moving in with her."

Mal snorted. He'd gathered that about Jo: that she was not always nice, but frequently kind.

"You know, I had this big group of friends back home before moving to Chicago," Dahlia continued. "When things started going south for me, they disappeared. Not a single one of them would've sent me money. They couldn't even offer me a couch to crash on when my ex started bringing his new girlfriend over. Lots of thoughts and prayers, with no substance. And here's this girl who I haven't even met in real life, throwing me a life raft just because." Dahlia ground her chin into the heel of her hand. "She's a special person, you know. Like, who does that? I paid her back, but I feel like she wouldn't have pushed me to. It was like . . . she couldn't help but help me."

"I know," Mal said quietly. His fingers tangled on themselves, and he remembered how, not long ago, Jo's had curled between his, how they'd settled into the grooves like they belonged there. How effectively she blasted away his moments of self-doubt.

"So," Dahlia said. "What's the game plan?"

The game plan was simple. They drew up shifts: Dahlia covered most days, Mal most evenings. She sent an email to Jo's therapist seeking guidance; he stopped by the grocery store to stock her empty pantry. Jo seemed to be subsisting on Ritz Crackers and dry ramen noodle packages, and so they split meal prep too: Dahlia handling lunch, Mal dinner.

"Don't make me regret this," Dahlia said, dropping her spare key fob into Mal's palm. To her credit, she'd taken a picture of his driver's license and his license plate as collateral—*Just in case this is an elaborate attempt at burglary.*

One thing they didn't agree on was the talking thing. Dahlia might have found it weird, how Mal puttered around her apartment and made himself at home while she was gone, his conversations with Jo that were really with thin air. He liked to imagine that Jo was listening, that the shift of movement he heard through her door was her turning over with amusement.

"I'm making the tortellini I told you about," he announced to no one as he mixed together the cheese filling. "Brought over my stand mixer and everything. I know you don't cook, but you should get one."

Then, as he passed dough through the pasta attachment: "My dad used to color it with natural ingredients, back in the day. The blue tortellini was my favorite. He used purple cabbage for that, added baking soda to it. I used to think it was magic. I thought about making it today, but I figured I shouldn't feed someone blue food without their consent."

As he cut the dough into strips, added the cheese fillings: "We skipped over a lot of the basics while getting to know each other, you know. Like, what's your favorite color? I'll guess. Orange? Or is that just that you look good in it? What are your favorite foods? What type of music do you like to listen to? I know what you like to read. Can't say I'm surprised to see James Baldwin in your bookshelves . . . but Octavia Butler? Didn't know you were a sci-fi girl. Which is your favorite Butler? Everyone talks about *Kindred*, and I see you've got *Parable of the Sower*, but I'm a big fan of the *Xenogenesis Trilogy*, actually . . ."

Finally, as he lowered the folded tortellini into the boiling water: "You know, my dad's family had a soul food restaurant, back in the day. He was supposed to take it over. He never went to culinary school, but he could make everything on the menu and then some. And then he met my mom, and he realized that if he wanted to be with her, he had to leave his small town. My grandpa understood, but my grandma was so pissed off that she didn't speak to him for a year. But my dad did it anyway. He was always brave in that way."

Mal left the tray by her door, with a side salad ("Don't be too impressed, this one's from a bag," he qualified.) and a glass of water, and then stretched out onto her couch and turned up his music (Frank Ocean's "Ivy") just loud enough for her to hear.

"I'm going to attempt to start my second book now," he said. "You can come out and join me, if you want."

She didn't. When he looked up from his computer, the tray was gone, spirited away like an offering.

That was okay, Mal thought. He would be back tomorrow to try again.

CHAPTER TWENTY-NINE

Mal

On day three of Operation Smoke Josephine Out, Mal finally made contact.

Mal knew Jo was eating his meals. She usually waited until he went to the bathroom or returned home for the night before snatching her tray into her room. Dahlia sent him pictures of the rinsed dishes in the sink the morning after, with the addition: Poor thing. She tries so hard not to turn the faucet on all the way so I won't hear it running.

"I'm back," he said. "I picked up Thai. I asked Dahlia what you like, and she said you'd probably be good with red curry, so that's what I got."

From through the door, a soft voice. "Thank you."

It was a good thing Jo couldn't see his jaw drop, or she might have run away again. After days of talking to a wall, it felt like he'd just heard a ghost.

"It's no problem," Mal said, tiptoeing toward her closed door cautiously.

"It is," she said. Her voice was scratchy with disuse, and she cleared it. "You're doing too much."

"I'm doing exactly what I need to," Mal said. "Not my fault you aren't used to being taken care of." He slid to the floor, dropping his head against her door. "Why don't you come out? Eat with me?"

Jo made a sound that could have been a laugh, could have been a sob.

"No," she said. "Sorry. I don't think I can. Not yet."

"It's okay," Mal said hurriedly. "I'm sorry. Didn't mean to rush you—"

"You're not rushing me," she filled in quickly. "I'm just"—she paused—"embarrassed."

"Embarrassed?" Mal repeated.

"Yes, of course," Jo said. "You'd understand, if you could smell me right now."

"I'm sure I've smelled worse."

Jo laughed, a small huff of a sound. "I hate that you're seeing me like this."

"Technically, I'm not seeing you," Mal joked lamely. He opened his mouth to offer up something else, thought better of it, bit his lip, then decided, *Screw it.* "I ever tell you about what happened with my ex? After she left?"

"No," Jo said. "Not in detail."

Mal sighed, straightening out his legs. As Dahlia had strictly informed him, the joint Boateng-Cortes household was firmly anti-shoes-indoors, and so he focused on the design of his socks, the thin line of white that demarcated the gray toes from black body.

"We owned a photography studio together," he confessed. "When we were in college, we always dreamed of working for ourselves. We took a loan out from my parents, moved up to Chicago to be close to her family, and opened our studio. She did the marketing, got the clients, and I did the shoots. It was a dream come true for me.

"But Porsh wanted more. From the business at first, and then from me. And when she didn't get it, she got frustrated, and then she got mean, and eventually, she left." Mal swallowed, remembering those first few days after he'd returned home to find her gone. At the time, he had felt like he'd failed—at being a partner, at being a man. "We'd been together for so long that I think I lost sight of who I was outside of her. And when I realized she was gone for good . . . I broke."

The stillness of the air between them felt potent, like they were both holding their breath.

"How?" Jo asked, after a moment. "I mean. What did breaking look like for you?"

Mal told her. He realized that he'd never told anyone this story before, aside from his therapist, because everyone who was still in his life had been an active player in it. He'd shut down his website. Unplugged his phone. Stopped taking bookings entirely. Google marked his business as closed, and he didn't refute it. For two months, he let every day meld into the next, playing video games online with potty-mouthed tweens until the sun came up, consuming nothing but takeout and cheap beer, becoming one with his couch. He'd spilled shit on his floor and not wiped it up. Let the vegetables in his fridge develop their own ecosystems. It had taken a surprise visit from Kieran, Kelechi, and his very concerned parents to whip him back into shape. They'd practically forced him into therapy, into the gym, out of his apartment, and stayed on his ass until he emerged from his cocoon with a vision of a future for himself that for once, seemed crystal clear.

"If I'm honest with myself, I probably had been depressed for a while," Mal confessed. "Definitely anxious. It kept me from taking risks, asking questions, pushing myself harder. I had this constant refrain in my head telling me that I shouldn't bother, and sometimes I listened to it, instead of listening to the people I loved. I had to get to a pretty dark place before I accepted that I needed help. And when I got it, it was all-hands-on-deck." He knocked his knuckles back against her door, one after the other. "So here I am, being your hands."

He remembered the chokehold of depression. It was hard to admit now, how much of his youth had been eclipsed by it, how, despite his loving family, he'd always felt it layered on his skin like a fruit mold. He'd gotten better, then worse, then hit rock bottom, and he knew better than anyone that climbing out of the pit was a Sisyphean task. Every day it took work, and some days more work than others, and most times being loved the way he, honestly, had always been wasn't enough.

But every now and then, it got close. Kieran's voice on the other side of his apartment door, his parents flying in from Texas, the whole crew pitching in to help clean the biohazard zone he'd created—it had been the gust of cold wind he needed to jolt him back into reality. And reality was what Jo needed. He couldn't imagine how she felt, under the onslaught of online attackers who made a game out of diminishing her. But in the real world, she was loved. If not by everyone in it, by him. And he would do whatever it took to break through the noise.

The hardwood underneath them creaked; Jo, adjusting herself

on the floor. If he concentrated, he could almost hear her breathing.

"Thank you, Mal," she said, after a moment. "For everything."

"Anytime," Mal said. He closed his eyes, considering his next ask. "But can you do something for me?"

Jo snorted. "I don't think I'm in a position to deny your requests after all you've done for me," she said. "What is it?"

Mal tilted his head toward the ceiling.

"Can you turn on your phone?" he said. "I just . . . want to be able to get a hold of you."

The silence stretched on for so long that Mal feared it might be permanent, and he bit down on his cheek, already regretting making the request. They'd made headway today. Maybe this was too much pressure too soon. Maybe asking her to pick up for him would give her another thing to feel guilty for, an additional task for her already overburdened mind. But when Mal was about to take everything back and excuse himself from the premises, Jo cleared her throat.

"My phone's a scary place right now," she admitted. "It's pretty hard to convince myself that I'm not a piece of shit when tens of thousands of people are assuring me that I am. I got a bit hooked to feeding the beast. Had to put it away."

Mal started. He hadn't considered that.

"Oh," he said. "Oh. That's probably smart. Don't worry about it. I'll be here, anyway—"

"But. Maybe my computer? The trolls found my work email, but my personal is still intact."

"Are you asking to be my pen pal?" Mal teased, biting back his self-satisfaction when he heard her snicker through the door.

"Yes, I think," she said. "Do you accept?"

"Of course, Dr. Boateng," he responded, "I look forward to our correspondence."

AMPERSAND SCREAMED AT the door when Mal returned home. Despite being generally aloof, she preferred Mal's presence to his absence, and his daily trips to Lincoln Park had clearly been ticking her off. He scooped her into his arms and carried her to his desk, shaking his computer awake.

"Behave," Mal instructed, and, in a rare display of agreeableness, Ampersand obeyed, stretching out like a sphynx on his lap.

Today was, he thought, a good day. He'd spoken to Jo, then gotten the first chapter of his second novel done. He texted Dahlia (She talked to me today), and she responded with a string of excited emojis and a WHAAA AMAZING in all caps.

When Mal volunteered to be Jo's hands, he'd meant it. But there was another set of hands that were noticeably absent, and those ones, Mal thought, had the ability to put an end to all of this.

What had happened between Ezra and Jo the night of the health benefit had clearly been monumental: the video of their embrace was seared into the back of Mal's head. But for as many times as he watched it, it didn't look romantic. The glimpse he'd caught of Jo's face when Ezra turned to look at the camera had shown sadness, not longing. And there was the context: at a hospital in the early hours of the morning, after Jo had visited her estranged mother.

Mal would've been more curious if he weren't so annoyed. Because really, what was the point of being best friends with a billionaire if he couldn't shut down a media circus?

Mal opened his email to a few new messages, then snickered when he saw the sender.

FROM: mojojojobee@gmail.com
TO: malcolmjwaters@gmail.com
SUBJECT: Hi

Don't even know what I'm meant to say here. Thank you. I'm sorry. Honestly don't know why you're still around. I'm sure I've gone and made your life a living hell. You hate being under a spotlight, and I've pushed you right under it. But I appreciate you being here regardless.

I never told you how good the tortellini you made the other day was. No wonder that was all you ate growing up. If they packaged the joy I got from every bite into pill form I'm pretty sure I wouldn't be depressed anymore.

FROM: malcolmjwaters@gmail.com
TO: mojojojobee@gmail.com

You haven't made my life hell at all. Actually, according to my agent, you helped me sell a ton of books. Which is a bit disturbing, honestly.

And you didn't push me anywhere that I didn't want to be. You know how many times I've watched that video of you telling a whole room of people that I was yours? So many times it would make you sick. You would run away from me, if you knew.

My tortellini always hits. That's why I made it. Happiness in every bite.

Anyway. Don't worry about me. I'll be okay. I want you to be too.

P.S. Ampersand says hi.

P.P.S. Your email handle made me laugh. How old is this account?

P.P.P.S. When you're ready, can you tell me how things went with your mom?

FROM: mojojojobee@gmail.com
TO: malcolmjwaters@gmail.com

To answer your question, ancient. Made it in high school. Applied to college with this address, if you would believe it. Nobody told me any better. I still think it's cute tho.

To be honest, not sure what okay feels like. Have I ever been okay? Maybe not. I just kept myself so busy that I barely gave myself time to think about it. I used to be so much more resilient, I think. I was a stony-ass kid. Nothing anyone could say to me could shake me. And now look at me. Stuck. Did all this work and I have nothing to show for it. I told Denise I wasn't going to do social media anymore. But who's going to hire me to be their doctor now? When they google me all they'll find is this shit.

OH. Speaking of you in the spotlight. Were you on Lana Porter's show??? And why did I have to find that out on a post calling me a dumb cheating bitch????

Can tell you about mom stuff now. In summary:

She had a heart attack, then a stroke. Got most of her mobility back, has started speech therapy. Her boyfriend has been emailing me updates. And yes, she has a boyfriend, and yes, they are living in sin. Who would've thought.

More Ampersand, please. I think that photo generated at least three more molecules of serotonin.

FROM: malcolmjwaters@gmail.com
TO: mojojojobee@gmail.com

I can understand that feeling. When you've been living in darkness so long, you learn to function within it. You start to feel like the light is just a myth, like everyone else squints their way through life too. But it doesn't have to be that way. You deserve more than a perpetual dusk.

And, at risk of overstepping my bounds, I don't think you were more resilient. I think you had no choice but to keep moving, and when you hit the finish line, you ran out of gas. Like those people who collapse right after they finish a marathon. But you'll get up again. I know you will. You're Dr. Jojo. You can do anything.

On that note, you know you don't have to work in a hospital, right? Maybe seeing patients isn't for you. I really liked what you said, about wanting to educate people. Maybe that's something you can explore more, when you're in a better place. (Also, as my publicist said, controversy sells. I'm sure if you want a job, you can get one easy. Even with all the BS going around.)

Re: your mother. TBH I'm not sure how to respond to this.

It sounds like communicating with them is giving you peace, though, and there's beauty in that.

Also, yes, I was, I was going to tell you about Lana, and I hate that you found out how you did. She sprang the clip out of nowhere.

Re: cat pics: I will consider this permission to empty my entire camera roll into this email.

FROM: mojojojobee@gmail.com
TO: malcolmjwaters@gmail.com

Omg Ampersand is TEARING UP that catnip. You've got a little fiend on your hands. Look at her eyes.

Thank you for that. Made me laugh.

I don't have time for exploration. I still need to pay the bills. Time to put on my big girl pants and stop wallowing.

Rochelle emailed me this afternoon to check in. She says I have good friends. She's proud of me for building "healthy relationships." So there! You have my therapist's approval.

TO: mojojojobee@gmail.com
FROM: malcolmjwaters@gmail.com

You know. Not to freak you out. Even though it will freak you out. But you know when it comes to money, I got you, right? I want you to be well. If you need time away from everything to get there, I'm happy to help.

Jo didn't respond to that, but he hadn't expected her to. For a woman who extended a helping hand at the first opportunity, she was terrible at accepting the same for herself. But Mal found that, for once, her silence didn't hurt him. His plan hadn't changed. Today's dinner was salmon and broccoli. Today's soundtrack, Nina Simone. Today's mission: trying to sweet-talk Jo into eating with him. Eventually, he'd get her to let him take care of her too.

But for Josephine Boateng, all his best-laid plans would always be for naught. She always managed to be one step ahead.

"Hey," Jo said from the couch when Mal pushed her front door open.

Mal blinked at her, and Jo stared blandly back. She looked tired, a little hollow eyed, but every bit as beautiful as he remembered.

"I was thinking," Jo continued, like she hadn't isolated herself for the past week, like they were picking up on a conversation had over coffee rather than through a door. "You should bring Ampersand over. She was probably just starting to feel secure in your presence, and if you keep leaving her like this, she might think she's been abandoned. Obviously we don't have a litterbox, but we can set one up in my bathroom. I'm pretty sure Dahlia won't mind. She loves cats—"

Mal couldn't quite remember crossing the room or dropping his tote bag at the door. His body snapped to hers like a magnet, and he felt the breath push out of her chest as he squeezed her close. Until that moment, he hadn't realized that his desire to see her again had been more of a desperation, that a part of him had feared that this time, when she broke, it would be permanent.

"I think she would appreciate that," he said.

CHAPTER THIRTY
Jo

It took me ten minutes into my medical school lecture on depression for me to realize I had it. The lecturer had listed the diagnostic criteria—insomnia, excessive guilt and worthlessness, depressed mood, loss of pleasure or enjoyment, difficulty concentrating—and I'd ticked them off in my head impassively and thought, *Huh, maybe I need to get checked out.* Six years prior to my matriculation, a former student died by suicide after failing an important exam, and thanks to his parents' impassioned advocacy, our otherwise garbage student insurance covered four free counseling sessions a quarter. And so for a year, I sat in front of a fortysomething-year-old white woman who reacted to my least troubling childhood anecdotes with abject horror and offered little more than breathing exercises and a psychiatry referral to get me on meds, and waited to get better. Then residency started, and there was no time to be depressed, no sick days to call out on the mornings when just existing felt onerous, only phone calls from exasperated night floats asking when I was coming to relieve them.

Depression was a luxury, I realized quickly. People like Ezra, people with trust funds and pseudo-employment, could afford to sink into melancholy. But the rest of us had to eat. Ezra had a whole host of resources—twice weekly therapy sessions, bimonthly psychiatrist visits, weeklong mindfulness retreats—none of which fit into my schedule. And so I'd filled the hole in my heart with work, scheduled virtual visits with Rochelle in times of crisis, and convinced myself that I was okay, most of the time.

And I *was* okay, until I wasn't.

"How are you feeling?" Mal said. He grasped my shoulders tight, like he thought I might pull away. Which was ridiculous, really. Pulling away from Mal felt impossible now. His voice had been the only thing to reach me in the darkness, an unrelenting reminder that I wasn't alone, even when I wanted to be. "Did you eat?"

"What, aren't you going to feed me?" I said, screwing up the corner of my mouth. "Pity. I'm too useless to figure it out for myself."

Mal's expression soured. "Don't call yourself that," he said. "It's not a joke."

I held back a laugh. I felt tired, giddy, and so desperately, vacuously empty, which was still better than how I'd felt for the last few days.

"Come on, Mal," I said. "It's objectively true. I'm unemployed, and I'm so completely incapable of taking care of myself that I apparently need two grown adults to babysit me."

I surveyed Mal's face for his response, expecting annoyance, disgust, irritation. A part of me hoped for it, really. *You're too good for me*, I wanted him to realize. *You should go find someone less broken. Someone who can take care of you too. Not someone like me, who intermittently ceases to function.*

But instead, what I got was concern.

"I hate how you're talking about yourself right now, you know," Mal said. "But fine. You think you're useless? Let's fix that. I'm putting you to work."

Standing, he walked to the kitchen. I followed, bemused by his conviction and the aggressive way that he tossed a head of broccoli and fileted salmon onto the counter.

"You'll handle the broccoli," he said, bending to retrieve a cutting board from the sink. I watched him with a mixture of fascination and guilt, stunned by how comfortable he looked in my kitchen, the ease with which he procured supplies I'd probably have to ask Dahlia to find. Silently, I took up the task, washing the broccoli before picking up the knife.

It took only a couple of chops for Mal to snatch it right back out of my hands.

"It's better if you cut the florets off the base. Cut the bigger pieces in half. Like this," he said, stepping in close beside me to demonstrate. His arm brushed against mine, and I nearly jumped back, startled by how the simple, inadvertent touch left my skin buzzing. Good god, was I this touch starved? Were my neurons so scrambled that they were starting to mix up self-loathing with horniness?

Mal, for his part, looked unaffected. Which was annoying, because he also looked hotter than I remembered, the veins and sinews in his forearms bulging as he worked. He looked down at me, his expression tender, then bumped me with his hip.

"Your turn," he said, handing back the knife and heading for the spice cabinet.

Pouting, I went back to work. By the time I was finished, Mal had already prepped and seasoned the salmon and was laying the fillets side by side in the foil-lined basket of Dahlia's air fryer. He started it, washed his hands, then walked back over to me.

"Much better," he said, scraping the florets into a bowl with a quick flourish. He gave me a curious look, then said, plainly, "You really weren't joking about not knowing how to cook, were you?"

"I had no one to teach me," I said plainly.

Mal nodded sagely, tossing olive oil, salt, and a rapid sequence of added spices to the bowl. Then he leaned in close and pressed a tender kiss to my forehead.

"Well, you do now," he said. "We have a lot of meals ahead of us. Just you watch, I'll make a chef out of you yet."

Tears pricked my eyes. *There you go again*, I thought. *Doing the most*. Just like yesterday. I got you, he said in his email, offering to financially support me through my crisis.

"Why are you doing this, Mal?" I sighed, throwing the broccoli into the oven with a clatter. "Why are you here?"

"Hmm?" Mal hummed. He'd brought dinner rolls with him and organized them onto a baking sheet. Then he smiled at me and said lightly, "Come on, Jo, you know why."

"Because you love me?" I said, watching his feet as they stepped closer to mine. "I'm not sure if I know what that means."

Mal cupped my face, and, unbidden, I leaned into the warmth of his hand.

"It means I want to see you happy," he said gently. "It means I want you to win, and that I want to be the one beside you when you do, the one to comfort you when you don't. It means I don't go more than an hour without thinking about you, and when I think about where I'll be next year, or in the next five, or the next ten, you're always there with me."

My tears pooled into the crease of his palm, and he wiped them away, pulling me into his chest. It must have been the writer in him that gave him the ability to say the exact right thing to me at the right time.

"Me too," I whispered. "That's how I feel about you too. I want you to have the world, Mal, and you *can* have it. I mean, look at you. Look at how many people you've touched with your work. You love me because you think I push you forward, right? Because I *see* you? But what if that's an act? What if I end up holding you back instead?"

I could feel the exact moment that Mal's heart stuttered under my cheek, felt his arms tighten around me just before he pulled back to look me in the eye.

"It's not possible for you to hold me back," he said. "Even if you can't do anything for me ever again. Even if I take care of you like this forever. I'll be happy to just be yours."

I'd never cried as a kid. It was as though the part of me that was supposed to feel had gone dormant after age ten. Prudence had told me to make myself useful, and so I did, ensuring I inconvenienced her as little as possible before disappearing altogether. My emotions finally woke up in college, but even with Ezra, I knew not to take up space. To him, my slumps were short-lived and self-limited, small periods of exhaustion-induced gloom from which I would assuredly bounce back. And I always did, like a ball against a hard wall, a rubber band stretched thin and then let loose again. He'd never seemed to wonder if I would snap, because I had never let him in close enough to worry. I was the *strongest person he knew.* Little did he know that the love he had for me was based on a lie.

But Mal had seen me at my lowest. He'd smelled my Frito stink. He'd seen me bedraggled, dressed in my last clean shirt, and he was still holding me like I was the most precious person in the world. My chest throbbed, and I sucked in a breath, looking everywhere but at him, at our tile floor that needed cleaning, the heathered pattern of his shirt.

"Ezra's in love with me," I said abruptly, unsure of how else to respond, how to communicate the transfiguration his words had triggered in my soul. "That rumor is true. He told me himself Sunday morning."

Mal nodded, his expression curiously passive. "I figured," he said.

"I don't love him anymore," I said.

The smile that broke out across Mal's face was sunlight therapy, a lightning flash in the midst of my melancholy. He dropped his head against mine, and for a moment, I couldn't tell whether the heartbeat I felt galloping against my chest was his or mine.

"I figured that too," he said.

And then he kissed me, and for a brief moment, the world seemed a less desolate place.

CHAPTER THIRTY-ONE

Mal

Jo got a little better, day by day. As promised, Mal brought Ampersand over to her apartment, and the two of them became thick as thieves, Ampersand curling at Jo's feet as they watched their respective favorite comfort films (Rodgers & Hammerstein's *Cinderella* for Jo, *The Bodyguard* for Mal) or beat Dahlia at her own overcomplicated board games. Jo was still too anxious to wander outside for fear of being recognized, but she had started heading downstairs into her apartment's gym again and occasionally down to the mail room. She'd even ordered Ampersand a name tag with an *&*, under the auspices that a "chic little thing like her would prefer it."

And while Jo healed, Mal kept an eye on the news cycles.

To his horror, they'd only gotten uglier. The *Post* article had uncovered several potential controversies, and every patchy-bearded man with a podcast mic and woman with a webcam had a hot take about the situation that required four minutes of ranting and two hundred comments worth of discourse. The Adelmans were racist because Paul had assaulted his Black assistant, or they weren't racist because they'd donated to this or that Black people in tech organizations. Jo was a conniving, capitalistic opportunist because she allowed them to use her for PR, or an unsuspecting victim who had found herself immersed in an unscrupulous billionaire family's business. There was talk about whether her medical admission had been bought, which then spurred an internet-wide debate about whether such nepotism was only being considered a problem because a poor Black woman was benefiting from it. And of course, the speculation on her love life, with Ezra worshippers flooding her inactive page with vitriol and original Dr. Jojobee fans defending her honor in the comments section.

It was simultaneously horrifying and fascinating to witness, like watching the aftershocks of a tsunami. Jo had been right to turn off her phone.

"So . . ." she asked, leaning against her doorframe, fresh from a shower. She wore a fluffy lilac robe, her hair held out of her face by a matching headband. "How bad is it?"

Reflexively, Mal grimaced, and Jo sighed.

"Yeah, I figured," Jo said. She stretched, and he followed the rise of her chest through the fluffy opening of her robe. "Well. On the plus side, Denise has informed me that my follower count is currently at seven hundred thousand. Granted, two hundred of those are probably just waiting for me to post something so they can find something wrong with me, but, you know. All press is good press, and all that."

She'd said it with bite, and Mal sighed, placing his laptop on her desk before opening his arms for her. She hopped onto his lap, and he dropped his head onto her shoulder, pulling her close.

"Denise isn't giving up, is she?" he said. She smelled sweet, like the lavender body wash she favored and the ginger spice underlay he had only recently realized was her natural scent.

"Nope," Jo said, sagging into him. Mal nipped at her neck, and Jo sighed, angling her hips into his. Then she leaned away, smirked down at him. "Are you seriously hard right now? Reading all those terrible, awful things about me get you going?"

Mal laughed breathlessly, parting her open robe farther to weigh a breast in each palm.

"Oh yes," he said. "You're a very bad woman, according to all the reports. Downright villainous, actually."

"And you like that?" Jo said, arching into his hold.

"Of course," he said, leaning forward to kiss her. Jo's sigh washed over his face, cool and minty, and then her hands were scrambling for his drawstrings, loosening them, drawing him out. He groaned into her mouth as she encircled him, stroking him firmly from base to tip, her grip sure like she'd been doing it forever.

"What do you want?" He breathed into the shell of her ear. "My fingers? My mouth? Want me to eat you?" He grazed his teeth against her lobe. "Want me to fuck you?"

Jo shivered—she liked when he talked, he'd realized, the filthier the better—then, without preamble, lifted her hips up and lowered herself onto him. Mal gasped against the sudden, unexpected heat, but she didn't give him a moment to adjust, pushing him back onto the bed with a gentle hand on his chest. The smile she gave him was beatific, made more so by the halo of light formed behind her by the ceiling fan lights.

Goddamn. It was hard to believe that this was what he was coming home to these days—a gorgeous girl with a heart of gold and the libido of a teenage boy, who fucked him like she had something to prove. Jo dragged his T-shirt up to his clavicle, leaning forward on her knees to kiss her way up his neck, and he bit down hard on his lip as pleasure spiked through him. There was something about seeing her undulating above him that got him going a little too quick, the visual stimuli of heaving breasts and thighs and her gasping, euphoric expression too overwhelming when paired with the exquisite clench of her around him. He reached for her, hooking his thumb into her mouth, and she gave him a coy smile before sucking it deeper.

Fuck. At this rate, he wasn't going to last another minute.

"Slow down," he begged. He grasped at her hip, gripping it beseechingly, and she interlaced her fingers in his. "Jo, please, I'm going to come."

Jo grinned down at him with all of her teeth, but she didn't let up. Instead, she leaned back on her haunches, plunging herself onto him relentlessly, and he realized, too late, that he'd been ambushed.

"Then come," she said sweetly.

She might as well have snapped her fingers. One second, he was gritting his teeth, rubbing circles around her clit to catch her up, and the next he was lost to sensation, his vision blurring before turning white, his whole body tightening as he emptied into her, over and over again until he had nothing left.

They lay there, panting, for several minutes, Jo's shoulders sloped backward, her face tilted up toward the ceiling. Eventually, she tucked her head down to give him a small, indulgent smile, as if she hadn't just ravaged him.

"I'm not saying sleeping with you is fixing my depression," she said, dismounting. "But I feel really good right now. It's the endorphins, I think."

Mal tucked her under his arm, tugging his shirt back down and his pants up.

"Glad to be of service," he said, pressing a kiss to her neck. She nestled into his side, leaning into his embrace.

"I had an epiphany," she said suddenly.

"Sleeping with me give you that too?" Mal said. "Damn. I'm more powerful than I thought."

Jo shoved his chest playfully.

"My mother's boyfriend emailed me yesterday," she explained. "He found my account. He and my mom have been watching my videos. He said . . ." She bit her lip, suddenly shy. "That the ones on heart disease especially have been really helpful. And I guess, I don't know, it made me not want to give up."

"Oh." Mal held her closer, feeling a conflicting clash of emotions. On one hand, after all Jo had told him about her childhood, it was hard for him to feel any sort of positive feelings toward her mother. On the other, he was relieved that she finally seemed to sound optimistic about her future. "That's good."

"And . . ." Jo said. "Denise sent me an email. From Lana Porter."

If Jo hadn't been weighing down his arm, Mal would have sat up in surprise.

"Lana reached out to you?" he said apprehensively. "Why?"

Jo shrugged, then reached for her laptop on her nightstand. She opened her email, scrolled, and handed it to him.

The email was a forwarded thread, and he scrolled further to read the messages chronologically. The first message came from Lana's assistant, a simple request for a virtual meeting. Denise responded with a not-quite rejection, explaining that her client was not taking meetings at the moment, but asking her to circle back in a few weeks. ("It must have killed her to say that," Jo said, snickering, at his side.)

Then came a message from what appeared to be Lana Porter herself. Please pass this on to Dr. Boateng, it started.

> It isn't often that I feel compelled to reach out to talent directly. But it is obvious that your client, Dr. Boateng, is something special. People who desire the spotlight do all they can to remain in it. But no matter how she may want to avoid it, the spotlight is trained on Josephine. She has a compelling image, a fascinating backstory, and what appears to be a healthy dose of ambition. She is magnetic in a way that simply can't be taught.
>
> I make it a point to identify and uplift talented Black women and would very much like to discuss having her on my show as a physician correspondent, with the hope that she could eventually remain on as a regular contributor. Please let my team know if this is something she would be interested in.
>
> Best,
> Lana

Multiple things ran through Mal's mind: First, that by mentioning her in his segment, he might have actually done something good. Second, that Lana had recognized Jo's inherent magnetism on sight. And finally, that Jo seemed to be sharing this email with him because she was considering saying yes.

This should've been a good thing. It was a path forward, and he could understand how a place as a physician correspondent on Lana's show aligned with her mission. But he'd seen how badly being under severe public scrutiny had affected her. Had watched her suffer. The idea of her being under a magnifying glass all the time, not just by virtue of her connection with the Adelmans, but through reach that exceeded her own, terrified him.

"This is good, right?" Mal said hesitantly. "I mean. It's an incredible opportunity. But it's also a lot of exposure. Are you sure it's what you want?" He wondered if she could hear his silent, tense *Will you be okay?*

Jo kissed him, gently, on the cheek.

"It'll be different. I'll have you." She shuddered, chuckling to herself. "Blegh. Gross. Can't believe I said that out loud. Your sappiness is rubbing off on me."

Mal laughed, but her assurances eased his anxiety some.

"Should've warned you that it was contagious," he admitted. Then, more seriously: "But how do you think it will be different? Lana's audience is massive."

"Well, for one, I'll be teaching," Jo said. "You said it, remember, at Il Latini. It's what I'm good at, and it's what I like. It's what I've always liked about medicine. Talking to people, helping them navigate and take charge of their own health. And it's why I think I'm struggling to go back to clinical practice, because that isn't always incentivized or encouraged there." She inhaled, but she sounded excited, the way she had when they'd sat across from each other at the coffee shop, planning out her shoot for the Tantra. "But I couldn't help it. So I tried hard to make that a big part of Dr. Jojo. But my engagement was always higher when I made it less about facts and more about me. My opinions. My life. My vulnerabilities. I was selling access to myself, not to my knowledge. Lana, on the other hand . . ."

"Doesn't sell herself," Mal finished, understanding. "She sells topics."

Jo sat up fully, her grin vibrant.

"Yes," she said. "Lana is funny. She's beautiful. She's magnetic. But what do we know about her? I mean, if we looked her up, we'd probably find some personal details, but mostly we'll learn about who and what she's discussed. She's a public figure in the truest sense. If I could eventually do something like that, but with health care, where I talk to different specialists, cover a disease process, or a patient's story, it would be perfect. Call it something like Ambulatory . . ."

"You could start off as a correspondent, like she's asking," Mal continued, "and if all goes well . . ."

He almost laughed. It was a brilliant plan. Ambitious, sure, but this was Jo, and so it was possible. He told her as much.

Jo put her laptop aside, then draped herself over him, nuzzling her nose against his. He laughed, roping his arms around her, relieved to find that, for once, her happiness didn't seem filtered through a layer of melancholy. She kissed him, once, twice, cradling his face between her hands.

"I couldn't have gotten to this point without you, you wise old man," she said.

"Yes, you would've," Mal said. He believed it. "You were already extraordinary. I just provided a little support."

Jo laughed, and then her gaze grew tender, her thumbs tracing a path around the angles of his jaw.

"I love you, Malcolm Waters," she said, and Mal froze.

That Jo loved him wasn't news, exactly. She'd skated past the words themselves, found ways to show him that fell just short of a declaration. But now she was saying them out loud, and he understood just how much she meant them. They weren't just *I love you*, but also *I trust you, I accept you, I understand you*. Not just a feeling, but a choice, because nothing Josephine Boateng said or did was ever without intention.

And that intention surged something inside of him, crackling through him like a lightning bolt. Suddenly he felt powerful, capable. He could do more than just sit and hope for the noise to settle. He could force the quiet to come.

"I love you too," Mal said, and later, when Jo settled in to sleep at his side, he sent his own email, this time addressed to Renata Kovalenko.

CHAPTER THIRTY-TWO
Mal

"Malcolm Waters," Amelia said, barely holding back the fury in her voice. "What the hell do you think you're doing?"

It had taken Amelia approximately nine hours and forty-five minutes to blow up his phone, about nine hours and forty-four minutes longer than he'd expected, considering the nature of the email he had sent to Renata and the En Garde team. I try not to involve my personal life in matters of business, he'd written. But unfortunately, I can't in good conscience move forward with this agreement while my affiliation with your family is causing harm to someone I love.

Renata's response had been prompt, a quick Are you free to discuss tomorrow afternoon? followed by a note to her assistant to clear her schedule for him.

"I'll pay back your percentage if I have to," Mal said to his irate agent. "And don't worry. I'll make you more money later. I can write you a second book. And then a third." The door to Renata's office opened, and a reedy man that Mal recognized from his last visit stepped through to tell him that "she's ready for you." Mal stood. "Sorry, Amelia, I'm about to go into the meeting. I'll call you after."

The last time Mal had entered Renata Kovalenko's office, he'd done so with a great deal of unease. He'd looked at her long conference table with trepidation, stared through her massive floor-to-ceiling glass windows and thought, *How is it possible that I'm here right now?* Renata herself he had regarded like he might a biblical angel, with a pounding heart and an averted gaze. But this time, when the model-turned-reality-TV-judge-turned-entrepreneur stood to greet him, he looked at her and saw a human being who was not doing enough.

"Hello, Malcolm," Renata said, gesturing toward the seat across from her. "I'm sorry that we're meeting again under these circumstances. Please, sit."

"Me too, but it is what it is," Mal said. He crossed his legs and waited for her to speak. Renata looked, as always, annoyingly perfect, not a dark circle under her eyes to indicate sleep lost, not a lock of hair out of place, even her white sheath dress bright and unblemished.

"This is about Jo, isn't it?" Renata said. "How is she doing? I haven't been able to reach her."

"Not well," Mal said simply.

Renata swallowed, her expression contorting into one of true sorrow. She tapped her fingers against the sleek surface of her desk, then sighed.

"I assumed as much," she said. "What's happening is terrible. My team released a statement yesterday, but I fear it may have just fanned the flames more. Unfortunately, we may just have to wait this one out."

Mal looked at her, stunned, then furious. Anger wasn't an emotion that came easily to him, but he felt it now, building in his bones so rapidly that he had to set his jaw to keep his teeth from chattering. It was the Adelmans' fault that Jo's name had been dragged through the mud, and all its matriarch could think of to rectify matters was to wring her hands, have her PR team draft a pithy statement, and wait? They hadn't been there when Jo locked herself in her room. When she'd been so terrified of her phone that she had to throw it in her closet just to keep from having her internal thoughts about her own worthlessness echoed by legions of strangers online. Even with all of their means, they'd done the bare fucking minimum. No wonder Jo had trouble depending on others. If this was the family she'd chosen, she had no reason to trust that her best interests would ever be met.

"Your husband gets involved in a scandal every other week, and that manages to get cleaned up pretty quick," he said.

Renata's blue eyes iced over like Lake Michigan in the dead of winter.

"What are you implying?" she said.

"I'm just wondering how much of what they're saying in these articles is true," Mal said. "About your family only bringing Jo close as a cover for your husband beating on a Black man. About you *using* her. Because it seems really convenient that you were able to cover up something like that, but that *this*"—he spun the globe on her desk—"is out of your hands."

Renata sat back in her chair, her expression suddenly blank. She folded her arms across her chest.

"She hasn't told you," she said.

"Hasn't told me what?" Mal asked.

Renata took a swig from her bottle like it was hard liquor.

"You're a creative, with a vast imagination," Renata said. "I won't keep you from thinking whatever you want. But be assured in one thing: I love that girl like she's my own. If there was anything more I could do, I would do it. But there are many things money can't buy, and the silence of millions is one of them."

Her refusal resonated like a slammed door. Mal gritted his teeth. He wanted to fight her harder, but he realized that they'd reached an impasse.

"Now, on the topic of our business together," Renata continued. "I understand your concerns about continuing to work with En Garde. But I would like to give you some unsolicited advice." She paused, but not long enough to give him time to interject. "Be choosy about when you let your personal life interfere with your business. En Garde has full intentions to bring *Dusk* to the screen within the next year. You'll make a million dollars when we do. If your goal is to be the best partner possible for Josephine, it might do you well to have that money in hand. So why don't you sleep on this for a few days and reach out to me again if you still think it best that we part ways."

"I'm good," Mal said.

Renata raised both eyebrows. "Mr. Waters," she said. "Do you understand what you're doing?"

"You said it yourself. You're a small production company, just starting out. One of your jobs is to shape perception of my project. If you're telling me you can't influence a little controversy, maybe you can't manage my work as well as you think." Renata stiffened, her smile a stricture on her face, but he continued. "I've already told my agent. You just need to get your assistant to send me the bank info, and I'll return the option money."

His piece said, Mal stood, smoothed his hands down his pants, and made for the door.

"Malcolm?" Renata called, when he had nearly reached it. Mal turned, looking back at her.

"Thank you for looking after Josephine," she said. "Seriously. I'll admit, when I first heard you were together, I worried that she might need someone a bit more . . . ferocious by her side." She smiled, as if fully aware that her compliment was backhanded. "But now I see that you are more than up to the task."

Mal nodded, then threw the door open.

"You here about Jo?"

It shouldn't have surprised him, that Ezra Adelman was leaning against the wall across from his mother's office. If he were in Ezra's shoes, he would be stalking him too.

Except maybe he wouldn't. Except, if he had Ezra's power, a meeting like this wouldn't be necessary, because he would have already put the rumors to rest.

To his credit, Ezra looked like shit. Unlike his mother, who seemed to be made of marble, his skin was wan and slack, his normally artfully rumpled hair unkempt. Mal would have felt sorrier for him if he hadn't been paying attention to the headlines. For all intents and purposes, Jo's downfall had been great for Ezra's image. He'd fallen for a relatively ordinary woman, his best friend even, only to have his heart dashed into the dirt. It was the perfect scenario for a romantic male lead, the tragically handsome aristocrat awaiting comfort from a woman who could heal his wounds.

"I can't reach her," Ezra said. "I was an ass to her after the hospital. Messed everything up." He gave Mal a beseeching look, and he realized that despite his assumptions, Ezra wasn't here to pick a fight. "Can you tell her I'm sorry?"

Mal stared Ezra down, unmoved. After she'd told him about Ezra's confession, Jo had informed him of how he'd reacted to her rejection by blocking her number. *I know he was hurting*, she said. *But I really needed him.*

"I'm not a messenger pigeon, Adelman," he said simply, then made for the exit. Ezra shifted to stand in his way, and Mal bristled, resisting the urge to push him aside.

"My mom's not just bullshitting, you know," Ezra pleaded. "We've thrown money where we can. Talked to our lawyers, put out statements. I don't know what else there is to do."

The amount of grief Ezra had given him was laughable now. Not so long ago, Mal had worried that he could never give Jo what Ezra had at his fingertips. He needn't have wasted his energy.

"You don't actually love her," Mal said. He watched Ezra's expression tighten with indignance. "Because if you did, you would have figured something out by now."

Then, bumping his shoulder, Mal walked away, leaving Ezra behind to ruminate. He was almost down the hall when he heard Ezra call out his name.

"Malcolm," Ezra said. "Wait. I have an idea. Can you help me?"

CHAPTER THIRTY-THREE

Jo

My first Adelman family dinner was not at a high-end restaurant, or even in the ornate, rarely used dining room of their Chicago penthouse. Instead, it was at their large kitchen island, seated on the high leather-cushioned barstools. I had nowhere to go for winter break my freshman year. The dorms were closing, and in preparation for my temporary eviction, I'd found a cheap sublet near campus. Back then, my friendship with Ezra was new and intense, his omnipresence in my dorm room causing a visible tension between me and my roommate, who seemed disturbed that he didn't seem to remember her, despite being the one to "introduce" us. I hadn't yet fully trusted him with the details of my estrangement from my family. When he discovered my plans to be alone for the holidays, he subverted them immediately.

"Are you kidding me, Jo?" Ezra had said, righteously indignant. "I'm not leaving you here alone. Just come home with me."

Renata was Jewish, Paul Christian, and so the Adelman residence was decorated in themed rooms to celebrate both religions: an elegant golden menorah in front of the grand stairway, a gargantuan Christmas tree almost scraping the twelve-foot ceiling of the living room. I hadn't been quite sure what to expect; my interactions with Ezra's father had been minimal and awkward, and Renata, though she'd never been anything other than doting toward me, still terrified me.

But then we'd arrived in the home to find Renata behind the stove, her usually elegantly coiffed hair tied into a messy ponytail high on her head, a violently stained apron tied around her waist, and what appeared to be a bloodbath in her kitchen. The moment we entered, suitcases squealing behind us, Ezra laughed so hard that he nearly choked.

"Are you . . ." he said in horror, "cooking?"

Renata folded her arms, successfully smearing what I realized was beet juice onto the unshielded sides of her shirt.

"What?" she said. "Why can't I cook? How do you think I survived before you?"

The oven beeped, and she ran across the room, pulling out a lumpy piece of what was supposed to be challah bread from within it.

"We needed a home-cooked meal," Renata explained. "I told Charlotte"—their cook—"that I could do it. I used to make borscht with my mother, you know. It tastes better when you do it yourself."

It did not taste better, but the warmth that had traveled from my throat and into my fingertips had been worth the damage the rock-solid bread did to my teeth. I'd never had a meal like that. The three of us, sitting at an island, giggling in between oversalted slurps. Not trying to scarf my food down as quickly as possible. Feeling safe. Loved.

Mal's roast, on the other hand, was delectable. The meat was perfectly melt-in-your-mouth tender, the potatoes well-seasoned and crispy, even the carrots flavorful. In a sharp departure from our many cooking lessons over the last weeks, he had insisted on making everything himself, and once he'd finished up writing for the day, tied an apron around his waist and got to task. Across the table, his gaze was plaintive, eyebrows turned up, brown eyes wide like a child caught in his mess.

I lowered my fork, sighing. "What did you do?" I said.

Mal jolted.

"What do you mean?" he said, and I comforted myself with the knowledge that he would forever be incapable of hiding anything from me, by virtue of being the worst liar I'd ever met.

"You're being weird," I insisted. "Acting guilty. Can you please fess up? Did you talk to media, or—"

As if on cue, Mal's phone buzzed. I peered at the screen, seeing a name that looked suspiciously like *Ezra Adelman* flash across the screen.

"Why is Ezra texting you?" I asked, stunned. I knew that they'd run into each other before, but there was no reason for Mal to have Ezra's contact.

"Ah," Mal said, his eyebrows traveling even farther into his hairline, just as the notifications began to roll in.

They came fast, buzzes, dings, and pings, banners in all colors of the rainbow flashing across his screen. I sucked in a breath, disoriented by the onslaught. My panic crystallized, lodged itself in my throat, and I looked to Mal, searching for an explanation.

"Mal," I said, my fork falling to my plate with a clatter. "What is going on?" When he didn't answer, I ran to my bedroom, stepping through my newly organized closet until I reached the phone that I'd tossed into the back weeks ago. My heart leaped in my throat, and I didn't bother counting out my pulse, didn't try to counteract my dread as I waited for it to turn on. Miraculously, it did.

"What the hell," I said, scrolling through my own notifications with my mouth ajar. My phone, despite my many fail-safes, had blown up similarly. My work email in particular. Denise was passing on interview invitations like her fingers were on fire, every subject line with a copied and pasted I just think you should see this!

Then there were the news headlines, the social media posts, tags more numerous than I could count. My Instagram ballooning to nearly nine hundred thousand followers, another two hundred thousand people appearing on my page like they'd materialized out of thin air.

And finally, there was Mal, sitting at my dining table and looking unsurprised by all of it.

"Are you going to explain what's going on?" I asked him.

Mal exhaled. Then, silently, he pushed his phone toward me.

It was a video. Ezra Adelman, sitting behind a desk, looking almost angelic in a white linen shirt. He smiled at the camera. His blue eyes squinted to jewels, the corners of his mouth pointing upward.

"I thought long and hard about making this," he said, and as if my body already knew what was coming next, tears dripped, ready-made, onto my plate.

I WAS THE campus paramedic on duty the day that Ezra died.

It had been two weeks since our fight in the Sheridan Student Center, when Ezra had declared himself my friend and I had told him to kick rocks, and in that time, my life had calmed down. Dark-haired heirs no longer plopped themselves next to me in class or overloaded my text thread with links to songs he thought I might like. The rumor mill had died down, and my roommate had stopped giving me dirty looks. I was finally living the college life I had dreamed of; the one in which I could mind my business and no one else's.

It was quiet. It was lonely.

And then, at my hip, my walkie-talkie went off.

"Jo, do you copy?"

"This is Jo. I copy," I said into the walkie-talkie. "What's going on? I didn't get an alert?"

"This is the alert," the voice responded—Mike, our dispatcher. "I just got a call from campus police. An anonymous caller just requested a wellness check on a student. They want to know if either of us is available to accompany them."

I was already diving into my jacket.

"I got it, Mike," I said, throwing my med kit onto my back. "Where am I meeting them?"

"On the quad," Mike said. Then he paused, a little uncomfortable. "But just a heads-up. The student . . . it's Adelman."

My stomach sank. "Shit," I said.

"Yeah, I know, no pressure, right?"

Our team was composed of two campus police, Dave and Winston, and Patrick, the private security Renata hired to aid the search.

It had been only three hours since he was last seen, a somewhat reasonable time for an eighteen-year-old boy to go wandering off without his phone, but the last person to see him had said he'd seemed not quite in the right state of mind. He'd left his house before the rager he was hosting could really start, but not before sending his mom a text saying, cryptically, "Love you. Forgive me." No one knew where he'd gone.

Had he been anyone else, emergency services might not have gotten involved. Dave would have probably rolled his eyes and put off the task until the morning. Patrick wouldn't be harassing the "guests," who hadn't even noticed that their host had disappeared while they trashed his house. Winston wouldn't be writing citations that would be thrown away for the juniors caught snorting lines on Ezra's glass desk.

I wouldn't be whisked among them, seeing Ezra's features in every strobe-lit face.

"You said Josephine Boateng?" his mother had said over the phone, after we'd left his house. I recognized Renata Kovalenko's voice from an episode of *Project Runway*; it was bizarre to hear it over the phone, addressing me. "I knew that name sounded familiar. I'm so glad that the person looking today is his friend."

How could I tell a grieving mother that, actually, she was mistaken? That I wasn't her son's friend, that, just two weeks before, I'd told him as much? What comfort would that bring her?

"Maybe we should file an official report," Patrick said, when an hour later, we had nothing, no leads, just more concerning details from the few party guests sober enough to describe Ezra's behavior before he'd disappeared ("weirdly chill, like, more than he usually is").

I tilted my head back, watching my breath form clouds before my eyes. The cold nipped at my nose, the tops of my ears, and I followed the blinking course of a satellite across the cloudless sky. Even in the suburbs, Chicago's light pollution made it hard to see the stars, but here, in this small, quaint college town, there were more than I could ever have imagined, less the scattering of lights I was used to, more the dense splatter of solar systems far off—

"The observatory," I said. "He's in the observatory."

Dave and Winston blinked at me ghoulishly, but Patrick was quicker on the uptake, and when I set off toward the astronomy building, he was only steps behind me.

The Adelman family had chosen a home for their only son just a few blocks away from the astronomy building. Whether Ezra had found his place of solace before or after matriculation was up for speculation. But he'd found it regardless, and I knew he returned to it often.

"I can take you there someday," Ezra had said, what felt like a lifetime ago, in our SSC booth.

"No thanks," I'd responded.

Joke's on me, I thought, as we waited, huffing, for the night shift custodian to let us in through the building's enormous carved wooden doors. *Guess you brought me here after all.*

There was a single rickety elevator shaft that took us to the tenth floor of the building, the highest it could go without a special access keycard. I pulled my medical kit to my front, taking out a vial of naloxone, a syringe, a needle. We'd practiced administration on a dummy before, but never a real human. To think, I'd known what he was doing all this while, and I'd done nothing to stop him. I'd looked him in the eyes and walked away.

I should have said something then. I should have *done* something then.

The elevator opened, and I stepped through it, finding the door that marked roof access, pushing through.

The roof was more of a balcony, a thin rim around the tenth floor, with rusting iron railings and concrete flooring that needed sweeping. My heart rate ratcheted up to my throat as I turned the corner, praying to all the gods that I would find him there alive, well. Hoping that my impulse to draw up a vial of naloxone had been out of an abundance of caution, that I would have to explain to the Elion EMS coordinator why I'd prepped one in the first place ahead of time and wasted supplies. That this nightmare of an evening would come to an end, and I would wake up to find it had all been a dream, that everything was okay, that Ezra was still harmlessly annoying and—

"He's here!" Patrick bellowed.

It was late, dark, but the light from the full moon was just enough to cast Ezra's sunken silhouette in a soft silvery glow. He'd always been ethereal, but there was something tragically romantic about how he looked then, his legs splayed, his head lolled to one side to expose a long, pale neck.

I didn't remember closing the distance between us. Didn't remember placing my fingers on that neck to feel his steady pulse still thrumming, didn't remember counting his breaths to find them slow and hesitant or screaming for Patrick to help me strip him of his jacket. Didn't remember stretching the collar of his shirt until it tore to reach the meat of his shoulder or slipping the safety off the hub of my needle, pushing it through his skin, pressing the plunger.

What I did remember was the wait. A minute was a long time when you were counting it down. Sixty seconds of praying, of holding this stupid boy in my arms, of realizing that if he were to die today, I would mourn him. Of wishing that when he'd told me I was his best friend, I'd admitted that he was mine as well.

And then, at the sixty-seventh second, something incredible happened.

Ezra opened his eyes.

"Jo?" he croaked. He sounded like he'd swallowed glass.

"Yes, you colossal idiot," I said. Tears trailed down his chin; mine, dropping onto his face.

He smiled, a quirk of his mouth that didn't hold a candle to his usual smirk.

"I feel like shit," he said.

I laughed, bowed my head. "Narcan will do that to you," I said.

Ezra nodded, his head beginning to loll, and I raised my needle, prepared to administer another dose.

"Stay with me, Jo," he said.

"I will," I promised.

CHAPTER THIRTY-FOUR

Jo

"I n my freshman year of college, I tried to kill myself," Ezra said, to no one, to everyone. "I don't think anyone really noticed that there was something wrong with me. I did a good job of hiding it. Had good grades. Friends. I don't even think I understood what I was feeling fully. Just that, most of the time, I didn't feel real. Like I was just putting on a show. Performing all the time felt exhausting. And one day, I decided to just . . . stop.

"People talk about suicide like it's this split-second decision people make, a final act of cowardice. But deciding to die, at that point, felt like the bravest thing I'd done yet. It felt like a choice I was making for myself.

"But then someone found me. A girl from my class. I'd always admired her. She had no one but herself, but she made that enough. The world was constantly trying to tell her that she didn't matter, and she asserted that she did, and made her place in it.

"I call Josephine Boateng my angel because she literally is," Ezra continued. His voice was steady, stable, but I could see the sadness in his eyes even through the screen, and it made me want to reach for him. "She was the first person I saw at the end of that tunnel. The one to call me back."

He was saying so much. How I consistently refused his family's monetary assistance, how his mother had given the money to my medical school in secret after my acceptance when she discovered that the scholarship they'd intended to give me was only partial. How, with me, he'd finally been loved for who he was, how my drive made him want to do something for himself and do it well.

Ezra was addressing the world, but it felt like he was speaking directly to me, his eyes creasing at the corners, an old pain evident in the tensing of his jaw.

And then, suddenly he was.

"Jo," he said, "if you're watching this, I want to say . . . I'm sorry. You've had to suffer so much because of me. Because of assumptions others have made because of my actions, opinions they've formed because they couldn't see you for you. And you deserve none of this. You deserve the world, you deserve the love that you're experiencing right now. I feel so lucky to have been able to stand in your light. And if you never want to speak to me again, if the damage I've done is too great, I'll understand." He cleared his throat. "And Malcolm . . . thank you for pushing me to do what I thought I couldn't. You were there for Jo when I wasn't, and even if I had a shit way of showing it, I'll forever be grateful to you."

I wanted to scream, but all that came out was a whimper. What was Ezra doing? Why was he putting himself on the chopping block for me? Why now, when all of his dreams were just starting to come true, when Zachary from *One True Kiss* was becoming a household name, when new roles and opportunities were just beginning to compile? He could've said nothing, let the news fizzle out, or done something more subtle, maybe post a picture of me, him, and Mal together to show that we were all cool, release my transcripts to prove that I had more than earned my spot at Herrick School of Medicine. Denise and I could've worked out a solution—it was what she was for, for crying out loud—or maybe I could've made something work with Lana. Hell, Renata's public relations team was like an army; surely they could've come up with something. He didn't have to put his entire heart out on display like this to save me. We could have handled it. Hadn't I told him that we would always be friends? Hadn't we promised that much to each other?

In the corner of my eye, I could see Mal shuffle in his seat. Turning away from him, I dialed Ezra's number, held my breath until he picked up.

"What is wrong with you?" I said into the phone.

Ezra laughed, a hollow sound.

"I see you saw the video," he said. "Did you like it? I thought it was pretty brilliant. Everyone knows you're a hero now."

"This isn't a joke, Ez," I said, my throat constricting.

"I'm not joking," Ezra said matter-of-factly. "I'm a coward, Jo. I couldn't tell you how I felt for years. When you were hurting, it took me way too long to figure out how to help you. This is the bravest thing I've ever done."

"The dumbest too," I said. I thought I had no more tears to cry, but there they were, flowing down my face.

"The *second* dumbest, at least." When I didn't laugh, his voice softened. "Just so you know. I'm leaving the country. Just to get my head together. And to escape my mother, who is probably contemplating my murder right now. I'm going to be intention- ally hard to reach. But I want you to know that I'm okay, or at the very least, I will be. If you're worried about my safety, I've got other people keeping tabs on me. I don't need you to take care of me anymore."

"I will always take care of you," I said, hysterical. "Do you understand? I saved your life, Ezra Adelman. It *belongs to me*. You don't get to decide what to do with it by yourself—"

"Of course I do," Ezra said. "And I should have realized that sooner." He paused, took a deep breath. "I love you, Jo. That hasn't changed. Probably won't change. But I'll do my best to love you in the way you want. Though, um, tell your boyfriend to be good to you. Because if he fucks up, I *will* provide a shoulder to cry on."

"I won't give you the opportunity," Mal said from across the table, finally breaking his silence.

Ezra laughed, and then he hung up, and when I tried to call him back, his phone went straight to voicemail. A second later, my phone buzzed with a text: Careful, Jo. Call me again and I'll think you're flirting with me. Followed by: Seriously. I'm putting you on mute though. Catch you in a few weeks, by which point I hope to be over you too.

I stared at the screen, stunned, until a hand covered mine, Mal's, lowering my phone back onto the table.

"I'm not sorry," he said solemnly, not breaking my gaze. "I know you're upset, but I won't apologize."

"I didn't need you to save me," I said. "I can handle myself. I've *been* handling myself, before you showed up."

"We know that," Mal said, and it was strange to hear him refer to a "we" that wasn't him and me, but him and Ezra. "But Ezra wanted to do everything he could, and I agreed that was the right course of action. I didn't know that he was going to do *this*, honestly. But even if I did, I wouldn't have stopped him."

"I didn't ask for this," I said through a tightening throat. Not even an hour ago, I'd imagined picking out another movie to watch, maybe taking Mal up on his invitation to put me through one of his more punishing workout circuits, or perhaps even inviting him back into my bed. Now I couldn't even bring myself to touch him. I squeezed my eyes shut. "I think you need to leave."

Mal seemed to sense my hesitation, and, to my relief, he didn't fight me. I was tired of fighting.

"Take whatever time you need," he said, and even his consideration managed to piss me off. "I'll be waiting. You know where to find me."

A romance writer through and through, I thought. I nodded, then turned tail, feeling miserably that the spell we'd woven together had already been broken.

IN TOUCH: Knydus Heir Confesses to Funding Heroin- and Cocaine-Fueled "Ragers" at Elite Private University in Shocking Video

TMZ: In Depression Awareness Month Post, One True Kiss Star Talks Suicide and Salvation

BUSTLE.COM, ASHLEY BIERNACKI: Accepting that I was the villain in Josephine Boateng's story required taking a hard look at myself—

merecedes_johnson: the rich white kids are always on the hardest drugs. Saw it in my college too. They throw black boys in jail for a bit of weed, but hamilton bartholemew the third could be snorting lines on the dean's desk and they'll be talking about his potential.

pilatesrn: i was an EMT in college too. Mostly got drunk kids but I was always so scared of a situation like that one. Bravo @drjojobee

futuredoctorwilson: i've actually met @drjojobee before. She's super sweet. A lot less scary than she seems online

beyoncesgivenchydress: @futuredoctorwilson y'all really need to stop calling every confident Black woman you see scary

@futuredoctorwilson: No, i didn't mean it like that

@futuredoctorwilson: She's just really nice

@futuredoctorwilson: I'm sorry. I may be white, but i'm committed to self-examination and even went to the BLM protests in my city. I'm always trying to learn.

xX_liliana_Xx: click on my profile to have a fun time;)

scarlemsfinest: This whole saga has been more entertaining than the last season of Love Island, tf

wonhosbabymama: @jenkiesjenkins, yoooo did you see that Adelman was dating her childhood bully too? Go to the Bustle @ashleybiernacki. Shit is craaazzyyy

margedonaldson: Dr. Boateng saved my husband's life. We were out at the zoo when he suddenly collapsed. She didn't hesitate to start CPR on him and assembled a team to help him immediately. He's doing well and recovering at home now. The ICU doctors told me that if she hadn't acted so quickly, he could have died or had significant brain damage. I'll forever be grateful to her. I don't know if she'll ever read this, but if she does—thank you. Because of you, I have my family.

CHAPTER THIRTY-FIVE
Mal

"You said what?" Kieran said in disbelief, his voice as booming and bombastic as if he were sitting in Mal's living room.

"If you loved her, you would figure it out," Kelechi repeated, deepening her voice in mimicry of his. "Come on, Mal, you write love stories. You should have known better than to give your rival that kind of encouragement. And now look what he's done with it."

Mal covered his eyes with his arm, miserable. He'd known that there was a chance Jo wouldn't take too kindly to the fact that he'd been the impetus for Ezra's public confession, but facing the reality had been harder than expected. Returning to his quiet, empty apartment hadn't helped. He'd spent yesterday pining and trying to distract himself with emails, work, and one brutal two-a-day at the gym before giving up and calling his friends.

Who, unsurprisingly, were definitely making things worse.

"You think I pushed them together?" he said miserably.

"Of course you pushed them together," Kieran said. After watching the Em-Dash book event, he'd switched to being staunchly Team Jo. *Like, damn*, he'd said, covering Harvey's ears.

I get it now. "Like. What'd he say? 'I was so lucky to stand in your light'? Bars. I teared up."

"Thanks, man, I feel so much better," Mal said sardonically.

"We're just messing with you," Kieran said, his tone mollified. "It's just . . . this is crazy right now. First Lana, now this. You're like, *famous* famous. Do you know how many people from college have hit me up to ask about you?"

Mal shrugged. His phone hadn't stopped ringing all day, calls from everyone from his agent to reporters to curious acquaintances suddenly interested in "catching up," and he'd already cleared his voicemail twice.

"It'll die down soon enough," Mal said. "I'm not all that interesting."

"I would have said the same a few months back, but that was before you managed to steal Ezra Adelman's girl," Kieran said.

"If I haven't already messed things up," Mal said with a sigh.

"Um, Mal," Kelechi said, her voice high the way it was when she had made a discovery. He could see her face in his mind's eye, the sideways tilt of her head, her eyes wide with thinly veiled delight. "I don't think you messed things up."

"And how would you know that?" Mal said, suspicious. "You hack into her phone somehow? Tap into her Alexa?"

"Nope," she said brightly. "I just checked her page. You should do that. And then call us back. Or maybe don't. You'll probably be busy."

And then, abruptly, she hung up.

Mal looked down at his home screen, dumbfounded, and then opened up his Instagram. To Amelia's naked delight, @malcolmj waters now had a following forty thousand large, with Ampersand's linked personal account sitting close by at twenty-eight.

He blinked at the number, bewildered, then, biting down on his tongue, he navigated to Jo's page.

There was a new post.

Mal sat up in bed, tapping it open with bated breath.

The photographs in the carousel Jo had posted were uncurated and unedited, a far cry from her typical well-manicured content. If Mal hadn't explicitly sought it out, he would have assumed he'd scrolled past a high school friend's post, except none of his high school friends ever got anything close to two hundred thousand likes. He recognized a few of the shots as his own: Ampersand curling into a ball at the base of a rumpled white bedsheet, dark, pink-toed feet peeking out in the background behind her, a portrait of Josephine in profile he'd taken during one of their many breakfasts together that focused on her neck. But most of them were Jo's: Mal typing at her dining table, his face tense with concentration, his and her shoes arranged over her "As Featured on MTV Cribs" welcome mat. A silver serving tray with a glass of water, a plate of tortellini, a side salad that probably came from a bag, taken from inside a dimly lit room.

And underneath that, the caption:

Hi. It's been a while. If you're new here, you know why I've been gone so long. If you're not, well, thanks for sticking around.

For the last few weeks, I've let other people tell the world who I was. Scream as I might against the noise, I knew and felt like I couldn't be heard. I felt lost, misunderstood, hurt, discouraged.

But in that cacophony, I found something incredible. I found courage. I found clarity. I found love.

Malcolm Waters, my knight in shining armor. Thank you for weathering this storm with me. You saw me at my most broken and decided to love me all the same. Thank you for reminding me that I deserve shelter too. That I deserve to be protected, and cherished, and loved.

I don't need time. I need you. Come outside.

Emergencies notwithstanding, Mal made it a rule to run every day. This was not out of concern for his physical health, though the benefits were not lost on him. It wasn't even for the aesthetics, though the combination of lifting, boxing, and running had given him a physique worthy of an appreciative thread on r/onetruekiss. It was because his brain was hooked on the endorphins that came with exercise, and without them, it tended to break.

Despite this, his lungs burned as he sprinted down his condominium's stairs. Why hadn't she called before turning up? Texted? Something? From his bedroom window, he'd made out Jo leaning against the iron railings of his stairwell, her butterfly locs up in two high ponytails, and he'd had to blink twice to make sure he hadn't imagined her. When she didn't disappear, he threw on a clean T-shirt, tossed this morning's cereal bowl into the sink, and ran out of his apartment like it was on fire.

When Mal threw open the door, Jo was right behind it, dressed in a white ribbed bodycon that hugged every curve. She gave him a wry smile, then tucked her phone into her purse.

"There are easier ways to get my attention, you know," he said, catching his breath. "You have my number. You could've called? Texted?"

What Mal wanted to say: *You look gorgeous, I know it hasn't even been two days but I missed you, did you really just hard launch me on social media before telling me you still wanted me?* But the adrenaline of realizing she was *here* had still not worn off.

"I could've. But this way was more dramatic, don't you think?" Jo said. She pulled her arms over her head in a stretch, smiling beatifically up at him.

"What if I hadn't seen your post?" he said, irritated by her carefreeness. Like she'd spent the last day completely at ease, while he'd worried and fretted that he'd overstepped, that maybe he'd lost the ground they'd gained. "What if I checked tomorrow, or the next day? You know I'm not on social media like that."

"I would've come back," Jo said. "Or just hit you up directly, honestly. But today's a beautiful day. I didn't mind waiting."

"I mind making you wait," Mal said, and Jo laughed, winding arms around his waist. With her body pressed against him, her face turned up to his with mischief, he felt his hackles lower.

"I wouldn't have to wait if we lived together," she said plainly.

Mal blinked down at her, then laughed out loud. This was the Josephine Boateng he knew, the one who could always leave him speechless, whose audacity knew no bounds.

"So, what, you're going to ditch Dahlia?" he asked, pulling back to look down at her face properly, the creases at the corners of her eyes.

"Dahlia's been thinking about leaving the city," Jo said. "She's been wanting to try homesteading. We spent an hour last night looking up chicken coops." She tilted her head. "I don't take up that much space, my skills in the kitchen are improving. I don't clean much, but I can cover the maid service. I make a pretty decent cohabitant."

As her hands folded at the small of his back, Mal studied her face, sensing that she was trying to tell him something else, something harder.

"You're not angry," he said.

Jo bit her lip. "No," she confessed. "But I am sorry. I should have tried to talk things out with you. Communicated, like you said before. I'm just so used to processing my feelings by myself, and so I did what I always do and ran away. But I promise I'll work on it, and you should absolutely call me out if you catch me doing it again—"

"You missed me," he interrupted.

"Desperately," she confirmed.

Her agreement and apology left him giddy, and he cupped her face in his hands, rubbing slow circles along her temples. She closed her eyes, easing into his touch.

"I missed you too," he said. "Which is ridiculous. It's been one day."

"Absolutely ridiculous," Jo said, practically purring under his ministrations. "Clearly just a honeymoon phase on steroids. Got me thinking the wildest thoughts."

"Not as wild as mine," Mal said, catching on to her game. "I'm thinking I want to spend every waking moment with you."

"Ha!" Jo said, but her smile stretched wider, and when she opened her eyes to look at him, they were dewy with adoration. The way he'd always wanted someone to look at him, like they couldn't believe he was theirs. "I think I've got you beat. 'Cause I want that, but, maybe, like, forever."

Something inside his chest cracked, and Mal tugged her close, as if she alone could fill the gaps. He remembered, not for the first time, the errant, irrational thought he'd had when she took his hand in her bedroom at the Adelmans': *I'm talking to my soulmate.*

"What if I don't think that's wild at all?" he said. "What if I want that too?"

Against his chest, he could feel Jo smiling, and there, under a beating late-afternoon sun, he felt like his life was beginning anew.

"Great. We're in agreement." She lifted her arms. "Now, if you please, I would like to be carried upstairs to be ravished, thank you."

The laugh that bubbled in Mal's chest was one part disbelief, the other part delight. He bent down and scooped her up, giggling, into his arms.

"As you wish," he said, and then he was fireman-carrying her over his threshold and into the permanent home he'd made for her in his heart.

EPILOGUE

FROM: mojojojobee@gmail.com
TO: malcolmjwaters@gmail.com

*I will never get over how much New York stinks. Like,
seriously. The studio? Pristine. Everyone in it? Gorgeous.
Then you take two steps outside and there's a heaping pile
of trash and a rat the size of a dinner plate wearing timbs.
Lana says I'll eventually get used to the stench, but I don't
know. You know how in those period pieces they used to put
perfume on their handkerchiefs to cover up other people's
BO? I think I'm going to do that.*

*How is planning going for launch? Do not stress about it.
I know you will anyway, but chill. You've done events before;
this one will be a piece of cake.*

*Speaking of cake: do not try and buy yourself one.
Because I have definitely not already taken care of that.*

Tell our daughter I miss her.

FROM: malcolmjwaters@gmail.com
TO: mojojojobee@gmail.com

Ampersand doesn't miss you at all. In fact, she's taken over your side of the bed, and I don't think you're getting it back.

NYC is like that. Still one of the most magical cities on earth. I need to drop by, meet up with my publicists. They've been putting in work; they deserve a dinner or something.

I am not stressing about launch. I promise. Momma, on the other hand, is losing her mind. She just asked if we need a florist for the event.

Speaking of flowers. Guess who sent me some for the event. Starts with an R. Ends with a Kovalenko. They're on the dining table right now. They're, um, a lot.

How's Ezra? He's done filming, right?

What time do you land again?

FROM: mojojojobee@gmail.com
TO: malcolmjwaters@gmail.com

I land at 10:00 a.m. Do you love me enough to pick me up from O'Hare? Or should I plan on finding a ride? (Note: no pressure at all on this, I love you too much to subject you to that drive.) Ezra's right here. Says he's good, and that his mom is going to be overcompensating for pissing you off for the rest of your life. Send me a pic. Are there ostrich feathers in it? Pearls? If not, it's at best a four out of ten in the Renata extraness scale.

You are definitely stressing.

FROM: malcolmjwaters@gmail.com
TO: mojojojobee@gmail.com

Fine, I'm stressing. But all things considered, I'm doing pretty good. This is just the second most stressful thing I'll probably have to do in my life.

Three hundred people bought tickets. The fuck. We're legit at capacity. How am I supposed to talk in front of three hundred people?

FROM: mojojojobee@gmail.com
TO: malcolmjwaters@gmail.com

Three hundred people is a lot, but your crowds are only going to get bigger, darling. Prepare thyself.

And I did not realize you had a ranking for "stressful things you'll have to do in your life." What tops that list?

FROM: malcolmjwaters@gmail.com
TO: mojojojobee@gmail.com

Proposing, probably. Though "birth of our child" comes pretty close. Actually maybe that should be number one. The maternal mortality rate for Black women is through the roof in this country.

Jo: . . . Malcolm James Waters. I am switching to text because how dare you!

Jo: Did you seriously just ask me to marry you over EMAIL???

Jo: And you write about love. You should be ashamed of yourself.

Mal: Jesus, Jo. This obviously doesn't count

Mal: God, does it count? It doesn't right?

Mal: Forget I said anything. Erase this completely from your memory. I'll do it better later

Jo: excuse you! who said I want to forget?

Jo: I'm a bougie bitch who's hard to impress. You're right to be scared.

Jo: Sooooo I'll make it easy for you. My ring size is 6.5, and I want a 2 to 2.5 carat Asscher cut solitaire. Think Liz Taylor. Lab diamond, no colored stones, nothing from the ground. Yellow gold, 18k. No dinners, no public places, somewhere pretty and private. And I want a photographer hiding in the bushes.

Jo: If these conditions are met within the next . . . nine months, I will most likely say yes. Potentially.

Mal: All right, bet. 😂😂😂 Now you got me excited

Mal: How about we make it six, and we have a deal.

Jo: I think I can work with that.

ACKNOWLEDGMENTS

For my tenth birthday, I asked my parents to host a book signing. In accordance with my request, my family and friends lined up at a small bowling alley in Hinsdale to purchase bound copies of my actual debut novel, "Tears of Happiness, Tears of Grief, Both I Cannot Handle." Now, twenty-one years later, I'm still the same girl with the same dreams, and it is honestly incomprehensible to me that so many of them are coming true.

So first, I would like to thank my readers. I can't possibly know all of you, but you are precious to me. You could spend your time doing just about anything, but many of you decided to spend it with my work, and for that I am so grateful. I hope you find a piece of yourselves in this book.

Next, my publishing team. Lucia, my OG editor: Thank you for believing in me and making everything I write so much better. I hope you are enjoying retirement and can't wait for you to read the final version of *BFL*. To Erika: In the short time we worked together, you managed to help mold this novel from a good idea to something I can be proud of. Thank you. To Priyanka: Thank you for taking me on with open arms and for advocating for this book. To Mumtaz: You blew this cover out of the park! It is beautiful; thank you for bringing it to life. To Emily, my publicist:

Thank you for the immense amount of outreach and coordination you do to ensure that people actually know that my work exists. To Rachel, DJ, and the rest of my marketing team: You rock, you work so hard, I appreciate you so much! Thanks as well to my UK team for bringing *BFL* to readers around the world!

Jess: Thank you for being my champion. For the countless hours spent talking me off various ledges (some of them imagined), critiquing my drafts, quieting my fears, and generally for being the best agent a girl could have. Also, for introducing me to one of my best friends.

On that topic: Riss—not just my writing partner, but my soul sister. Everything I write has so much of you in it. Thank you for marching through the trenches with me. For four-hour-long writing dates inevitably followed by four hours more of voice notes, for stuffing me full of empanadas and chicken chili, for reminding me that I wasn't alone during some of my darkest days. I love everything you've ever written, but I can't wait for *A Love Like the Sun* to take the world by storm. I love you booski.

Jenny: Hello, angel! We literally fell in love over the page, and I think that is just so apt. *Everyone Who Can Forgive Me Is Dead* is incredible. Thank you for your support, love, and podcast-length voice notes.

Shruti, Ijeoma, Grace, Satish, Nolan, and Ross: Thank you for getting me through the craziness that has been the last couple of years. Shruti: Thank you for reading multiple iterations of *BFL* and being fervently team Mal the whole time.

Ehigbor and Rebecca, thank you for reminding me to dream big and to not be afraid to "want it all." You inspire me always.

Chris D: Thank you for helping me create the whole sweet, jacked, anxious Black boy vibe for Mal. Rooting for you always.

Mom, Dad, Humphrey, and Sam: Thank you for loving, understanding, and supporting me, your workaholic daughter / big sis. I'm so lucky to be yours.

Finally, to the 30 percent of medical trainees who struggle silently with depression: I see you. You are not weak. You are not less capable. You are human, and that is your greatest superpower.

ABOUT THE AUTHOR

SHIRLENE OBUOBI is a Ghanaian American cardiologist, cartoonist, and author who grew up in Chicago, Illinois; Hot Springs, Arkansas; and the Woodlands, Texas. She appeared on *Good Morning America* to promote her debut novel, *On Rotation*, and is a regular contributor to the *Washington Post*. When she isn't in the hospital, she can be found drawing comics, writing on her phone, and talking to everyone who will listen about women's heart health.

READ MORE BY
SHIRLENE OBUOBI

"As a fan of *Grey's Anatomy* (and *Chicago Med*!), I couldn't put down *On Rotation*, and you won't be able to, either. Shirlene Obuobi makes you feel as if you're actually right there with the lovable Angie, and I personally couldn't get enough." —Meg Cabot, *New York Times* bestselling author

This dazzling debut novel by Shirlene Obuobi explores that time in your life when you must decide what you want, how to get it, and who you are, all while navigating love, friendship, and the realization that the path you're traveling is going to be a bumpy ride.

"Smart, funny, and utterly swoonworthy, *On Rotation* is a layered and deeply compassionate novel of navigating life and love in your twenties. Angie Appiah will be your new best friend." —Grace D. Li, *New York Times* bestselling author of *Portrait of a Thief*

"*On Rotation* is a charming story from start to finish. The ending will melt your heart!" —Tracey Livesay, award-winning author of *American Royalty*